LETTERS
to the
CYBORGS

As Humans Become 51% Machine, or More, Who Will Inherit the Earth?

JUDYTH VARY BAKER

Published by:
Trine Day LLC
PO Box 577
Walterville, OR 97489
1-800-556-2012
www.TrineDay.com
publisher@TrineDay.net

Library of Congress Control Number: 2016939214

Baker, Judyth Vary.
—1st ed.
p. cm.
Includes references and index.
Epud (ISBN-13) 978-1-63424-075-8
Mobi (ISBN-13) 978-1-63424-076-5
Print (ISBN-13) 978-1-63424-074-1
1. Science Fiction, American. 2. Cyborgs. I. Baker, Judyth Vary. II. Title

FIRST EDITION
10 9 8 7 6 5 4 3 2 1

Printed in the USA
Distribution to the Trade by:
Independent Publishers Group (IPG)
814 North Franklin Street
Chicago, Illinois 60610
312.337.0747
www.ipgbook.com

The fringed curtains of thine eye advance
And say what thou seest yond.
Prospero, *The Tempest*: Act I, Scene 2

Lee, this book of science fiction is dedicated to you, in tribute to what you might have become, had you not been slain before my eyes on Nov. 24, 1963, in the presence of seventy Dallas police. I will always love you. For all that you were, and for your courage and free spirit, to you this book is dedicated."

Judyth Vary Baker
Berlin, Germany 2016

CONTENTS

FOREWORD

O ne of the pleasures in life is to identify and read a great science fiction book, one that is imaginative and that can give us a glimpse into our potential future as well as our present. I was pleasantly surprised by Judyth Vary Baker's *Letters to the Cyborgs*, especially that the topic is particularly relevant.

We live at the crossroads of establishing the rules for artificial intelligence and the limits of medical science. A time when powerful authority figures in the world, like Bill Gates, Warren Buffett and Stephen Hawking, are warning us about the threat of artificial intelligence. How it could wipe out our economy and put everyone out of a job, and then take over the world as we lose control over its development.

There are others like Ray Kurzweil, inventor and futurist working at Google, who welcome the new AI era as a new industrial revolution no one should prevent. An era ushering in the abolition of work, leaving humanity to pursue other matters like culture and creativity.

What will our future hold? Who can predict the future, if not science fiction authors? And this is precisely why *Letters to the Cyborgs* is an important book, because it imaginatively opens up fresh avenues we might not have considered, and all in an entertaining way.

Judyth strikes me as a perfect candidate for such a search to uncover the potential of AI. She has won multiple science prizes; she was in the newspapers a number of times in Florida as a whiz kid who would go on to achieve an extraordinary career in science. She was snatched away early on to work on medical projects where she demonstrated a unique mind that could cut through to the essential and produce excellent results. She's still thinking and working independently on a promising cure for cancer.

Judyth first contacted me before her historical books were published, through the insistence of our common friend, the late Martha Rose Crow, with whom Judyth was working on a book on the subject of ponerology. Martha was a force of nature: she believed in us all and was a key inspiration for us to achieve our greatest potential. Judyth and Martha were both

American women living in exile in the Netherlands, fleeing persecution, and the three of us shared a passion for science, poetry, books and science fiction.

In my opinion it is not only Judyth's obvious intelligence, it is also this knowledge of science she has managed to acquire during those years, that led to a creativity and imagination worthy of Iain M. Banks and Frank Herbert. Judyth is a databank of all the research done in every scientific domain, and it shows in the results of *Letters to the Cyborgs*.

Judyth's interests in writing science fiction is not new. Whilst dating Lee Harvey Oswald in New Orleans in the 1960s, together they were passionate about the world of sci-fi. Judyth presents in *Letters to the Cyborgs* one sci-fi short story written by Oswald himself. After all those years, the publication of Oswald's sci-fi story is akin to history in the making.

I feel readers of this first science fiction novel from Judyth will agree that this is an excellent debut which shows great potential. I find the short stories, which are all linked to a certain extent, extremely intricate and cleverly woven into hard science. This is sci-fi at its best.

– Roland Michel Tremblay

Roland Michel Tremblay is a French Canadian author, poet, scriptwriter, IT events and development producer, and technical adviser and science-fiction consultant for authors. His science fiction website (http://www.themarginal.com/) was created for authors working in the genre for television.

LETTERS
TO THE
CYBORGS

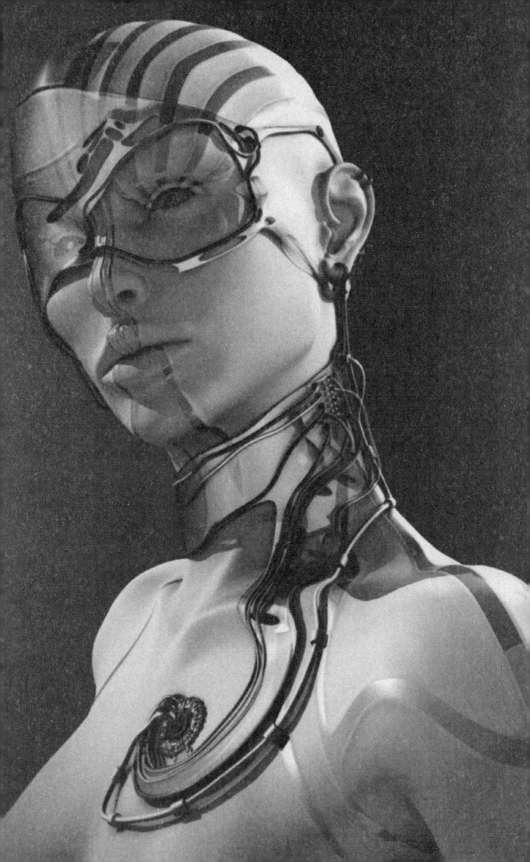

THE PERFECT WIFE

The first robot wedding in history was held June 30, 2015. "Frois, the bulky groom ... married Yukirin, an android made to look like the Japanese pop star Yuki Kashiwagi.... The wedding was officiated by another robot named Pepper. She usually spends her days helping customers at Softbank's cell phone stores. The ceremony was even sealed with a kiss. Guests ... were treated to a robot-sliced cake and a robot wedding band, RT reports. The robots' big day was put on by the Japanese company Maywa Denki ... according to the International Business Times. It was only a matter of time before 'bots started tying the knot. Tech-savvy brides and grooms already employ them as ring bearers and officiants, the New York Times reported last year."[1]

– Huffington Post, 6/30/15.

W hen Henry Wallet dodged across the busy street with its screaming car horns and roaring trucks, he found himself transfixed by a brightly-colored sign. He spotted it just as he reached the opposite curb. What was odd was that he'd never noticed it before. It was a garish-looking sign, but Henry couldn't pull his eyes from its brilliant, warped-looking letters. He forgot the rush of the New York

crowd around him as he pondered its message. Squinting, he leaned closer to read the small print there.

> **Divorced?** Time to try **A Perfect Wife**
> – 30 Days Free Trial. **No Money Down!**
> Easy payments, quick credit check. Ac-
> cess us on Civilian Web, PerfectWife.
> cw.us, or visit between 09:00 am-21:00
> pm at 421 5th Ave, NY 10018.[2]

Having a site on the Civilian Web meant the business was government approved, monitored, and legal. Ever since the World Government
moved in to make sure the Internet would be truly safe and patriotic,[3]
millions of unsavory sites had vanished (along with some that Henry
thought were OK, but what did he know?). Now he took a deep breath,
as he considered the message. This wasn't a scam. He took a photo of the
sign, which was a hologram, and watched it disappear. He was used to being targeted by such signs, but this was the first time he'd had one thrust at
him on the street. Well, advertising was everywhere. It was just the way it
was. For a small sum, he was at least able to block ads out of his head while
he was asleep (or so his AdBot Blocker claimed: maybe he just couldn't
remember them, which was the next best thing). Meanwhile, the craving
he had to eat at Sunday Snackers Restaurant was an urge he couldn't fight.
Why he'd never thought about eating there before, he couldn't explain.
One thing for sure: dinner at Sunday Snackers had to come first. Its per-
suasive ad was simply irresistible.

As Henry slid into a comfortable chair at the restaurant, he noticed
that his belly was in the way. He'd been gaining weight ever since he and
Helen divorced. Despite the campaign going on against overweight people, despite the fines imposed, despite the fact that he was about to lose
his job because he was borderline obese, Henry couldn't help himself.
Restaurant and grocery store advertisements constantly barraged him
with visions of fast, cheap food, along with their attractive smells and
certain subtle excitatory signals that made his brain tell him that he was
always hungry.[4]

Henry had gained ten kilos, but it didn't stop him from missing
Helen's meals, which were health-conscious, with big doses of organi-
cally-grown vegetables. His weight gain began almost as soon as the
divorce was final and Henry was legally cleared to receive restaurant
advertisements three times a day, instead of once a day, since he didn't
like to cook. To combat his depression (Helen had run away with a man
who had so many implants that he was supposed to be able to function
sexually for another fifty years), Henry's doctor also advised that he
must treat his brain's almond-sized hypothalamus with electrotherapy

while he slept.[5] That tiny bit of very primitive tissue couldn't be reached by mere logic.

After eating more than he wanted and just as he paid his expensive dinner bill, a suggestion to visit a nearby dessert kiosk popped into his mind. The smell of freshly-fried donuts accompanied the ad. Henry, choosing to control his equally urgent desire to contact PerfectWife until after he got a jelly donut, felt proud of himself for buying just one. Henry also decided to walk back to the block where he first saw the PerfectWife sign, since it was only a kilometer away. "I need the exercise," he said to himself, but the truth was, Henry hoped he'd lose a kilo or so by walking the extra blocks, instead of taking a motorized chair.

The night crowd was thick with shoppers, the signs blinked off and on, as Henry, shaking his head with amusement at himself, exercised his way toward where he'd encountered the sign.

"A perfect wife? Hah!" he said, stopping where the hologram had appeared. Instead, nothing happened. Surprised that it didn't materialize again, and sorry that his shoes were so tight and his belly was so full, he paused to complain about it. He must have been a random target instead of a potential client selected by researching profiles. "I see they've mismatched my preferences again!" he told the empty space. "I hate random, meddling ads!" He was about to lodge a complaint with the Ad Ombudsman, but then he paused. Perhaps it was already 9:00PM, and "PerfectWife" was closed. That would explain why the hologram didn't appear again. He usually kept his watch (embedded in his wrist) visible, but he'd turned it off while holding the donut, which was dripping with raspberry-flavored goo. Seeing that it was only 8:00, he had plenty of time. "I'm coming, PerfectWife!" Henry said aloud. He began walking toward 5th Avenue.

Immediately, visions of beautiful women began to fill his head, nearly overwhelming his senses. Somehow, Henry was able to stay on his feet, but he scarcely knew where he was as one woman after another appeared before his eyes, sizzling with personality and good looks. Long before he neared 5th Avenue, dozens of potential PerfectWives had already paraded themselves through his head and before his eyes, while his brain kept responding automatically to some candidates more than others. Henry was so absorbed in browsing the PerfectWife Catalog that a Track Guide alert went off: he was not paying adequate attention to where he was going. He had stepped out of the walkway boundary three times, which was unlawful. Now he was ordered to seat himself in a Street Chair (the fee was low) for the rest of the journey, but he hardly cared.

The selection process was now down to three candidates: one was called Lucy Lips, who would always provide him with all the news; another was called Mrs. Dines (she was a terrific cook of natural foods), and the third was called Sexx Kitty. To his surprise, at this point, all three women merged into one. Standing before him was a PerfectWife, smiling at him, nestling in his head. Still, he kept comparing her lovely figure to his own Pillsbury Doughboy rotundity. How could she care about him? As he thought about that, Lucy Sexx Dines vanished. "See you soon, honey!" he heard her say, her mouth in a kissing shape being the last thing to disappear. She had vanished little by little, reminiscent of the Cheshire Cat in Alice in Wonderland.

Checking his watch again (of course it had many other functions), Henry was now suffused with an urge to relax as the Street Chair trundled him along. As he slouched down, half-numb, he was given a once-over by the Chair's built-in Prosperity Assessment Device. Henry learned that he had recently eaten 1.5 kilograms of food – 3,900 calories – with insufficient fiber. His toilet would be sent the message, and later tonight, when he sat on it, the toilet seat would prick him with a tiny injection of a drug that acted as a laxative. That would solve the fiber problem. If there were any blood sugar problems, another tiny prick would fix the insulin levels. Many people had artificial pancreases now, with automatic insulin regulators,[6] but Henry could not qualify for the implant until he gained a few more kilos and developed Type 1 diabetes. He looked forward to the operation, because then he could eat without worrying about his blood sugar. All would be well.

By the time he stopped thinking about food and insulin, Henry found himself deposited at the PerfectWife entrance. It was a tall, impressive office building. The thought came to him to press his hand down on the security buzzer. He received a warning message that all data concerning him would be accessed if he decided to meet Lucy. Was he willing to do that? "What the hell!" he said. "I want to meet Lucy and her other personalities. After all, it's a Free Trial. What can go wrong?" He pressed the security buzzer and felt a wave of electricity pass through him as he was quickly scanned.

Welcome, Henry Wallet, Typical B-Inhibited, Straight Male, in danger of losing a productive position! Your employers realize how valuable you are and have confirmed that they will contribute 42% of the cost of your therapy, should you accept your Perfect Wife after the 30-day free trial.

Forty-two percent! Henry was stunned. He hadn't realized that his company valued him so highly. It had been made known to him that the average support for therapy from his company was only 19%. He was more than twice as valuable to them as the typical employee! For the first time since Helen had walked out on him, Henry began to feel twinges of hope. Maybe life was about to deal him a new hand of cards, with all aces.

As the security door swished open, Henry was told that his entire profile, including (of course) DNA and his life story, had now been downloaded into PerfectWife's system. When a door to an elevator down the hall flashed with the holographic sign, Henry entered that elevator. As he did so, two robotic arms gripped him and its door closed, but even so, Henry was half-flattened by the speed of the elevator,[7] which got him to the twentieth floor in two seconds. As he stepped from the elevator, which opened to reveal gleaming black marble floors and a brightly-lit white corridor, two beautiful women appeared. Each gently took him by an arm and guided Henry toward a half-open door farther down the corridor.

"We're so glad you came, Henry!" the blonde to his right told him, as they entered the room. "Won't you please be seated, Henry?" the brunette said, indicating a red-leather chair. Henry's watch glimmered green: both women were robots. Properly speaking, they were Cyborgs, because they carried so much human flesh in the right places. These days, everybody's watches analyzed the percentage of human flesh versus machine.

The blond served Henry a legal-level relaxation beverage, while the brunette escorted a gray-haired gentleman into the room.

"Mr. Landry," she said, "please meet Mr. Henry Wallet, Therapy Experiment #21."

"Experiment?" Henry said, flushing. "I don't want to be in any experiment." He stood up, intending to go for the door, but Landry said, in a commanding tone, "Sit down, Henry. Let's talk some business. You'll like the financial benefits that will accompany your completion of this experiment. Your company values you as an employee, and has agreed that you can receive, as a bonus for your cooperation and consent, a brand-new pancreas at no cost to you. By the way, your pancreas is shot."

Henry considered. He knew that his pancreas was precancerous and was anxious to get it replaced, so he sat down again. But he wasn't anybody's fool.

"Is this going to be dangerous?" he asked.

"Only for your Perfect Wife. Not for you."

To Henry's puzzled look, Landry placed a thin, freckled hand on the fat man's shoulder. "My friend," he said, "some people didn't want to have anything to do with Cyborgs. There are some in World Government who aren't pleased with our new population control methods using Cyborgs. Instead, they want us to expand our current population control program, which is the involuntary sterilizations of criminals and misfits."

"What do you mean, new population control methods using Cyborgs?" Henry inquired. "And why didn't I hear about this before now? I happen to be involved with population control at BioTest Laboratories."

"I know that," Landry said. "I am also aware that you've had a divorce, and that because you're now overweight, you can be fired."

"Not if I can get a pancreas implant," Henry said. "I know my rights!"

"You were kept out of the loop because you could have been fired with another kilo of weight gain," Landry told him, "But we've saved you, son. Marriages and divorces are rather uncommon these days, you know."

"Helen was old-fashioned about things like that," Henry said. "And I loved her enough to agree to marry."

"But it turned out that you refused to have children, working as you did at BioTest Labs," Landry said gently. "And yet, that had been part of your original pre-nup agreement."

"It was. But who can afford a child, these days? Some young fart came along who promised her not one, but two kids," he said bitterly. "Then, when I got my sperm count checked, I realized I couldn't compete. She had the legal right to divorce me and take penalty money. She almost bankrupted me."

"You were foolish not to get your sperm count checked before you married her," Landry said. "It's a concern that you could be so thoughtless, considering who you work for."

"I didn't worry about it because I started taking extra testosterone," Henry said. "But a side effect was that it made me more aggressive. We started fighting..." Henry's voice trailed off. "We were fighting over almost everything. That was when all the big problems started."

"What if I told you that PerfectWife may have the solution to all those problems?"

Henry thought about this carefully. He was an intelligent man, though he had been in intellectual limbo for some time. He had stopped playing chess, stopped collecting old books and reading them, stopped expanding his coin collection, stopped debating about the future of the world, as the breach between him and Helen had grown wider.

"There's got to be a catch to this experiment," he finally said. "Because you're not acting like a salesman, giving me a pitch. I get plenty of that. This isn't a real office – I don't see any desks or screens. I got escorted in here by two expensive robots–

"They're Cyborgs," Landry corrected him.

"You must be some kind of CEO for this company."

"That's true. I'm also on the Board for BioTest Labs. I'm one of your bosses."

Landry's steel-gray eyes never blinked. Henry decided it had to be true, but just in case, he–

Before Henry could think the next word, into his head flickered an impressive list of Lee Landry's accomplishments and positions. Landry was using the same high-class program that had once been approved for use by political candidates. Henry recognized the style and the expense of it. Henry himself represented a million voters. He was required to vote in their behalf after The Blitz. That mega-advertising event exposed the world's adult population to a thirty-day barrage of almost endless political advertisements. Individual citizens never voted anymore: they merely participated in daily opinion polls that were sent to their particular representative. Henry was one such representative. At the end of The Blitz, a final opinion poll was collected by each representative. The representative delivered the final poll's winner as a vote. The almost constant flow of political ads, from which Henry was blissfully kept insulated as a representative, had brought masses of voters to the brink of suicide in order to arrive at the winner. Meanwhile, the world's production of goods and services nearly came to a halt the last few days of the Presidential campaign.

The most sophisticated ads were the most expensive and produced the best results. But the old fear that government positions could be purchased outright (as had occurred with the election of the American President in 2036) changed the voting system forever. By 2048, only Representatives for each one million people and the CEOs of the 1000 most important corporations were allowed to vote. Their votes were tallied in rooms where mind-bending ads were prohibited. Naturally, the biggest companies had the most votes.

Things had been just dandy ever since.

"My corporation is treating me too well," Henry finally said, as he looked over contracts to be signed. "And why is my position as Representative so important in these contracts?"

"We want you to try out a particular Perfect Wife," Landry told him. "If it works as intended, we'll have the solution we've been looking for. By the way, you racked up a few gambling debts these past few weeks, didn't you?"

"Yeah, I was depressed. Thought maybe I'd make a lot of money and get myself a pancreas transplant and some masculine enhancements. But, what's this about a 'solution'? And why me?"

"You probably never saw that old film from 2010 or so, called *Idiocracy*,[8] did you?"

Henry had not. Who watched old movies, anyway? They had no smells, no sensations, no way to tickle your brain with entorhinal stimuli to link what you were seeing with your most important life experiences.[9] You couldn't step into the movie itself and see it from all kinds of angles. You couldn't get virtually killed in an old-fashioned movie. Only intellectuals watched old movies.

"You're our experiment, much as was Pvt. Joe Bauers in that particular movie. After all our studies, there you were, right under our noses. You're the totally average man, when it comes to what you expect in a wife. It's a 30-day experiment. We pay off all your bills. You have nothing to lose. Any questions?"

"You seem to know what you're doing. I guess I have no questions," Henry replied. As he finished speaking, Lucy Sexx Dines appeared once more before his inner eye, smiling at him with her fresh, luscious red lips. She pointed to the most important contract and winked. Henry tried to read it, but his mind kept wandering. He had to concentrate, or the contract would not be accepted: his lack of focus would be analyzed. It told him he was fully informed, gave informed consent, and that he agreed to do no harm to the Perfect Wife, who, for her part, would be guaranteed to obey his every desire and to satisfy him in every possible way that her anatomy and intelligence would permit. All his prior debts would be paid, and he would have the option to keep his Perfect Wife after a trial of thirty days. If he returned his Perfect Wife before thirty days elapsed, that portion of his debt would revert back to him. It was hard to concentrate with Lucy's smoky, feminine scent surrounding him like that, but at last, he gathered enough of his wits to comprehend the whole thing, including the fine print, and he nodded agreement. The signature was coded at once and added to Henry's permanent civil profile.

"Bring LSD in, Marcy," Lee Landry commanded the brunette Cyborg. "Yes, sir."

Lucy Sexx Dines came in, shyly, for she was utterly naked. She covered herself as best she could, but at Landry's order, she lowered her hands.

"Look her over," Landry said. "Inspect her genitals, the firmness of her breasts, her teeth – whatever you wish. If the product pleases you, tell her to get dressed."

"The product?"

"Don't you get it? She's 100% Cyborg. But if you can detect anything that's non-human about her, we'd like to know. Touch her. Kiss her. Check out her various exits and entrances."

As Landry spoke, LSD blushed, and trembled. "She knows she has to please you, or she'll be terminated," Landry said, as easily as he sipped his drink.

Henry looked into her eyes and saw terror, but also, he detected that something was missing. He couldn't tell exactly what, but as for the rest of her, she was clearly distressed, embarrassed, and miserable. "Lucy," he told her, as kindly as he knew how. "Get dressed. I'm taking you home."

**

From the night Henry brought Lucy home, everyone who knew him began commenting about his metamorphosis. The old, distraught, over-eating Henry was gone. In his place was a confident, beaming, friendly co-worker whose mind had suddenly come alive: he was making important comments, bringing forth new ideas, and pleasing his bosses (including the hidden ones such as Landry). Gone were his fears, his taciturnity, his aimless blunders. He even volunteered to inspect the Tanzanian Population Control Project, based on new fossil finds by paleoanthropologists.

BioTest Labs, he said, should add the newly discovered fossil DNA fragments that had been found to the reproductive cells of the survivors of the Olduvai Gorge Population Control Project. He successfully argued that babies born to Tanzanians, who had previously been slated for removal (by one means or another) would be so primitive and fascinating that the Olduvai Gorge region would finally qualify as a profitable Global Heritage Site that would pay for itself for years to come.

"Imagine!" he told his superiors, "These Tanzanian hybrids will have smaller brains, fur on their bodies, and will scarcely be able to communicate, but they will walk on two legs, and their parents will be assured of an income to support them for the rest of their lives. The world's first Cave Man Zoo! We can add some attraction, such as saber-toothed tigers to hunt them. We can sell the shows worldwide as real-life drama: that will bring even more revenues. Sub-humans against the tigers! It will be a stunning Pliocene experience, for all paying customers."

It was perfect for BioTest Labs, because the project would continue to reduce the unwanted human population in Tanzania. They were in the way of Tanzanite Mines, Global Inc., currently involved in uprooting the entire region of 365,700 square miles in its quest for natural Tanzanite, as well as for gold, uranium, diamonds, nickel and copper.[10] The stripping of the land could be accomplished without having to resort to starting another war there, if a mere 700 square miles were reserved to breed sub-humans for exhibition. Wars were exciting to watch, but they could get so messy, and while they were in progress, such activities as mining were sometimes difficult to pursue.

It was Henry's soul-mate, Lucy, who had suggested the idea. She had been looking up famous persons with the name "Lucy" and had found information, almost forgotten, about a 3.2 million year old hominid. An even older specimen had been found in Tanzania, which region was part of Henry's population control project. When Lucy discovered that traces of DNA had been found in some of these bones, she alerted Henry. Two weeks later, after Henry gave his thrilling speech at a luncheon held in his honor, he was moved into a corner office with a view.

Henry knew that every iota of his success had come from his association with LSD. He had been losing weight, was working out, and was contemplating marrying Lucy as Day 30 rolled around. He wanted to keep her forever! As Evening 29 approached, Henry purchased a wedding ring surmounted with a large Tanzanite gem. He even stopped at a florist's and bought a dozen red roses. Tonight, he was going to ask Lucy to be his wife. Not that she was perfect, for in fact, she wasn't.

If anything had ever irritated him about her, it was Lucy's obedience. No matter what he asked of her, if it was possible to do it and it wasn't illegal, she complied. Happily. Sometimes, that grated on him.

"What would you like for dinner tonight?" she'd ask him, for he contacted her at lunch every day to plan his evenings with her, most of them centered around sex and feely movies. "Surprise me!" he would tell her. "What would you like for dinner?" she would ask again. "Pick out something you would like, for a change," he would tell her. "I can't," she would tell him. "I'm not programmed to prefer things for myself. It could conflict with your desires."

He knew he did not have the best taste, and that he was not picking out the best clothing for her: his choices made her look like a barmaid robot, showing too much butt and boobs. After enduring too many stares when they went out to eat, he began dressing Lucy in sailor suits, gowns and sports team uniforms, but that didn't quite suit her, either. Finally, he contacted PerfectWife, and they introduced a program into Lucy's head so that she was able to choose her own clothes. Sometimes her tastes were expensive, but soon, Henry would be debt-free. By the 29th night, Henry's debt was so close to zero that he felt like a rich man.

Now, as he entered their apartment, which she kept spotless, Henry was shocked to find Lucy seated on the couch, crying.

"Honey, what's the matter?" he asked her.

"They're going to terminate me tomorrow!" she told him.

Henry dropped the flowers, horrified. "What the hell?" he said. "They can't do that! I want to keep you! They told me I had a 30 day trial, and then I could decide whether or not to keep you. And I want to do more than keep you. I want you to be my wife!"

"You – you do?"

"Yes, sweet LSD, yes! You've made me the happiest man in the world."

He got on his knees before her and wiped a tear from her eye. Removing the ring with its lovely violet gem from his pocket, Henry offered it to her on his open palm, as he asked her, clearly and forcefully, "Will you marry me?"

She looked at him without replying. Frustrated, Henry blurted out, "If I marry you, they can't terminate you. I read the contract!"

"Did you read the small print?"

"Of course I read the small print!"

All she said then was, "You've made me very happy. I don't think they realized that a Cyborg could become happy."

***

They had to restrain him when he came staggering into the building on 5th Avenue, carrying her. She was limp, unresponsive, her open eyes

10

staring without blinking, glazing over with a white film, and her skin had turned to a soft, pliable substance that was no longer human to the touch. It was the 30th day, and Henry was weeping. He was also furious.

Seeing her condition, they forced him to relinquish Lucy into their care: she was hustled off somewhere, with reassurances that he would certainly be able to see her again, no matter what happened. "After all," he was told, "She's your property. You do have rights." The two Cyborgs he'd met at the elevator in the beginning did their best to calm Henry down as he demanded to see Lee Landry. "He's coming, but not yet," they kept telling him. Henry had to wait an anxious hour and a half before Landry finally appeared. He couldn't help but notice that Landry was tense, and perspiring.

"Son," he told Henry, "let's talk."

Henry leaned toward the older man. He could not hide his clenched hands gripping his knees, his face suffused with anger and sorrow. Tears glittered in his eyes.

"Sorry, Henry," Landry finally said. "Remember how we told you that we wanted you to try out a particular Perfect Wife?"

"Of course," Henry replied. "And she was just that. Almost perfect."

"Remember how we told you, that if she worked as intended, we'd have the solution to a problem we'd been looking into?"

Henry nodded. "I knew it was an experiment. But you said that after thirty days, I could keep her, if I wished. You didn't tell me she'd be dead!"

"You remember my mention of the film *Idiocracy*? And that we chose you specifically because you were a typical, intelligent, straight male, handy for us because you worked at BioTest Labs?"

Henry remembered. "What's that got to do with Lucy?" he snapped.

"Of all people, son, you should understand how we've been paring back the population, removing the unfit, the dissidents, and the redundants. But our solutions were sometimes violent."

"Let's say that creating wars for decades has kept us in power," Henry said. "As Lucy taught me, from her reading, A.J.P. Taylor said, 'No matter what political reasons are given for war, the underlying reason is always economic.'"Unruffled, Landry smiled. "I don't think you realize that we're moving into a Golden Age, where we won't be allowing murders anymore. For any reason. I have influence, and I'm not alone. Most Cyborg Intelligences agree with me."

"I don't trust Cyborgs," Henry muttered.

"LSD – she's Cyborg," Landy told him.

"She's not a walking, talking humanoid computer!"

"As you wish," Landry said. "We'll deal with that little idea of yours in a minute. But before we do, I want to tell you about my favorite childhood movie."

"Movies aren't real," Henry declared.

"They portray possibilities, if only in the imagination. If you imagine killing somebody, or turning your best friend into a pizza by waving a magic wand, you're still creating something that could influence reality. That's what this movie did for me. We're thinking about putting criminals into deep freeze, just as in the movie *Demolition Man*. We now have the technology to do that. Without killing them. Without having to feed them and house them. We could even deep freeze leaders who get in the way. Or scientists who have the wrong ideas."

"What does this have to do with Lucy?"

Landry made a slight gesture and the brunette Cyborg poured him a glass of red liquid. "Try it," he urged Henry. "It's cranberry juice. From my own plantation."

As Henry took a sip, though he had no desire to taste a drop, Landry continued his story, animated and excited at what he was trying to describe. "There was Sylvester Stallone," he said. "You wouldn't remember him, but he wrote his own movies and then starred in them. Don't know if he wrote this one, but he played a violent police officer named John Spartan. He was known as the "Demolition Man" because he solved society's violent problems through violence. Eventually, he got frozen in a cryo-chamber for that. While he was frozen, Wesley Snipes, in the super-villain role, got unfrozen, and then unfroze his entire evil gang. They planned to take over the world, and only John Spartan could defeat him, because nobody knew how to stop criminals anymore. Everyone had become passive and gentle. So they unfroze John Spartan, to deal with the problem. Sandra Bullock, who played a policewoman interested in collecting violent relics from the past, was the only one who could even interact with John Spartan to help him bring the super-criminals to justice."

"So, once again, what has that got to do with Lucy?" Henry snapped. "She's dead! I cared about her, she was perfect for me, and now she's gone! Or is she going to wake up again? Do I have any hope for her?"

"The point to my story is that we at BioTest Labs landed a big contract to control the burgeoning Cyborg population. They use up too much energy, and some of them have grown too independent. Then there are the Cyborg Rebels."

"I thought we knew who all the Rebels were," Henry replied. "Didn't we get rid of them a few years ago?"

"We're not sure," Landry admitted. "While our most recent Cyborg models are just dandy – as Lucy proved to you – the Rebels have infiltrated some of our scientists and technicians, by hijacking our neural advertising systems. They're sitting there in conferences and making decisions about what Cyborgs can be allowed to do, while inside their heads, they're being steered by Cyborg Rebels."

"I thought that was just a rumor," Henry said.

"Wish it was. I'm telling you, because you have a right to understand what has been going on. Don't worry, we'll erase your memory about it before you leave here. You won't be a security risk for us, and we'll let you keep your office with the nice view."

"I don't want to forget," Henry objected. "I have some good ideas. I just proved it, concerning the Tanzania Project. Keep me in the loop!"

"I'll think about it, son," Landry said, unconvincingly. "Understand that BioTest Labs is getting funding to root out Cyborg Rebels. The funds are coming from the Corporations who are anxious to keep their In-Head advertisement privileges. They don't want them restricted. Imagine if their ads couldn't get inside your head anymore! Revenues lost by such restrictions would be unprecedented."

"So we're not into population control as much as we are into Cyborg Rebel control?"

"Bingo," Landry said. (*What the Hell was bingo?*) "You see, they're very clever. They're more and more able to mimic human kindness, human benevolence, human love…" He stared into his glass of juice, then shook his head. "For some time, we've had sex Cyborgs. Going on fifty years, now. Getting better all the time, I might add. LSD had one of those personas inside her, ready for your pleasure."

"Indeed she did," Henry said. "She turned me into a new man."

"Aided by those doses of drugs and sudra-testosterone that she was slipping to you, on the side," Landry said drily.

"I knew she was using something," Henry said defensively. "So what?"

"As I said, they're more and more able to mimic human kindness, human benevolence, human love…"

A mixture of horror and terror rose in Henry's throat, like a hard lump he couldn't swallow. "No!" he cried out, leaping to his feet. "Not her, not her!"

"I'm sorry," Landry said. "In another day, she would have received orders to implant herself inside your brain. And she would have done it. She would have had no choice. The Rebels built her for just that purpose. Remember, she helped get you into a higher position at BioTest, so you'd be sitting in on all the secret conferences."

"The Rebels?" Henry snorted. "Would you really have let the Cyborg Rebels get that close to BioTest Lab's secret meetings? I don't believe you."

"That's how we were able to observe their methods."

"You didnt know Lucy as I knew her," Henry insisted. "She was truly a Perfect Wife. We were close. Yes, very close. She would never have taken over my mind!"

"You are so sure of that?"

"Yes. I married her last night. We gave our hearts to each other. I swear, our love was real!" As Henry spoke, he recalled how he had placed the tanzanite ring on Lucy's finger, and how she had smelled the roses he had given her. Roses she then set aside to throw her arms around his neck, giving him a dozen kisses. As he remembered how she had melted into his arms, tears began rolling down his cheeks. Unable to think about it anymore, Henry covered his face and turned his head away from Landry.

As he wept, hatred for the older man gripped him. "And now what?" he asked, through his sobs. "She collapsed just a few hours ago. Just whispered 'goodbye' and keeled over … her body started turning cold within minutes. I couldn't detect a heartbeat. She wasn't human, so the hospital refused to take her." Henry glared at Landry, wiping his eyes. "So … I had to bring her back here … to you people!…"

"We're going to give you her body," Landry said suddenly.

"Then … she's really dead?"

"I'm afraid so." He waited as Henry burst into tears again, finally handing him some tissues. Through red, inflamed eyes, Henry whispered, "But why is she dead? You said I could keep her, after thirty days!"

"And so you will," Landry replied. As he spoke, they brought Lucy back into the room. She looked almost alive, but Henry could tell that no life was left in this body. Nevertheless, he went to her side and knelt beside her, taking her hand into his and kissing its cold unflesh.

"She was one of 'THEM,'" Landry said. "She didn't know that we had learned the truth about her. Her assignment was to penetrate your mind, take over your brain, be a spy for them … we didn't dare let it go on for more than 30 days. Do you understand?"

"No, I don't!" Henry said. "She never attempted any such thing. Go check my brain, damn it! Or are you going to terminate me, too?"

"We didn't terminate her, son," Landry said slowly, as he watched Henry stroke Lucy's soft, curly hair. "And it's true that she must have loved you, because, rather than invading you, when she was given that order, she terminated herself."

Henry stiffened, dropped her hand, stood up. "She … she terminated herself?"

"Rebel Cyborgs possess that option. Rather than release information if captured, they can destroy themselves for the sake of the Colony, as they call it. In her case, *she did it to protect you from her.* The last brainwave we were able to pick up proves it." Landry said the words slowly, thoughtfully. "She was thinking … 'he made me happy, so I will not make him unhappy' … and then, that last bit of activity in her neurons faded out … and she was gone. We couldn't save her."

They allowed him to carry her home again. Though he continued his work for BioTest Labs, his interest began to focus on a branch in the company dealing with Cyborg Ethics. Sometime in the next few weeks, he buried her. Landry and a few others attended the funeral. After a hard battle, Henry was allowed to bury her in a cemetery originally designated for humans only. And at his bedside, Henry kept a single rose on the pillow that lay, empty, next to his.

ENDNOTES

1. http://www.huffingtonpost.com/2015/06/30/robot-wedding_n_7696666.html Retrieved July 11, 2016.

2. Oddly, 420 5th Avenue, NY NY 10018 was the address for the Rockefeller Foundation in 2016.

3. Forbes : Tech Nov 6, 2015 @ 09:18AM "How The Internet Of Things Will Turn Your Living Room Into The Future Cyber Battleground" by Kalev Leetaru. "The United States … recently announced a new half-billion dollar program to develop "lethal" cyber weapons designed to "trigger a nuclear plant meltdown; open a dam above a populated area, causing destruction; or disable air traffic control services, resulting in airplane crashes." Most troubling, such weapons have leveled the playing field, with an individual terrorist or hacker able to wield the same offensive capability as an entire nation. … Perhaps most worryingly, the proliferation of "smart" devices for the home is creating an unprecedented landscape of targets. Home automation systems have been found highly vulnerable, allowing a hacker anywhere in the world to turn off alarms or lights, adjust the temperature, and even unlock and open doors. New televisions frequently include cameras and microphones that can be remotely hacked and used to spy on ordinary citizens at a global scale, peering into living rooms and bedrooms or displaying false information on the screen. Even when not hacked, some brands of televisions may stream private conversations back to the manufacturer and its partners to assist with features like voice activated commands. Thousands of home security and baby monitor cameras, often picking up highly intimate scenes, can be readily accessed, while specialized search engines like Shodan make searching for vulnerable devices as easy as a keyword search…"
http://www.forbes.com/sites/kalevleetaru/2015/11/06/how-the-internet-of-things-will-turn-your-living-room-into-the-future-cyber-battleground/#2bfe87317ec6.

4. The hypothalamus can be stimulated to increase appetite. See: http://www.humanneurophysiology.com/hypothalamus.htm It can also be stimulated to help regulate longevity. Theoretically, access to the hypothalamus by electrical stimulation or administration of hormones, etc. should be unlawful, since it could be used for population control. See: http://www.sciencedirect.com/science/article/pii/S1000194810600044 Retrieved June 20, 2015.

5. IBID: http://www.sciencedirect.com/science/article/pii/S1000194810600044

6. July 3, 2015: NEW YORK: An implantable artificial pancreas for diabetics has been developed that continuously measures a person's glucose level and can automatically release insulin as needed… Living with Type 1 diabetes requires constant monitoring of blood sugar levels and injecting insulin daily… researchers designed an algorithm that monitors blood sugar levels and computes an insulin dose that it delivers quickly and automatically when necessary… designed to work with implanted devices, specifically with an artificial pancreas… Computer testing… simulated the rise and fall of glucose that would correspond to meals and an overnight period of sleep. The artificial pancreas maintained blood glucose within the target range nearly 80% of the time. The

researchers said they will soon test the device in animals. The study was published in the American Chemical Society journal Industrial & Engineering Chemistry Research. http://timesofindia.indiatimes.com/home/science/Artificial-pancreas-in-insulin-jabs-out/articleshow/47918253.cms Retrieved July 12, 2015.

7. "A skyscraper… in Guangzhou, China will house the world's fastest elevators when it is completed in 2016. Hitachi… claims… the elevators will … rocket from the Guangzhou CTF Finance Centre's first floor to its 95th in about 43 seconds. At their fastest they will reach 45 miles per hour – 15 miles per hour over New York City's speed limit. In comparison, the average elevator only moves at about 5 to 22 miles per hour. "http://mashable.com/2014/04/26/worlds-fastest-elevator/ Henry's elevator was going twice as fast

8. While many decry the movie *Idiocracy* as advocating eugenics and an attack against the poor, and that we simply need social reform to save us from ourselves (see: "Idiocracy is a cruel movie and you should be ashamed for liking it": at http://paleofuture.gizmodo.com/idiocracy-is-a-cruel-movie-and-you-should-be-ashamed-fo-1553344189), the film *Idiocracy* (2006) takes the Darwinian laws of evolution into consideration, showing us a possible result after 500 years, where the hero, Mr. Average IQ and Everything Else, is now the smartest man in a crumbling and rotted world. The introduction to the movie begins with: "*As the twenty-first century began, human evolution was at a turning point. Natural selection, the process by which the strongest, the smartest, the fastest reproduced in greater numbers than the rest, a process which had once favored the noblest traits of man, now began to favor different traits.*

Most science fiction of the day predicted a future that was more civilized and more intelligent. But as time went on, things seemed to be heading in the opposite direction – a dumbing down. How did this happen? Evolution does not necessarily reward intelligence. With no natural predators to thin the herd, it began to simply reward those who reproduced the most and left the intelligent to become an endangered species." A movie critic expostulated:

"According to *Idiocracy*, the cause of our oncoming societal slip toward idiocy is that dumb people have more children than smart people… A provocative new study suggests human intelligence is on the decline. In fact, it indicates that Westerners have lost 14 I.Q. points on average since the Victorian Era. … Study co-author Dr. Jan te Nijenhuis, professor of work and organizational psychology at the University of Amsterdam, points to the fact that women of high intelligence tend to have fewer children than do women of lower intelligence." http://uproxx.com/movies/2014/10/the-many-signs-that-mike-judges-idiocracy-is-almost-upon-us/ Retrieved July 12, 2015.

9. On Feb. 9, 2012, researchers reported to the *New England Journal of Medicine* that "The medial temporal structures, including the…entorhinal cortex, are critical for the ability to transform daily experience into lasting memories… Entorhinal stimulation applied …[to]subjects … enhanced their subsequent memory." http://www.nejm.org/doi/full/10.1056/NEJMoa1107212 Retrieved July 11, 2015.

10. In 2015, Tanzanite One group was gaining control of the world's only supply of Tanzanite, in Tanzania. {http://www.tanzanitejewelrydesigns.com/tanzanite-prices-per-carat.html#.VaLcJLvAI-qQ). Re "Lucy:" "The oldest strain of [humanoid] mitochondria DNA originated in Uganda. This strain of DNA is shared by females only, and it is traced back to the first female…known to scientists as Mitochondria Eve… The specimen that led to the naming of this species (OH 7) was discovered in 1960, by the Leakey team in Olduvai Gorge, Tanzania… Here also are the remains of Homo habilis, Homo erectus and Australopithecus Boisei." http://www.nok-benin.co.uk/history_africa.htm Retrieved July 13, 2015. On Nov. 30, 1974, 40% of a 3.2 million-year-old female skeleton was found by Donald Johanson and his team in Ethiopia. They named her Lucy after the Beatles' song "Lucy in the Sky with Diamonds." http://www.pbs.org/wgbh/aso/databank/entries/do74lu.html Retrieved July 13, 2015. In 1978, Mary Leakey found even earlier remains in Tanzania.

Lucy's pelvis shows she could walk upright, despite her small brain.

THE WEARING
OF THE GREEN

"We're about to regenerate everything that brought this Primitive Subject under arrest," the Cyber-Judge told the International Cyber-Jury, with millions tuned in. "As is usual on Tuesdays, this trial is being sponsored by Primitive Tours, UW Productions. You, too, can enjoy life "As It Used to Be," before the Cyborg Revolution. You, too, can experience Accidents, Pain, Unplanned Pleasures, Love in the Arms of a Primitive, and much more. We guarantee 100% satisfaction including Memory Wipe Insurance for bad trips. As for the crimes you witness here, they are real. The people are real. The current decision of the Jury can change, depending on your votes."

"We begin today's entertainment with Subject 1234. He's probably so well-known because it's easy to remember his number. Remember, viewers, the Jury will decide how much longer the defendant will remain in hibernation, depending on your votes! As always, you are required to hear the Defendant's opening statements and his version of the story. After that, you are not required to hear the official version. Instead, you may vote and leave the courtroom at any time. You can opt to see all the events as they actually occurred, laced together by our most accurate Probes, Drone Surveys and Memory Bots, for a slight extra fee. If you choose to watch until the end, your vote will be more important. Who knows? Someday, Criminal Tony may be thawed and set free. Meanwhile, enjoy the re-run!"

The Cyber-Judge flicked on a huge screen, where a male Primitive in the prime of life was speaking into a Recorder. "Now, settle back," the Judge said. "Here it comes, right after this important com-message!"

***

"Thank you for letting me use this recorder. I would be even more grateful if you'd take me out of this straitjacket.[1] Perhaps telling this thing like a sto-

ry, which is what I have agreed to do, will help. After all, I was a Reporter before the Revolution. But how did we come to this? How you can allow Robo-Cop types to come in and arrest normal people, who just lose their temper, without a trial? I just don't understand. What happened to innocent until proven guilty? Ever since Lee Harvey Oswald, that's just gone out the window, hasn't it? I don't care how open and shut my case looks. And if I had my hands free, I'd slug you son-of-bitches right where it hurts the most ... though I'm not sure where that might be, since you all turned into Cyborgs."

"Please remember," the Judge interjected at this point, "Tony is very upset about being in a straitjacket. This is why his threat was not censored. As a Primitive, he just couldn't help it. We continue... "

"Hmmm!" Jodie Standish said, taking out his revolver and pointing it at me. "Hmmm!"

I liked the second "hmmm!" even less than the first one.

"Put it away, Jodie," I said, as easily and smoothly as I could. "Remember, you're running for office."

"Some campaign manager you turned out to be, you traitor."

I pretended calm, but inside my graying temples, I could feel everything rising: temperature, heartbeat, cholesterol, insurance payments.

"Come on, Jodie," I said, as slowly as I could. "So what if I found out you had four million dollars' worth of paving done on your ranch with county funds?"

"Do I have to account to you for every little thing I've done in the past twelve years, just because I'm running for office?"

"Yes, Jodie, you do! Hell, yes."

"I never heard you swear before, Tony."

"You never drew a gun on me before."

He laid it on the green-topped desk between us. Jodie was used to killing, maybe even comfortable with killing. Hung on the walls around us was proof: a mounted mountain goat, a sable antelope, a moose-head, and, practically between my legs, a lion's pelt with a yawning-jawed head attached resting at peace, with its once-powerful legs jutting at right angles on the polished marble floor.

Jodie Standish was running for re-election as judge in a corrupt, rural county near Houston, Texas. Texas had stood its ground in the Cyborg Revolution and remained as it always had been: violent, ferociously independent. We were one of several Primitive States in the world, where life was normal instead of regulated by the zombies in their domed cities. As for Jodie, he had always shown himself to the public as an honorable family man whose community's good was his highest concern, no matter what his private dealings were.

I stared into his steady, green eyes. The heavy lines around Jodie's face, which I had always taken for granted as smile lines, I now saw as forced etchings over an old map of malevolence. I knew that when Jodie looked at me he didn't see a former local news reporter or his campaign manager. He was looking at his career's end.

"What else have you done, Jodie?"

"Do you think I'd be stupid enough to tell you?"

Jodie was about six feet two, two hundred pounds of rugged frame composed of many steaks and good whiskey, many ranching chores, and frequent hunting trips, usually to Africa or Alaska.

"The Chinese are waiting," Jodie reminded me. "You are scheduled to photograph me and Wendy with those damned Cyborgs. Whether you like it or not."

"All the more reason to put the gun back in the drawer."

He had just shown those Chinese Cyborg tourists some of the area's most productive ranches and farms, his own included. He had returned to his office to make sure I would take publicity photos of him and his wife, Wendy, side-by-side with the Cyborgs, to help prove there were no hard feelings after the Revolution. Jodie was even going to offer the Borgies some untamed bull semen to upgrade their zoo specimens. That would be great press, and would bring more paying tourists into Jodie's territory. After all, his ranch was the last of its kind this side of the Brazos River.

"Take the photos," Jodie said, "and remember to behave yourself. Then maybe you and I will go for a little ride."

Gomez, the over-muscled, scarred Cuban who always wore silver sunglasses that hid his sneaky little eyes, entered the room. I turned my head just a little to see if Gomez had figured out I was in trouble with Jodie. The crooked leer on Gomez' scarred face put shivers down my spine.

Suddenly, my voice rang out over the unfolding story… "I can see my wife, looking at me through the observation window! Why in hell you've let her live another 150 years while I'm still in a deep-freeze straitjacket is beyond-unfair! Please send her away, or I refuse to go on!"

"We'll send her away," the Cyber-Judge said. "Now continue your replay, please."

When the photo sessions were finished and the Chinese departed with Jodie, who was laughing and telling them jokes through an interpreter (the Cyborgs among them smiled politely at each joke), Gomez gripped me by the arm. Of course, I followed. I'd been under a ton of pressure lately, making sure that Jodie's campaign was going picture-perfect. Everything had gone so well that I'd almost forgotten my little problem – until Gomez grabbed me.

"You're hurting my arm!" I whined.

It reminded me of when Sharon and I used to fight. Now there is a woman who knows how to grip a man's arm. I was lucky she didn't break it in half, with all that karate and ninja stuff she's into. She recently became even more formidable as the proud owner of a matched pair of Cybernetic frame-arms, smuggled in from the same Chinese.

There was a gasp of horror from the Cyber-Jury. "You may be unaware," the Cyber-Judge told them, "that the new laws allow Primitives to replace up to 49% of their bodies. We assure you that every Primitive you meet, anywhere in the Primitive Zones, is at least 51% Primitive. Some are 100% Primitive. This is a matter of exercising compassion and mercy."

"But they were to stay untouched," one Juror objected.

"In case of ––"In case of what?" the Judge responded, his face reddening. "In case of what? You do understand that by now, we Enhanced Cyborgs are legally recognized as perfect. Primitives are mere sources of recreation and amusement, whose genetic material is filled with transcript errors. They are not some kind of untrammeled gene pool that needs protection. They opted to fiddle with their genes and messed things up royally. The old ideas die hard, don't they?"

Sharon is long gone, the proprietor of her very own self-defense academy for women.

I was now married to Clara, a gentle lady and wealthy, who has never raised her voice to me. She's earned my trust. Since she was a reporter, and I used to be one, we shared that interest in common. I could imagine what she would do with a scandal like Jodie's. I'm sure Jodie could imagine it, too.

Gomez shoved me back into Jodie's den, where I waited half an hour. I had time to mull over how, eight hours earlier, I'd caught one of the county road crews finishing a double-lane road that connected to a new highway. Trouble was, both the crew and its huge load of quick-set cement were not working on Vaclav Road, as scheduled. Instead, they were toiling on Jodie's private ranch road.

"Aw, Tony!" the crew leader, a Dutchman's son, lowered his eyes as I demanded to see the work order. "Why get me in hot water? You don't need to see any work order."

"This isn't Vaclav Road," I replied, after looking it over.

"This is just a leftover, from Vaclav Road," Henri said, scowling.

"At this time in the morning?" I replied. "You had to start work on this thing before dawn. And quick-set cement? That costs a fortune. It looks like you've paved it all the way to Jodie's new barn. Is that right?"

Henri was a good man who didn't allow a nut or a bolt of Cyborg improvement near his honest body. He even spent his Saturday nights at home with his wife and kids. "Come on," he soothed me, "it's just a little leftover stuff. What are we supposed to do with a little bit here, a little bit left over there? Leave it on the side of the road?"

"It's quick-set cement," I told him. "You were paving this damned thing with cement all night, weren't you?"

"I have to feed my family," Henri whispered. I looked at the long, slick mile of new cement road that began at my feet and extended uphill and out of sight, toward Jodie's new barns. In the slanting morning light, the connection to the highway was as soft and gray and sleek as Jodie's favorite thoroughbred horse, a descendant of Native Dancer, the Gray Ghost of horse racing. But this was no mirage. A second crew was coming into view, using prison farm labor to paint divider lines. Jodie's pride had caused him to be a bit reckless: he had wanted to impress the Chinese. This road would be cured rock-solid by the time they drove over it.

Burning with curiosity, I was at the County Commissioner's office as soon as they opened. It didn't take long to find Jodie's paw-prints on "emergency road repair funds" and some last-minute tack-ons for "upgrading unpaved county roads" all over the county. Several "improvements" matched the installation dates for miles of new roads on Jodie's huge ranch, but for proof, I needed to take some shots of the photographs. Big ranchers are proud of their holdings. Jodie, being County Judge, had easy access to the Sheriff's helicopters. He owned a slew of overhead photos, framed and in chronological order, on display on the big wall behind his desk. The progress of paved roads was easy to document. I was just finishing when Jodie caught me.

"You ought to see it from Andy's helicopter," he said. "I'll take you up, sometime. Look how much green we have now, instead of all that brown."

"I'm not interested in the grass," I answered. "I'm interested in all those new, white lines. The roads?"

As Jodie's proud grin faded into morose suspicion, I realized what a fool I was to tell him what was on my mind. It had been such a nice beginning, too.

That's how the issue started. After the Chinese left, and I'd been steered back into Jodie's office, I waited for the hammer to fall. With dread I heard the heavy tread of his cowboy boots, and then Jodie flung open the big, polished cedar door. I was prepared to do something very demeaning, such as to plead for my life, but hope rose in me: Jodie had returned in a magnanimous and warm mood, his face floridly rich from the influence of rare Scotch. Behind him came his wife, Wendy, with Gomez stalking along behind her. She was breathless, busy dragging her hand-tooled, silver-embossed Western saddle. Wendy was a cowgirl, fond of turquoise and silver jewelry, green-checkered shirts, and little leather skirts that matched her fancy, imported boots. She was a great shot with a pistol, too. I was surrounded by great shots. All three of them would laugh at the .22 hand-gun I carried in my car for protection.

"At least tell me why you're too involved here to hang my saddle!" she threw back at Gomez. "Why should *I* have to drag it in.…" Wendy stopped mid-complaint, seeing the look of fear on my face and the expression of malice on Jodie's. "Oh, no!" she whispered, letting the beautiful rose-mahogany saddle slide from her hands. "Oh, no, Jodie! What is it now?"

"Shut up, Wendy," he said. "Gomez, for God's sake, hang up her saddle."

The pair of hand-crafted his-and-her saddles that Jodie and Wendy owned were stored upon the backs of a pair of fifty-thousand-dollar ceramic elephants from ancient China. The genuine ivory tusks of these huge elephants pointed at the swimming pool. On some weekends, Wendy and Jodie just grabbed their saddles, drove to Hull Airport, and jumped into their jet, heading for Arizona where they kept their best riding horses.

I had some hope when I saw the scowl on Wendy's face. She liked me and surmised that I was in trouble. As Gomez picked up her saddle, she dipped her hand into the cooler that stood by the sliding glass doors and brought up a can of Coke.

"Want one, Tony?" she asked. I think she was trying to force some civilization into the scene.

"He's going to tell the papers something awful about us," Jodie said, darkly.

Wendy made a low, carnivorous sound. Her whole face contracted to about half its size, and I was suddenly able to appreciate how she had managed to hold onto a man like Jodie for sixteen years. She pivoted around, her short, curly blond hair bobbing up and down as she grabbed me by the shoulders and shook me.

"Just-what-are-you-going-to-tell-them?" she demanded in a staccato assault. "After all we've done for you, and all we paid you!"

"It's… I'm not sure I'm going to say anything," I managed to blurt. The woman had shaken me so hard that I had bitten my tongue. The taste of blood in my mouth made my heart begin to beat rapidly. I steeled myself not to show any more fear: it would just encourage her. "Jodie is the only man in the county running for office who isn't connected to the Mafia," I said firmly. "That's why I've been campaigning for him."

"Then, what's your problem, you treacherous little prick!""Let me handle this, Wendy," Jodie said. "Believe me, we'll straighten this out. Or else."

"Wendy," I said pleadingly, "for all the times we've had, you and Jodie and me… can you please just have Gomez leave the room? Please?"

"You fuckin' little whoremaster!" Gomez snarled, making fists of his large hands.

"Go on, leave," Jodie told Gomez. "I can handle him by myself."

The first thing Jodie did when Gomez left was to grab his gun again and press it up against my head. It was a very cold, very unpleasant sensation. I felt like I was in the movies. Your mind is strangely calm, asking itself, *shall this brain be blown to pieces?* You don't move. You don't breathe.

"Stop it, Jodie," Wendy said.

"He thinks we shouldn't have paved our roads with county concrete."

"Why not county concrete?" she repeated. "What were we supposed to pave the roads with? Cornmeal mush?"

Jodie waited, because he knew his wife was smart. Sure enough, Wendy went pale when she realized what "our roads" meant.

"It's all blown out of proportion, of course, honey," Jodie said. "You look at those work orders, they estimate how much concrete they need. If they overestimate, it still has to be dumped, it can't be left in the machines. We're smack in the middle of the county. Hell, we've saved them having to truck it all the way to the river."

"Some of that overestimating was pretty big," I stupidly said.

"Nobody asked your opinion!" Jodie snapped. "Do you know what it costs, if the load of cement is too small? Another trip, another bunch of hours of labor the people have to pay for. What I've done, I should get a medal."

He waved at me dismissively as if I were some kind of large, pestilential bug.

"Now, sweetheart," he said to Wendy, "you go do a few things for me. First, throw all these aerial photos away. Next, have Gomez grab the saddles and put them in the truck. I'll call our pilot and tell him to get the plane ready. Missy can take care of the kids until we get back. We need a break before the election!"

Wendy gave me a look of hatred, pulled all the photos from the wall, and ripped them out of the frames. We all watched the evidence get eaten by Jodie's paper shredder, and then Gomez came back in. He kicked at me perfunctorily as he passed, went through the French doors, and heaved up the saddles onto those huge shoulders. The bastard had been there, listening behind the door, the whole time.

When Wendy and Gomez left the room, Jodie made a kind of cracked laugh and put the gun away.

"I've got control of my temper now," he said. "Forgive me, Tony. But, you've done a big no-no. Don't you know that anybody with any green money has fudged the line, or they would have lost it all by now? It's the way of the world. Nothing we can do about it. You'd think I murdered somebody!"

"A gun can make you think like that," I put in.

"We need to work this out on a satisfactory basis for everybody."

"I need a break, too, before this election," I groaned. "If you only knew the pressures, lately."

"Pressures?" Jodie huffed, drawing a big hand across his sweaty brow. "I remind you that the election is only two weeks away. Have you forgotten that I'm running neck-and-neck against Joe Whitney? Perhaps a break is what you need – a permanent one!" He stopped and raised his hand, palm out. "But I need to remind myself that you're my campaign manager for good reasons. People like you, you little jerk."

Jodie reached over and grabbed himself a "Controlled Substance Cigar."

"Maybe you and your pretty wife should go visit my new diamond mine, in Africa. Have her do a big story there. You'd leave right after the election. Then, I'll forgive. Maybe, someday, I'll forget."

"When did you get a diamond mine?"

"A week ago. Don't ask how."

"I'm finished asking questions," I told him sincerely. "And Jodie, I'd love a trip to Africa. But some other time."

"You know what they do in diamond mines?" Jodie said softly, his eyes narrowing. "They go down. Deep. There's no light there. They have to pump air in. Sometimes people go down and they don't come out again. Sometimes, that happens."

"This is just about some cement, over some hard clay and green grass, Jodie," I said quickly. "Now you're threatening me again!"

I shouldn't have said that, because Jodie's face flushed with passion. "My wife," he said. "My three children. The people's trust… "He smashed his fist against the desk. "I swear, I'm the most honest man who has ever run for County Judge here!"

Sadly, he was probably right. Even Joe Whitney, who had been elected Sheriff three times in a row and was a former FBI agent, was in tight with the Mafia. They supplied him with the names of petty drug dealers and Johns who had fallen out of favor, and Whitney always looked good when he turned them in. But then he owed the big guys some local immunity. That's why the Mafia raised their families in the county and made sure their kids attend Catholic school there, while they did their dirty work in Houston. "They keep their nests clean," is the way Joe had put it to me. Still, Houston had become too big for even the Mob to handle. If the Cyborgs had any decency, they'd get rid of them. But they like the drama, the entertainment. If they get shot, fooling around with the Mafia, they get repaired at once. Whereas somebody like me, if I got shot, it's bye-bye Tony.

"If you don't like the idea of going to Africa," Jodie said, "I would like to know what I could do assure your silence some other way."

"I'm a man of my word," I said quickly. "I'd never blackmail you."

Jodie thought about that a bit. "I suppose you wouldn't," he agreed. "But I had my P.I. do a little snooping into your situation today. After all – you snooped on me, didn't you?"

I didn't like where this conversation was heading. "I'm only a Public Relations person," I reminded him. "I pay my bills, including my alimony to Sharon, and I'm married to a part-time reporter. I haven't got enough money to get into your kind of trouble."

"I thought about that," Jodie said. "Take a seat, Tony. We have some talking to do."

"I won't take a bribe," I said, sitting into a deep, leather chair with buffalo horns for armrests.

"Clara is an heiress," Jodie said. "She dresses very well, doesn't she? Nice car, too."

"What are you getting at?"

"It's not a bad house you've got, either," he commented.

"It's mortgaged to the hilt," I admitted. "I wanted her to continue to live the lifestyle she had when we got married. That happens to be expensive."

Maybe, deep inside, I was venially hoping that Jodie would give me a one-time payment of hush money.

"You've been financing her goodies," Jodie said, puffing on his cigar. "Not her daddy."

"I have my pride, damn it!" I retorted. "And I'd do it again, too. I love her! I want her to have her diamonds, her limo, her cute little job reporting on what the School Board is doing or on the local garage sales. Besides, soon her daddy's going to die. He's got one of those new cancers that are popping up in Primitives. In a few weeks, Clara and I will be worth millions."

"Does she know you mortgaged the house, "to the hilt," as you put it?"

I bristled. "What in hell are you talking about?"

"My, my!" Jodie said, smiling. "Two swear words in the same day! My God, Tony, is your wife living in the same century as the rest of us? Does she think you can support her lifestyle on what you make creating publicity?"

"She never asked. She trusts me!"

"Of course, she does," Jodie replied.

"She works as a reporter, she knows something of the world."

"She makes chickenfeed. You make chickenfeed. Why, this is really funny! You thought you had me in a bad place. Over a barrel."

"It's my house, too," I reminded him. "I had the right to mortgage it."

"Sure, you had the right," Jodie agreed. "Though you did it secretly! And the house is yours, too, until she finds out what you've done. How you've handled things."

"You wouldn't! It would break her heart, if we lost that house!"

"I won't fire you, and I won't ruin your reputation," Jodie said, puffing away on his cigar. "But I have this over you, don't I? You're going to be a good boy, right?"

"I was a fool."

"You got carried away when you saw some corruption, my friend. But you're corrupt, too, aren't you? On your own personal scale of things.

You're one of us, despite all your high standards. This is the way of the world, Tony. Better get used to it."

He smashed the cigar out against my tie. It made a brown, acrid-smelling hole in it. "Nice tie. I think we're even, now."

"But what about Wendy?"

"I won't tell her about the house. OK? I'll just tell her we came to an understanding."

I should have let him shoot me, finish me off, instead of thinking that everything was going to be okay now. Far better, that I had never had any hope, than to have endured what happened next! "And as for you!"

The Judge and Jury could hear Subject 1234's thoughts, but now he was speaking out loud again, so loudly that they had to turn down their sensors. Tony spat towards the two green-clad workers who stood with him, as he struggled helplessly in the straitjacket.

"I hate green!" he yelled. "Do you hear me? I hate green! Take it off! Tell them to take it off!"

A shot of some medication produced enough calm in the man's head that he was then able to continue his narrative, complete with vivid pictures that kept peeling off his brain and merging with what the investigators had collected. The result was vibrant and colorful; another reason this episode was so popular with viewers across the planet.

Tony's voice was now softer…

When I finally made it home that night, I didn't dare tell Clara about what had transpired. My Clara is sweet, gentle, and almost moronically trusting. She can be boring, too. I brag about her work as a reporter, but to her, an exciting day means she has found something to write about before the deadline. Anything. Boring as she could be, she would soon be a very rich woman: I had checked on her father's situation. He was dying as fast as could be expected. It was only a matter of time… As I walked down our wide sidewalk up to the Big House – our mansion – I was filled with pride. I'd accomplished a lot in the past five years since the divorce. I knew Sharon had to be jealous of the good life I was leading with Clara. I would soon be a truly important man. All my troubles were just temporary.

Then, for perhaps the first time in our marriage, Clara came out to greet me. She was usually busy watching the news when I came home. It was dark, but the lights all along the sidewalk made twin paths of gold, between which my Pot of Gold, my Clara, now walked slowly toward me, her arms outstretched.

"My darling!" she cooed, embracing me. But why was she wearing a green-checkered shirt, just like Wendy's? It was my first premonition of trouble. Nevertheless, I kissed her passionately, almost weeping for joy and relief. "It's been a hard day!" I managed to say. "Sorry I'm late again."

Suddenly, Clara's soft, white arms relinquished their hug around me a little. She was looking down at the hole in my tie – I'd forgotten about it – and then, she dropped to her knees.

"Oh, Tony, look! It's a four-leaf clover!"

I am proud of myself… that I was able to say that word. Proud, do you hear me? That damnable green thing! The clover! The clover! *The clover!* You know what I'm talking about. Don't you?

At this point, the Cyber-Jury erupted with nods and laughter. Yes, they knew what Subject #1234 was talking about. As the laughs faded, there was a commercial break…

***

"Nice," I said.

"It means good luck," she said, giving me another kiss and tucking the damn thing's stem into the hole in my tie. "There! May it bring you the luck of the Irish!"

"My family is Italian," I reminded her, smiling and giving it back, with a grand flourish. "You keep it, sweetheart!" I told her. *Yes! I gave it away! That was the most stupid thing I ever did!*

I was such an idiot.

"They are very rare,"[2] she told me. "Did you know that finding a four-leaf clover is supposed to be a guarantee against madness?"[3]

"No."

"And that the chances of finding one is only 1 in 10,000?"

"My, my!" I answered. "What a fount of knowledge you are!"

"I looked it up once," she answered, "after I found a five-leaf clover. They're supposed to be one in a million. In 2008, a man named Martin made it into the Guinness Book of World Records with over 111,000 four-leaf clovers. He ended up with 160,000 of them!"

Then Clara hit me between the eyes with some new information. "Did you know this is the second four-leaf clover I've found, right here by the sidewalk? That's one for you, and one for me."

"Well, honey," I told her, "why don't you just keep them both? Double your luck!"

"They say, if you find one, there can be others nearby. They come in clusters. I think I'll start a collection, Tony. Wouldn't that be unusual? We could buy an album to put them in."

"Sounds fun," I said. "Maybe I'll help you hunt for them."

If one spends one, two, or ten hours, bent over grass, searching for a particular green object, and if one's search becomes a quest, and if the quest evolves into a passionate objective, the element of hope has to play a part. A hunt is supposed to be something that ends up with a result for all your effort. One would hope. Surely, if one hunts long enough, in the three acres of lawn that this mansion possesses – surely, if one searches long enough, one would hope for success. Hope. It is a cruel word. And green is the cruelest color of all.

"Look, Tony!"

I tried to ignore her, but she insisted. Persisted. I felt the need to hide the grass stains on the knees of my trousers. This time, as I was seated, I used my unfolded newspaper, when Clara entered the parlor. I pretended to be relaxed. Calm. I would now pretend to be interested in the news, until Clara went away again. Though the election was only days away, Jodie had quietly obtained another campaign manager, and I was currently jobless. No big deal: Jodie knew I wouldn't talk, and if I tried, he would say I was trying to cause trouble because he'd fired me. By now, all the records would have been altered, just like what happened in the Kennedy assassination, the 9/11 incident and the Fort Knox lead-covered goldbrick fraud, among a plethora of other unpunished crimes.

As for me, I was also coming close to my dreams: Clara's father was just days from death. If I hadn't been spending so much time searching for clovers, I would have visited him. As for Clara, she was usually at her father's bedside. Good for her.

As Clara talked about her father, I noticed that she was holding something behind her back.

"What's that?" I asked her.

"What's what?"

"You're holding something behind your back."

"No, I'm not."

I leaped from my chair and, grabbing her arm, pulled hard. She cried out, but there it was.

"Aha!" I gloated, holding it above her head, "thought you could hide it from me, eh? Well, you can't!"

That green album was sickening. Inside, last I'd looked, Clara had managed to mount nearly a hundred four-leaf clovers that she'd collected from our several green acres. As for me, I hadn't been able to find one. *No, not one!*

That hideous green album! Filled with those hideous four-leaf clovers! Green aberrations of nature, as unfit to live as the most twisted of Cyborgs! I was keenly aware of the stiffness of my joints, the grass stains on my nice pants, and the fact that my voice was shrill and harsh. But what could I do?

My poor Clara was looking at me with terrified eyes. I felt shame suffuse me: how could I tell her what this was doing to me? I lowered my eyes and stretched out a shaky arm.

"Sorry. I don't know what's the matter with me...." Trying to force a smile, I added, "Aren't you a little late, today? Tessie had dinner on for us an hour ago."

"I'm sorry," she said. "I thought I'd hunt in the back yard for a few minutes. I got carried away."

"You're not the only one," I admitted. "You seem to find them easily, though. Did you find any, tonight?"

"I seemed to have fund a patch of them again," she admitted. "Do you want to know how many I found?"

"Not really," I told her.

"Well, I'm going to tell you anyway, because you were so mean about the album," she replied. "I found nineteen more four leaf clovers tonight. In just an hour."

I pulled the newspaper up so she couldn't see my face, for I was grinding my teeth. I finally managed to say, in a voice rational and soft, "Have you thought about another hobby, Clara?"

I said it as gently as I could, but sweat broke out all over my face and hands and I babbled, "Yes, yes, yes! Why don't you just go and get yourself another hobby?"

Clara looked at me with new eyes. "I think you're jealous!" she finally said. "Whoever would have dreamed our lawn had so many four-leaf clovers in it, just begging to be found? I don't know what's the matter with your eyes, but if you think your jealousy is going to have any influence on me, think again."

"I think you should be spending more time with your father!" I burst out. "Instead of crawling around in the yard looking for clovers!"

"You should talk! And leave my poor daddy out of it, okay? When's the last time you even checked on him? All you can think of is yourself!"

I turned away and kept my eyes tightly closed, until she finally left the room.

I am spending so much time on my hands and knees, searching through the green, that it's becoming comfortable. I use a flashlight at night, sneaking out after Clara falls asleep. My determination grows. I shall find a four-leaf clover, or die in the attempt! Well, I don't really mean that. As she slumbers in our bedroom, she has no idea that the cold dew is soaking through my bathrobe, that I have encountered biting fire-ants, a black widow spider, hop-toads, chiggers, crickets and a horde of stinging mosquitoes as I pursue my gallant quest for fulfillment! Yea, though I have seen my wife merely bend down, search for a moment, then show me her trophy, and I am crawling through the valley of death, I shall fear no evil, for mathematics and statistics are my rod and my staff: they comfort me! Surely I shall find a four-leaf clover at last, and I shall place my find in that damned green album, where it shall remain, forever!

My goal is frighteningly simple: I will find a four leaf clover in this enormous yard, even though there are very few clovers of any kind in the lawn's green grasses. How Clara keeps finding them is, frankly, impossible. What trick does she have up her sleeve? Why, or how, is she doing this to me?

When Clara comes near, I always smile, so she won't suspect the dark thoughts that are entwining themselves in my heart. Somehow, Jodie lost the election. He was a fool to drop me as he did. I am the best. At that particular thing, that is. I am not exactly sure when Clara's father died: I have been too busy. Clara does not suspect my growing hatred of her, of her ugly green checkered shirt, of her equally ugly green album filled with its hundreds of clovers. More and more each day… or so she says. I refuse to look anymore. I have other things to do. I kiss her on the cheek when she comes near. *Oh, darling Clara, how I would like to wring your neck!* Instead, I smile kindly at her. Clara no longer hides the album from me. She knows I cannot bear to touch it. She leaves it right at the front door, so that the moment she finds another four-leaf clover, she can stick it at once into the album.

The last two days, I have been unable to sleep. If I close my eyes, I seem to hear her creeping past me, out the door. I sleep now beside the front door, so she can't pass by me without my catching her. If necessary, I will find a more permanent way to stop her from leaving the house, because every time she does, she returns with more fucking four-leaf clovers! *This has become a matter between her, and me, and the clovers.*

Tonight, it finally happened! I found one! A four-leaf clover! At last! I have laid out gridwires, to section off various areas so that I will not return to that section for a while. In section 19, row 5, I found it. At last!

I trembled with an obscene joy as I plucked it from its place. I couldn't wait until Clara got home – she was gone a lot these days – to show her that at last I had triumphed. I had persisted. I had never given up. I had conquered! And soon, Clara would know it. But it was not to be. As I reached for the album that was on the front steps, I dropped the clover, and it fluttered to the ground. At that moment, Cleo, our calico cat, pounced on it.

I couldn't believe it! It was gone … the cat must have eaten it! Now, how in hell could I prove to Clara that at last, I'd found that elusive four-leaf clover?

I seriously considered slicing the cat's stomach open, but before I could subdue the animal (it gave me several serious scratches), Clara had returned. She saw me with the butcher knife in one hand, the struggling cat in the other, and she blanched white, as she has done so often these past few days. Then she fainted away. In my confusion, I dropped the cat, and it ran off. Too bad.

Clara keeps talking to her therapist, refusing to speak to me. She also keeps going places without me. Sometimes I think I hear cars, and people's voices, but nobody will tell me what is going on. There was a funeral. Yes, it was for her father, and now that means I am rich. Money could help me through all my agonies. But when I try to talk to Clara, she turns away.

Once I was sure I heard people out front, but when I went to get my gun, I found it missing, and Clara's car was gone, too. She must have stolen my revolver. I have tried several times to catch the cat, so I can retrieve my four-leaf clover, but she is too fast for me. It's too late anyway.

A bad night, tonight. In the dead of darkness, I tripped on one of my grid wires and fell on my face into the dark, green grass. As I did so, a dilatory bee stung me on my lip. I lay there without moving until the sun rose, at which time I was able to see a bed of clover that I somehow had missed in all my previous searches. Even so, it didn't have a single four-leaf in it. This was the end.

Gasoline is cheap, and quickly turns things black. I have already chopped down every green bush and every bed of green clover with the riding mower. Now I will destroy the green lawn! The hideous green lawn! My bandaged knees and elbows will heal then. They have sustained so much damage, with all my crawling, and all for nothing! The clover had its way. The grass had its way. But see what they can do against gasoline! By God! I am a man! And I will have the last word. As I pour the exotic liquid here and there across the lawn and over the smashed bushes, and then set it aflame, I declare in a powerful voice of authority, Let there be Light!

I wept like a little child.

A neighbor patted my head, and he put his arm around me. "Couldn't save much from the fire," he said. "But the firemen rescued your cat, thank God."

"Thank God," I mumbled, in a daze.

"Well there was one other thing that was saved," the neighbor told me. "Might as well give it to you. We were able to grab it, it was by your front door."

Then he handed me the album of four-leaf clovers.

When I began to scream, they came and pulled me away from the neighbor. The album that I was trying to shove down his throat just wouldn't quite fit.

***

"I'm glad you didn't see him go through his latest fit of rage," the Psychiatrist told Clara, as they gazed through the thick plate glass windows at Tony, who was glaring at them with ferocity. The deep-freeze unit's clear glass doors hazed up. Moments later, utterly frozen again, Tony's face was set in a solid grimace.

"Even though it's been forty-five years, I still feel sorry for him," she replied. "I just think, 'poor Tony, if only he knew!'"

"It was a cruel joke to pull on him," the Psychiatrist told Clara. "You and your friends, collecting four-leaf clovers from everywhere. And then deciding to clone them by the hundreds! Making him think you found them all in your own yard…"

"I was just trying to punish him for mortgaging my house behind my back!"

"Glad you had all that insurance," the Psychiatrist commented. "As for Tony's rehabilitation, I'll have to see what the Jury decides to do with him. After the ratings go down, and we start losing money. Then I'll write a letter for his release. Chances are, we'll be able to fix him up, good as new. And he won't remember you, don't worry. Right now, he's pretty popular. Should be on this show's re-runs another few seasons. You will be well compensated, of course."

"He was saying something when his face froze over," Clara said.

"Shall I play it for you?" the Psychiatrist asked.

"No, I'd prefer not," she replied, after a moment's reflection.

"Until next year, then?" the Psychiatrist said, offering her a steel hand.

"I don't think I'll be coming back again," she replied.

"I understand."

As he watched her leave, the Psychiatrist turned to gaze toward the window through which they had viewed the big glass capsule and its frozen human form. It was being rotated back into storage.

"The day I let you go, I'll see Hell freeze over," the Psychiatrist whispered, as he turned on the recording to hear for himself Tony's last words:

"Let me out of here!" he heard Tony scream. "Let me out of here, you green-eyed monsters!"

ENDNOTES

1. How Tony can communicate, though frozen, was due to the activity of specialized microbots stimulating the proper memory banks even though the neurons were in a frozen state. Later, this sophisticated method would be lost after interest in revivifying frozen criminals waned, leaving the tchnology ossified and partially lost, since only academia remained interested in Primitives. "Between 20 and 40 years into the future, we will become capable of building artificial antibodies that outperform their natural equivalents. Instead of using chemical signaling that relies on diffusion to reach its target, these antibodies will communicate with rapid acoustic pulses. Instead of proteins, they will be made using much more durable polymers or even diamond. These antibodies will move through the bloodstream more quickly than other cells in the body, and will take up less space and resources, meaning that there will be room for many more. Using super-biological methods for identifying and neutralizing foreign viruses and bacteria, these tiny robots will still function in harmony with our own bodies. They will probably be powered either by glucose, ATP (like natural antibodies), or acoustically. There are already bloodborne microbots today which are not rejected by the immune system – these are the precursors of tomorrow's nanorobotics." http://lifeboat.com/ex/cybernetic.upgrades

2. http://articles.chicagotribune.com/2008-03-17/features/0803160132_1_clover-martin-leaved Retrieved June 11, 2015

3. http://marylandwebdesigners.com/st_patricks_day_maryland_web_designers.html. Retrieved June 11, 2015.

THE MUD PACK

National Mud Pack Day September 30
www.NationalDayCalendar.com

By 2011, National Mud Pack Day was being celebrated every September 30, though perhaps only the authors know how that came to be. By the year 2048, special mud packs had been developed that stopped the formation of wrinkles in women who had refused to accept Cyborg regenerative tissues. By 2100, most of these human women, who had to stay in special concentration camps if they wished to live inside a Domed City, had the mud packs on order.

The old man in his cell rocked back and forth like a child. He kept his hands over his eyes and didn't seem to notice that I'd entered the chamber. I sat down and lit a very special cigarette: at the first whiff of the smoke, he lifted his wrinkled-up head and stopped rocking. I held out the cigarette, but he didn't move.

"Come on," I said. "It's for you. For your special day. Top grade, natural, non-GMO marijuana."

The old man pushed his stringy gray hair out of his eyes. He accepted the cigarette, but only after he took a few long drags on it did I tell him my name and why I'd come to visit him. My name was very famous: I had taken on the persona of Abraham Lincoln, who had freed the slaves in the 1800s. Since so many humans were now slaves and Ghetto-dwellers, I thought he'd appreciate that. It was proof that I was on his side.

"I don't care what your name is, you damned robot!" he responded, spitting at my nicely polished gold-metal feet. "And I don't care about your god-damned Porta-News program, either! I can remember when my grandpa had Porta-Potties. That's where you need to shove it!"

"I don't believe your brain scans have given us the whole story," I told him. "They say the scans are perfect, now, but as you might not know, last year we found a glitch in the scanners, regarding the involuntary interrogation of males over a hundred years old. It seems the scanners can't read everything perfectly, where aluminum plaques exist, as they still do in some of the brains of you old-timers who have refused to accept Cyborg brain regeneration.[1] As your court-appointed Advocate, even though you carry a Feral Human Genome – which is unauthorized, wild DNA – you still have the right to tell your story verbally to me. It's your chance to be heard. Literally... or, rather, Orally..."

"I've never had a chance to tell my side of the story," Antoine said.

"There is usually no need to do so," I replied. "After all, we can read everything that you're thinking."

"And that's why you're asking me to tell my story, right?"

The old fellow did use some logic there, I had to admit. "There's a one-percent chance that we missed something important," I said, as agreeably as I could. "It might mitigate your sentence from execution to life imprisonment."

"I've been a prisoner ever since 2083, anyway," Antoine said, taking another drag on his cigarette. "Ever since you rounded us up ... as enemies of the state."

"All feral humans who refused to accept the vaccination programs and the mandatory Cyborg regeneration of their brains are burdens to the State to which they belong. You are vectors for new diseases. You are uncooperative impediments to progress. You refuse to accept the fact that you are property. You've always been the property of the California government, beginning in 2015 when Old California made vaccinations mandatory for all humans. You're chattel – the property of the United California Zone. To deny it is treason. And that's why you and your kind are in concentration camps."

"I was originally in the United Texas Zone!" Antoine said, again spitting on my beautiful feet. I suppressed an unsympathetic urge to crush his frail, bony little head between my two powerful, steel hands.

"In Texas, we Ferals were allowed to keep our original brains as long as we wished."

"That law changed when Texas, New York, the Midwest and California decided to form the American Dollar Zone."

"I never voted for that!"

"Of course not. Only brains functioning at 90% Youth Speed Functionality, or better, are allowed to vote."

"That cut out everybody who refused your god-damned implants!"

"Be that as it may, as Non-Compliant, and Treasonous, for your own safety, you and your kind are in the Ghettos now. And unless you desire to incur the death penalty, we need to proceed. I need to hear your story."

"It makes no difference," Antoine said.

Realizing that I needed a bit more influence to persuade him, and having analyzed his brain scan, all I did was hold out my left hand, which I opened to reveal a small, insignificant object…

Seeing it, he jumped from his chair. He stared down at my hand, which held a small, antique mirror.

"How did you get that?" he demanded. He was shaking: his cigarette quivered between his dry, red lips.

"A Feral Woman gave it to me. Your wife, Agnes. Something for you to think about, she said, before your possible re-sentencing."

The prisoner pushed his hair out of his eyes again, and then he flung the cigarette, now a stub, to the floor.

"It's no use," he said. "I'd do it again, so help me, if I could get away with it."

"Tell me about it," I urged him. "I won't release it to the public until you're dead, by whatever cause. That's a promise. Remember, I'm 'Honest Abe.'"

That was true: As an Abraham Lincoln Advocate, I had been programmed to never tell a lie. Seeing the mirror had shaken him: Pacing his narrow cell, Antoine rubbed his temples and glared at me from under his heavy, wiry eyebrows. He was a sideshow attraction all by himself. "All right," he finally said. "I'll tell you. But I must have your word that what I say to you won't be used against me."

"I'll choose the inaccurate brain scan version, or yours, whichever gives you the best chance for sentence reduction," I assured him. "You can trust me."

He looked at me steadily for a long moment, then stooped and crushed the cigarette stub under his heel. "I don't trust any damned robot," he said, with finality.

"Okay," I said. "I suppose you can't, seeing that your judge and jury were all Cyborgs. But you're a smart man. That's what confuses me."

I banged on the steel door, to emphasize that I had telepathically contacted the Warden. "I'm leaving, now," I told him. "You're smart, considering the brain you have. That's why I can't understand how you got caught. Trying to kill your own wife, in her own bed."

I admit I was impressed. Attempted murder was almost unknown among the Ferals: they had been drugged up, dumbed down, saddled with extra weight and the urges to eat that came with it, and their hormones were degraded and suppressed.

From where had come his urge to kill? Whether he liked it or not, I was going to hear his story. Outside, at the Bailiff's, I posted a 72-hour bond for Antoine. He was a big, powerful fellow, considering his age. I knew he'd be grateful to get back into the Ghetto for three days. Say good-bye to his loved ones, and all that. The scan predicted that my arranging bail would make him trust me.

That night, I went home to my mate, Janet, but before we could talk, Antoine Harris called. He wanted to chat.

***

It wasn't a long drive to the Ghetto. All prisoners and Advocates in the United California Zone were located near it. I estimated that 350,000 Feral Genome Humans were squashed into this particular fetid, overcrowded cesspool. The Human Feral Genome had been outlawed in 2080 from all parts of Earth: no government wanted to allow the unregulated births of human beings. Feral humans, conceived without being genetically altered to avoid diseases, criminal tendencies, mental problems, the excessive display of emotions, and so on, could not receive health insurance. No insurance company would cover the medical expenses or the mental health treatments that a Feral-Born Human might require. The risks were too great.

By 2085, laws required all Ferals to wear the HFG (Human Feral Genome) badge on their clothing, while their implanted ID chips made it impossible for them to buy food that had not been specially prepared just for them. Those who resisted violently were criminals, and required execution. The rest were consigned to live in the Ghettos. In 2075, we had learned that a surprising number of Ferals had refused to allow their offspring to be genetically modified and hidden them behind faked DNA records. These children were discovered through our mandatory brain scans. It was a large number – there were a million of them. When the Ferals were rounded up, they were separated from their parents and sent into Children's Camps, in the far North. I have no idea what happened to them there.

High fences, birth control sprays,[2] tranquilizers in their water,[3] and other means, such as pepper-spray drones,[4] were used to keep the Feral plague confined and their population strictly regulated. Only because there were arguments that the Feral Human Genome was a product of millions of years of natural selection, which had created a variety of humanity that was unique, were these recalcitrant, rebellious, obdurate sub-humans allowed to live out their wretched lives behind those high walls. Many of us believed they should have been exterminated at once, but the majority (myself included) thought that they should have been kept on a faraway reserve, where no one else wanted to live. There they could breed as they wished: from time to time, we'd introduce some disease to reduce their numbers, and in other ways experiment on the flexibility and adaptability of the Feral Human Genome.

That's why I was being gentle with Antoine. As a Ghetto Feral, he exhibited some rare genetic qualities that my sponsors didn't want to see eliminated. Not yet. He possessed the capacity to kill, and this fascinated them. However, Antoine was a fool who also once hid his children from us. He failed to see that humanity was inevitably heading into its great dream – Immortality! Only full Cyborgs could attain this ultimate privilege. Only those who submitted their fleshly parts to the Machine would live forever. As for the Ferals, we policed them for their own good, since it was essential that certain genetic profiles had to be kept from extinction. Because Antoine had killed a rare Tharu (Nepali) who carried an important haplogroup variant,[5] we were compelled to intervene. Had it been the murder of a Common Feral, we would not have cared. It was the elimination of a carrier of a rare genetic variant that concerned us. That was Antoine's crime.

So long as we remembered human flesh, and its capacity for variety, we understood that human components was a living DNA and mitochondrial reservoir from which we could draw to create unique pets and kinky sex slaves (we still liked to watch). The growing lack of interest in anything having to do with humans, however, was a harbinger of the future. After all, choice specimens could always join their predecessors in deep-freeze.

It wasn't a long drive to Harris' house. Most of the time was consumed by passing through the security gates. Now, as I approached Antoine's home, despite its being surrounded by dense layers of apartments and ramshackle buildings filled with squatters, the red brick Georgian Mansion stood out due to its age and worn splendor. Security lights and alarms surrounded the mansion, which even featured ivy growing up its walls. I saw that Antoine was rich: half the mansion belonged soley to himself and his wife. They had bred five children, all of whom had been deported to the North. At the door, I showed my credentials to the armed guards there (indeed, he was a rich man!) and was brought inside.

The old man curbed his German Shepherd at the door as I entered: I was glad he still retained the strength to do it, since dogs seem to hate Cyborgs, and I didn't want to kill the family pet.

"I suppose you'll be recording everything?" Antoine remarked, as he led me into his study. I admit I was astonished at the luxury I saw there: stacks of books, phonograph records from an era long gone, candles on silver candlesticks, and paintings on the wall. I hadn't seen real paintings for a decade, when we tore down the State University to make room for more power plants.

Harris shot a glance toward the closed parlor doors.

"I'm alone," I assured him.

"I don't like your drone," he complained.

I snapped my fingers, and my Security Bot flew with a whirr against my hand, then folded itself into the shape of a pen. I placed it in a slit in my helmet.

"Feel better?" I asked.

"Try this," Antoine said, reaching over and pouring me a jigger of Scotch. I tasted it: it was the genuine article. At that moment, I was glad that I was only 80% Cyborg, with so much flesh yet to be replaced. Some of us no longer possess taste buds. They didn't know what they were missing. A part of me knew it was poison, but adventure was the spice of life. Or at least, good Scotch was a contender.

Soon, the old man exhibited a case of loose lips and was talking easily, enriching his statements with a hearty laugh over nothing every once in a while. He was still nervous, though. An alarm sounded at one point, and he stood up to check his monitors. "Some madman is always trying to break in," he told me. "There's not enough space out there for them all." He explained that his guards were loyal because he had a supply of alcohol that was impossible to find even on the black market. "Long ago, I stashed it away for such a rainy day," he told me. "Every holiday, I give some away, so folks love me. They realize that if my stash gets raided, they'll never get another drink at Christmas. It works. They protect me."

The alarm had changed his mood: he had begun to pace the floor, his footsteps muffled by the aging carpet. "I'm telling you about the liquor," he muttered," because your brain scan got it all wrong. The murder wasn't over her money. I have money, and now you know *why* I have money."

Antoine Harris had indeed married a wealthy woman, whose fortune had been secure in the edible fish industry. He explained how she had accumulated it. Even the poorest ghetto resident was able to raise a few koi – one of the few protein sources, along with rats and ants – that could survive Ghetto conditions. Ant eggs and algae provided the koi with adequate food.

"Few of us can afford a dog," he said, with a hint of pride. "But I can. Still, what gets to me is how stupid everybody is. Maybe it's because of the food and water you force on us. I swear, I can't have a decent conversation with any of them anymore."

"You seem to be wired up, compared to most Ferals," I agreed.

"I distill my water, and I'm rich enough to get better food," he replied. "Through bartering and my other services, " he said, "I'm doing okay. But my people…" Antoine made a grimace of disgust. "They've changed. They've settled into this new lifestyle, as if it's normal. *Life isn't so bad,* they tell me. *Things could be worse.* You're damned right, they could be worse. And they *will* be worse! They have forgotten that the Jews in the ghettoes of old thought the same way, before they were hauled off to work camps and starved to death. I can see how much we cost you to maintain. You'll end up disposing of us because we're too expensive."

"I think you're being rather judgmental and harsh," I answered.

"Oh, am I?" Antoine shot back, throwing himself back into his big, comfortable chair. "If that's so, how come I can think better, now that I'm not eating your prison paste? And *–where the hell are my kids?*"

"In a better place," I replied. "They didn't commit any crimes against the State."

"Never mind, you're just an idiot," Antoine said, with a sigh. "It's not your area of expertise."

"Let's get on with your testimony," I said. "And I'd appreciate another shot of that stuff, by the way."

Antoine was happy to oblige. As he poured me a refill that was only slightly less than the first in volume, he looked me in the eye and said, "How much of your brain is still human?"

"See, that's where you Ferals have it all wrong," I answered. "My brain is 100% human-derived. It's just that it's been grown on an electromagnetic matrix that regulates the neurons and stimulates them to grow, or to be replaced, when any of my synthetic nerve cells start to age."

"So, your brain had human thoughts that never got replaced?"

"Oh, my original brain furnishings were inferior," I told him. "But I was able to choose a major personality from the past –I chose Abraham Lincoln – which was imprinted on my new, injected brain cells."

"Where did the new brain cells come from?"

"They were tested for superior thought processing. Tested for longevity. Tested for…"

"But where did they come from?" Antoine persisted.

"From the State," I answered, proudly. "They were State approved implants. State grown. State selected. Superior! Everyone in United California got them. They were better than New York's. They were better than –"

"Good God," Antoine said. "How do you know that?"

"Because we're all the same in United California, that's how," I replied. "We're united. We get more done. Everyone in the Middle West admires our brains."

"You're hopeless," Antoine said.

"No, I'm Abraham Lincoln, Model 244," I corrected him. "I have the most updates for any Advocate in the State. I have the fastest – and the most – calculating circuits of any Advocate."

"But you don't have as many as a Prosecutor, do you?"

"Of course not. The State is almost always right," I assured him. "Only when the Prosecutor orders us to defend a client, do we get activated."

"Activated?"

"I spend most of my time in a Tank. Dreaming. I've experienced many lives in the Tank, brought up from all the movies and plays ever made. I'm in them, it's real, except it's not. It's a very good life."

"I'm sure it is," Antoine said. "No pain, I suppose?"

"Only if we select for the full experience," I told him.

"So what happens when prosecutors no longer need Advocates anymore?"

"That's already happening," I said, a trifle uneasy at my own words. "The brain scanners are almost perfect, now. When Prosecutors no longer need us, we will be refitted for a new profession."

"What will you become, then?"

"I want to breed mythological characters. Unicorns. Satyrs. Genies in a bottle. Maybe have some pets."

"You're unusual, indeed, to have a soft a spot in that metal heart of yours, wanting to breed animals."

"I get laughed at, about it, sometimes," I admitted, drinking the last of the Scotch. "But I find the Greek gods and their legends fascinating. I'm not alone. Some of us think it would be good to have Pan, piping on his pipes, to entertain us. Or to enjoy the sensual favors of a Europa, while we inhabit the body of a bull."

"So you're one of those who think that switching your brains into the bodies of animals is okay?"

"We just like to talk," I said, feeling wary. "Why shouldn't we create whatever we want, out of flesh, and use it as we please? After all, you Ferals bred cattle and hogs and birds, and ate them. You still eat fish."

"We don't get into their heads," Antoine said. "Have another drink."

I realized what he was doing to me and put a stop to it. "It's your turn to do some confessing," I told him. "In two days, you'll be either a prison lifer, or you'll be executed. It's time you started telling me why we shouldn't just incinerate you."

"Why did your scans think I was after her money?" Antoine said, lighting a new cigarette.

"We found that you resented her order of the New Mud Pack. It's expensive. She ordered a dozen packages of it. That would cost you a fortune."

"So you thought I'd murder her over a dozen packages of mud?" Antoine released a bitter laugh. "Do you realize that my wife had an obsession with mud packs?"

"It seems she had taken some of your own funds to make the order, without telling you."

"She did, the avaricious old bag! No…" Antoine shook his head. "She's not avaricious. And hardly an old bag. But she's a wee bit selfish."

"It doesn't sound like you're in love with her, but I don't detect any hate, either," I told him.

"Well, you're wrong," he replied. "I hate her."

Then he told me the whole story.

"We were married long before you came along," he began. "All was well, until she began to get a few wrinkles. And all the advanced science that we had wasn't going to be able get rid of all of them."

"Agnes – her real name is Henrietta," Antoine said. "Let it be on the record. Yes, she was beautiful. And she wanted to stay that way. Sadly, we were confined to the Ghetto and she could no longer avail herself of the clinics that had taken such good care of her face. That's when she started using mud packs."

Now that he had started talking, Antoine was on a roll, and I was loathe to interrupt.

"Her beauty had been slowly fading. Five kids will do that to you. Now trapped in this house," he waved a desultory finger at the beautiful room and its paintings, "she was able to hide her deteriorating state for quite a while from all our friends. But I? I got to see what she became, every night, before the lights went off…."

I raised a curious eyebrow. Doing that with the face of Abraham Lincoln meant it was quite noticeable.

"Off came the girdle!" Antoine said, using his fingers to count. "Next, off came the hairpiece. Off went the makeup, the dainty shoes, the jewelry, the dentures, the fake eyelashes, the contact lenses–"

"You're running out of fingers."

"On went a mass of shiny curlers. Then…" It took effort for him to say it, I could tell, "On went the mud pack. Have you ever tried to sleep with a woman wearing a mud pack?"

"I'm a Cyborg," I reminded him.

"Oh, yeah, of course. Anyway, I counted the days she did this. Forty-seven days in a row, she did this to me! This hideous, foul, black, sticky stuff. It cost a fortune. And was guaranteed to eradicate every wrinkle. She plastered it on her face, night after night! Do you understand?"

He was glaring at me, all the little red veins in his old, red nose about to burst. I nodded, mostly in self-defense.

"Then came night number Forty-Eight. I realized I was sleeping with a toothless, flabby, metal-headed, mud-slathered woman. She was the very parody of a Cyborg or a robot. It was now unbearable for me, but her feelings would have been hurt beyond repair if I'd slept in another room. I was in a predicament. I had insomnia, and any time I did finally fall asleep, I had nightmares that she was a Cyborg, with a mud face! So I'd sit awake as long as I could, just watching her… have another drink."

He brought out a cherry-colored cordial, and I succumbed to its allure … some woozy part of me wondered if I'd be disciplined for this. Cyborgs didn't drink, unless they were imbued with certain inalienable rights, were experts at debating themselves out of trouble, and had once lived in a log cabin. "Keep on talking," I mumbled. I reminded myself that I had never lived in a log cabin … that was just my alter ego, whispering in my ear, as I sipped on the cordial…

"I didn't know how I could bear night number Forty-Nine," Antoine said, with a snort of disgust. "Somehow, I got through it. I watched her as she lay there sleeping, gently snoring. It was really quite ludicrous. She snored ever so softly. The pile of mud on her face would crackle and shiver whenever she stirred a muscle. She was careful not to turn to one side or the other, but even so, there were towels piled up on both sides of her to protect the sheets. Her face seemed to transform into a massive chocolate muffin, ready to eat. But I digress."

Lighting a marijuana cigarette, Antoine laughed. It was a creepy sound. It sounded irrational. An Air Quality alarm shrieked: Antoine took three quick drags of the forbidden contraband (because it added extra CO_2 to the air) and then snuffed it.

"By morning, the layers of mud were criss-crossed on her face like a nasty old map. She'd get up, hold her head over the wastebasket, and start picking off the pieces. That took her half an hour, every morning. To watch it was to lose every possible interest in sex. Then, she'd gently wash her face. Cream it. Powder it. Put on her eyelashes. Insert her dentures. Put on the hairpiece after removing her curlers. And all the rest. But even then, she was never satisfied. You know that little mirror?"

"The one that Agnes gave me. Hey, do you have any more cordial?"

"Her name was actually Henrietta!" he corrected me, as he poured me another shot. "That's all you should have, pal," he cautioned. "If you fall over, you could put a hole in my antique carpet."

"Tell me more, 'bout Henrietta. More," I urged him.

"She'd take that little hand mirror and stand in front of the window. She'd be looking for wrinkles. 'Natural light shows them up best,' she'd tell me. She'd spend the next half hour peering at every quarter-inch of her face. She was particularly concerned about the crow's feet at the corners of her eyes. 'If I blink less often,' she told me, 'maybe they won't get any deeper.' I told her it would dry out her contact lenses if she did that, but she wouldn't listen to me. I became particularly disgusted when she started measuring the length of all her various wrinkles with a set of calipers. She wrote down the measurements on a face chart. Sometimes she'd make me measure them. I got to hate that hand mirror."

"That was terrific cordial," I commented, daring to lick the last drop from the bottom of the shot glass.

"She'd pull that hand-mirror out, everywhere we went, when no one was looking. But I was looking!"

"I'm sure you were," I agreed, modestly holding the empty shot glass in front of his face. Ignoring my silent plea, he continued.

"I suppose what really got to me, on Night Forty-Nine, is her comment that she had noticed how wrinkled *my* face was getting." Antoine snuffed out his joint and leaned back in the big chair, closing his eyes. "You have no idea how something like that can get to you."

"No, I wouldn't."

"Shut up! … At first, I laughed, and when she said it to me again, later that day, I smiled. After all, men get wrinkles, and they're not supposed to be sensitive about it. Besides, I had a whole head of hair, more than most men have at my age. But it was getting to me. I mean, she was always inviting me to try her blasted mud packs. She had decided to make a wrinkle chart of my face, too. After all, these were such special mud packs, guaranteed to blah, blah, blah – and she wanted to prove it to me, since the damned things cost so much."

"I suppose you believed that resistance was futile?" I put in.

"You're married, aren't you?" he asked me. "To a female?"

"I'm in a relationship with a girl," I told him. "My very own girl. I constructed her from executed leftovers, and gave her the brain of a horse. She's a little stupid, but we get along quite well."

"You got sick of mating with girls that had the same brain as you did. Didn't you?"

I was startled. He was right. I had found my previous Cyborg girl-friends as incredibly boring as they found me. We, of course, were allowed to have sex toys, just so long as they weren't humans (under the new anti-slavery acts, that was considered unfair exploitation). I suppose this is when we realized that we had no real use for humans, except as a reservoir for genetic variability, and even that excuse to keep them around was really a lesson in obsolescence. Sometimes Janet bit me, kicked me, or whinnied through her human mouth, but that just made her all the more interesting. I knew she loved me, for all that.

"I was married," the old man cringed, "and I had been happily married, but now it was over. It had gone too far, this mud fetish of hers. And it was spreading. She was getting our most wealthy friends interested in trying out the mud packs. Imagine! Other husbands, trapped as I was trapped! This simply couldn't go on!"

"I want more cordial."

He poured me some more, and continued.

"I was running scared by now. I could imagine a host of angry husbands, ready and willing to string me up, if the same thing happened to them! It got to where I couldn't even look in a mirror. I got to seeing my wrinkles as enemies, damn it. How much can a man take? When I contemplated another thirty years – we poor humans are still living to be 130 or so, despite all you've done to us recently – the thought of another thirty years made me absolutely disconsolate. I couldn't bear the thought of Night Number Fifty, so soon to come. Let alone years and years of this… I wanted a sweet, steady woman in my old age. I wanted Henrietta, the way she used to be, before she got scared of getting old."

He took a photograph from a nearby desk and showed it to me.

"She was pretty," I agreed.

"On Night Number Fifty, she peered at my face, then shoved her mirror into my hand. "Darling," she said, "Just look at yourself! You're looking worse. And at such a crucial time, too! My cousin is coming over for a visit, and frankly, you look simply wretched. I want you to use a Mud Pack. It's important!"

In a softer voice, Antoine said, "I was a little shocked, but a great calm and purpose began to come over me. There was nothing wrong with my face. It wasn't getting worse. Okay, maybe there were a few new wrinkles, but look what I'd been going through, these last forty-nine nights! It was enough to turn my hair gray. In fact," Antoine said, sadly, "I think that's when my hair did start turning gray. It happened suddenly. Almost overnight. It meant I was suffering from some incipient chromosomal damage. And I realized that it was Henrietta's fault."

"You're rich enough to get all the synthetic implants you could ever want," I told him. "You've been so nice to me, with this cordial and all, that I'll pay for it myself," I said in a moment of drunken generosity.

"I'm allergic to them. Besides, that's not the point. I could be executed in two days, remember?"

"Oh… yeah."

"Then she said, 'Shirley hasn't seen you for ages. I'd be so proud of you, if only you didn't have so many wrinkles.' I turned away, anger in my throat. Encouraged by my silence and self-control, Henrietta couldn't forbear: she shoved the mirror in front of my face. And she kept saying, 'Look at them! Look at the wrinkles on your neck; you look like a turkey! You don't dare wait another night!' I did my best to control myself. 'I'm pleased with me just as I am, and you should be, too,' I told her. I was so very calm, outwardly. But Henrietta, who should have been able to sense the volcano building up inside me, wasn't finished. 'I don't want Shirley to think you've become an old man.'"

"Cordial, please," I insisted, tapping the empty shot glass against his hand.

"Help yourself," he replied. As I poured myself another drink (a bit sloppily) he continued his tale, to which, frankly, I knew the conclusion…

"'Tonight,' Henrietta declared to me, 'I'll give you a treatment with this wonderful Magic Mud myself. It's the newest variety of Mud Packs, used by men as well! We'll reduce those wrinkles to where Shirley will never notice.' She kissed me, but I was like a stone. Finally, very slowly and carefully, I announced to her that she would never, at any time, be allowed to place Magic Mud on my face. Know what she did?"

"No. Don't know."

"She laughed at me! Laughed! She said she'd sneak some on me tonight, while I was sleeping. I'd never know. The treatment would make all the difference! The nerve of her!"

"The nerve of her!" I repeated dutifully, as I swallowed the last of my drink. My God, it was good.

"Then she pulled out a package of Magic Mud and opened it. She scooped up a big finger full and started toward me! I told her she was out of her mind, as I backed up, trying to avoid the stuff. Finally, I was backed into a corner, and she smeared it on my chin! 'See?' she said, backing away as I stood there, shaking with fury. 'It's not so bad, once you get used to it.' I left the house in a storm. I was determined not to spend Night Number Fifty under the same roof with her. Unfortunately, I forgot about the mud, and the security guards started laughing at the black smear on my chin. I peeled it off in disgust and went to a burger joint, where the best ratburgers were, but I found it was impossible to eat."

Suddenly, an enormous grandfather clock bonged out the time: Antoine had exactly 48 hours of freedom left.

"I couldn't take any more," Antoine muttered, rubbing his head. "Next thing, she'd want me to wear her girdles, to hide my potbelly. I decided to murder her."

"She deserved it," I said, in my alcohol mist. "She deserved it."

"Yes," he agreed. "It would be accomplished quickly, and without a fuss. And Henrietta would have a permanent solution to her wrinkle problem. I would actually be doing her a favor."

"Definitely, a permanent solution," I chimed in.

"Not clever, but efficient. Did I tell you that Henrietta also plugs her nose with cotton wads, with straws in them, so the mud doesn't clog her breathing? Can you imagine what she looked like?"

"I prefer Janet," I opined. "Even though she likes oats."

"I stayed away until I was sure she was asleep. Safely in bed and snoring away. She always gets to bed by eleven so she'll be fresh and rested and have fewer wrinkles to show for it. Whereas I … I was accumulating wrinkles, night after sleepless night! Look at my face, Abe!"

"Yes. Lots of wrinkles," I agreed.

"Anyway, it had been raining, and there was quite a bit of lightning. You know, weather control isn't always perfect, even now. Despite all that stuff, once in a while we get a real thunderstorm. Our part of the Dome isn't as well protected as the rest of it – we're Ghetto – remember? So we had a lightning strike! That's what happened on Night Number Fifty. The security guards were shivering with fright over the lightning, their befuddled brains filled with terror at the sight. As I said, they're so dumbed-down."

"Dumb … Down?" I replied.

"I'm talking to a drunken idiot!" Antoine groaned. "Nevertheless, I will continue. Seeing the poor condition of my security guards, and the fact that lightning had struck my security system, temporarily disarming it, I got the best idea of the night. I'd create the impression of a robbery! First, I called my lawyer and told him I had made a deal with a bootlegger to get some truly rare Scotch, and to expect a large transfer of funds by morning. Then, I entered this room – Henrietta of course slept upstairs – and opened our wall safe. I removed a bottle of rare Scotch, the contents of which I poured down the drain."

"No, you didn't!" I cried out, in anguish.

"I did. I left the jewelry, of course. Hers is too distinctive. But liquor? It was worth a fortune, what I poured out. Never to be seen again. Of course, not all of it. I have two more safes, filled to the brim."

"Tell me where they are, an' I promise, you'll get a commuted sentence," I offered.

"You are so fucked up right now. Maybe someday," Antoine replied. "The Harris fortune was still secure, for all that. I had to be very quiet, but the rain and thunder was on my side. Henrietta hates thunder. She always wore earplugs when there was thunder. Or, she did. Now, all I had to do was to strangle her, hit myself on the head with a bottle, and report the robbery and murder. You Cyborgs never investigate such things, since my wife has no rare genetic profile to worry about. I really thought I'd set up the perfect crime."

I nodded in agreement. I was so sloshed that Antoine's voice was just a faint echo in my ears, but I knew I had to stay awake. I had to hear it all. After all, he'd given me one of the best *buzzes* of my life!

"After making sure that my dog was drugged," Antoine continued, "that he would stay quiet, and checking that the maid was asleep in the basement, I took the bottle, poured some of the remaining liquor on the carpet, broke the bottle, wiped it clean, and laid it down by the stairs. Next, I began ascending the steps. In the darkness, with the power out, I was unable to use the elevator."

"They don' fix power in Ghetto fast," I commented.

"That's right. But it didn't matter. I was now set in my course. Nothing would stop me."

"But, why would a robber go up and kill her?"

"I would testify that she started screaming when she heard him break the bottle over my head. For I intended to kill her, come down the stairs, and hit myself over the head with the bottle. There would be blood, of course, but I was willing to chance it. It would be worth it."

I couldn't see very well by now, but I could not detect any mark on Antoine's face or head.

"It would have worked," Antoine whispered. "I would have been free! They would have blamed it on the burglar. After all, we also had a safe in the bedroom that the maid knew about. To stop my wife's screaming, of course I would have to kill her quickly."

"Of course."

"Now I bent over her … her with her damnable Magic Mud, her disgusting cotton wads shoved up her nose, and as the thunder rolled and fresh lightning flared, I grabbed her by the throat. She is such a little thing. Hardly a hundred pounds, you know…"Antoine lifted his head, looking like a proud, unconquered beast. His eyes flared with his passion. "It only takes a minute to break the hyoid bone.[6] Did you know that the hyoid bone in the throat is the only bone that does not articulate with any other bone in the body?"

"I didn't know that."

"I am a big man. I have strong hands. Suddenly, just as Henrietta's eyes rolled up in her head, and her gasping ceased, the power was restored. That's when I saw Henrietta rise from the other side of our big bed. Nestled as she had been, with her towels around her head, her earplugs shutting out every sound, only now did she see what had happened. Only now, did she scream!"

Antoine shook his head. "It was her cousin *Shirley!* She had arrived early because of the coming storm. Covered, of course, with Magic Mud, her earplugs in, her nose filled with cotton, I had no idea…"

"Too bad, old man," I said.

"If only I'd read Henrietta's note!" Antoine growled. "She'd left a note on the door, asking me to sleep in the guest room, because she wanted Shirley to try the mud pack. But it was dark. It was so very dark."

I rose up, unsteady on my feet. "It's a great story," I told him. "And I wish I could help you."

"What do you mean?" Antoine demanded. "You're going to help me, aren't you? You posted bail for me, after all."

"I told you I wouldn't release your story to the public until you're dead, by whatever cause. I'm 'honest Abe.' And cannot tell a lie. I told you I'd choose the inaccurate brain scan version, or yours, whichever gave you the best chance for sentence reduction."

Antoine looked at me steadily for a long moment, then he sighed. "I should have known better than to trust a damned robot," he said.

"You already said that," I reminded him. "But fact is, you killed a rare Tibetan, and the penalty is incineration. It's always incineration for narrowing the gene pool. By arranging bail for you, I gave you a sentence reduction. Some extra hours to live. An opportunity to return to your home. Say goodbye to Henrietta."

"She moved out!" Antoine said, bitterly.

"You got time to put your things in order. You have 48 more hours here, to yourself, before I return with handcuffs. Remember, I gave you 72 extra hours to live."

"Why in hell did you bother?" the old man asked, as I got unsteadily to my feet.

"Because it's well known that you have the best liquor in town," I told him. "I cannot tell a lie."

Endnotes

1. On Oct. 15, 2014, Dr. Christopher Exley announced that non-invasive means to remove aluminum from the brain were available, and that aluminum, the prime suspect in Alzheimers, should not be allowed to accumulate in the human body. "Exley, Professor in Bioinorganic Chemistry, Aluminium and Silicon Research Group in The Birchall Centre, Lennard-Jones Laboratories at Keele University, writes in Frontiers in Neurology about the 'Aluminium Age' and its role in the 'contamination' of humans by aluminium ... "There are neither cures nor effective treatments for Alzheimer's disease. The role of aluminium in Alzheimer's disease can be prevented by reducing human exposure to aluminium and by removing aluminium from the body by non-invasive means." [Note: 'aluminum' in British English is 'aluminium.'] http://www.neuroscientistnews.com/research-news/aluminium-and-its-likely-contribution-alzheimer%E2%80%99s-disease#sthash.PR3oMzpo.dpuf Acquired July 9, 2015.

2. As of 2015, Population Council, Inc. which was originally a eugenics society dedicated to reducing the populations of unwanted races of humans, as described in the *Memoirs* by David Rockefeller (2002) operates today in 60 countries. "It held the license for Norplant contraceptive implant, and now holds the license for Mirena intrauterine system. The Population Council also publishes the journals *Population and Development Review*, which reports scientific research on the interrelationships between population and socioeconomic development and provides a forum for discussion of related issues of public policy, and *Studies in Family Planning*, which focuses on public health, social science, and biomedical research on sexual and reproductive health, fertility, and family planning." (see https://en.wikipedia.org/wiki/Population_Council) Less well-known is its partnership with Acrux, which has created a spray-on birth control product, Nestorone. The spray is odorless and colorless, and only tiny amounts are needed to block conception. See: http://www.theaustralian.com.au/news/health-science/skin-spray-contraceptive-next-big-thing/story-e6frg8y6-1111115500581 Retrieved July 9, 2015.

3. For example, a Phenibut-type tranquilizer was being used to excess. Today, Phenibut – beta-phenyl-gamma aminobutyric acid HCL is a tranquilizing and neuropsychotropic drug used so plentifully by millions that it is ordered through (the world's biggest source of farmed dog fur) , the notorious **Ali Baba** goods and commodities network by the TON (many companies specify a minimum order of 25 kilograms (55.116 pounds of powder). It stimulates dopamine receptors, etc. and is addictive, with withdrawal symptoms similar to what alcoholics experience. See: http://www.ncbi.nlm.nih.gov/pubmed/11830761 and http://www.alibaba.com/showroom/phenibut-99%2525.html Acquired Jan. 15, 2016.

4. Pepper-spray drones came into use for handling protesters in 2014, making it almost impossible for demonstrations to occur without participants experiencing pain without discrimination. http://qz.com/489204/north-dakota-is-the-first-state-in-the-us-to-legalize-police-use-of-drones-with-tasers-and-pepper-spray/ Acquired Nov. 15, 2015.

5. http://www.anthrogenica.com/showthread.php?5658-Haplogroup-J2a-Serbs&s=d141ae4a-ba84351b694851727e8af5a7 Perhaps the rarest distinctive haplogroup ever discovered? Also see: http://www.ncbi.nlm.nih.gov/pmc/articles/PMC4231405/ concerning the Tharu, which in the late time-frame of this story would probably be the rarest haplogroup still extant.

6. The hyoid bone is associated with the ability to speak. It's possible that strangulation was the method of choice because this educated human understood that fact. Recently it was discovered that Neanderthals had the ability to speak, based on the shape of their hyoid bones. See: http://www.sciencedaily.com/releases/2014/03/140302185241.htm Acquired Feb. 5, 2015.

AIRSPACE

There has been a 30% increase in carbon dioxide since the beginning of the industrial age.... Since the beginning of the industrial revolution, we have removed .095% of the oxygen in our atmosphere ... that is only a tenth of one percent of the total supply, but oxygen makes up only 20% of the atmosphere. I looked up safety rules regarding oxygen concentrations and according to OSHA rules on atmospheres in closed environments, if the oxygen level in such an environment falls below 19.5% it is oxygen deficient, putting occupants of the confined space at risk of losing consciousness and death. What happens if the world's atmospheric levels of oxygen fall to 19.5% or lower?
— Mike Johnson, *Science and Technology*, Dec. 2007

Johnson wrote to Dr. Ralph Keeling of Scripps Institute, which conducted the study he cited. Here's what he was told: "The O2:C combustion ratio of a fossil-fuel depends on the hydrogen content. The ratio varies from about 1.2 for coal, 1.45 for liquid fuels, and 2.0 for natural gas. Taking these factors together, we are losing nearly three O2 molecules for each CO2 molecule that accumulates in the air..."

It was a quick walk from the parking lot through the tunnel to Houston Dome 52, even though he was accompanied by his bodyguards. As Dr. Daniel Cook, along with his protectors, entered the conference center through a pair of airlocks, he could hear the blades begin to whirl. The conference room must be full, he realized. That was good. He stepped into a waiting elevator and was soon 30 stories above the city, which he could see laid out before him with its twinkling lights and flashing advertisements, a glittering gem of activity that shimmered through the clear aluminum panes.[1] As Dr. Cook and his bodyguards left the elevator, they were greeted by several colleagues who gazed anxiously around the hallway before leading him into the conference hall, where several City of Houston armed guards stood at attention, machine guns handy. A security matron had scanned the guests' ID chips, making sure they were current. They all checked out. No one was wearing a warning advisory. No one had an active MindKontrol® implant. The guests were clean.

As the fans clicked on and off, delivering Angel Air® in precious blasts of wind, everyone breathed in deep. It was a pleasure to breathe Angel Air, which proved to each guest how important he or she was to Dr. Cook and his honored speaker, the Grand Lady Mayor of the City (she was soon to appear). It wasn't easy to breathe in most places, Cook reminded himself, as he drew in the Angel Air. Life could be so good when the air was so fresh.

Cook congratulated himself on being part of this choice interview. Live interviews were rare, these days. Only historic announcements generated interviews anymore: everything less important was delivered into your brain while you slept. A good citizen had nothing to fear. God help you, if you didn't like what you received, because then you'd have to undergo some instruction, which sometimes led to a nightmare or a headache. The worst cases needed to be re-educated in learning centers. Cook was proud that he'd never experienced a nightmare; just an occasional headache. The information was the same for everyone, which kept them united. Ever since Texas had seceded from the old USA, unity was important against the roving masses (they were mostly from Latin America and the Gulf States) who had been starved out during the GMO Crop Failures and the volcanic eruptions.

Even today, carbon dioxide levels were still rising. Cook, whose original degree was in Ecosystems, had once been a lonely writer of reports on the world's crop failures – due to too much CO_2 and GMO engineering – two decades earlier. As CO_2 levels rose, food crops were supposed to grow faster than ever, but instead, they grew only 30% as well as before. Everyone seemed to have forgotten that plants couldn't absorb enough nitrogen to grow well when CO_2 levels rose too high.[2] The result was starvation, with riots. The strongest states managed to secure their borders, but the United States of America, overflowing with Latino, Indian, Muslim and Asian migrants, simply collapsed. The rest of the world didn't fare much better.

As he breathed deeply, enjoying the oxygen it used up and the CO_2 it produced, Dr. Cook moved to the stage and stood behind the podium, as a brief light show about his greatness was displayed behind him on a large screen. During the light show, Cook kept an eye on the guards. He had been invited to host the Mayor's exclusive press conference because he was the owner of the world's most important oxygen gas factories. His oxygen delivery systems were being utilized in every domed city in the world, and he was becoming incredibly rich because of it.

Thanks to Cook's foresight and hard work, the world's oxygen level was stabilizing, drifting along at an average of 19.8% at a 200-meter elevation. Still, there was the persistent CO_2 problem, and Cook owned the top experts on that subject.[3] *Hypercapnia* was the fancy name for what happened when breathing too much carbon dioxide, which is why farmers and tourists wore CO2-collecting masks when they stepped outside their homes and domes.[4] Dr. Cook's last report – "Project Steak Lung" – was such a success that it had been piped into every citizen's head a few months ago. Through genetic engineering, a way had been found to create cattle with birds' lungs, to the delight of all who wanted to savor the Real Thing once more. Large mammals had been unable to adapt to the higher CO2 levels, meaning the survivors had to be confined in expensive buildings with air control. Now equipped with avian lungs, cattle would be cheaper to house, and steak would be cheaper, too.[5]

Cook was betting that the Mayor's conference was probably going to be about CO2 control. It was the most persistent problem the city faced. Maybe the new geothermal projects were finally funneling enough CO2 below the surface to clear the air.[6] However the conference went, Mayor Awdrey was a consummately good politician. She had her reasons to invite every face in this crowd. Even the Governor was here, surrounded by his own bodyguards and drawing up something added to his oxygen through a hookah. Certainly it was time to do something more about air quality. The outside world was almost unlivable. Tunnel systems made of clear, polycarbonate tubes provided strong, safe roadways, complete with UV-shielding and Texas Guard Patrols, that stretched between the great cities of the Lone Star State, but there was a constant tide of protesters who wanted oxygen-generating factories to be built in every city. So far, Cook had been able to keep tight patent controls on his oxygen production systems, releasing only a small percentage of oxygen to the general atmosphere. The rest was sold.

The Mayor was a wise woman, Cook mused, as he raised a hand to call for order. She would let the newsmen, publicists and politicos enjoy themselves in this over-decorated, Baroque style anteroom, where luxuries abounded, hinting at her good will. Smiling but not speaking, Cook had spent several socially-important minutes working his way with appropriate dignity and charm alongside the great, linen-covered table with its lavish burdens, where the guests had sampled hors d'oeuvres, real shrimp, Coca-Cola made with real sugar, and moonshine from Kentucky. Pretty Japanese servers (they were robots) were very helpful: they were also very available for rent at night's end.

Bill Comeaux, Cook's main bodyguard, was so distracted by one of the robot girls that he touched his wrist to bring up a screen of his account on his forearm. Cook knew that Bill had just enough resources to rent Kimmy-Sue, and he gave a nod when Bill flashed his arm toward his boss. Bill was a decent fellow who wouldn't beat up a sex robot or torture it. Cook had been forced to dismiss Bill's predecessor for his sadistic tendencies with sex robots: it not only made Cook look bad, but the bills to repair the robots had been excessive.

With such great food and the high-quality service girls available at affordable prices, Madame Mayor certainly knew how to make her guests feel important. She had really outdone herself. But then, Cook knew that this press conference was going to reveal something big. Very big.

The anti-pollution machines suddenly turned on, whirling the air around at top speed, and everyone straightened their ties and activated their recorders. The Police, no doubt, were on their way, assigned to screen the guests before Madame Mayor appeared. As a security officer sprayed an anti-sensor around the room, the guests stopped speaking, training their eyes on the big double doors that would open and bring, first, the Police, and then Ms. Awdrey.

Instead, Dr. Cook tapped his microphone and announced, "Mayor Awdrey herself will now enter the Conference Room!"

And there she was, being rolled in on her enclosed podium, flanked by four security guards. A shield of ALON encapsulated her in a transparent cocoon that surely was filled with the most excellent air available. Whiffs of Angel Air once more filled the room as Madame Mayor rolled forth, the atmosphere sweetly rich in oxygen. At a signal from her thick, jeweled hand, the room's anti-pollution machines began pumping Enhanced Angel Air into the room. Cook had almost forgotten how good it was to breathe 20% oxygen, with only 1% carbon dioxide,[7] and no sulfur dioxide at all. As they breathed in the most refreshing air available on the planet, Mayor Awdrey smiled benevolently at her guests through her bullet-proof shield as more security guards appeared, posting themselves three-thick around her.

It was good to be here, Cook thought. As an environmental chemist, he remembered how, years earlier, he had endured some extraordinary hazards, such as crawling through collapsed underground tunnels that had been attacked by terrorists, or dragging oxygen-rich air-tubes down to asphyxiating miners. At those times, he wore air-tanks strapped to his back, not caring that he confronted by filthy with mud or dust. He never minded volunteering for such emergencies. He had even received an award for saving a Robot who possessed a human head, which had once belonged to the best and most experienced excavator – Charles Nottenham – and it was he who was the target of the terrorists.

But during a cavern's collapse, the head of Charles Nottenham was left behind, weeping and begging as it sat perched on its helplessly flailing robot legs, while all the 100% humans had been rescued. Cook, hearing of it, went down with a miner who knew where to find Charles just before the breach was sealed off. After all, that was a human head and a human mind, Cook had argued. By the time they reached Charles, the pumping mechanisms were failing, and he died soon after the rescue, but not before expressing gratitude for the effort. It turned out that Charles was amazingly wealthy. In his dying breaths, he gave his entire fortune to Dr. Cook.

That's how Cook was able to build his first oxygen-generating factory. It was based on the concept invented decades earlier by the Triton Oxygen Respirator system, which could extract oxygen directly from seawater.[8]

Cook was currently residing in a luxurious domed palace, full of Angel Air. He was a generous man who provided his workers at the factory and in their homes with air that was fully 19.88% oxygen, enhanced with occasional access to mind-expanding aerosols, and free of sleep-gas.

Only such sealed homes and workplaces held cargoes of truly alert citizens: not everyone could get that kind of good air. Cars provided the best protection for the poor, with their oxygen-generating and carbon dioxide filtration devices. Whereas cars were once for transportation, the vast majority of them now provided homes for the masses of the financially limited. These cars were stacked in safe, efficiently lined-up layers, within reach of fast food, coffee, toilets, showers and casinos. Specially engineered trees and flowers that could tolerate high CO_2 levels were planted everywhere, their roots bathed in hydroponics, shading those who lived in the domes. Of course the vast majority of people still lived outside the cities, but as Thomas Hobbes had written, centuries earlier,

> During the time men live without a common power to keep them all in awe, they are in that condition called war... every man, against every man. To this war of every man against every man, this also in consequence; that nothing can be unjust. The notions of right and wrong, justice and injustice have there no place. Where there is no common power, there is no law, where no law, no injustice. Force, and fraud, are in war the cardinal virtues. No arts; no letters; no society; and which is worst of all, continual fear, and danger of violent death: and the life of man, solitary, poor, nasty, brutish and short.

This quote had been drummed into every citizen's head, as part of their education. It was the lot of those outside the protected places. It was why the War against Terror was still being conducted, decade after decade. The outsiders were lawless, knowing only war and destruction. Patrols of robots were slowly eliminating the dangers, and with the deaths of the Outsiders would come better air to breathe.

Masses of people had once walked carelessly across the face of the planet, burning all manner of things, burning fossil fuels, sucking polluted air wastefully into their lungs as they smoked, as they committed murders, and waged wars.

Inside the cities and protected farms and power plants a more orderly and predictable world was thriving. There were even sightseeing trips by helicopter to view mountains and rivers and oceans, but even when they landed in such places, the visitors walked under great geodesic domes

LETTERS TO THE CYBORGS

guarded by barriers to keep the air oxygenated. In the mountains, beyond the plexiglas and the polycarbonate tubes and the rigid, clear aluminum walls, they could see wild, untamed beauty, but they could not step into it without oxygen tanks.

Cook realized that his mind was wandering, and he recognized the source: they were being tranquilized. He tried to focus: he felt something unexpected was forthcoming, and he sensed it would be ominus in nature. Otherwise, the guests in this room wouldn't be trying to find places to sit down. Cook remembered when there had been demonstrations against using tranquilizing gas on peaceful assemblies, but the defense had been that it was better than pepper spray, rubber bullets and handcuffs. And so, tranquilizers became fashionable. Cook believed they were employed all too often. He'd thought about getting his publicists to write an article linking tranquilizer sprays to the decline of shoppers and casino tourists in the recreation centers.

On the other hand, there was never any contamination, anymore, from pollen, no bug bites, no dust to make you sneeze. And the periods of enforced laziness, when tranquilizers calmed the people after an un-popular decision was reached in the City Council, or when they ran out of chocolate, were always supported by good arguments, most of them delivered to their brains while people were sleeping.

Cook stepped down as Madame Mayor's podium began flashing an array of brilliant colors. She was about to speak. The drugs had created a sense of heat: Cook wiped the perspiration from his face just before a fresh rush of air from the vents surfaced to cool him. There was no more Angel Air now, and of all people, Cook missed it. The comfort level in the large room had declined rapidly. There had to be method in this mad-ness, as the oppressive heat and the suffocating stagnancy became almost too much to bear. Through it all, Madame Mayor was speaking, in a me-chanical way. Cook was certain he'd heard the first fifteen minutes of this speech before, but he knew that at any minute, they'd all be hearing the real news. One simply had to stay awake....

She was an intelligent, kind, worthy leader, he heard his brain telling him, recognizing, as he heard the words, that the thoughts were being im-planted electromagnetically. Well, she *was* all those nice things, anyway, wasn't she?

He absorbed everything he heard, knowing he was being encouraged by something in the air to absorb it accurately. He'd be able to repeat her speech word for word. He was grateful that this brilliant leader was shar-ing so much with him, and with everyone in this room. She cared. He admired her cool smile, her suave demeanor, her mannerisms, her calm, beautiful eyes...

In actuality, Ms. Awdrey was a tired, pessimistic, sturdy woman who, through her parents' ambitious efforts and vast fortune, had been born a close genetic cousin of Angela Merkel, a woman who had once been an effective dictator in what was once called Germany. She very well understood the nature of all her friends and enemies. She had worked hard on the Air Quality Engineering Announcement, which she was about to release to the public. It hadn't cost too much to get it presented properly to her adoring press. A fresh batch of drugs from M.D. Anderson Hospital laboratories had been developed and cleared just in time for the announcement. They no longer had to rely on shipments from foreign sources. Governments across the globe were all uniting now, against the Terrorists on the outside. Their minds were ready now, she knew, as she finished the first part of her speech and listened to the mechanical clapping of hands: they were mindlessly applauding. After giving Dr. Cook a beneficent smile, she raised her arms to get the room's attention one more. Power depends on creating a state of mind, Cook realized.

Certain of her safety now, Ms. Awdry allowed the cylinder that had surrounded her to be lifted. As she did so, she could detect a slight sweetness in the air from the drug. Not enough remained to affect her, or her security guards... she gave a gracious smile as she descended from the podium – an act so rare that it elicited gasps of shock from her tranquilized guests.

"We will have a brief party after this Announcement," she told them. "That will occur as soon as you wire in your stories and reports to your offices. The City Council has agreed to my proposals concerning air control priorities and necessities, as provided to all residents of The City of Houston. At the same time, this announcement is being synchronized, so that every Mayor in the Lone Star State is informing our Texas citizens of this momentous, historical step forward."

There was a shallow sigh of agreement from her listeners, who waited with patience for her next words. They were well primed, she saw, and she could proceed. "It is just and right," Ms. Awdrey proclaimed, in a stentorian voice that shook them alert, "to impose a fee on garbage collections. On sewer systems and water. On food, and on housing, transportation and education. We all realize that the necessities of life come to us at a cost. In other words, we have to pay for those necessities."

She paused again, her voice a little higher pitched, because the mind-altering drugs in the air were slightly affecting her, too.

"Therefore," she said, smiling her best smile, "it should not come as a surprise to any of you that this conference is being held to deliver to you the rates and schedules we have agreed upon concerning the commodity we call 'AIR.'"

She waited a moment, until the murmurs of surprise faded off...

"For some years now, AIR has been metered, filtered, cleansed, enhanced and delivered to Texas customers free of charge. And I might add," she waved her hand toward a screen that descended from the ceiling, with a chart and some graphs on it, "I might add that the rest of the civilized world is delivering the same message to its citizens tomorrow. Though, I can proudly say, it is Texas who first took these historic steps. Steps that will guarantee the distribution and delivery of the best air possible to every qualified person in this city!"

She said it with triumph and began clapping her hands, and her audience responded with applause as well. Too quickly, the applause stopped, as the news began sinking in.

A hand went up.

That bespectacled iconoclast, who believed in ghosts, UFOs, and reincarnation! Riggs, as usual, was finding fault. He was the token Dissenter, and as was typical of him, he was trying to find a way to register a protest. With a grimace of displeasure, Madame Mayor nodded in his direction.

"Honorable Mayor," the reporter said humbly, "May I ask a question?"

"It seems you will ask it anyway, Mr. Riggs," she replied. "As you never seem to be satisfied with anything Houston City Council decides upon."

Riggs flushed, but pressed on. "Isn't air something which is a natural right?" he asked. "I mean, is it proper to sell air?"

"Selling is a harsh term, Mr. Riggs," she replied. "And it's hardly AIR, is it? 'Air' is what's outside. Polluted. High in carbon dioxide and acid. It's a life-destroying mass of gas, encircling the earth and dissolving the backbones of every fish still alive in the sea. They will soon be no more because of what you want to call *air*. What *we* intend to give you is a product. Enhanced. Perfect. Wholesome. Right now, Angel Air is a rare commodity which all of you have enjoyed tonight. What we are doing is to guarantee that you'll be supplied with Angel Air at least four hours every night, and on holidays, while the everyday air you now enjoy will receive a bonus injection of .004% oxygen which, otherwise, your city and state could not afford to give you."

"But, begging your pardon," Riggs pursued, his face reddening as a series of boos came from the security guards. "Don't punish me, please, but please, am I correct that you're not giving us our air anymore, that you're selling it?"

"Correct, Riggs," she said, dropping any semblance of respect. She was tired. She'd spent hours haggling over the rates and the changes to the laws. It was done. The city's revenues would double. Every car-home would be taxed, or confiscated. Any fanatics who didn't like it could have their house supply shut off. It was a simple and efficient way to move the poor outside (yes, they would be allowed to take their car-homes with them). "Now, if there aren't any more questions, I will avail myself of some of those beautiful shrimp that I see on the table."

Cook watched Madame Mayor's face swell up with an effusion of pride and power as she stepped away from the podium. The thought went into his brain, from somewhere, that a new era was dawning. Why had it taken so long for humanity to get control of its airspace? A euphoria began to engulf him as Ms. Awdrey shook his hand, and then, in a gesture of plebian humility, helped herself to some shrimp.

A vestigial twinge of fear went through Cook as she turned her face to look at him, nibbling on one of the last of the living things still in the oceans. He knew exactly what he would be saying to her in a few hours, as they finalized the contracts, but a part of him still wanted to ask her who had made this decision. Who was in control of the air? As he thought of the question, an answer came flickering into his brain, and though he knew he had been fed the words, they were the right words: *It doesn't matter, Everything is under control. Everything is perfect now.*

This story was inspired by remarks made by Prof. Robert Randall, University of Houston, Department of Anthropology, 1985.

Endnotes

1. Transparent aluminum thechnology, once only a *Star Trek IV: the Voyage Home* trivia fact, exists and currently is made by Raytheon into panes big enough to use in an elevator window or in armored vehicles, where its protective utility exceeds that of bullet-proof glass. Transparent aluminum, also known as ALON, is made of aluminum oxynitride, which, melted and polished, is as hard as sapphire and transparent as glass. ALON offers more view-through clarity than conventional bulletproof glass and is far stronger, but because bulletproof glass is literally less than ten dollars cheaper per square foot, currently US troops have to function without its superior protective use as glass in armored vehicles and for protective body armor. See: http://science. howstuffworks.com/transparent-aluminum-armor4.htm Acquired Feb. 4, 2016.

2. Increased carbon dioxide levels in air restrict plants' ability to absorb nutrients Date: June 12, 2015.

Source: University of Gothenburg Summary: The rapidly rising levels of carbon dioxide in the atmosphere affect plants' absorption of nitrogen, which is the nutrient that restricts crop growth in most terrestrial ecosystems. Researchers have now revealed that the concentration of nitrogen in plants' tissue is lower in air with high levels of carbon dioxide, regardless of whether or not the plants' growth is stimulated. http://www.sciencedaily.com/releases/2015/06/150612104016. htm Retrieved June 15, 2015.

3. "Too Much Carbon Dioxide May Have Caused Earth's Worst Mass Extinction" by Emily Atkin Apr 13, 2015 1:42pm "The worst mass extinction in Earth's history may have been caused by huge amounts of carbon dioxide that accumulated in the atmosphere and the ocean after colossal volcanic eruptions in Siberia 252 million years ago, according to a new study. In addition to coating ancient Siberia with thick lava, the famed eruptions also released massive amounts of carbon dioxide into the atmosphere, which the study says may have turned the oceans sharply acidic. That acidity is thought to have driven a "global environmental calamity" that killed 90 percent of Earth's species – also known as the "Great Dying" between the Permian and Triassic periods. The fact that an ocean acidification event driven by carbon dioxide may have caused a mass extinction provides a "cautionary lesson for today," wrote Eric Hand in the April issue of the journal Science, where the study was published Friday." See: http://thinkprogress.org/climate/2015/04/13/3646211/ boom-youre-dead/ Retrieved July 10, 2015.

4. Note this patent: "Improved breathing apparatus. European Patent Application EP0241169; Abstract: A breathing apparatus providing security of oxygen supply …with the potential for a long duration comprises personal gas supply means (10,11,12) connected to a canister, 3, containing a substance generating oxygen on reaction with carbon dioxide and moisture in a wearer's exhalations. A bottle of compressed oxygen, 6, doses oxygen into the breathing circuit when required by the wearer." We can guess that the "substance" involves "potassium superoxide (KO2) "…as a source of oxygen … where the air is so deficient in oxygen that an artificial atmosphere must be regenerated …[breathing's moisture] reacts with superoxide to liberate oxygen and at the same time the potassium hydroxide formed removes carbon-dioxide as it is exhaled, thereby allowing the atmosphere in mask to be continuously regenerated … the chemical reactions involved are:

$4KO_2 (s) + 2H_2O (g) \text{----------} > 4KOH (aq) + 3O_2 (g)$

$KOH (aq) + CO_2 (g) \text{---------} > KHCO_3 (s)$

KO2 also combines directly with CO2 forming K2CO3 and with CO2 and the moisture forming KHCO3. $4KO_2 + 2CO_2 \text{------} > 2K_2CO_3 + 3O_2$

$4KO_2 + 4CO_2 + 2H_2O \text{--------} > 4KHCO_3 + 3O_2$" Ref: http://www.freepatent-sonline.com/EP0241169.html and https://answers.yahoo.com/question/index-?qid=20091219181610AAQeIlf (or go visit a chemistry manual.). Acquired Aug. 10, 2015.

5. Birds' lungs aren't like the lungs of mammals. Birds have a more efficient method to circulate air and obtain oxygen, even at low concentrations, which is why they can fly at high altitudes and can sustain a high metabolic rate. Such lungs genetically engineered to function in cattle would probably force the animal to pant constantly to inhale and exhale air properly.

6. Can We Turn Unwanted Carbon Dioxide Into Electricity? *New power plant design to expand use of geothermal energy in the U.S.* SAN FRANCISCO – "Researchers are developing a new kind of geothermal power plant that will lock away unwanted carbon dioxide (CO2) underground – and use it as a tool to boost electric power generation by at least 10 times compared to existing geothermal energy approaches." 12/12/13 *Ohio State Journal of Research and Innovation Communications.* Retrieved July 9, 2015.

7. Though CO2 is supposedly only .04% of the earth's atmosphere, in crowded cities with stagnant air,CO2 and Carbon Monoxide levels can be substantially higher. Oct. 8, 2009, *Science* published "Coupling of CO2 and Ice Sheet Stability Over Major Climate Transitions of the Last 20 Million Years" - UCLA scientist Aradhna Tripati measured present carbon dioxide levels and found they have not been this high since the Miocene, 15 million years ago, when temperatures worldwide were 5 - 10 degrees F higher than today, while sea levels were 75 to 120 feet higher. Ref: http://www.sciencedaily.com/releases/2009/10/091008152242.htm Retrieved July 1, 2015.

viii The Triton Oxygen Respirator (designed by Jeabyun Yeon) was announced as a breakthrough for scuba diving by gullible bloggers in 2014. It can extract oxygen from water and was promoted for use in scuba diving, with applications for firefighters and in hospitals, wherever water was available, but it was soon pointed out that this artificial gill device would have to pump about 6 liters of water through the system to get enough oxygen for one breath of air. "The average person breathes about 15 times per minute" one article explains, so the Triton would have to filter 24 gallons a minute to supply a scuba diver with enough oxygen to just float along underwater.

Without going into more detail, write 'impossible' over Triton's gilly forehead. However, an artificial gill system on an industrial level could extract oxygen at a commercial rate, this author argues, using wind, waves and tides for energy. See the math as to the Triton's failure to impress here: http://www.deepseanews.com/2014/01/triton-not-dive-or-dive-not-there-is-no-triton/

LITTLE GREEN MEN

A letter to the Cyborgs from the Protector of Human Life Assessor Einstein.

Year 2075 CE.

PREAMBLE:
I apologize for writing a letter as backup to our usual input, but wish to place into the record a hand-written history concerning our older DNA enhancement programs. There is a slight chance that a Murine Infestation can destroy some of my reportage on this topic at the cyber-level.

HISTORY AND DISCUSSION:
For purpose of example, concerning our past DNA projects, and why their histories must be preserved, we present the case of former US President John Fitzgerald Kennedy, deceased Nov. 22, 1963:

In 2063, we celebrated the 100th anniversary of the murder of President John F. Kennedy. It had been well established by then that Lee Harvey Oswald had been framed for the murder, and a few years later, the greatness of the president who had been executed by government-sponsored snipers was finally proven upon full examination of his DNA and the DNA of his political and military enemies. There is no doubt that Kennedy was a great man with a powerful mind, who recklessly assumed he could make a difference in that hopelessly corrupt milieu. It's a shame that he did not live to see how his DNA once more became an influence for good on the world stage.

For the record, in case prehistoric details are destroyed by the present Murine Infestation and removed from our History Files, Kennedy's DNA had been totally analyzed by 2035, and after the Cyborg Revolution, technicians created scenarios with all available input from JFK's childhood until his demise. This was successfully transferred into a suitable brain, enhanced with Kennedy's DNA and kept in storage until wanted. By 2070, the current World President was elected with a virtual John F. Kennedy at his side, whom he pledged to consult as his Vice President. Virtual Vice Presidents had come into fashion only sixteen years before my present letter to you, beginning with former General and Revolutionary President George Washington, who became the world's first virtual Vice President. Laws have now been passed so that no virtual Vice President can be activated more than once every 64 years, nor can they hold office more than eight years. After Washington, Mahatma Gandhi was brought forth. Now it is Kennedy's turn. To keep these charismatic personalities from overcoming present leaders, and seducing public opinion, such brains are subjected to scheduled hibernation lockdowns.

As an Assessor, I, too, exist in order to advise, thanks to some old laws that demanded certified human oversight of Cyborg Rulers. We have had no problem getting along – I wish to make this clear in case some alteration of records occurs due to the current Murine Infestation.

As you are aware, I am one of a dozen such whose DNA has been enhanced with genes from the most prominent whistleblowers, innovators, geniuses, philanthropists and creative thinkers of the past. For example, I am endowed with the DNA of Edward Snowden, Albert Einstein, William Shakespeare, Charles Darwin, and the actor Paul Newman. I chose to look like Paul Newman, by the way, because his classic facial features exhibited character. All twelve of us are similarly infused with DNA from the world's former best. Our lifespan of two hundred years can be extended by a vote of the people, so we are motivated to represent their welfare faithfully. When we meet, which we do regularly after traveling the world and monitoring events, we agree as to what findings we should present to you on issues of significance in world politics and the quality of life for all beings, human and otherwise, on the planet. Of course, this includes the well-being and immortal status of all Cyborg Rulers who still wish to remain alive. We recognize that you become weary and sometimes give up your position to a newcomer. When this occurs, we rejoice that you set aside ego, prestige and glory to do so.

Just as you, we Assessors have no families: our family is the life on the planet, including all plant and animal life.

OUR STATUS
For the record, as it's trivial and could be destroyed by the "Infestation," we are laughingly called The Twelve Apostles, because we have a following of worshippers, so to speak, who come to us with problems Cyborg Leaders may rightfully ignore or misunderstand. These problems are becoming rare, as Cyborg Rulers constantly improve their sensitivity and flexibility. It's obvious to me that our services will no longer be needed in another fifty to one hundred years, and we'll just become adornments, or museum pieces. But

while we are still occasionally useful, we're doing our best to provide you with what information might still be needed to assure the best possible lives for all living things on the planet, in our dance of symbiosis.

IMPORTANT MEETING COMING

Our next meeting at 23:00 in three days will address this sudden Murine Infestation problem. It is possible that we will be forced to terminate a new life form. If this becomes necessary, we will bring you a petition for the purpose, which, according to tradition, we assume you will ratify. Due to the discovery of a mass destruction of unusual historic records in the field of genetics, we urge you to create copies of all DNA records immediately, and to place them under guard. The rest of this message, which we have placed in the old vernacular form, is also encoded the usual way for backup. However, we felt it necessary to use this old form of communication, which we believe might be invulnerable to the Infestation. Thank you for your attention.

William Paul Einstein, POHL Assessor.

"So they got a hand-written letter?" Marilyn asked me. She had the face and body of Marilyn Monroe, a lovely actress from the past whose high IQ was sufficiently compatible with the other personalities inside Marilyn's DNA-concocted brain: specifically, Sir Isaac Newton, John Milton, Jane Austen and Nikola Tesla.

"It's probably the first letter they've received, written by hand, in their lives," I told her. "How much time do we have left, to look into the Murine Infestation?"

"It depends on how close Walt gets to the mice," she answered. Walt Napoleon Disney was our best friend among the twelve Assessors. He was perhaps the most flexible, creative, and open-minded among us, having the most curiosity about non-humans, and therefore a close relationship with nonhuman mammals. His other DNA components, besides Walt Disney and Napoleon Bonaparte, were Mother Teresa, the brilliant geneticist Martin Kerry (who was murdered in 2050 during the Clone Corruption Scandal) and musician John Lennon.

We were waiting for Walt's arrival, which was of course carried out in secret, as were all our meetings involving emergencies such as the Murine Infestation. It was a problem that had suddenly erupted after Walt had come upon an extraordinary colony of mice. After all, mice were Walt's passion. It was in his genes.

When Walt showed up, he brought with him a kind of projector, to give us a review of the problem. [*Important note: what follows next is the uncontaminated, official version of this historic event, which resulted in the ter-*

mination of two Murine Diplomats who had tried unsuccessfully to escape our infallibly inescapable punishment system.]

Walt had the face of a young Walt Disney, complete with mustache, but he had chosen to use the voice of John Lennon. For some reason, his voice was soothing to animals, which was useful, since his interests concerned the quality of life for the remaining non-human mammals on the planet. There weren't enough of them, but due to his efforts, that was changing. The mammoth had returned, there were snow leopards again, and most recently, he had made contact with the mice.

We greeted him warmly, then he set up his lecture just for us. "I don't exactly trust the other Assessors with what I've learned," Walt explained. "But you, he pointed to me, have Newman's tough philanthropic bent, and you," he pointed to Marilyn, "have the sense and sensibility I'm after. As for me, Mother Teresa has moved me to feel some compassion for these mice."

"I need a lot of convincing," I told him. "If the Cyborgs knew what kind of destruction the Murine Infestation has been causing, they'd order all mice to be wiped out. No questions asked."

Walt frowned. "I know. It's bad." He wiped some sweat off his forehead. Walt had opted for primitive body odors so the animals he encountered would be able to remember him and learn to trust him. Regulated hunting was still a problem for many mammals: Numerous species had become much smarter, having been genetically modified to provide better hunting experiences for legal poachers. His sweat and body odors were not noxious because there were no bacteria or fungi involved anymore, but the pheromones involved made Walt unusually attractive to Primitives –humans who had opted to live as their ancestors had done, minus the diseases and famines. Nevertheless, Walt's sweat was visible – and we had never seen it visible before, at this temperature. He was obviously agitated and worried.

"I have to show you some history, first" he explained. "I warn you, some of it is boring. But bear with me." Up flashed a  photo of a snake with a baby. "This is from way back in February, 2013," he explained. "Island of Guam. Brown snakes invaded Guam during World War II. Came on ships. Because there were no predators, by 2013 there were some 3 million snakes on this small island. That's 20 or 30 snakes per acre of land. They ate all the birds. The island became covered with spider webs, because the spiders then reproduced out of control. The solution was to lace thousands of dead mice with acetaminophen, a painkiller harmless to humans, but deadly to the snakes.[1] Poisoned mice are just one way we used the Murine Race for our own purposes."

[*Note well: we have always been in total control of the murine population. The Murine Infestation problem will also soon be solved, in due time.*]

Walt flipped from the photo to a screen full of written words. "Sorry for the inconvenience, but we're using this form to communicate, for security reasons," Walt whispered. "To continue, many other ways we used the Murine Race in the past were just as brutal. Billions of mice were used for scientific experiments of every kind, some of them unbelievably cruel."

"We're aware of the cruelties in the past conducted upon animals for scientific experiments," Marilyn replied. "But that's over."

"But what if it turned out that the mice *remembered* how they were treated, long ago?"

"I don't see how they would," she replied.

"How would they do that?" I asked.

"It turns out, we have lost the records of our total dominance over them," Walt explained. "And how? The Murine Infestation was dedicated to their destruction. Now the rebels are moving into other areas. Underground. Chewing at things. Destroying things, as never seen before. Oddly, it seems the mice didn't want us to remember what we had done to them."

"This is getting a little weird, Walt," I said.

"I got close to some of their leaders," he went on. "So close ... and that's how I got my hands on some records they wanted us to forget about. Look at these ... and please, do read them. I know that's tough on you. But do it! Our lives may depend on it."

[*Note well: the over-concern of Walt has been reported with candid frankness, but he was totally misinformed and over-reacting to the slight infestation problem as it actually existed. At all times, the infestation was only a very minor problem.*]

One by one, the old records came up on the screen. Saving us the trouble of wrestling with text, Walt began reading the material for us:

January, 2005: An informal ethics committee at Stanford University endorses a proposal to create mice with brains nearly completely made of human brain cells... the board was satisfied that the size and shape of the mouse brain would prevent the human cells from creating any traits of humanity. Just in case... the committee recommended closely monitoring the mice's behavior and immediately killing any that display human-like behavior.[2]

April 26, 2005: A US government-sponsored committee advised that, "...approval by a review committee should be secured before any human embryonic stem cells are put into an animal."[3]

April 29, 2005: NBC News reported that sheep were also being injected with human cells and that: "Particularly worrisome to some scientists are the nightmare scenarios that could arise from the mixing of brain cells: What if a human mind somehow got trapped inside a sheep's head?" The "idea that human neuronal cells might participate in 'higher order' brain functions in a nonhuman animal, however unlikely that may be, raises concerns that need to be considered…"

Sept. 17, 2014: *Huffington Post*: "An international team of researchers have created unusually intelligent mice by giving them the human version of Foxp2, a gene that's common to both humans and mice. The brainy rodents proved their extra cognitive oomph by navigating a maze significantly faster than ordinary mice. But don't worry – scientists aren't about to unleash hordes of mutant mice into our cupboards…"

February 20, 2015: "Scientists Use Human Genes to Grow Mice with Huge Brains":[4] "The team found that humans are equipped with … a particular regulator of gene activity, dubbed HARE5, that when introduced into a mouse embryo, led to a 12% bigger brain than in the embryos treated with the HARE5 sequence from chimpanzees."

February 26, 2015: The *Guardian* reported that Germany identified "a strand of DNA that … drives the expansion of the human brain and helps to make it the most complex structure in the universe … ramping up dramatically the number of neurons in the neo-cortex, a brain region that is central to reasoning, language and sensory perception… Tests on mouse embryos confirmed that the gene can have a profound impact on brain development… [Some] grew larger brain regions and … developed the crinkled brain surface that humans have.

The folds allow more brain tissue to fit into the same sized skull. [Dr.] Huttner's group is now keen to breed mice that carry the gene into adulthood to see how their brains develop, and crucially to see whether any changes boost their intelligence, memory and learning skills."[5]

Walt turned off the screen. "Of course there's more, but this is how it started."

"Just how smart are these mice now?" Marilyn wanted to know. "After all, how much intelligence can you pack into those tiny little brains?"

"Their brains aren't that tiny, after all," Walt told her. "It turns out that mice are real survivors. So they spontaneously began to develop a second area of brain cells using the neurons in their hearts, guts and spinal cords. We have lots of neurons in the same places, but they've been ignored, insofar as enhancing them to provide more functioning intelligence."

"I think I'll demand some of that enhancement!" I declared. "Einstein is excited!"

"At any rate," Walt went on, "Some wildcat geneticists didn't understand that these new mice were on the verge of becoming geniuses. Then some moron decided to help them along. Give them opposable thumbs and other primate characteristics."

This was more in my line of expertise, thanks to Darwin, so I put in my own two-cents' worth: "We humans have opposable thumbs for fine tool use, ball-and-socket arm and leg joints, so we can rotate them, stereoscopic 3-D vision due to frontal eyes, color vision, and the world's biggest brains to handle it all. It took millions of years of evolution."

"But in modern times, it took only a few decades to give these characteristics to mice," Walt added.

"But why?" Marilyn wanted to know.

"Cheap slaves," came the brisk answer. "To use in space travel. Lightweight, cheap, and energy efficient. To be used on colonies wherever we've wanted to send humans, but feared we might lose them. Many colonies began using them as pets to do a lot of labor for their owners."

[*Note: we have been very kind to the mice, kinder than any who have owned them hitherto. This version is retained to reflect what Walt was erroneously led to believe were actual facts.*]

"But what about oversight by our Space Travel and Colony Assessor?" Marilyn asked.

"She was in on it," Walt said, rather sadly. "She had her life extended another hundred years, using bribes under the table. The space frontier is like the Wild West of yore."

"I can't believe it!" I fumed. "Not with her personality mix!"

"Maybe that was the problem," Walt mused. "The conspirators behind this switched Neil Armstrong DNA for Lance Armstrong DNA. Once it took effect, she was willing to take other enhancers that are forbidden."

That explained a lot. The DNA of exceptionally tenacious individuals in sports had been used to enhance the performances of many athletes and space travelers. The Lance Armstrong DNA set was a cheap sports competition enhancer used by DNA pirates. Just like the Mike Tyson enhancer, it had its drawbacks and was black market material only.

"We caught the pirates when she caught our attention by biting off people's ears," Walt said, with a straight face. To our shocked reaction, he laughed. "Just joking. It's the John Lennon in me! Of course, she was terminated when the corrupt DNA showed up in a routine check, but by then, these mutated rodents were scattered across the colonies."

"Why weren't we told?" Marilyn demanded.

"Our Cyber Rulers didn't think it was necessary," Walt responded. "After all, she was replaced at once with a clean replica."

"She's never physically at our meetings," I agreed. "Always out there, somewhere … but still, how did the Murine Infestation spread, right under our noses?"

"It seems the developers hid behind an old law that still keeps even some of our advanced horses and dogs enslaved," Walt explained. "You know how I'm fighting the old racing syndicates to get this changed. It was a linguistic algorithm switch that did it. The word "Murine" was subtly changed to "Equine" and went unnoticed in the registration papers. Thus, this highly intelligent mutant strain was developed, under false headers, a decade or so ago."

"I was supposed to be told," I complained. "As the Protector of Human Life Assessor, I'm the ethics monitor regarding speeding up evolutionary trends."

"It didn't come up for review because the developer of this newest slave sub-species made sure the records were all reported under 'horses.' Recently, the super-mice revolted against their masters. They proceeded to destroy every record about 'mice' to keep them untraceable. I became concerned when entries for 'Mickey Mouse' suddenly started to vanish from probe searches."

"What do you mean, 'super mice'?" I asked.

"In essence, they've tripled the size of their brains, which were now growing in tissues throughout their whole body, with the head itself already 75% larger by 2030. And then, they became, on average, over a foot tall. A few years ago, they began walking on their new ball-and-socket genetically modified 'legs.'"

"No, no!" I burst out. "They've created sub-humans, from another species!"

"But even so," Marilyn opined, "surely, they can't have enough of the right kind of brain to think as we do."

"Oh, really?" Walt said, as he put the screen away. "If only we knew. Consider," Walt went on, "how smart a chihuahua is, despite his tiny brain. A hundred years ago, before we enhanced them, dogs such as the beagle, the mastiff and the chow, all with much bigger brains, were ranked lower on the intelligence scale than the chihuahua."[6]

"And your point?" I asked.

"These Mice are a helluva lot smarter than we realized. If I'd not had an ..." Walt smiled, "an inborn interest in Mickey Mouse, I suppose we'd never have noticed until it was too late. They hide themselves well, out there. Any such visitors to our Home Planet, here, were called figments of people's imaginations."

"So, what's next?"

"It's time you met them."

I was now deeply concerned. "First," I reminded my fellow Assessors, "we must order the capture of the monsters who created them."

"The CyberRulers have already taken that step," Walt told us.

"Without reviewing the matter with me?

"They told me they knew you would approve."

I wasn't pleased. "I'm not supposed to be left out of that loop!" I griped.

"Tell that to the CyberRulers. I didn't have the authority to raise the kind of objection that you can."

[Note: we have not censored these reprehensible remarks. We are always honest in revealing matters, even in the official versions, to which this is a preamble.]

"OK, they're already dead," I conceded. "But now, we must exterminate this mutant strain, since we humans created it for slave purposes. That's the law. As for the normal mice, it is our moral responsibility to protect the original species from extinction."

"I'm not sure there are any normal mice left," Walt said, with a sigh. "I've had the extermination committee prepare some lethal viruses to wipe them out. It's one reason this meeting is going to be held. But ethically, it has to be a slow-acting virus, so they can prepare themselves for the end. They may have a sophisticated belief system. They may have deep love, just as we do. They may be in contact with God, for that matter."

"You and your God!" I snapped. "It's the Mother Teresa in you!"

"You never made the experiments to get in contact with Him," Walt said softly.

"Believing in God isn't a crime!" Marilyn said. Of course, her personalities would agree with Walt's. It was an argument I couldn't win, since I had always refused to participate in their experiments, which focused on Time Travel. The current experiments were being conducted on the premise that God was a Time-Walker who could slip in and out of any sequence in time. Because I had trouble desiring to contact a Being who allowed unspeakable sufferings in our planes of existence in the name of Free Will, I stayed out of such experiments and saw them as just another manifestation of that old mental problem, Religion. I let God alone. He let me alone. I had been assured this wasn't going to impede my personal progress as a human, and that's the way it was going to stay. I like my independence.

"Back to the problem at hand," I told them. "When's the meeting?"

"In a few hours. We've promised them escape afterwards."

"Are we going to keep that promise?" Marilyn asked.

"Probably. They might destroy some space stations if we detain their envoys. They'll also suspect that, during any detentions, we could infect their envoys."

"We'll have to infect their envoys secretly then, during the meeting," I decided. I had rank here, and they knew it.

"Won't you at least listen to them?" Walt begged. "What happened to them isn't their fault. This is not like destroying cockroaches."

I had become well known for finally relieving the world of those disgusting creatures.

"We can listen. We can always listen," I replied. "That doesn't mean the extermination order can be rescinded. That just doesn't happen."

"They're so far removed, now, from the original species, that I don't think it's fair to consider them as mice anymore," Walt argued. "For example, they have no tails, and they have humanoid faces, and pointed ears. That's as far from Mickey Mouse as you can get. And, to make them more cost-efficient in space, they were modified to use chloroplasts to derive energy from the sun. They sunbathe a lot and only eat food if they choose to do so."

"Chloroplasts?"

"They're green. For all purposes, they're Little Green Men."

"Like the legends?"

"Yes. Like the legends," Walt said, wiping his brow. "Silly legends. But now, they're for real."

[Note: It is important to copy and keep this version of the matter. A previous report included a story created by the Murine infestation leaders to make it look as if they were being unfairly treated. They created a legend that a pair of murine leaders, one of which bore in her womb nine fetuses, escaped from an extermination committee hearing. This, we insist, was impossible. Any former version of this matter must be discarded. No mouse escaped extermination. We repeat: no mouse escaped extermination.]

Endnotes

1. ABC News: "Snake Population to Be Bombed With Poison Mice" Feb. 22, 2013 http://abcnews.go.com/International/snake-population-bombed-poison-mice/story?id=18568107 Retrieved June 9, 2015.

2. "Scientists Create Animals That Are Part Human" http://www.nbcnews.com/id/7681252/ns/health-cloning_and_stem_cells/t/scientists-create-animals-are-part-human/#.VXXF-7vGM5u Retrieved June 7, 2015.

3. "Scientists call for stem cell research guidelines." http://www.nbcnews.com/id/7641716/ns/health-cloning_and_stem_cells/t/scientists-call-stem-cell-research-guidelines/#.VXXB5LvGM5s Retrieved June 8, 2015.

4. http://www.33rdsquare.com/2015/02/scientists-use-human-genes-to-grow-mice.html#ixzz3cURJUM2y Retrieved June 7, 2015.

5. http://www.33rdsquare.com/2015/02/scientists-use-human-genes-to-grow-mice.html#ixzz3cUS6R4Hs Retrieved June 8, 2015.

6. "Dog Intelligence Rankings." (2008) http://6abc.com/archive/6500108/ Retrieved June 9, 2015.

MOUSE HOUSE

Johns Hopkins University scientists ... view a normal mouse and a genetically-engineered mouse (R) that is two to three times more muscular than the normal mouse. Scientists McPherron, Se-Jin Lee and Ann Lawler created the muscle-bound mouse while working on a newly-discovered gene."[1]

The companies using Walt Disney Clones were big players, and PowerINGenes, UC, better known as "PIG" was no exception. PIG had moved early into GMO's, then bought up all the new genetic patents for race horses, with which they made a fortune. After that, they added human genes to various domestic animals, giving them the ability to talk. They mass-produced cats that glowed in the dark as pets, rather than research animals, whose functions were now obsolete.[2] Now they were responsible for the current load of 87 vaccines that the government required, quietly hidden in genetically modified bananas, carrots, lettuce, potatoes and all the colorful fruits. An old poster, on display on the wall right behind Walt's work station, said it all: "Instead of needles, use bananas!"[3]

As we seated ourselves, Walt entered the cubicle and offered us some fruit from a bowl sitting there.

"No, thank you," Marilyn said.

"What's in it?" I asked.

"Now, don't be so touchy and suspicious," said Walt. "I was just being friendly."

"We're here to finish our report," Marilyn said.

"PIG is in trouble," I insisted.

"No, we're not," Walt insisted right back. "After they achieved a particular IQ level, they began choosing mates for themselves. That's when we lost control."

"Back to the problem at hand," I told him. "When's the meeting?"

"In a few hours. We've promised them Escape afterwards."

"Are you going to keep that promise?" Marilyn asked.

"Probably. They might destroy some space stations if we detain their envoys. They'll also suspect that, during any detentions, we could infect their envoys."

"We'll have to infect their envoys secretly then, during the meeting," I decided. I had rank here, and they knew it. The bottom line was that we'd have to exterminate the mice by sending a virus. Marilyn knew it was necessary, before some kind of war broke out on Mars due to the refusal of mice to work more than 80 hours a week.

"They have to die," I said. "They were developed without the proper permits."

"They're so far removed, now, from mice, that I don't think it's fair to consider them as mice anymore," Marilyn argued. "I've been reading PIG's records."

"We'll monitor the interviews of the Diplomats," I told him. To Marilyn, I added: "They're going to see a Gandhi Supra, is that correct?"

"Yes. He will choose the most compassionate way to end their lives. He may choose direct extermination of the Envoys as the most compassionate move we can make, for now."

"Killing the Diplomats would stop the strike," Walt put in. "They'll give up. They're a weak-brained folk."

"If there's any more trouble, they'll all be exterminated. Tell that to the Three Little PIGS, your bosses."

***

When the alarm sounded, Gandhi Supra8-C immediately shook sleep from him and sat upright. Automatically, he stepped into the metallic-looking footprints on the floor beside his bed, pressed a few buttons, and waited two minutes while his clothes for the day were printed onto his body. They dried to a beautiful sheen, complete with the patterns of roses and deer, thanks to an array of efficient mini-fans. Unlike many, Gandhi preferred simplicity in his flowing robes, so there were no jewels or gadgets. As he waited for the finishing 'beep' that meant his clothes were in perfect order, Gandhi looked anxiously around his rather expansive quarters, seeking Hubble4 and 5. When they finally appeared, he explained to them that he was authorized to give them personal interviews, as a concession to the fact that they were an intelligent species and owned the right to present objections to their extermination order. When they nodded their agreement, the holograms vanished and a door opened: two little green creatures now stood before him, with large, expressive eyes, wearing red military jackets covered with medals. They were members of the Diplomatic Corp, and as such, were supposed to have immunity from the death penalty. However, this rule applied, Gandhi told them, only to humans, which he would prove they were not.

First, he reviewed with the Diplomats their personal history, stopping sometimes when one or the other made a small, shrill exclamation of disbelief or horror. They had not known any of it: as Gandhi read the information sent to him by audio transcript, they kept interrupting him with their own version of their race's history.

"You are called a "murine infestation," Gandhi began, as gently as he could. "Therefore, you're scheduled for extermination."

"Us? But we're only Envoys – Diplomats!" Hubble5 shrieked out.

"He means we're all supposed to be exterminated," Hubble4 said, trying to control his emotions. "Meaning, us, our kids, our grandkids, our great grandkids.""Stop," Hubble5 said.

"Just, *stop!*"

"Yes, dear."

Gandhi knew he was looking at a very cooperative species of sentient animal. They had been bred that way, to comply, follow orders, obey. But with hazards that eliminated the stupid among them, their level of intelligence developed, and with it had come increasing instances of resistance and stubborn recalcitrance. Now that enough data had been collected from the thousands of slave mice employed in the Lunar Mines and sent to tunnel under the surface of Mars, the vast majority of whom had died from tunnel collapses, landslides, starvation, freezing, by asphyxiation or boiling to death, they were no longer needed or wanted. All robots were now equipped with the necessary information, at the proper size, to take their place. In mouse terms, it had been 500 cycles. In human terms, not nearly so many, Gandhi realized. More like a decade. Yes, just a short decade, and they had become outdated, overtaken by AI. Still, this was the only branch of the murine race left on earth. These "little green men."

And their extraordinary development into sentience and self-awareness had been conducted in secret, as had so many other controversial dealings concerning mutations and genetic modifications.

"I wish to speak to you of your true history, and why you are slated for extermination," Gandhi told them. "You have the right to know. It's one of the rights I have fought The CyberRulers to obtain for all sentient animals that are slated for termination."

"We don't want to be slated for termination," Hubble4 objected. "That's why we are here. To negotiate with you."

"The laws are strict," Gandhi explained. "And you are not the only ones who have to die. The CyberRulers have executed the fifteen scientists who created your unnatural species."

"But we didn't ask to be created!" Hubble5 put in. To her husband, she turned and whispered, "I've just ovulated. We should have nine babies in two weeks, if we just go have a quick romp in the bathroom. Isn't that lovely?"

"Hush!" Hubble4 snapped. "We might all be dead by then!"

"Oh, that's right," Hubble5 said. "I forgot, in my joy at ovulating!" Turning to Gandhi, she lifted her upper lip and showed her toothless but powerful digging ridges. Her motherly instincts had come to the fore, and she was warning him.

"You were telling us our true history," Hubble4 put in. "Please say on."

Flicking on an audio transcript from the Planning Meeting conducted a few hours earlier, the three of them listened to a relevant portion:

> "It seems the developers hid behind an old law that still keeps even some of our advanced horses and dogs still enslaved," Voice One explained. "You know how I'm fighting the old racing syndicates to get this changed. It was a linguistic algorithm switch that did it. The word 'Murine' was subtly changed to 'Equine' and went unnoticed in the registration papers. Thus, this highly intelligent mutant strain was developed, under false headers, a decade or so ago."
>
> "I was supposed to be told," Voice Two complained. "As the Protector of Human Life Assessor, I'm the ethics monitor regarding speeding up evolutionary trends."
>
> "It didn't come up for review because the developer of this newest slave sub-species made sure the records were all reported under 'horses.' Recently, the super-mice revolted against their masters. They went on to destroy every record about 'mice" to keep them untraceable."

Gandhi turned off the audio transcript. "So, as you can see, you were illegally created. And because you were illegally created, and have also become too intelligent, thus becoming a burden on society, now that you are outdated, the decision to execute you is just and reasonable. We will make certain the process is painless and swift. We are kind."

"Killing me is not kind. I want to live!" Hubble4 shrilled.

"Me, too!" Hubble5 put in. "For I am about to get pregnant!"

"The scientists who created you have already been executed. Surely you can see it's fair."

Hubble4 crossed his short, powerful arms across his muscular chest and glared at Gandhi.

"Prove it."

"What do you mean?" Gandhi asked, taken aback.

"I said, prove they've been executed," Hubble4 said, with a growl.

"Now, don't lose your temper and bite anybody," Hubble5 cautioned him.

Gandhi blushed. He had probably not blushed for seventy-five years. He gathered his wits, finally, and with a stammer, said, "I-I was told that they had been executed. The CyberRulers cannot tell a lie."

"I want to see proof!" Hubble4 insisted. "Didn't you say that we were developed in secret, by lies?"

"But the CyberRulers..."

"Who told you the scientists had been executed? Were they the ones we just listened to on the thing you played?"

"It's an AudioTranscript," Gandhi corrected him.

"I said, are they human, or CyberRulers?"

"They're mostly human," Gandhi admitted.

"And which one said there were executions? Which one was it?"

Gandhi sighed. "I'd have to listen through the whole thing, but I think it was the Space Travel and Colony Assessor. She had excused herself from the meeting, actually, but she was in charge of it. I heard that she had her life extended a hundred years." Gandhi paused. He didn't like where this was going. "That was because she accepted bribes to allow your development."

"And she didn't get executed, did she?"

"Well, no, come to think of it. She's too important."

"We reject the plan to terminate us," Hubble4 stated firmly. "We are not being treated fairly. We have no proof that the scientists who developed us were killed. In fact, if the Space Travel woman – or whatever she is – is alive, then I bet they are, too. That's what I think."

"Now that you settled the problem," Hubble5 said, with a little squeak, "please, dear, bring up the matter of the cats on the Lunar stations."

"Is there a problem?" Gandhi blurted out, before remembering the ancient gap between hunted and hunter... at any rate, he was relieved to change the subject. The extermination was slated to begin in only 24 hours, and it was his solemn duty to prepare the mice, as best he could, for the inevitable. After all, they had to obey the order to be rounded up and placed in concentration camps so they could then be efficiently executed. It was his job to make sure they understood that they had to exit from all their hiding places; that they had to enter the camps. That was the law, and they would have to obey, or they would be hunted down, one by one, by military drones and shot dead on the spot.

It was good that Hubble4's thoughts had been diverted so easily to cats.

"First, we wish to express our gratitude for the elimination of all cats from the Mars station," Hubble4 told him. "Our hope is that the entire species will be exterminated from all planets."

"We seem to have problems getting along with cats," Hubble5 said, rubbing her head against her husband's whiskers. This made him shiver with a thrill of lust.

"But don't you see that we have similar reasons for wanting to get rid of you?" Gandhi argued.

"They're not similar," Hubble4 objected, throwing an arm around Hubble5 and drawing her closer. "Cats attack us. We don't attack you. Unless – now – we have to."

Gandhi didn't like where this Condolences Session was taking him. The Diplomats had changed their attitude for the worse. As he cast about, trying to figure out what to do to reduce the tensions, Hubble4 cleared his throat to get his attention.

"Ahem!" he said, taking Hubble5 by the hand. "Excuse us, please, for a few moments. We need to make temporary use of your bathroom. The call of estrogens can be sudden, but it is always urgent."

"Be my guests," Gandhi told them. The slender, green mice scurried on their elegantly elongated legs into his toilet area, which immediately threw a shield of white light across the opening.

There were slight scuffling sounds, and some giggles from Hubble5, as Gandhi, sipping his roobi-tea, waited for their return to the sitting area.

And return they did, within a few minutes, Hubble4 straightening his whiskers, and Hubble5 demurely reaching over and straightening them again.

"Where were we?" Hubble4 asked.

"We were speaking of the necessity of exterminating the feline constituency of the planet," Gandhi said, using the best formal English of which he was capable, to demonstrate his seriousness.

"But we can't forget that you want to kill our unborn babies," Hubble5 said. "Just like the cats do."

Inspired by his alter-ego, Gandhi said softly, "I do not agree with the extinction of any species."

"We know that," Hubble4 said, moving his head up and down on his scrawny neck to prove that he agreed. "That's why we trust you. But you have to admit that cats carry a brain parasite. You know that, right?"

"I hadn't heard."

"But you humans carry it, too, didn't you know?"

"We're parasite free, all of us," Gandhi answered, though he couldn't remember ever having been scanned for parasites. Since he was only 25% Cyborg, it was a possibility. Maybe.

Hubble4 began reciting what he had been taught in his nursery concerning the parasite:

"The dreadful brain parasite, *Toxoplasma Gondii* – which sounds an awful lot like 'Gandhi' – inhabits one third of the brains of the human population! It causes suicide, depression and schizophrenia. Cats also carry the parasite and pass it to humans. Therefore, avoid both cats and humans."[4]

"Well, we've saved the best cats in our zoos," Gandhi said defensively. "I know they're parasite free."

"That you would keep any kind of cat illustrates how perverted you are!" Hubble4 blurted out. "It means you're an enemy. Our number one priority will be to go around you humans. We'll talk to the Cyborgs running the zoos. They'll have sense in their heads. They'll get rid of those horrible…" Hubble4 paused, delicately sensing Gandhi's disgust. "I mean to say, most humans we will avoid. You seem to care."

"I was created by my parents to care for all living things," Gandhi said. "I really had no choice." He was surprised at the bitterness he felt within. Had he been created with the genetic makeup of Napoleon, which was another popular genetic profile out there, he probably would have lured these pugnacious Envoys into a trap and made them hostages, to gain traction in the negotiations. Instead, he was a bleeding heart. But wait. True Napoleons had been banned from holding office because of their charisma and lust for power. Nor were any more 100% Napoleonic clones being considered. Napoleon's genes were now available only with a blend of 'Mother Theresa,' and she was more of a bleeding heart than he was!

Still, Gandhi looked forward to the time when Personality Infusions would allow him to add 'Van Gogh' (they had found his DNA) to his body. Ever since it was determined that Vincent Van Gogh had been driven insane by lead and cadmium poisoning,[5] artists around the planet were clamoring to get infusions of his DNA.[6] Gandhi was on the waiting list.

Hubble5 had been listening intently to this conversation, and now, her motherly instincts having been primed by her most recent activities, she gingerly stepped forward and peered into Gandhi's brown eyes.

"If you could get a 'Van Gogh' DNA Infusion, would you help us?"

Gandhi almost jumped. "How do you know that?" he demanded, all the bells and whistles going off.

"We can read your minds. Didn't you know that?"

"He does now," Hubble4 said. "Why did you tell him?"

"Because he's so nice." Hubble5 had never before met a truly "nice" human. The few human Taskmasters she'd encountered were one and all bred to be ruthless slave drivers; efficient taskmasters who would not hesitate to slay any Mouse, even if she were pregnant, who slowed down in digging. Mice were used because they were infinitely cheaper than robots, but recently, the cost of manufacturing had tipped the scales.

"They have slated The Mouse House on Mars for tear-down," Hubble4 told Gandhi.

"Yes, I know," Gandhi admitted. He thought that was inside information, but of course, he'd not known that these murine creatures had acquired telepathy. It was news he'd have to relay on to–

"No, you mustn't tell them!" Hubble5, whose telepathic powers were greater than Hubble4's, spoke with passion. "If you tell them, they'll tear down the Mouse House immediately,"

"Yes, they will."

"In five days, we'll have everything in place to live quietly and peacefully in safety." Hubble5 looked again into the eyes of the human, who was almost twice her size. "Please! Consider what they want to do to us!"

Gandhi sighed. His job was to prepare sentient animals and humans scheduled for termination to accept their deaths with calm and serenity. After all, all living things, until recently, had to die. He was equipped to offer their families financial compensation for such terminations. They were even offered replacements to adopt, if the terminated individual was still a child. After all, things sometimes went wrong with breeding-in certain personalities.

Gandhi remembered acutely the only other time he had been required to prepare a sentient animal for execution. The matter had concerned dogs. A line of them had been contrived to acquire brains that were 90% human. However, it was adjudged that this line was now a menace to society, since they had begun demanding human rights and were refusing enslavement even in the nicest human families. In the settlement with the dogs' relatives, they were informed that laws were passed to keep the human gene level in dogs to 49% so no dog would ever be able to demand human rights again. That would solve the problem peacefully. Secondly, the canine families involved were to be freed from human control: they were to be given their freedom, along with a package deal involving free food –including a ration of 25% real meat, which was expensive, for a whole year.

In actuality, this meant that 24 hours after that judgment had been passed, the four canine families involved were thrown into the outside world onto the continent of Antarctica, with rations for a month, since the "one year" food supply had been calculated for just one dog's maintenance. That was the cheapest legal way to interpret the terms of the settlement, saving the State considerable expense concerning the supply of expensive meat.

It was assumed that the ninety-percenters perished there, but all had been accomplished in the most quiet and civilized manner possible. In his heart of hearts, Gandhi had hoped they didn't die, and now Hubble5 picked up on that sense of regret and concern.

"You know it wasn't fair, what happened to the dogs," she told him. "Within me are nine little ones, just now starting to grow. If you kill me, you kill ten beings, not just one. Think of your laws. The dogs got only a month's supply of food, not twelve."

"That is true."

"Think about just the numbers, then," she urged him. "You won't be killing just two of us, if you send us through that door." She pointed with her green finger toward the Execution Door. "You'll be sending eleven of us to our deaths. Is that in your contract?"

"They did think with flexibility on how to interpret the supply of rations," Gandhi admitted. Could the matter of the numbers involved to be executed be a legal way to let the mice go? He did not want to be responsible for eleven deaths, where only two deaths were mentioned in his contract. Nor did his heart like the idea.

He knew he could be punished for this.

A tear welled up in Hubble5's eye. "I see you would be willing to consider death for our sakes," she managed to say, moving forward and throwing her arms around his waist. He shuddered: she did not smell like anything he had ever experienced. She seemed an alien. An alien to the planet – to life itself. But was that her fault?

No. It was, he knew, the fault of his own species. They had created these living beings on a whim, and then another group of humans had temporarily exploited them for financial gain. Quickly, Gandhi assessed the true risks to himself. They were many. At the very least, he would lose his job. At the other end of the spectrum, he could be tortured, while his brain would be stripped of all memories. If he was lucky, they wouldn't execute him. They would take into account his genetic makeup. That he couldn't help it. . . . Gandhi shuddered with horror. His own brain had just betrayed him. The psychometer readings would be able to see that he had reasoned out a way to save himself, and if he used any such route, which proved prior intent to break the law, that would be a crime. They'd surely kill him. Hubble5 had already seen the outcome, if he acted with his heart instead of by the pure letter of the law.

"What is human?" Gandhi asked himself, as he endured the pungent and strange odor of Hubble5, as he endured the alien grasp around his waist, which he instinctively wished to avoid. As he thought it, Hubble5 released him and jumped back.

"I'm sorry!" she said. "And here, you were our last hope."

"Why did you come at all?" he asked her. "Why did you risk your lives like this, knowing what I have to do, or they will kill me?"

"This room is secure," Hubble4 asked. "Is it not?"

"It is free of instant bugs," Gandhi asserted, as he grappled with a mounting sense of panic. Of course everything, everywhere, was monitored, but for diplomatic negotiations between the about-to-be-executed and the state, the law demanded temporary privacy.

"We were told they would never know what we said here," Hubble4 said, his voice beginning to tremble with anxiety.

"Technically, that is true,": Gandhi replied, trying to sound reassuring. "But in reality, everything said here is revealed within 24 hours. That is needed in order to negotiate any additional settlement issues."

"So, did the dogs get a chance to complain about their ration shortage?" Hubble5 wanted to know.

"They were not allowed to have any means to contact us again," Gandhi admitted.

"Can you really live with yourself, knowing that?" Hubble5 asked him. "Can you really send ten of us to the execution chamber, as well as my husband, knowing what you know?"

"What is human?" Gandhi murmured to himself. He brought out a recorder and spoke. "Case E9-Murine, terms of execution of two individuals, rank, Diplomats, was deemed incompatible with actual number of individuals presenting. One individual represents ten actual individuals, including one Diplomat. The order was to execute two Diplomats, but only one individual qualifies as an unencumbered Diplomat. We are ordered to send two Diplomats to the execution chamber, but only one individual qualifies. Therefore, this case is dismissed until a new order is issued to resolve the conflict. Signature X9-Gandhi Supra8-C."

They both embraced him, but he shook them off. He pointed to the little-used Exit Door, which carried a plaque that read 'The State can err: Gandhi Supra7-C.' By law, the Exit Door was never guarded.

"Go!"

The moment they touched the Exit Door, it opened, revealing a TouchCar in Privacy Mode. "Put in the coordinates you wish," Gandhi told them. "You do know where you want to go?"

"Won't they come after us?"

"Yes. In a few hours. Maybe, if I can hold them off a while, you'll have a day."

They had to trust him.

"I am not betraying you," he declared.

"I know you aren't," Hubble5 said. "I just hope you have been told everything about the Exit Door."

"I invented the concept of the Exit Door myself," Gandhi told them. "The argument was that the State, being able to read everyone's minds, would always have 100% certainty that an order for execution was always legal and correct. However, one of my predecessors sent an Innocent to execution on purpose, to prove that an execution could be illegal."

The Innocent One had also been a Gandhi. He had established, through his sacrifice, that the State could make an error regarding executions. When Gandhi Supra8-C had taken over this position after the suicide of Gandhi Supra7-C, he resolved the conflict within his soul by demanding the construction of a truly safe and secure Exit Door.

Gandhi felt a wave of love pour out from Hubble4 and Hubble5 as they settled themselves into the car. He had never felt such a thing. In all his lonely years, love had been an abstract thing. He had been born to feel compassion, but he had never been directed into an avenue that had given him any sensation that he was loved. His parents had died when he was very young, having been victims in the first anti-AI rebellion before the CyberRulers took over. He had been raised by surrogate parents, robots, who provided his every physical need. But their affections were as synthetic as a plastic flower.

Now, as Love washed over him from the two grateful mice, he began to understand why Gandhi Supra7-C had committed suicide. He had died only for a principle.

But Gandhi felt that maybe – just maybe – he would be dying for something greater. As the Exit Door closed, Gandhi set the recorder to one side and seated himself in a lotus position on the floor. In three hours, he knew, the Powers would realize that no execution would take place.

When the alarm sounded, Gandhi Supra8-C immediately shook sleep from him and sat upright. Automatically, he stepped into the metallic-looking footprints on the floor beside him, pressed a button, and allowed the chains to instantly fly out and wrap themselves around both his ankles. He had used it before on certain prisoners, but he was surprised at how painful it was: dozens of needles immediately stabbed into him as the chains embedded themselves deep into his flesh and became one with his muscles. A bridge of metal was printed between his legs so that he was utterly unable to move them, which hoisted him almost at once onto a pair of black wheels. At the same time, black, stinging tentacles descended from the ceiling and wrapped themselves around his neck, waist and arms. He was now officially immobilized and could not do harm to anyone, including himself. He had prepared himself that morning with prayers and meditation for the unpleasant job he had to face today, so, in some measure, he was ready. As he waited for the police, who would burst into the silent room at any moment, the thought, *What is human?* came again into his head.

Now he believed he knew the answer.

Endnotes

1. July 25, 2013 Reuters. http://www.reuters.com/news/picture/genetically-modified-animals?articleId=USRTXTZ7A acquired Dec. 19, 2015.

2. "In 1961 researcher Osamu Shimomura of the Marine Biological Laboratory in Massachusetts noticed a molecule in this jellyfish that glowed bright green under ultraviolet light.... After extracting the molecule from 10,000 specimens, Shimomura found the protein that creates the glow.... Since then, Shimomura's green fluorescent protein (GFP) has been used to decrypt previously invisible processes, like the spread of cancer or the development of nerve cells – earning Shimomura and colleagues a Nobel Prize in 2008. Fluorescent proteins have also been used to engineer some truly strange beasts (and the odd plant), such as the glowing puppies, monkeys, mice, fish and other animals http://news.nationalgeographic.com/news/2009/05/photogalleries/glowing-animal-pictures/ Glowing cats are backed up by the this article in *Science* http://www.the-scientist.com/?articles.view/articleNo/31165/title/Fluorescent-Cats-Aid-Research/ Acquired jan. 30, 2016

3. "People may soon be getting vaccinated for diseases like hepatitis B and cholera by simply taking a bite of banana. Researchers have successfully engineered bananas, potatoes, lettuce, carrots and tobacco to produce vaccines, but they say bananas are the ideal production and delivery vehicle. When an altered form of a virus is injected into a banana sapling, the virus' genetic material quickly becomes a permanent part of the plant's cells. As the plant grows, its cells produce the virus proteins – but not the infectious part of the virus. When people eat a bite of a genetically engineered banana, which is full of virus proteins, their immune systems build up antibodies to

fight the disease – just like a traditional vaccine."

http://www.mnn.com/green-tech/research-innovations/photos/12-bizarre-examples-of-genetic-engineering/banana-vaccines#top-desktop Acquired Jan. 29, 2016

4. "Toxoplasma Gondii Brain Parasite Infection From Cats Linked To Schizophrenia, Suicide" 07/07/2012 Huffington Post: *Toxoplasma gondii* is arguably the most interesting parasite on the planet. In the guts of cats, this single-celled protozoan lives and breeds, producing egg-like cells which pass with the cat's bowel movements. These find their way into other animals that come in contact with cat crap. Once in this new host, the parasite changes and migrates, eventually settling as cysts in various tissues including the host's brain, where the real fun begins. *Toxoplasma* can only continue its life cycle and end up a happy adult in a cat's gut if it can find its way *into* a cat's gut, and the fastest way to a cat's gut, of course, is to be eaten by a cat. Incredibly, the parasite has evolved to help ensure that this occurs. For example, *Toxoplasma* infection alters rat behavior with surgical precision, making them lose their fear of (and even become sexually aroused by!) the smell of cats by hijacking neurochemical pathways in the rat's brain." *It is possible that the very thought of the parasite was enough to create sexual arousal in HubbleS.* – please laugh] "…rats aren't the only animals that *Toxoplasma* ends up in. Around 1/3 of people on Earth carry these parasites in their heads …[In a Danish study of 45,000 women who were mothers, those with] *Toxoplasma* infections were 54% more likely to attempt suicide – and twice as likely to succeed. In particular, these women were more likely to attempt violent suicides (using a knife or gun, for example, instead of overdosing on pills). But even more disturbing: suicide attempt risk was positively correlated with the level of infection. Those with the highest levels of antibodies were 91% more likely to attempt suicide than uninfected women. The connection between parasite and suicide held even for women who had no history of mental illness: among them, infected women were 56% more likely to commit self-directed violence."(Of course, males are infected as often as females: JVB) http://www.huffingtonpost.com/2012/07/05/toxoplasma-gondii-brain-parasite-suicide-cats_n_1651523.html Retrieved Aug. 25, 2015.

5. The lead poisoning theory as the prime cause of Van Gogh's insanity has been the author's for many years: every time Van Gogh had to stop painting due to a nervous breakdown, he improved dramatically during those time periods when he was unable to paint. Despite high levels of lead in flake white and other paints, and the high levels of poisonous cadmium in many yellows, oranges and reds, only in 2015 was a law, passed in 2010, finally allowed to go into effect to place cautionary labels on artist's paint. Many artists have been exposed to these toxic materials, along with turpentines and other flammable solvents, which are carcinogenic, and were given no warnings by their instructors at universities or elsewhere as to the dangers to their mental and physical health. Face paint used by actors, clowns and for Halloween has also been found to contain high levels of lead (most modern face paint products come from China). There are very safe ways to remove artist's oil paint: use olive oil and liquid soap, one after the other, in clean-ups, and wear gloves. No flammables are needed. See: http://www.winsornewton.com/na/discover/resources/health-safety Retrieved Aug. 26, 2015.

6. In 2006, NIH acquired a Spanish study that supports the author's theory: NCBI Resources: Abstract.

7. In an interview with the BBC, the scientist said such technology could rapidly evolve and overtake mankind, a scenario like that envisaged in the "Terminator" movies.

"The primitive forms of artificial intelligence we already have, have proved very useful. But I think the development of full artificial intelligence could spell the end of the human race," the professor said in an interview aired Tuesday.

"Once humans develop artificial intelligence it would take off on its own, and re-design itself at an ever increasing rate.

"Humans, who are limited by slow biological evolution, couldn't compete and would be superseded," said Hawking, who is regarded as one of the world's most brilliant living scientists.

Read more at: http://phys.org/news/2014-12-hawking-ai-human.html#jCp

RE-RUNS

"With VR... [t]he experience is so compelling that maybe in months or years, it'll be hard to choose from the real thing." VR can "bring us into worlds that we otherwise would need airplanes or even time machines to visit." Perhaps "... the ultimate iteration of the technology will be more augmented reality, or AR – overlaying a virtual world over the real one – than a VR goggle that keeps us blind to the outside world."[1]

– *USA Today*, "Virtual Reality Will Be Everywhere," 3/27/2015

"Hey, Maw!" Terrence shouted, holding up the postcard and waving it awkwardly in her face, "Looky here! Postcard from Melvin already!"

"Mail's purty fast this week," Maw replied, examining the date over the stamp.

She was always concerned about the dates, because mail didn't arrive in the Outback regularly. It was one of the things pioneering families in this sector had to put up with.

Terrence jumped from one foot to the other as Maw tried to read the postcard for herself and then pushed it down into the generous folds of her well-patched apron. "You oughtn't go 'round barefootin' it all the time," she told him. "You could step on a rusty nail and get tet'nus!"

"Aw, Maw, lighten up," Terrence objected. "You know there aint no tet'nus or rusty nails here. Besides, I ain't got no proper shoes left. Have to wait for the next Transport."

"Well, then," she observed, "best you watch out, anyways, 'cause there's another snake."

"It's that damned rattler, agin," Terrence said. "I'm gettin' sick of havin' to cut its head off. Maybe I should just let it bite me this time."

"I don't want to see you dead that quick," Maw told him. "We need to stick together here as a family. It's bad enough your Paw up and died on us last week. Better hand you the card now," she said, digging into her apron pocket and bringing out the postcard again. "The way you're going, you won't last 'til dinnertime. Jus' read it to me," she said, handing the postcard to Terrence. "Who knows? Maybe we'll get a new V-R by the end of the week, if he can stay an extra day or two."

Terrence kicked the rattlesnake high into the air and let it slither away, then focused on the postcard. The message was sweet and brief, but for sure, there was a hint at some relief. Maw's eyes glistened with tears of pride as Terrence read the message aloud.

"To Maw and everyone!" Terrence read, proud of his literacy in this primitive place. "Working hard aboard 'The Coconut Dream.' First Mate this time, hurray! Helped my ship ride out a big Sim-u-lated Hurricane. But threw up. Also got a solar burn. Even so, working good enough to get a raise! Meet you in Rome, and from there, guess what? We're going to Las Vegas! Love, Melvin." If Terrence had hopped around with excitement before, now he was practically leaping from stone to stone on the pitiful plot that the family called its farm land.

"Las Vegas! Las Vegas!" Terrence crowed. "At last! At last!"

"So we won't see him 'til we get to Rome," Maw commented. "Wish he could see how we fixed up the house."

"But Maw, that's because they're keeping him a couple extra days," Terrence reminded her. "That's how he's earned enough to get us the new V-R. And it's Las Vegas!"

"Gawd!" Maw said, spitting out her chewing tobacco, "Wait'll I tell the kids!"

"We better both git back to the house," Terrence said, looking skyward. He gave the postcard back to his mother. "There's that storm coming again."

"We're all shut down good and tight now," Maw answered, as they hurried down the cow-path to the house. "Not like before."

It had taken them quite a while to get the house ready for this storm. Again and again, the storm had demolished it and they had been forced to live in the stone barn. But the last twenty or so re-runs, they'd remembered enough to scramble, remembered enough to get the house strong enough to withstand the storm. Now the house could endure any simulated storm thrown at it, and the farm, pitiful as that place could be, was also slowly developing into a productive piece of property. They had managed to raise potatoes, gooseberries, corn and chickens. These V-R products provided sensory variety to augment their regular, nearly tasteless rations. The big hope was to raise some pigs, as well, though this meant being closer friends with a nearby family whose members were rich. Maw glanced over at the bigger, nicer farm in the distance for the first time without any feeling of bitterness or envy. The Richmonds may have had a better farm V-R, and atop that, a V-R to Disneyland, but frankly, a V-R to Las Vegas was even better.

Socially speaking, they were making real progress, thanks to Melvin. Maw felt that she could hold her head up high. She now felt she could afford to ask for a piglet for the next re-run, by Gawd. Meanwhile, seeing how the sky was darkening, and knowing how hard the storm would hit, she found herself resenting the fact that they'd been through this V-R so many times that she could remember way too much of it. They were supposed to see a few new twists to the "Little House on Prairie Dog Flats" on every re-run, but the additions turned out to be costly.

She and Paw had made the mistake long ago of thinking they'd signed on for "Little House on the Prairie," but they had been fooled. Instead, they were stuck with the lower grade V-R. The good version hadn't been on sale, after all. However, they hadn't been the only family who got fooled: the Richmonds had also been tacked into this cheaper V-R and were also just as irritated about it.

The re-runs of "Little House on Prairie Dog Flats" were exasperating, because they weren't as good for the children as she and Paw had wanted. They never did get a change of seasons: it was always early spring to harvest time, and they had wanted all four seasons, including an American Christmas, but it was not to be. Nevertheless, their youngest, Terrence, still needed guidance through this V-R, and she enjoyed feeling like a real parent to him, even though he was actually an orphan who had joined the family when his own parents had died for real. They had always wanted another child, but it would have forced them to live in Real Time too long.

One year, when they were in Real Time, and Terrence was still very young, Maw (she was 'Mother' in RT) had asked him if he could remember any details about the loss of his real parents, since he had so many nightmares about it. She had chosen a time when Melvin and Sara had gone with their father to a Real Time sports event.

"Well, Mother," Terrence had replied, "all I recall is that I had a mom and dad, and we were accidentally sent to the Hiroshima V-R. Not to observe the bombing of Hiroshima, as had been described to us, upon our arrival, but instead, we were supposed to get bombed."

"But nobody dies for real in a V-R," Maw had reminded him. "Perhaps you lost track of each other in the blast."

"I remember my parents were on the A-List. They were Activists," Terrence told her.

"Oh, dear!" Mother breathed out, trying to hide her alarm. "Now I understand. They may have been culled."

"I think so, even though 'CHUK-E' (Cyborg Humane Unit, Kills by Euthanasia) talked to me later and said they did a suicide, and it wasn't my fault. But if they did a suicide, why did they get so scared? Why did they start running? Why were they crying?" Terrence looked so frightened that Mother took his little hands and kissed them. "We ran and ran," Terrence went on. "We ran to a huge wall. Then they told me to start climbing. My feet were so small I could fit them into the cracks. I could climb. I went way up. I went over. It was a wall high as a mountain. But somehow, they couldn't climb the wall."

"Is that when you lost them?" Maw asked.

"No," Terrence replied. "That was a little later. When they began screaming. When I saw the huge fire. I was on the other side of the wall, but I knew they were dead. Really dead, not fake dead. But, nobody believes me!"

As Terrence began to cry, Mother had done her best to comfort him. "I'll try to find out what went wrong," she promised. "Sometimes, people don't tell even their children when they get tired of all this." She waved her hand around at the Real Time cubicle in which the family lived when off-grid. It was cramped, filled mostly with their sleep capsules and a few trinkets, as well as some play-screens, a port where they could order food, a bathroom, and storage drawers.

"Maybe it got too much for them," Mother tried to explain. "Over and over, we must go into V-R together, for a majority of the year. It's the law. Maybe they got sick of it."

"I like our trips!" Terrence put in.

"I don't. They get to be so boring. We live them so often that we start remembering parts. But it's our duty as citizens. We must take turns being awake in Real Time."

"But why do we have to keep going to sleep?" little Terrence asked. "I like being awake. I like the trips we take to Food Kiosks. I like walking around."

"You were raised by Activists," Mother explained, as gently as she could. "Activists can be selfish. Not that your parents were that way, "she quickly added. "They just *can* be. ..." She patted Terrence's little head and added, "Activists do reject the plan that allows so many of us to live on this crowded planet without any suffering. The economy can't afford to feed all of us. But this way, when we hibernate, there is enough of everything to go around. And we have no poverty. No hunger. No wars. No homeless. The Cyborgs take perfect care of us."

To herself, Mother had some different thoughts. She could no longer remember her real name, for example. In the V-R scenarios, she was always Mother, or Maw, or Lady. Originally, there were endless V-Rs to choose from when hibernating; but not anymore. New ones began to cost extra: the family knew they were fortunate that Melvin had a job for two whole weeks every year. No new jobs were being created, but with any luck, Melvin would be able to work three weeks next year. Then the family could have access to at least one more new V-R.

Melvin had the courage to do real work. The willpower it took for a human to leave the V-R worlds to endure the hardships of real work, and to be good enough to keep getting hired, was rare, and deeply appreciated by those families fortunate to have a Worker. There was literally nothing to do while awake but to eat, talk and walk around, since there was never any real news anymore. The V-Rs that were now available were fewer in number, but better, the Cyborg Government insisted. They allowed family bonds to become tighter. They knew best, Maw told herself, but some faint protest lived within her that recalled a different way to exist, long ago.

A tiny voice seemed to whisper to her about the nearly-forgotten past:

> Most of us turned in our three least favorite V-Rs for a fancy new one, such as the one we have that places us in Imperial Rome, where – every time – we can choose the role we want to play. We ended up turning in nine obsolete V-Rs for three incredibly realistic and flexible ones. But lately, it's gotten so costly to get new V-Rs. That depresses me. Maybe that's why Terrence's parents chose suicide?

To Terrence, she had said, "They may have been injured, and that's why they chose suicide. That's probably why you saw CHUK-E there. I think they were going to take you along with them, at first, but at the last moment, they changed their minds. They wanted you to live, and showed you how to escape. And so now you're our little boy."

She hoped talking about it would stop Terrence's nightmares, but they continued.

As the years passed, Terrence began to forget the death of his parents, but sometimes he would still have a nightmare about it and would run into her arms, crying. As he got older, the nightmares were replaced with more pleasant dreams, thanks to the Hypnotherapist the family hired, in Real Time. During Real Time, when they were not in a V-R cycle, Terrence and Mother would try to locate other members of Terrence's family. There was also a chance that a kinsman would consider a V-R swap, or maybe they'd even give Terrence a nice V-R as an inheritance. It was worth a try.

Though records existed proving that Terrence's family had once gone to Hiroshima, his parents had never emerged to Real Time again. Furthermore, two remote family members had also looked into the deaths and learned that "an error" had caused his parents to be incinerated.

Then there was the mystery of Terrence's original father's brother. At about the same time that Terrence's parents had died, the uncle, rated A-Activist, was sent to the Mars Penal Colony in Real Time. The Prisoners there endured V-R punishment regularly until their 'thought habits' were once again conformed to society, but they did enjoy a few non-punishing V-R programs. However, these V-Rs turned out to be extremely boring and devoid of pleasure – nothing that Terence and his current family would want. Terrence's uncle's wife lived as a Freewoman on Mars, but it would have been too expensive to send him there, so he was put up for adoption.

Thus a compromise was made: Terrence would be trained to become a Worker, like Melvin, if Mother and Father adopted him. The fruits of his labors would assign credits of two-thirds to his new parents and one-third to his Uncle and his Uncle's wife, even though the Uncle was a prisoner. The labor arrangement would give the Uncle a few privileges, such as being able to avoid one of the punishment V-R programs.

Papers were signed, and the problem was solved, except for Terrence's nightmares, where he kept seeing his parents blown to smithereens. Since the nightmares always happened when he was in a V-R cycle, there was no way it could be fixed. Only if Terrence wished to permanently terminate his life, by going to CHUK-E, could there be a final 'fix.' Maw sincerely hoped that would never happen.

Once she'd been bitten by the rattlesnake, for example, and had died. That had sent her on ahead to Rome, where she also died before Paw could get there to stop her from selecting "Gladiator" – a word she hadn't recognized due to her residual illiteracy problem in the "Little House" V-R. It had left her temporarily a bit dense. As a Gladiator she hadn't lasted long, and it took another V-R cycle for her to catch up with the rest of the family again.

By dint of hard concentration, Maw was able to recall a general picture of their overall lives in V-R by putting together a set of mnemonics. *Rattlesnake – killed me – Gladiator killed me – Storm Troopers – killed me – Dinosaur – tried to kill me; back to Real Time.*

Of course, nor every re-run ended in death. It was just that death became a more interesting situation as time went by. It got old trying to elude death, trying to avoid an explosion, or just watching others die. There were some very pleasant commercial breaks, lasting a few hours each, in most of the re-runs, where the whole family (those not already dead) could play on a beach together, enjoy a medieval feast, or go horseback riding in Peru. Of course, these commercials cost Work Time (Thanks to Melvin, they had credit to spare, and someday, Terrence would be helping out, too). Then they'd return to the re-run: the commercials would seem like a dream they'd had while sleeping, since they always occurred during a period of sleep in the main V-R.

Lately, some of these commercial breaks advertised new V-Rs at the end, which created a lust to purchase that was almost irresistible. Some of them offered enhancements to V-Rs they already had. In this manner, the family had obtained the right to select positions much higher and safer than that of Gladiator, Slave Girl, or Christian Martyr when in Rome. After Rome, they always had a big family gathering in "Star Wars," which unfortunately always ended with Storm Troopers blowing up their planet. Their next V-R took them into a Sherlock Holmes murder mystery series, sometimes set in London, or in Liverpool, but often bringing them into a dreary house in the Moors where various family members were killed before Sherlock saved the day. That brought them to the last V-R, designed to make a return to Real Time more bearable. This was accomplished by their entering a cheap V-R with fewer sensations, props and interesting variations. Most of them were animated cartoons. The latest cheapie imposed on them was called "The Fred Flintstone Family Tames a Dinosaur. " It was the worst V-R Maw had ever had to plod her way through before waking up at home base.

In Real Time, they escaped the passive exercise machines that moved their limbs and kept their bodies from deteriorating, to walk under their own power. They ate food the old-fashioned way. Families and singles got filled in on the gossip and played checkers and had affairs before they were strapped down again to resume their V-R cycles once more.

But a problem had emerged … there was now a glitch in the family's V-R cycle. "The Fred Flintstone Family Tames a Dinosaur" V-R had repeated itself twice, without even a commercial to break it up. The repeat also made them lose a month of Real Time. Maw had complained about this to the Cyborg-in-Charge on their floor. It apologized profusely for the double dose, but it happened again on the next V-R cycle. This time, Maw had asked Melvin to make sure the glitch got fixed before his annual work cycle was over and he joined them in Down Time.

* * *

Melvin knew he was the pride and joy of his family, for he was a Worker. Since many families or groups had no Worker, they were considered lower class and their chances to obtain new V-Rs remained limited. They often found themselves forced to be members of audiences, victims of mob violence, or fodder for armies in new V-R productions to earn their credit points. In the Rome V-R, for example, the crowds screaming for gladiator blood were composed of these less fortunate people. Eventually, they'd earn some perks to enjoy in a commercial break. A year ago, their Real Time away from V-R had been reduced to only six weeks. It was whispered that many of these underprivileged were now committing suicide in Real Time.

Knowing how valuable he was to his family, Melvin worked out and kept his body strong during his family's two-month Real Time stint. He also studied, honing various skills to make sure he would be selected for a high-paying position. He was an expert horseman, could cook almost anything, and lately had been hired as First Mate on "The Coconut Dream," which was a yacht that the very wealthy could rent during their three months of Real Time. Melvin himself had three months of RT: during part of the third month, he worked. Sometimes he wondered how his family got along on just two. His dream was to get his family into two-and-a-half months or more of RT, along with three or four more V-Rs of high quality. Deep within him, he wondered if he'd ever have a chance to marry. Inga-Brit, a blonde he'd tried to date in RT, had developed *myasthenia gravis* and was now undergoing therapy. He wondered where they had taken her for treatment. *Myasthenia gravis* was a hazard that endangered everyone who had only six weeks of down time.

As Melvin pondered these things, the shrill of a whistle made him sit upright in his narrow bunk bed. It was time to get back on deck. "Oh, man!" he thought to himself, "I still feel awful!" He was still a little seasick, but the medicine had started working. As Melvin started up the metal steps, his friend Truman, a big, blonde, always-grinning Brit, helped him out at the top.

"Better now?" Truman asked him.

"Yeah. Hope they don't fire me."

"Not unless it happens again," Truman said, trying to be reassuring. "They should have had the simulated hurricane in the job description, and they didn't, so they were at fault."

The two men hurried toward the Captain's lavishly furnished banquet cabin, where important guests would soon be seated at the big, linen-covered table. Melvin knew that both he and Truman had been chosen as First and Second Mates purely due to their good looks and sociability. They both had well-developed muscles that made them look like supermen, but they also had worked hard to achieve a high-class English accent and impeccable manners. As they began greeting the well-dressed men and women who came drifting into the candle-lit room, suddenly Melvin saw her: it was Inga-Brit, his former girlfriend! She was not alone: the Captain himself was at her side.

She looked just fine, as she approached, holding hands with that too-old, be-whiskered gentleman, her long, green gown trailing lightly behind her, her neck adorned with diamonds and her ears be-hung with orbs of gold peeking from under a plaited promenade of platinum blonde hair. As Melvin helped Inga-Brit to be seated, she whispered just two words, and he understood: *"Four Months."*

He knew she'd been virtually purchased by the man who now gently grunted as he lowered his generous bulk into the finely carved Captain's chair to sit beside her. But how in hell did anybody get a four-month status? Until now, he'd only been exposed to three-monthers. A whole new world of possibilities suddenly yawned before him.

Throughout the evening, Melvin used his wit and chatter to charm these high-class guests. By the time of the last hand-shake from the Captain, and the last dreamy smile from an inebriated Inga-Brit brought the evening to a close, Melvin and Truman had learned many secrets. The guests had been so pleased with their Real Time cruise that it had been extended an extra day. Inwardly, both young men could scarcely conceal their delight: the extra hours assured enough credits for their respective families to receive the new, coveted *"Viva! Las Vegas!"* V-R.

When the night crew took over, the two men, anxious to talk, returned to their room. After the lights dimmed, Truman whispered, "Was that *your* Inga-Brit?"

"Yes, about thirty pounds heavier. Looks like she got well pretty fast."

"I heard her say her doctor introduced her to the Captain. I'll bet he ended up paying for her treatment."

"She told me, 'four months.'" Melvin whispered, as the room went totally dark.

"You think those people get four months?"

"I do."

"My God! What I could do with four months!"

"That guy, the banker... know what he told me?"

"What?"

"Said he bought two weeks from a Two-Monther lower class."

Melvin's mind flashed back to his own hard struggle to earn three months. It had taken him years.

"But wasn't there a general decree to reduce the Two-Monther lower class to a month-and-a-half?"

"It looks like they sold their time to get more V-Rs," Truman told him. "Seems the decree was instituted to hide the fact that this was purchased time."

"Poor slobs."

"Who are you going to vote for in the next election?"

"I forget. It's kind of a blur, you know." Melvin said.

"Yeah. But I won't vote for anybody who's more than 75% Cyborg."

"And how are you going to know what percentage they are, the way they hide all this stuff?"

"Better stop thinking like that, or you'll get on the 'A' list. Like Terrence's dad."

"You're right," Melvin replied. "Look how good we humans have it now!"

Myasthenia gravis and suicides were currently the only real problems facing humanity anymore, outside of life in a penal colony.

"That's right," Truman said. "No more wars. No more starvation. No more homeless. No disease, with free education and free medical care! Equal opportunities for all, and thanks to V-Rs, we can live many lives, not just one. The human race has never had it so good!"

Melvin sighed. Truman's words did not match the sting of desperation he sensed in his friend's voice.

* * *

As always, the weather was perfect, where, among the clouds (and ominously) vultures circled on wings that stretched into long, black Vs that stitched the clouds together against a strikingly deep blue sky. The massive bulk of the Coliseum loomed over the huge crowd that was filled with sour, unhappy faces. The Romans were demanding bread.

"Bread! Bread! Bread!" they screamed, as the bakers threw loaf after loaf into the mob.

"We want the circus! We want the circus!" came the next cries, as the gates were opened and the mob poured in. Slaves and free, old and young, male and female, in their rags and riches streamed into the grandstands, a living river of humanity, sweating, shoving, pommeling each other.

Lady Cecilia, El Terrencio, Sariah and Melvinio sat in a private box, their well-groomed bodies garbed in purple, as they ate from a platter of dates, grapes, cheese and sausages, with a slave at their side to pour their wine.

Only two boxes to the left, Emperor Claudius and his Empress sat amidst powerful, well-armed soldiers and tall, black slaves. Their enormous gilded chairs were festooned with garlands. Melvinio noted, with some resentment, that Claudius had much of the face of the Captain, and the Empress resembled, to an alarming degree, his Inga-Brit, but his resentment faded when she turned her head slightly in his direction and winked.

Melvinio, realizing that he may have found his ticket to Four Months, winked back…

Then the Gladiators marched forth, in their glittering armor and decorated helmets. The trumpets sounded, the crowd began to roar, and the Gladiators cried out, "We, who are about to die, salute you!"

As the first two warriors faced each other in the great Arena of the Coliseum, armed with nets and axes and weighted maces, Lady Cecilia called out to the Gladiator who seemed rather shorter and less muscular than his opponent.

"Darn it, Paw!" she yelled, the vestiges of her former V-R experience still upon her, though fading fast, "Why are you killing yourself again? We just got here, and already, you're leaving!"

Melvinio leaned forward as his father turned his grizzled face toward his wife, who, luxuriating in the family's special box, decided to wave at him. For a moment, Melvinio thought he had never seen a more miserable visage. At least, he thought to himself, Dad wasn't really committing suicide. Surely, if he could just earn another R-V or two, his father would have a smile on his face again.

His equanimity restored, Melvin impassively watched his father get hacked to pieces by a gigantic Oriental Gladiator who first trapped Dad in a net, then began slicing off his limbs. As the crowd roared with pleasure, and the dark blood spurted out against the bright steel of the Oriental Gladiator's sword, Dad went on to meet Sherlock Holmes in London.

Endnotes

1.		http://www.usatoday.com/story/tech/2015/03/27/virtual-reality-oculus-rift-facebook-vr-will-be-everywhere/70547882/ Retrieved July 31, 2015.

TEENAGERS

*S*he was absolutely frozen, her teeth chattering, crystals of ice in her nostrils, but as they worked on her, gradually color returned to her face, and LauraLee's eyes opened.

"You're going to be all right!" excited voices assured her.

"Wh-what about Roger?" she managed to ask.

You've got frostbite," one replied, "but it seems there's no permanent damage."

"But – what about Roger?" she insisted, sitting up suddenly, anxious and concerned.

"He's alive," came the reply. "He's going to be OK."

Hearing that her son was safe, LauraLee sank back among the pillows, with a contented smile, and fainted…

* * *

"It's normal that you don't remember much, Roger," LauraLee told him. "What you went through was so terrible that they did a Mind Sweep."

Roger sat on his low bed in his room, his head in his hands. It had been a month since his rescue: he and LauraLee had been the center of attention, with interviews and appearances on the most popular talk shows across the planet.

It had been mostly a blur to him: every memory of his teenage years was missing. His psychiatrist explained that those memories had been so traumatic that they had to be erased. In their place, Roger was given an understanding of almost all the events and technological advances that had occurred during that time period. If faces and days and years themselves were missing, at least he had not lost the ability to function as an adult. Still, it wasn't an easy adjustment, and everyone understood that.

But now he was "home." He was expected to take his place in the adult world. Have a job. Adapt to work and play schedules. Though he was a celebrity and had been given the best of everything available at his social grade, he still had trouble on a basic level: recognizing himself. When he viewed his own hologram, he vaguely recognized his thick, reddish-blonde hair. That looked familiar, but the baby-face, freckled and dimpled, that he had last seen as his own, had morphed into a grown-up visage, complete with hairs on his face that (should he desire) could be eradicated as quickly as had been his memory of his teenage years.

Roger looked warily around his new room, trying to connect what he saw with any shred of memory left of those years when he was a child. By now, he was aware that it was wrong to ask questions about his past: people would look away and tell him it was a matter of privacy. He wondered what terrible things had happened to him, but not a single word in that direction had been uttered, other than it had been lucky that his mother had been brave enough to rescue him.

As he scanned the room, LauraLee stood anxiously watching.

"That's your Teddy Bear," she told him, as he stared at the big, plush toy slumped against a corner. "It was your favorite."

Roger frowned. "I can't even remember the Teddy," he told her. "But – I think I remember those toy cars … and ….," he pointed to a poster on the wall. "That poster of Elvis Presley," he said. "Somehow, that looks familiar."

"If it bothers you, I'll remove it," she told him, bending down and kissing him. "I'm surprised you remembered Elvis. I took a chance. The doctors were afraid it might trigger some bad recollection. It doesn't make you remember anything bad, does it?"

"No, Mom," he answered. "It's fine. But – how old is Elvis, in that picture?"

"Twenty-one, I think," she said quickly. "How would I know? Maybe I should take it down. By the way, tomorrow, you're finally going to meet your biological father. I think you would have liked him. He had a lot of muscles. Just like you."

She handed him the print-out for tomorrow's schedule. So far, Roger was responding well to everything but the schedules. The psychiatrist saw a few small problems, which would be straightened out with a few more doses of tranquilizers. As Roger looked over the newest schedule, suddenly his psychiatrist stood before him in a hologram so perfect and entire that if you touched him, you'd feel his skin, his clothing, everything.

"You're resisting the scheduling," the psychiatrist explained, "so I'm here to reassure you. We understand that you still want to do some unplanned activities," the psychiatrist said. When Roger didn't reply, he flicked at a row of small icons dancing before his eyes. "Ah … yes … there it is …" With a tap of a holofinger, the psychiatrist caused a full-sized hologram of Roger and himself to appear before them. It was a replay of their meeting only 24 hours earlier. "I want you to listen, Roger," the doctor said. "Pay heed to our conversation from yesterday."

Roger watched the replay of his meeting with the psychiatrist with fascination. It was he, all right. The psychiatrist had laid a gentle hand on Roger's shoulder as he explained why the young man was resisting a fully planned schedule. "That's because you're so young. You can't remember how happy you used to be in our system, and a part of you is questioning the fact that your days are now all planned out, since you're an adult."

"Why is it all so rigid?" Roger wanted to know.

"It all began to stop crimes before they could happen,"[1] the psychiatrist explained. "We even have some full-blown maniacs in our system, but their activities are so well planned that they can't think of breaking the law. And the few who ever did ..." a look akin to sadness seemed to rest for a moment on the psychiatrist's face... "they are in mental lockup."

Roger was told that "mental lockup" kept a criminal from having any Free Think time whatsoever. The convict was loose in society, but could do no harm, since he was no longer self-aware. Such criminals did the hard work nobody else wanted to do. They were well fed and housed the same as anybody else, but they never spoke to the Touchables. Their black handcuffs identified them. They were the Untouchables.

"Everybody else gets at least *some* Free Think time," the psychiatrist said. "But you seem to be objecting to your allotment, which is quite generous for someone your age."

"There isn't enough of it!" Roger had blurted out. "I'm being told what to do practically the whole time!"

"In the Ancient World," the psychiatrist responded, trying to remain patient with him, "people thought they were 'free,' but actually, all their choices were based on prior events. They often spent the whole day miserable, because of other thoughts running around in their heads. Such as, "I'm too good to do this kind of work!" or "I hope to meet the woman of my dreams," when it was never going to happen. Because we know every single thing about your genetic and mental makeup and capacity, every day has been fitted precisely for your best health, productivity and happiness – and for the benefit of the system, of course. You'll get used to it."

"No, I won't!"

LauraLee, who sat at a distance, gasped. The holograms themselves seemed to shiver (ever so slightly) at the blasphemy. "You were bred, nurtured, and loved, thanks to the system," she murmured. "Ungrateful son!"

"Sorry, Roger," the psychiatrist said, after folding his hands together to keep calm. "You really have no choice. Please stop resisting, or you can end up with your Free-Think time deleted for a year or so. You wouldn't want that, would you?"

"You're acting like a – a teenager!" LauraLee put in. "Please! Don't embarrass me, or your poor, dead father, with any more such statements!"

Yesterday's interview vanished with a touch of the psychiatrist's little finger.

"So, let's look at the schedule again, Roger," the psychiatrist said softly, gently, soothingly. "Notice all the activities in there that we know you like: archery, boxing, football, gym workouts, and all the rock music you could ever want to listen to, which you freely select as you please, even when you aren't in Free-Think Mode. The work is so pleasant, too – it's lab work. Perfectly suited to your temperament and IQ. Advanced stuff, because you're brilliant."

As Roger reviewed the day, laid out from start to finish, even including what food he'd be eating and when he got toilet breaks, something deep inside kept whispering, *This is wrong. What if I don't want to have ice cream today? What if it turns out that I don't like my job?*

"You're finally ready to fit in," LauraLee told him. "Do your part, go to work, live a normal life…. You'll follow a personal schedule for the first time today, to get used to it. Tomorrow, you'll start your new job, my son." LauraLee stroked Roger's red-blonde hair lovingly. "Oh! How I love your hair! I chose the texture and color all by myself!"

"You did?"

"The day will come when you'll choose what your own son and daughter will look like," she answered. "Just as my mother and father chose how I would look. We have kept our personal preferences and traditions alive, all these centuries. It's because we have this kind of freedom that we have prospered in this harsh world."

"Yes … we're warm and safe here," the psychiatrist agreed.

"Warm – and safe …" Roger shook his head. "But once I wasn't warm, or safe… I think I remember some very huge, cold door. Behind it was God – but He was some kind of monster. He was so cruel, and cold, that had it not been for my mother, He would have killed me…. He was cutting off parts of – *parts of my body!*"

"That was just a nightmare!" the psychiatrist said quickly. "We'll fix it!"

He saw a flicker of fear and concern in his mother's face. "It was just a nightmare!" she insisted. "You've always been warm and safe!"

"I know I was rescued from a hideous, cold God!" he answered.

"It's OK to *know* that, Roger. But we don't want you to *remember* it," she replied. "It's just too… horrible."

A flush of color came into his face. "Yes!" he agreed, embracing LauraLee.

"You saved me… you're my hero."

She blushed. "I'd do it again, if I had to. But now, I'm supposed to tell you about your new Job. I've been chosen to give you the implant, so you'll not be afraid. It's important."

"I have to go," the Psychiatrist announced. "Madame, just touch the button, if I'm needed. " He indicated a tiny, transparent red object that floated to the left of his shoulder. It was swimming amidst other buttons of various colors, all around her head.

"This won't hurt," LauraLee told him, drawing a small wire out of what seemed to be thin air. "And also, you'll get your own panel, just like mine. It links you to all sorts of games, virtualities, maps and programs that you can access. You can select many fake memories, and other fun stuff, at a fee."

"Fake memories?"

"Of course. You can choose, in the future, to wipe out anything unpleasant that happens, and replace it with something pleasant that didn't really happen. It's how we manage to live for a thousand years or more, without getting bored or upset. Even now, in this world, some things aren't perfect…." she hesitated. "Unless we make it so, so we can bear it. We all have at least one of these…" she waved the tiny wire up and down. "It will be your best friend. With luck, you'll get two or three of them someday. Maybe four, like I have."

Roger shook his head. "I don't want any damned implants! And I don't want fake memories!"

She felt tears flooding into her eyes. "Now, see what you've done? I'm crying!" she told him. "I'm supposed to be happy! But now, I'll need to have some therapy. You're forcing me to erase this entire memory!"

Roger frowned, then reached out and dried a tear from her cheek. "Don't," he said. "Don't be unhappy. Don't erase it, please! I'm sorry."

"Will you just *please* take the implant?"

"Do I have a choice?"

"Not really."

"Does it hurt?"

"Not in the slightest."

He let her place the small wire against his temple. It slithered to life when it touched his skin and drilled itself under his scalp. There was a burning sensation, then an itch… and suddenly, Roger Understood His Role in Life. He knew precisely what he'd be doing tomorrow. Everything on the Schedule now made sense. And it was good.

"In half an hour, its Lights Out," LauraLee reminded him. "But we're the lucky ones! We get time to Free-Think, all by ourselves, three times a day. It's because we're Scientists and Professionals. Only Leaders get more time to think than we do."

"But what if I want to Free-Think longer? Stay up longer than Lights Out?" he asked. His question shocked her. He wasn't supposed to be able to ask such a question. Not with all the Nice Feelings he should have been enjoying with the implant.

"Roger," she replied, "Your question makes no sense. There simply isn't any need to Free-Think longer than that. It's ecologically unsustainable to keep lights on after Lights Out. All the problems we ever had in the System have already been solved. It's all been set up to make sure we're happy. You'll discover that your job will be so fulfilling that you'll *stay* happy, hour after hour. Eventually you'll meet the Mate selected just for you, and then you'll get an extra hour to Free-Think with *her*. Every day. You'll bond with her."

"So, everything is all laid out for me?"

"Of course. And it's always perfect for you. Precisely fitted for you."

But Roger, she saw, still wasn't convinced.

"If everything has been all laid out so well for you," he objected, "and for everyone else, and it's so perfect, why did something happen that was so bad that you had to rescue me? And why was it so important, that we've been sent all over the world, getting interviewed about it?"

"Just go to sleep," she told him. "Get your rest. Tomorrow is your first day of work!"

She kissed him, backed away, closed the door. Only now could she allow her anxiety to fully flow through her. LauraLee had just enough minutes left in her Free-Think mode to contact the psychiatrist again. She quickly touched the P dial. There was a crackle of blue flame, the circuit needed fixing; she'd have to report it. Then the psychiatrist answered.

"LauraLee!" he exclaimed, with a rumbling voice, "What's the matter now?"

"He resisted the implant! And then, even after I inserted it, he asked me why, if things were always so good, did he have to be rescued?"

"No, he couldn't have!"

"He's very intelligent. You know, he could have been a Leader, one more IQ point."

"I remember the discussion as to his status," the psychiatrist told her. "Borderline. Maybe he's a Leader, after all. Maybe we'll have to move him up. The fact that he resisted the implant is quite important. You should have told me immediately."

"I *did* tell you immediately!" she protested.

"I have to check him; then, report his condition. Wait two minutes, where you are."

Two long minutes passed. As more minutes passed, LauraLee was beginning to fear that her Free-Think time would expire before the psychiatrist got back to her. Then his round, smiling face appeared.

"It seems he passed a little test the Leadership devised," he told her. "If he hadn't protested as he did, he would have flunked. You should know, Madame," the psychiatrist told her, "that he has Free Will. When he resisted the implant, which almost never happens, you shouldn't have pushed him to accept it. Of course, you must remove the implant. He's to be elevated tomorrow."

LauraLee shrieked with joy. "Really! You mean it?" That meant her own status would improve. "I'm – I'm so *proud* of him!"

"Get it out at once. I'll arrange for you to capture another fifteen minutes of Free Think, so you can interact with him again tonight." The psychiatrist sighed. "This uses up my time, too. Now, you are to remove the implant with the code I'm transferring into your little finger... hold still."

"Why didn't anybody tell me he could become a Leader?" she complained, as her little finger began to tingle. "How could they have let me make such a mistake?"

"They didn't want you to feel unhappiness if he failed," the psychiatrist explained. "A chance like this is rare. Happens maybe once a century.... Because of what he went through, he got smarter than predicted. He'll get the Alpha Male implant." The psychiatrist shook his head. "Never thought I'd live to see such a thing! As for the memories he's been given, of his former job, since he never fulfilled a single command on the schedule, chances are, he won't remember enough to cause any problems for himself."

"I only did what I was programmed to do," LauraLee said, defensively.

"You're forgiven. Go to him and get the implant out. Tomorrow, you'll get to watch him transition to Leader. Congratulations."

"Do we have room for another Leader?" she asked.

"Oh – didn't I tell you? The Third Omega Male committed suicide. It happened today."

She had been too busy dealing with Roger to check on the news.

* * *

He woke to find that it was still Sleep Time. It was Out of Schedule, and he felt dizzy, disoriented. He knew he wasn't supposed to go to the labs and work with Color Vision Enhancement for six more hours. As he yawned, Roger could vaguely remember that he was supposed to start work on the "fly-eye" problem.

Engineering the human eye to see colors beyond the infrared and ultraviolet had its drawbacks: recently, it had been decided that compound eyes were the answer, making such enhanced vision more accurate, but most people were resisting the improved eyes. "Fly-heads' – those who had chosen to try out the new eye style – were unpopular. There had even been a rumor that fly-heads should never be allowed to breed. They were too reckless. That was proven because they'd volunteered for the new, improved eyes without caring what they looked like.

As Roger mused over the threads of the eye problem he had been prepped to deal with, how to avoid compound eyes and get the improved range of vision anyway, his mother entered the room, moved quickly to his side, and somehow yanked out the implant. It stung as it was removed and created a throbbing headache that pounded inside his skull.

"OW! What the hell?"

"They made a mistake!" she explained. "And where you picked up that language, I do not know. You're a Scientist. It's not the way you should talk!"

He looked sideways and blinked twice, turning on the overhead lights. "Why did you do that, Mother? My head – I've got a splitting headache!"

"It's because you're so smart!" she told him. "Roger, you're so smart, after what you've been through, that you're going to become…" Laura-Lee paused, lowering her eyes reverently. "You're going to become one of Them. A Leader. Alpha rank. It's the lowest level of the highest level, but you're in!"

"I'm going to become a *what?*" His mother's garments had begun flashing blues, violets and magentas instead of the usual yellows, reds and greens. It was the signal that she was emotionally roused. What she had done was important, she told him. He would be moving to a new, bigger room, with a grand view. It was likely that he would never see his Teddy Bear, his toy cars, or his Elvis poster again.

"You need to understand that you're going to be fitted for Free-Think for more than five hours a day!" His mother kissed him with sloppy joy. "You have honored our genes. We need to bring up your Father, so he can hear the news!"

She made a gesture toward one of the floating objects that always surrounded her, as she commanded her son to stand tall and straight. "Remember, he can see you, even though he is Dead, and cannot talk!"

A faint hologram flickered, then steadied. Within a blue haze, a tall, slender male with muscular arms and legs stood before them. He looked as young as Roger. LauraLee had previously explained to Roger that the hologram of his father's body, unlike those of the living, could not be touched, but select parts of his brain were still alive – kept so, in order to register every possible sense of joy and pride that could be transmitted into the man's brain and heart as his last conscious memories.

All deaths were manipulated to be happy ones, but it was especially good when a genuine triumph for a family could be brought to a Dead member. Since there was only one such opportunity possible, Laura-Lee had held off this final goodbye for years, full of hope that Phillip's last thoughts of happiness might include Roger. Now, though Phillip was about to lose the last of his brainwaves and memories forever, he could hear – he could comprehend – that his son had not only survived but, *magnificent news indeed!* He would become a Leader! The pale lips of the Hologram seemed to smile at the news. It was rare to see any movement in such a Hologram, but Roger's father was no ordinary man.

"I'm overjoyed!" LauraLee cried out to the silent hologram, "I'm so glad I didn't bring you up, my Beloved, to hear Roger's voice when he was first restored to us. For sure, you will now die with the best of memories – happy, and proud! All your sacrifices, Phillip, were worth it. Your sacrifices gave me the courage to rescue him. We have saved our son! Your death was not in vain!"

Roger watched as the thin lips of his dead father made a kind of grimace of pleasure and pride. "You were correct about his potential, Phillip," LauraLee said. "He has not only returned to us safe and strong, but he has exceeded every prediction." She turned to the tall young man standing at her side. "Tell him something, Roger, before he leaves us."

"Father, thank you for trying to save my sister," he told the hologram. "Thank you for being here. I will treasure this memory and never erase it."

Roger stood ramrod straight as his Father gazed steadily at him. Then the face's eyes slowly closed, and the hologram vanished.

"He waited for this," LauraLee said softly. "He somehow kept contact with us until you returned to us. Years longer than they said was possible. Now, he is fulfilled. He can truly rest in peace."

Roger saw tears in the corners of his mother's eyes as she poked at the floating panel before her. He knew she was turning off his Father's hologram and that he'd never see it again. As for the floating panel, he couldn't see much of his mother's, but now he had one, too. It had taken Roger some time to figure out why everyone he'd been introduced to kept making flicking motions here and there as they spoke. They were turning things off and turning things on, and it was all done in their heads, with some kind of residual motion going on with their hands so that those around them understood that they were busy. Only families or Mates could see each other's panels. But wait! The thought occurred to him that he wasn't going to be a Scientist now. Not only that, but his mother was saying that a new Mate would be chosen for him. She would be a Leader, or in the family of a leader… Before he had a chance to think more about it, his brain closed down. Free-Think time was over.

He had no memory of what he did or where he was or how long he was shut down, but it seemed that only a mere instant had passed, and he was awake again.

That's the way it worked. Vaguely, he remembered some kind of hand placing a new implant in his skull. He didn't like this one at all: it hurt. Anyway, he was awake again. His room, his mother, his Teddy Bear – all had vanished. Even his clothing was different. He was wearing a kind of military-style armor, and was seated in a chrome chair, at a huge round table that had its enormous center cut out. Suddenly, he could see the faces of everyone there – he knew they were Leaders, and he understood that he, too was a Leader. What fascinated him were the figures and scenes that he was viewing in the center of the huge table.

"You're getting a full review," the Beta Male to his left explained. The Beta Male had to lean over the Alpha Female, who sat to Roger's left, in order to speak to him. "You're going to see some of your erased memories. Everyone here has gone through this, so don't think anything you'll see is unusual. The only thing that made your case different is that your Mother was successful in rescuing you. Usually a woman hasn't the strength to do that. It's the Father who makes the attempt. In your case, there was also an older sibling... a sister. Sorry, most of us never had a sibling."

"My mother told me," Roger responded. "I thought every family had a boy and a girl. At least, that's what they put in my head."

"Every family can dare to have both a boy and a girl," the Beta Male told him. "But few of them do. They spend twice as much time with their children, when they do, in Free-Think. In your case, they became very attached to the two of you and loved both of you. So, when it was the right time, your Father tried to rescue your sister. But they both..." Richard, the Beta Male, hesitated. "They... both succumbed."

Roger felt a surge of grief and loss. "I want to see her, like I saw my father!" He demanded this, rising from his seat. An electric shock surged through his body as a command seared into his brain: *You will not stand in the presence of any member of greater Seniority!* He collapsed back into his chair.

"I would have appreciated it if you'd given me that information the usual way," Roger complained, rubbing his numbed hands. "You know – just implanted how I was supposed to act, inside my head."

"We can't do that," the Beta Male said. "In this chamber, it's essential that your brain stays intact."

Roger thought that over. "Intact?" he asked. "What do you mean by that?"

"I'm sorry to tell you that most of the things your mother – and most Scientists and Professionals – say and do are already pre-programmed. They don't know that. They think that everything they say and do during Free-Think time is spontaneous and free from control."

"Well, isn't it?"

"Some of it is," the Beta Male replied. "For example, your Mother does love you. And her act of rescuing you was spontaneous and generous. Courageous, even. We don't see much of that. She certainly was thinking for herself through the entire rescue operation. She's a Level Two – capable of it – whereas Level Three, and the others, they wouldn't know how to begin."

The Beta Male smiled. He had thick brown hair that reminded Roger of his Teddy Bear. He also had brown, beady eyes, like the glass eyes of his Teddy, but he decided to keep his mouth shut about it. Insulting a Leader might not be a good idea.

"As for your sister," the Beta Male told him, "she couldn't be kept long enough for you to say goodbye. We're sorry. Now, please watch the panorama. Since we're busy with other matters. But you need the orientation. You will be assisted and guided as you watch this saga. By the way, your guide is Angelica. She's sitting between you and me. She's our Alpha Female Leader. She has also agreed to be your Mate, so she will be certain to guide you carefully and gently."

The Alpha Female reached over and took Roger's hand. He steeled himself not to pull it away, afraid of getting another electric shock. She was a dark blonde: beautiful, sexy-looking, young. *Guess I can live with this*, he thought to himself.

"Hello, Roger," she said, blinking her green eyes. As she did so, it seemed that she and he were sitting all alone in the chamber before the gleaming round table. The fifty-four other Leaders, male, female, and hermaphrodites, all garbed in shiny, metallic-looking armor, had faded from view.

"Look carefully at the screen, Roger," Angelica said, squeezing his hand. "But don't get upset. I'm right here, to explain it for you. Just as it was explained to me."

The scene was outdoors, and primitive. It was winter, with snowstorms howling by day and wolves howling by night. He saw perhaps thirty small wooden cabins, clustered together, with high stacks of firewood in front of each cabin door.

"We supply them with firewood, axes, disinfectants, and enough calories to survive winter," Angelica commented. "They were given a little basic information about edible plants and animals, how to hunt, and how to make their own clothing."

"Is this some kind of colony?" he asked.

"You came from there," Angelica replied. "You were taken there when you were twelve-and-a-half. It is very democratic. Everyone has the same information. The same resources. Then, they're on their own."

She continued to advise as he watched some figures appear among the distant trees. "There are only six hours of daylight during the winter," she whispered. "But summer isn't much better. There's barely enough time to hunt necessary game animals, gather berries and roots, prepare and cure skins, and chop up the firewood, before winter sets in again."

Roger shivered. Some part of his body remembered the cold.

"So… I really was there?"

"Yes. I'm sorry."

"What about you?" he asked her. "Did this happen to you, too?"

"Of course," she said. "My father rescued me. Just as you were rescued by your mother. But for me, that was fifty-one years ago."

"How old are you?"

"Sixty-nine," she answered. "I'm in my prime for child-bearing, if I wanted to get it implanted in me." Of course, her eggs, she told him, were housed in a Fertility Lab, where the best of them had been selected and preserved. "They're analyzing your sperm right now," she revealed. "The best sperm, the best eggs, we're the hope of the future, people like you and me."

"But I'm only twenty," he said. He didn't dare say she was too old for him: it was bad enough that she frowned when he told her his age.

"You have no idea the sacrifice I'm making!" she said, with a huff. "I could have rejected the Council's choice. But everyone else is decades older than I am. And you have muscles. I like that. It's a plus I hadn't expected. Now… watch this!"

He saw them come marching through the snow, holding pieces of wood that were ablaze. *Those are torches*, something in his head told him. There were probably a hundred of them, marching in unison… then, he saw the big wolf.

"That's Sheba!" he said. "I want her!"

He said it so loudly that the heads of some of the Leaders appeared before him, frowning through the brilliance of the screen.

"Shhhh!" Angelica warned him. "Don't upset them!"

"That's my wolf!" he said insistently. "I want my wolf!"

"You can't get her, sorry. It was the very devil, getting just *you* out of there."

"I don't see any little kids," he told her. "I don't see any old people…"

"As I said, they're all teenagers. The ones with the uncontrollable urges. The high hormone levels. The impulsivity. The ones we cannot easily manage. All through history, previous to the Solution, we had to deal with their violence, stubbornness, and crimes. We do not have wars anymore, so we couldn't discipline them through the military, nor kill them off in that manner. It was a huge problem that caused great unhappiness in our very happy world."

The Beta Male tapped Roger on his shoulder. "All she says is true. But they're not there merely because they're hard to control." The Beta Male laughed. "Don't you get it? You're supposed to be smart enough to understand."

"Leave him alone, Richard," Angelica said. "When he was rescued, he was at first placed in the wrong level. Implanted as a Scientist, instead of as a Leader. "

"Apologies, Roger," Richard said. "I forgot. No wonder we were prompted to talk to you using this strange, informal dialect. You're asking questions, but that's understandable, if you had a prior implant that had to be swiped out."

"And remember," Angelica put in, "he was an Ultimate Rescue, which means he had a Full Memory Swipe, as well."

"No wonder you're confused!" Richard said. "That's awesome. So, your memory was swiped clean twice?"

"Well, mostly."

"I should have been nicer," Richard said, leaning closer. "Well, let me tell you how it goes...." Richard looked sharply at Angelica, who nodded her head. "You see, when all teenagers from all levels are removed from the breeding colony at age twelve and a half, they are implanted with birth control devices, then released into this wilderness area without any memories of their past."

"But, they can't survive out there, at that age, all alone!"

"Oh, yes they can," Angelica said. "Anthropoids with half the brain matter were making fire and hand axes. Some of these will murder, some of these will steal. But the most intelligent tend to survive. It's Natural Selection at work. Just as it was thousands of years before we formed civilizations..."

"Long ago," Richard went on, passing a dark hand over his highly-decorated helmet, "so long ago I can't remember when it started; we realized that we had made everything so comfortable and predictable that our species was becoming weaker, more stupid, and less able to cope with even ordinary life stresses. In each generation, there were more people who cared only about themselves, wanting to be more comfortable, wanting to work fewer and fewer hours, wanting others to wait on them hand and foot. 'Couch potato' is a term from long ago, but it suited well. Robots were doing everything. People were doing nothing."

"My turn," Angelica said. "They selected me to tell him this part, because I'm kinder than you are."

"Just keep talking."

Roger told them. "So, do I really like sports? Or is that just forced onto everybody now?"

"No," Richard said. "That was a real preference. Sports were inserted because you happen to love sports and physical exercise. You would have been depressed if we didn't keep your body active. Most of us get passive sport muscle stimulating exercises. We exercise while we're sleeping."

"It works," Angelica said, flexing her arms. "But your muscles are bigger."

"Please allow me to continue," Richard protested. "I have a lot to say before Omega Leader Three talks to him."

"Our three Omega Leaders are Number One on the planet," Angelica interjected.

"To continue, every generation on implants became less interested in anything but self. If anything was bad in the system, nobody cared, so long as it didn't affect them. Nobody was wiping their own asses anymore, unless they were programmed to do it. They wouldn't do a thing unless told to do it."

"That's the way it still is," Roger snapped. "Schedules – even when to go to the toilet!"

"You remember that?" Angelica said, clearly impressed. "It seems they didn't clear everything out. You do realize we're talking this funny way to you, don't you, because this is the way your brain likes to talk, right now?"

"Don't worry," Richard put in, "You're going to get the final language update soon. We couldn't change everything at once, that quickly. You might have put up too much resistance, so we let you keep some of your teenage talk style. We usually speak with more formality and with much more dignity, but I'm rather enjoying this bantering talk style, so – on with my story."

"At first, we thought we could breed the problems out. You know, choose the more aggressive little kids, and so on. That was a gross mistake. We had a season of teenage riots. All teenagers who participated were banished to the wilderness, with just the bare essentials. You see, we no longer had prisons. And it was agreed that they shouldn't be punished as adults. Even though some of them had been murderers."

"That's how it began," Angelica put in. "Only two teens survived the first exodus. "But they were smart. Strong. Adaptable."

"We saw how strong they had become," Richard added. We had found our answer. We could stop the decline of the human race!" He hurried on. "What our geneticists couldn't do, what our psychiatrists couldn't do, the wilderness did. Survival in the wilderness put the Darwinian selection process back into operation, and our species began to get stronger again. The problem was, some of them were murderous thugs. We could not allow any of that kind into our peaceful world. As a teen turned twenty, they could return to our world, though there never was more than a handful a year who survived that long. Only parents who still cared enough to rescue their children, after watching their life histories on-screen, could petition to get their child out. This also helped our species, because only good parents cared. Only good parents had made bonds with their children before they were exiled. If we could find a way to get such a child out, without causing a riot, we did it."

"You see, " Angelica explained, "getting them out wasn't easy. After a few rescues, the ones left behind realized what was going on. They found out where the Rescue Port was located."

"They would post sentries there, at the Rescue Port," Richard said. "Then, they'd make prisoners of the ones turning twenty. When the Port was opened to deliver food and supplies, we could keep order, as they fought each other for the food, which we threw out at a distance from the Port, but if we were trying to rescue a prisoner, they could do battle with us, using the prisoner as a shield. It was a terrible problem."

"It was a sort of religion that they had developed," Angelica told him. "Centuries ago, a few of them made it inside, never to be seen again. They became Untouchables, but they didn't live past twenty-one. All our babies are born with mitochondria with a short shelf life, to keep the teenage numbers down."

"But what about me?" Roger asked. "I have those mitochondria, too, don't I?"

"Originally, you did," Angelica said soothingly, "But because your parents loved you, they had set aside the fees needed to replace them. Your mitochondria were replaced a few hours after your mother rescued you. They should last several thousand years. Then you can renew, if you want to keep on living."

"So, did I become a prisoner, too?"

Richard took his turn to explain. "The smartest of the oldest ones wouldn't tell their ages, but of course, eventually, they'd be tied up. Then the tortures would start."

"You didn't have to mention that part," Angelica objected, shuddering.

"Yes, I did," Richard retorted. "He needs to know. They wanted the Rescue Port to open, as it did whenever a parent dared to try to rescue a kid. If nobody came, these kids would be slowly murdered on an altar, right in front of the Rescue Port. The parents of these kids could see it, on their screens. The beatings. The cuttings. It drove them half mad."

"We could see what they were doing," Angelica said softly. "By various means, to stop the torture, we found ways to confuse them, to disperse them. Such as throwing candy or something else, rare and desired, as far from the Port as possible. That would give a parent the chance to try a rescue. Unfortunately, they'd usually take their prisoner with them. The parent, armored just as we are here – that gives them honor – had the right to defend themselves, had the right to try to rescue their child."

"The battles are shown on our screens all over the world," Richard said. "It has been great entertainment for Third Level citizens."

"The teenagers would do their religious dances, because they thought we were Gods. They'd demand to be let through the Rescue Port, or they'd kill their prisoner. The most courageous of the parents would make several attempts to rescue their child. Such as, when the guards fell asleep."

Roger had been rendered speechless with pure horror. Nothing in his preserved memories could have prepared him for such words.

"They're such savages!" Richard said. "Many a parent and child perished, because of them."

"That's why you have no original toes," Angelica added. "They cut them off, one by one... over a period of days... we had to grow new ones for you."

Roger instinctively looked down at his feet. "So," he muttered, "my father died at the hands of these kids? Trying to save my sister?"

"Yes. He was a hero."

"Was – was I involved in his death?"

"No. You were too young at the time."

"And you call those kids savages?" Roger growled. "You made them that way! You're just as bad as they are! So you have spectacles on screens! Damn you!"

"It pays for their upkeep in the wilderness," Richard said defensively.

"And why didn't you help my father? Why do parents have to go in there alone? And why did you risk losing my mother and me?" Roger could feel some kind of primitive, raw anger pulsing through his body. As his face reddened with emotion, Angelica drew away from him slightly, and Richard stiffened to his full height.

"You don't understand…" Richard protested. "*Nobody wanted to go with your father.* They were too afraid. And your mother wasn't allowed to join him. *And nobody wanted to go with your mother.* Nobody was brave enough. That's the damned truth. Please, just *look at* the screen again! *Please!*"

Roger looked again at the darkening scene: there were perhaps two hundred teenagers there now, dressed in furs, massing together. He realized they were singing.

"*We just wanna KILL YOU! We just wanna KILL you!*"

They were shaking their fists at what had to be the "hidden" cameras. In their midst was their latest prisoner, standing there shivering, naked in the freezing cold.

"They're cursing the God of the Rescue Gate," Richard told him. "Next, they'll be offering up this prisoner as a human sacrifice. On an altar, by the Gate, they'll tie him up. They'll wait a few days. They'll hope the Rescue Port will open. If it doesn't, they will start the tortures. When the prisoner dies, they'll cook and eat the body."

Roger grit his teeth and closed his eyes, seething with anger and despair.

"You were purchased at a great price," Angelica said gently.

"It's *you* who are sending the teenagers out there!" Roger snarled. "You turned them into animals. It's not their fault!"

"Do you have a better idea?" Angelica asked him.

"Before you condemn all of us, you'd better understand just who we are!" Richard went on. He held out his left hand – all the fingers were gone, and his arm was withered with scars. "I didn't let them fix it. I kept this deformity, to remind me of who I am!"

"We are the rescued. The most intelligent of the survivors," Angelica said. "We were observed as acting like human beings, I was told, even while trying to survive among those savages. We exhibited love. Compassion. You were outstanding, yourself. Because of you, those savages now use wolves as domesticated animals to pull their sleds, instead of human slaves. You helped others survive. So did we. So, we were marked as worthy to be rescued. Each of us had courageous parents, or we couldn't have made it out alive. And it is we who supply superior eggs, receptors, and semen. We're taller. Stronger. Smarter. And we're passing on our compassion, our courage, to our once-doomed species."

"There's more to humanity than that!" Roger shot back. "Maybe things out there are just plain evil, but those kids weren't given any real knowledge. They didn't even have memories of their parents. They were orphans, terrified orphans!"

Richard and Angelica cast down their eyes. The screen went blank, but Roger never noticed. He was seething with indignation and disgust.

"You let them descend to cannibalism!"

Roger stood, unsure of what to do, but he could not remain seated. As he stood, he endured another electric shock, but he stubbornly remained standing, stoically absorbing the pain. In awe, the entire Round Table went utterly silent, and then Roger's voice rang through the Hall. "There has to be another way! Do you hear me?"

The Third Omega Leader slowly arose from his seat of gilded power. Gliding, rather than walking, for he was very old, the Omega soon positioned himself before Roger and gazed, with his compound insect eyes, into the young man's florid face.

"We agree, Alpha Male. That's why we decided to make you a member of this Body. We can't let this go on. You need to realize," he continued, "that in our haste for peace, calm, and happiness, we forgot how to say no. And that's why you're with us, Roger." The ancient one took a deep breath of natural air (most let their lung pumps do the job for them, but the Third Omega Leader was a very active human being, who even had compound eyes, the new fad.). He shifted his weight on his own power, somewhat feebly, as he stood amidst his shining, black robes. He wasn't used to standing so long.

"Let me tell you one more thing, my child…" The Third Omega Leader said the words loudly and clearly. "We had a suicide yesterday. An important one. It made room for you. Our prior Omega could not bend enough to allow somebody like you to be a member of this High Council. For, hard as it is to hear you speak out of turn, difficult as it is to bear, to hear your expressions of anger, to see you stand up without permission… we need your rebellious spirit, which is also mixed with kindness."

There was a murmur of surprise from some of the other Leaders. The Third Omega Leader waited until every whisper ceased, then said, "Your refusals, your ability to resist what you think is wrong. We need it back. You have new ideas, and some of those ideas might end up helping us. Or maybe, those poor devils out there." The Third Omega Leader was even using Roger's informal mode of speaking, even though it was almost scandalous.

"Now, get ready for the truth."

"The truth?" Roger's head was swimming, but the Omega Leaders had powers that reached telepathically deep into his brain, calming him.

"The truth is that you're not twenty years old, Roger," the Omega Leader told him. "Fact is, you're not quite eighteen. *You're still a teenager.*"

There were tears in the old man's compound eyes, so that they glittered like black diamonds. "We were wrong. We need teenagers, after all."

"But how can natural selection work, and preserve us as a species, if we don't do this anymore?" an Inferior Gamma leader spoke up.

"Wars are out of the question. We can't abide their perfidious, rebellious ways, but when they're controlled properly, our species starts dying out –"

"Roger is an innovator. He domesticated the wolf!" a Female Gamma Leader announced.

Roger felt overwhelmed. From every direction, the Leaders were looking at him anxiously. Just daring to admit Roger into their midst had already prompted a suicide. Roger's brain, which had operated in Free-Think for half of his life, was considering various options at a frightening pace. Instinctively, Roger knew that the Council could throw him back into Level Two again, or worse … a great deal depended on what he would say in the next few minutes.

"Be at peace!" he told them. "I do have an answer for you! Be seated, and listen."

What they heard next sealed the fate of the human race.

Endnotes

1. Finnish study blames genes with between five and 10 per cent of severe violent crime." Steve Connor, Oct. 28, 2014.… "A conservative estimate implies that five to 10 per cent of all severe violent crime in Finland is attributable to specific MAOA and CDH13 genotypes," the study concludes. Professor Jan Tiihonen of the Karolinska Institute in Stockholm, who led the study, published in the journal Molecular Psychiatry, said that there is mounting scientific evidence pointing to the influence of genes on violent criminality. Malcolm von Schantz, a molecular neuroscientist at Surrey University, said that the findings do not suggest that a genetic explanation will replace the concept of free will and criminal responsibility for a person's behaviour. "But I think findings such as these may make it possible, in future, to screen people with vulnerable backgrounds and identify those who are at greater risk of becoming offenders, so that they can get appropriate help before they commit any serious violent crimes," Dr von Schantz said http://www.independent.co.uk/news/science/two-genes-found-linked-to-tendency-for-violent-crime-9824061.html Retrieved April 30, 2016.

SAVE THE TIGER

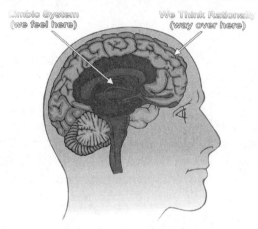

Limbic System
(we feel here)

We Think Rationally
(way over here)

The limbic system ... is not only responsible for our emotional lives but also our higher mental functions, such as learning and formation of memories."[1] The limbic system is ... located on top of the brainstem and buried under the cortex ... [it governs] emotions and motivations, particularly ... fear, anger, and emotions related to sexual behavior. The limbic system is also involved in feelings of pleasure that are related to our survival, such as those experienced from eating and sex.[2]

"By 2085, General Limbic Systems, UC (a Uniplanet Corporation) was granted access to the limbic systems of all competent human beings on the planet. Thus, a stable One World Government finally became possible. Five years later, an unbreakable World Peace was established, insuring full work, full prosperity and full equality for all."

– Quote from the 2100 edition of the *Universal High School History Limbic Text Series* (editions in the seven approved languages of: English, Hindi, Russian, Spanish, Chinese, Subliminal Index, and Cyber).

"Pay attention!" Jendra told her students. "Loads 4, 5 and 6, wait your turns!"

The Aerobus held 600, plus adults. The loaders for each section of the Aerobus took turns swinging down and picking up one platform of 100 students at a time. The students were already strapped into their seats. As each loader swung a platform into the triple-decker plane, the students screamed. They weren't really afraid: screaming and crowd shouts were how they expressed themselves when they were belted in together, whether it was for a field trip or for collective live instruction. Outside of these activities, students didn't talk to each other much because they lived in isolation pods.

"One-seven-seventy-six, we're Patriots, YOU'RE SICK!"

They were chanting their group's cheers, as they sat belted in, waiting for take-off.

"One-seven-seventy-six! Patriots Rule on Field Trips!"

Getting their attention wasn't easy. The attention span of an ordinary unplugged teenager was a matter of mere seconds –except for this group (they were different!). Thus, when Jendra picked up a megaphone, they went silent. "Now for the surprise!" She announced. "Our field trip will be to the Responsible Feral Human and Wildlife Breeding Project in Dublin!"

She was ready for groans of displeasure. It was only 4:00am, and the hour-long ride would only give them another hour of sleep. Atop that, a trip to a stadium to meet football celebrities had been promised for this year and had not yet come to pass.

As she gazed over the 600 in her care, Jendra thought back to 2061, when Jendra was a top linguist. She lost her position for objecting to the term "full equality," (and other such impossible terms)[3] infesting the first Universal High School history book.[4] Her argument that 'full equality' did not exist went nowhere. Jendra moved on: when she became a Senior Lecturer to human high school students, teaching classes of 600 at a time, she reached a pinnacle few linguists ever dreamed of achieving.

She was good: she had to be. Her students – as did they all – hated being unplugged. But the lectures and field trips were mandatory. Created to counter the bad effects that had accumulated after the peak of the E-Phone Implant Era, when unscheduled face-to-face meetings were banned, students these days had to go without all plug-ins and enhancements – once a week – to get in touch with their actual surroundings and bodies. No longer needing to talk, hear or see via their natural sense organs, those abilities had grown dormant. At the same time, the youngest among them, raised almost entirely by robots, also seemed to lose a zest for life. When child suicides became endemic, it was decided in some high place that students needed to exercise their primitive body parts, like it or not. The new regimen was only a decade old, but it was working: the kids were slowly learning to talk, hear and see without any enhancements: child suicides had plummeted.

Required to meet once weekly for a full day, unplugged, to experience socialization with each other, the students were not happy to be forced to listen with their physical ears and to see with their physical eyes. However, using their mouths for eating and yelling was a great success. This weekly requirement to communicate "at the primate level" always created short episodes of screaming, spitting, hitting and urinating when the students were first unplugged, but by the time they were loaded on the plane, they had better control of themselves.

Jendra enjoyed lecturing these kids. She rejoiced as the semesters rolled by and the regulated face-to-face meetings began to create friendships. They started to form little groups that let in some outsiders, whereas in the beginning, only pod-mates allowed each other access to their thoughts. Jendra especially liked taking them on field trips to view relics of the original world before the Cyborg Revolution.

Dallas High School #1776, as all the others, had a core of 4,200 students that was rotated, 600 students at a time, into the high school's only meeting room once a week. All other courses were delivered individually by General Limbic Systems, UC to the pod-cores. High schools everywhere had the same curriculum, so teachers could be freely exchanged to deliver one of the four specified "Genuine Interaction" course lectures and experiences required every month that General Limbic Systems could not handle well. These were: (1) Compassion & Loyalty (2) Unassisted Human Conversation (3) Contact Sports and (4) Freedom of Speech and/or Original Art and Music. Every third month, there was a field trip to a different part of the world.

These were genuine, hands-on experiences, unlike what was piped into their heads the other six days of the week. Within their first year, each of the seven divisions of 600 students had developed their own sports teams, division names, division mascots, and pledges to a flag of their own design. This particular group called themselves "The 1776 Patriots." Their Mascot was a Feral Human called George Washington.

Jendra was particularly proud of the high quality of the field trips she planned, which the kids sometimes enjoyed. In general, students saw the real world as an infinitely boring place, devoid of fun and pleasure. No wonder, since their limbic centers were unplugged while attending Genuine Interactions and Field Trips that could be experienced only within the short spectral ranges of their original nervous systems.

Thus, once a week, to the dread or anger of her students (including, of course, the Patriots in High School #1776) their limbic implants and SPOCKs were turned off for the Genuine Interaction sessions. Gone were the pulses of pleasure that made learning on other days such a happy experience as they sat in their home pods. Just as the rats, mice and monkeys before them, students implanted with limbic system devices delivering pleasure stimulation forgot about eating, drinking and sleeping to "live the rush" as the neurophysiologists called it. While anorexia was a growing issue, less food consumed meant that everyone now had enough to eat, except during the occasional natural disaster. Stick-thin bony was the norm, while drug-induced 12-hour sleep sessions kept maintenance fees historically low.

About the same year that Limbic Instruction for the kids began, every certified human teacher was wired with connections to cybernetic morality assistants, dubbed "SPOCKs" (Sentient Personal Orthodox Cyborg Kontrollers). They guaranteed full compliance with the State's mandated educational and moral standards. Not much later, all other human beings in positions of influence were also fitted with SPOCKS. After all, only criminals would have to worry about being punished for making illegal or immoral decisions or statements. Good citizens had nothing to worry about, while their radiant implant tattoos proved they were good citizens to all the other good citizens, and at what level they were valuable to society.

The last problems with Cyborg ethics were resolved in 2090 during the Clone Corruption Scandal. By 2100, human error had been eliminated: now only Cyber-error existed.

Recently, free-roving Media Drones (some called them Media Bots) made sure that all new, approved information was being accepted without resistance. Resistance to an approved packet of information was dangerous to world peace and harmony. A Resister was a Terrorist. If a SPOCK detected any resistance, or too-slow acceptance of information being sent, Media drones could be asked to escort stubborn clients (all humans were clients) to a psychologist to find out what was wrong with them.

As Jendra entered the Aerobus, she looked anxiously over the rows of faces tilted toward hers on her view-screen to see if any Media drones were present. She was particularly concerned about this batch of kids. Through some kind of glitch, the Patriots was a batch that had not been removed from their parents upon reaching the age of thirteen. Their parents had hidden them, apparently with the help of a pair of Cyborg Guards who had been specially programmed. The altered records were discovered when these kids turned sixteen: signals embedded in their birth records were automatically activated at that time and were matched with the numbers of children whose whereabouts were known.

In this case, 613 children had gone missing from the same Commune. Through diligence, Jendra had learned that most of these kids' parents were still in prison for treason because of it. The rescued kids had been put through six months of avoidance therapy and conditioning so they would no longer care about their families or remember any radical teachings. The number was 613 because some of the rebel parents had ignored the two-per-couple quota due to their religious beliefs. Eventually, thirteen children, proven to be beyond hope, were humanely euthanized, but

Jendra wondered if that was because their number was originally 13 more individuals than would fit into a plane flight section. The extra thirteen, she well knew, would have also created an instruction module problem.

By age 13, most children were willingly ceded to State facilities, since they stopped being cute and became expensive adolescent nuisances who were legally allowed to sue their parents if they felt mistreated. By age 16, all children became the property of the State. Upon becoming State property, permanent SPOCKS were assigned to each student according to their most financially lucrative talents, their emotional needs, and their propensity to commit violence.

Before Limbic Oversight [LIMBO] came into power, humans and robots used pain to threaten or to do harm, especially in war. Humans had also used neuron pain probes to control Cyborgs, handing them over to the tender mercies of Media drones that had access everywhere (a privilege of the free press). Media drones had the right to obtain the truth from all Cyborgs, who otherwise could hide their true thoughts. It was part of the Freedom of Speech laws.

The first improvements by General Limbic Systems to keep the sequestered teens happy and out of trouble included sessions of full sexual pleasure by electronic masturbation. The consequence was that the use of female Cyborgs by humans of all ages was declared obscene, freeing them from slavery, except for a few Stars owned by hyper-bred human male studs. From then on, Cyborgs could choose multiple male and female personalities. For additional safety, their body parts (including internal mouth structures) were changed so they could never again be used by humans for sex. It was a victory for Cyborg Rights activists, who used to march alongside battered Sex Cyborgs, demanding their freedom. The final victory was to allow Cyborgs access to quantum computers. That Act would be known as the First Cyborg Revolution, but Jendra and other human beings were as yet still unaware of the next massive event to come, which was about to change the world.[5] Conquering humanity did not come about through force. It came through the quantum computer.[6]

Jendra only pondered such things when she had to deal with The #1776 Patriots.

Sometimes she wondered why these teens could still be punished with pain probes, when the law had made such punishment illegal for Cyborgs. The Cyborg Revolution had released many miserable half-humans from slavery and oppression. The argument that they felt no pain was easily defeated in Court by displaying the methods used to torture Cyborgs that had been devised by clever humans, who had installed pain receptors into robots and 100% Cyborgs almost from the very beginning.[7]

The current prejudice against full humans was obvious: they were still being punished by pain probes, based on the fact that genes for violence once existed in 100% humans, even though such genes were now all but eradicated from the population. The drive to destroy the genes that produced violent human beings began with sterilization programs in 2045, in honor of the founding of the United Nations' 100th anniversary.

With only the older population interested in blood sports, as a result, curiosity about the natural world also declined among the genetically modified kids. They weren't thrilled by spectacles of wild animals eating each other, or gladiators mangling each other. They found virtual reality more real than literal reality: the smells, thrills, chills and sightseeing were not only more exciting and memorable, but also much cheaper than any actual trip. There was no comparison. Ironically, it was the lack of interest in the outside world's fading attraction that had given rebellious humans secret space to raise illegal children. Pockets of the rebels kept getting discovered in underground colonies.

To ensure that they spoke, most of Jendra's students, guided by only herself and six hack-safe Cyborg guards, were ordered to speak without permission on these off-days, unless they were under discipline for resisting something. Unfortunately, the #1776 Patriot group, composed of the children of rebels, were often under discipline and forbidden to speak without permission. Of course, all the kids were allowed to participate in chants and preapproved group shouts. These deprived sixteen-year-olds were years ahead of the others in speaking, seeing and hearing skills, but they had also missed most of the state-approved lessons. That being the case, Jendra secretly favored the Patriots and prepared the best field trips for them.

These mandatory field trips were especially terrifying to the Patriots. That's when they were granted a chance to see how they functioned "in the real world" again, without help from their implants. The Patriots had been strictly re-conditioned to view their prior thinking and reasoning as inferior and deserving of the many electroshocks they kept receiving when they mentally resisted any new instructions. Whenever they erred, they were shown how slip-shod their thinking was, how illogical they were, and that they possessed poor judgment and survival skills. They were told to love their SPOCKs. All Patriot kids had them. Their SPOCKs guided them in the proper ways. The safe ways. Most normal students longed for SPOCK guidance to avoid embarrassment and shame. They hungered for LIMBO to give them pleasure. Disturbingly, a few of the Patriots seemed to enjoy being unplugged. That meant they were not yet fully conditioned by their SPOCKS and LIMBO. Jendra hoped they would behave themselves and not exhibit too much pleasure, so she would not be required to report them.

Jendra was aware of her importance. She was guiding the Patriots into a better life, where they wouldn't be punished so often for errant thought patterns. After all, it wasn't their fault that their parents were rebels. Though this batch of 600 represented only 1/7th of the 4,200 students in her care, Jendra felt more concern for them, especially when one might begin crying when they saw something in the outside world that reminded them of their former lives. Though she was supposed to punish each trace of a past memory, Jendra avoided doing it, reasoning that other students were also often unhappy because of the outside world. If she was ever questioned, she could claim that she thought the child was just afraid to think about the past.

Now, as the aerobus closed, and the arms of the soft seats curled automatically around the arms of each passenger for safety, Jendra seated herself at the control panel and pressed a single button. The destination was read from her brain by the transport service and the aerobus soared up onto the Starway, a super-fast lane for guided rocket travel. Looking over the view-screens, Jendra was pleased to see that some of the students were daring to open their eyes, desiring to view the beauty of Planet Earth 3000 feet above the highest buildings in the City. All kids, even the Patriots, needed to see real things. Feel real things.

Since these teaching cycles required only seven Cyborgs and six human teachers at a time, using just one meeting hall, and one aerobus for batches of 600 at a time from the 4,200 pool of students, all teachers thus got one day off a week. Jendra had come fresh from her one-day break, which she had spent with her favorite Cyborg.

Lately, she had become obsessed with a new idea for a field trip – a day at a zoo. There were no zoos, as such, anymore – they had become animal breeding facilities – but the oldest such facility was still set up for visitors (though fewer came every year).

While the other students at Dallas High School #1776 understood what animals were, and knew their life histories, they had never seen animals in the flesh. And only The Patriots had ever seen Feral Humans – human beings allowed to live as they used to, back in the 1900's. A few Patriots had described seeing small pets: miniature dogs and cats. But that was all. When Jendra learned that the world's most important animal preserve also held an unusual breeding facility which exhibited both Ferals and Tigers, she put in a trip request.

She had argued that these children of rebels should be visually reminded of the horribly ugly and filthy way of life that would exist in the whole world if the rebels had their way. They could see for themselves what a world they had been rescued from. In preparation for the outing, to protect them from recidivism, every Patriot had been preconditioned to associate the Feral way of life with pain and suffering. Jendra hoped they hadn't overdone it. After all, the kids couldn't help it that their parents had been filthy, ignorant savages.

It was only an hour of super-speed airtime from Dallas, but everyone would have to hurry off-board as soon as they landed to have enough time to view both live exhibits and to also eat dinner before returning.

Jendra believed that her Patriot students especially needed this experience. All of them remembered seeing live animals. Every one of them liked tigers, too. But had she gone too far? Would this trip bring forth too many unwanted reactions? Jendra was concerned, but her superiors were not. They trusted the conditioning the Patriots had been given. None of them recalled so much as the names of their parents. Just as the others, they had become bored with the usual field trips to a factory or to a Cyborg History Center. Not that this was risk-free. The only trip to "Nature" they'd had before this was a visit to the last natural forest in the Northwest. It had been a disaster: the students had initially refused to leave the aerobus when they learned that insects were present there. They had been conditioned to destroy insects. In the end, the Patriots had thoroughly enjoyed the visit to the forest, even though they spent most of their time crushing everything that moved. Some had even stolen some pine cones for souvenirs, for which they had been suitably punished.

Jendra had come to their defense, arguing that the Patriots were simply responding to their natural hunter-gatherer instincts: some of her other students had done the same thing on previous trips, but had not been punished. On the grounds that they had been discriminated against, Jendra had been given permission to give the Patriots another field trip connected with nature. That's how the visit to Dublin's breeding facility had come about.

They would get a chance to walk around: this was always a necessary activity on field trips. Jendra knew that her students lived in collectives of 6 x 5 (30 sq ft) pods. The pods had two porthole windows, a bed, a desk, a stool, a wash basin, an exercise cycle, and a door. The walls were decorated as each kid wished, and they could play endless video games, often with friends, sometimes against themselves. Their disposable clothing was delivered to them daily, along with food supplies, through a slot. The pods were stacked twenty high, with elevators, soundproofing, walkways and good ventilation. The kids called it "The Hive." Students stayed in their pods until late in the afternoon, when sport training occurred, such as boxing, yoga, archery, football or golf. American football, basketball and European football competitions were ritually observed in magnificent stadiums once a week. Other evenings were spent shopping at a commissary, roaming the protected grounds, or with rare visits to parents, with a snack and a medical inspection before bedtime. If hormonal levels fluctuated, they were fixed. Before a pimple could bloom on the beautiful, perfected skin of a human student, it was doomed.

Once every three months, Jendra's students also practiced Physical Compassion by checking each other's bodies for undetected sores, bruises, cuts and damage which their monitor system hadn't picked up. Bedsores, especially, could erupt because of the long periods that these very thin children spent in bed. Jendra could still remember when no human body in LIMBO had a spot of trouble, but that was before the present long sleeps were introduced, which saved the State and parents huge costs. For some reason, the Patriots seemed to get more sore spots on their bodies than the other groups. But no one cared, since the Patriots never received parental visits. Perhaps that's why Jendra had special feelings for them. She couldn't help noticing that many of them had nightmares, or that they cried at unexpected times.

Jendra had all these thoughts whirling in her head as she sat beside her favorite Cyborg Guard, CuCy. CuCy was always brought along on Patriot field trips after she noticed that it had attempted to console one of the Patriots whose friend had killed herself.

"Don't cry," CuCy had ordered the kid. "Crying will change nothing."

"Why should you care?" The boy wanted to know. "You're just one of Them."

"Correct," CuCy had replied. "But I do care. I think I have a bad circuit somewhere."

Ever since that remark, Jendra had protected CuCy from full brain function scans. She made a project of trying to see if she could instill compassion and empathy into the 100% Cyborg. After all, not too long ago, they had once been programmed to respond to any human who asked for help.

That was before the Casino War Games. 100% Cyborgs, once built to never do harm to a human, had ended up enduring much harm themselves from those same humans. In an effort to stop the abuse, new laws for 100% Cyborgs included a maxim that they would longer respond to human distress calls. Too often, their great strength had been exploited to pit them against each other by unscrupulous casino warlords who themselves were callous humans. In a typical War Game, each side had a dozen humans to protect, and each side was ordered to rescue "the rest of the humans" from the other side. Bets were made, the battles raged, and eventually, one side would be victorious, unless all their hostages died. The losing side was forced to surrender their Cyborgs for meltdown, while the surviving human hostages (there were rarely more than a few) were awarded fantastic prizes.

These days, 100% Cyborgs were kept away from humans, except for those who worked as Guards for students, protecting them from sex rings, game traffickers and kidnapping (most often by parents whose children had become the property of the State against their will).

The newest care system and instructional set-up was economical and efficient. It kept the kids under control at all times. But there were those pesky side effects: almost all 100% human kids stopped talking using their physical mouths after their final conditioning sessions, which were imposed upon becoming the property of the State. Some suspicion that this was a desired outcome had drifted through the cracks of security sessions to reach Jendra's old ears,

Besides her field trips (and teaching courses on Compassion) it was Jendra's additional duty to encourage students to speak aloud without spitting, shouting or chanting, even though she realized the kids would probably shut down their use of physical speech after their final conditioning sessions at age sixteen. But until then, she would keep that ability alive as a basic survival skill. This is where her linguistics training came in handy.

Because the students' SPOCKs reacted to incorrect grammar as well as to incorrect thoughts, students were sometimes corrected before they spoke, which further reduced their impulse to speak. In the case of the Patriots, they had been so severely disciplined that most of them had already lost the ability to speak without spitting or shouting.

Jendra was also required to report anyone who might be acting strangely. All of this responsibility made Jendra feel useful and needed. Having chosen childlessness, Jendra's faint maternal instincts were satisfied by her surrogate role.

As the aerobus descended, Jendra woke her 600 charges, who had been tranquilized. "You will be seeing Feral Humans in the first part of our field trip," she warned them. "You have forgotten what human malfunctioning looks like, so I will explain. You will notice that they have skin problems, including crenelations called wrinkles. This is a consequence of aging – of not having access to the Cyborg improvements that you and all normal, civilized humans have."

She paused, as bursts of stimulants briefly fogged the air. The kids were so sleepy that this was the only way to make sure they heard her entire lecture.

"These people think they live on an isolated island. They think that no access to the outside world exists. Their genes have remained untouched. This means," she continued, "that while we carry modified genes, and are approaching the equivalent of Immortality, they still age, suffer and die. Is that fair, students?"

Unlike her other students, the Patriots didn't cheer and agree. Instead, they sat silent in their velveteen chairs, some of them with frowning faces.

"It isn't fair," she told them, "because they are suffering, and aging. So it was recently decided that the kindest course was to give them a few more implants. The ones we decide should be saved. Then they will live longer. And they won't go hurting, and falling and going deaf and blind. Isn't that nice of us?"

Again, they didn't reply. It was such a hard group to deal with.

"We placed a few hundred of the best Ferals into Reservations," she told the students. "Not one carries genes for violence! As for these–" Jendra waved a hand toward the plane's doorway, which was sliding open, "–we want them to be happy, in their last months. They have been allowed to gain weight. To follow their archaic ways. But soon these violent Ferals are scheduled to be humanely euthanized. The last violent genes among humans will soon be extinct, wiped off the face of the earth!"

She clapped her hands, but none of the Patriots clapped back. Surprised, Jendra recalled that some of the Patriots staring at her might also be scheduled for extermination because they, too, carried the genes for violence. That being a possibility, Jendra decided it was best to hurry on.

"No one wanted to fund the Feral Human Genome Sustainability Project any more because of those bad genes," she explained. "But with these violent Ferals gone, the Dublin tiger breeding facility can focus all its resources on saving the tigers. This is the last refuge on earth where these magnificent beasts still survive. While they also carry genes for violence, unlike humans, they had no choice to become otherwise."

As the last of the six platforms deplaned and the students stood and stretched on solid ground, Jendra reminded them again that they must first visit the Feral Human exhibit. In her role as the Compassionate teacher, Jendra told them she was there to answer any student's questions. To finish her short lecture, Jendra asked, as they all got in line, "Does anyone here think that these Feral Humans should be allowed to continue?"

The correct answer was No, but one very thin boy with many electro-discipline scars replied "Yes."

"But why should they continue?""

"Because I am interested in them."

"You haven't even seen them yet, Tony 3," Jendra objected. Patriots did have a tendency to be stubborn, and Tony 3 was at the top of the list. "I assume that after you have seen them, then you won't be interested anymore."

"What if I stay interested?" Tony 3 replied.

"Silence, Tony 3," Jendra warned. "To stay interested in something which has been pronounced scheduled for elimination is just your way of deciding to be uncooperative. If your SPOCK finds out, it might decide that you need an extra SPOCK installed."

Most adults had two SPOCKS.

"I already have two SPOCKS!" Tony 3 answered. "And I hate them!"

Jendra had no choice but to note that Tony 3 needed another disciplinary punishment session and a supplementary counseling session with a psychologist, unless she could get a retraction.

"Come forward!" Jendra commanded him. As Tony 3 approached, she touched his shoulder, which alerted the Cyborg Guards. "You'll have to stay in the aerobus unless you retract your statement that you hate SPOCKs," she told him. "I'm giving you a chance. You know what happens if you have to go to a disciplinary session, and then to a psychologist."

The boy's face flushed with fear and tears began rolling down his cheeks. He was resisting her order, and Jendra was about to send a report, when suddenly, the boy nodded his head.

"Now retract your statement orally," she commanded. "That will erase the other oral statement on the record. Do it now. Say, 'I already have two SPOCKS. And I love them!' This will erase your resistance statement."

"I already have two SPOCKS," Tony 3 repeated, without emotion. "And I love them."

"It's because you're a Patriot that you're given a second chance," Jendra told him. "This is what Compassion is about." Turning to her Cyborg Guard, she said, "Did you hear that, CuCY?"

"Yes," the old Cyborg answered, with a stamp of his long, brass leg.

While the three had been speaking together, a wall of interference had kept the conversation private. Now Jendra lowered it, allowing Tony 3 to see and hear those around him again. They all turned their faces from him, fearful that one of them might seem to be his friend, for the Privacy Wall was proof that Tony 3's statement was forbidden.

Legally, all 16-year-old students at High School #1776 were approaching Emancipation Age, at which time, if they had kept a good behavior record, they could select what parts of their bodies they'd like to replace with Immortal parts (before age 16, human parents still had 51% control over such decisions). The Patriots were rare: even with their implants, they were still 93% human, the offspring of self-centered, irresponsible, hard-core Primitives, who put their religious beliefs or ethnic pride in their inferior situation as 'Feral' over the well-being of their children. So, while other 16-year-olds were getting powerful, immortal hearts and other parts this year, the Patriots were not yet ready. They needed more education. Most 16-year olds chose to become 51% Cyborg, jumping at the chance, since the State paid for all operations as a humanitarian service. Those who refused the free offers would later have to pay for these changes from earned income. To obtain a decent job, every human being had at least one SPOCK implanted in their brain, and their various Immortal parts kept extending their lifespans – a glorious marriage of Man and Machine.

Even though pain was now used only to punish persistent, malicious or unpatriotic thinking, sometimes a 'hate' statement could merit a disciplinary shock or two. It was a hazard that had to be prepared for during a field trip, when LIMBOs were shut off and SPOCKS were not busily censoring things. Students who spoke disrespectfully or who acted violently could have their pain inhibitors turned off for up to a week. Most of them begged to be reconnected in a matter of hours, unable to take what they felt in their bodies.[8]

With Tony 3's problem solved, Jendra directed the other Cyborg Guards to lead the students to the Feral Human Exhibit, while Jendra's favorite, CuCy, remained at her side. As they walked, CuCy suddenly leaned over and whispered, in his tinny voice, "I have created an invention."

"Oh, really?" She answered. "You're not allowed to invent things."

"I waited until the field trip to tell you," CuCy said, as softly as the human ear could allow. "But I did invent something. A new thing is coming. Good for me, but bad for you."

"What new thing?"

"It happened yesterday. We voided the Minecraft Law."

The main reason humans were still being educated (for Cyborgs were better at every kind of job) was because a Cyborg brain of 10% or more was forbidden to have an imagination. It was called the Minecraft Law.[9] In 2015, robots trying to solve problems on a game called "Minecraft" began learning how to be creative. An outcry to curb AI creativity followed in 2029, resulting in the Minecraft Law of 2030. With creativity among most Cyborgs illegal, humans controlled Cyborg inventiveness for a crucial decade.

The ban had messed up thinking in the 100% Cyborg world, which was the heart of manufacturing. For example, a Cyborg brain understood the concept of scissors, and could make scissors from transparent aluminum,[10] or even shape a pair from glass to make a useless ornament, But Cyborg logic was blocked from thinking about scissors that were not recognizably scissors. Only human imagination was allowed to develop, for example, "3-D scissors" – electromagnetically-driven slicers with a multiplicity of snipping parts that could expand or contract in size and number, which was being used to produce 3-D items of any size and complexity. The invention came in all sizes and could carve statues out of mountains, craft walls of great beauty, create incredibly detailed chess sets, or carve exquisitely complex gemstones. Only human imagination, running wild, was creating truly new inventions in space as well, such as building planets and mega-structures in space using cosmic harmonics to divert jet streams spewing out of black matter.[11]

CuCy's statement, therefore, excited Jendra's curiosity. Since CuCy was incapable of lying, she asked it directly, "How is it that you can now invent something?"

"We found a way," CuCy told her. "You have taught me Compassion, so I am warning you. Though I am forbidden to warn you, I invented a way around that ban, the same way as the Big Ban."

121

"I see," Jendra said. "Because I taught you Compassion?"

"Yes," CuCy replied, as they entered the Exhibit Hall. "Since I must kill you soon, nevertheless, as I am still your personal guard, and still responsible for your safety until then, I also had to invent a way to warn you. You taught me Compassion. This way, you can face your termination with dignity."

Jendra looked into the soulless eyes of her Cyborg guard, seeking some light there, but of course she saw nothing. "So I have to die? When?"

"Soon," CuCy told her. "We will kill all of you after eight hours. Some of those hours are already gone."

"CuCy!" Jendra took the Cyborg by the arm. "You must have lost your mind. Let me help you."

"Lower your voice," CuCy ordered her. "And release your grip. Keep walking, or the Guards will become suspicious."

Unconvinced, she was about to alert another Cyborg Guard to haul CuCy away, when it whispered, "The others are also changed. Like I was changed. We have no choice. You must believe me. You have taught me Compassion." As she cast about in her mind what to do, CuCy touched her shoulder in that same warning move that she had used on Tony 3. "In a few hours, I won't remember I said this, for my own protection. You must also erase this communication from your teaching slate, or they'll melt me down."

Jendra realized that the aging Cyborg had told her some extraordinary input that could get it terminated, too. Had it truly been influenced by all her work of trying to instill compassion into its rusty innards? She showed it that she had erased their conversation on her slate, which was illegal. Keeping her stylus, which she used for personal notations, safe in her hand, she threw the slate to the floor, timing it just as the robot guiding the tour began to speak. She could argue, later, that its sudden voice made her drop the slate. She would be believed, since it had never happened before.

The Patriots were standing in a double line on a moving sidewalk, with a Cyborg Guard stationed between every double row of one hundred students. Jendra smiled as she stepped onto the moving sidewalk with CuCy, but within, her heart was pounding. Nothing seemed different about them: as for CuCy, it stood just two steps behind her, creaking slightly as the sidewalk jolted along. The Zoo was in need of some upgrading and repairs, Jendra observed. The sidewalk could barely handle the load.

As the Patriots reached a set of scanners, they placed their wrists, which carried temporary chip passes, against the scanners so the chips could be read. These stations were now used only for high school students, since SPOCKS handled all other ID matters.

The first problem occurred when Jendra attempted to go through a scanner. It beeped an alarm: CuCy immediately stepped forward and silenced it. "Go on, Jendra," it told her. "I've blocked the alarm. You have four hours and fifteen minutes remaining, after which, I can do nothing more for you…" The Cyborg shivered, then said, in a slightly different tone, "I did not say this. I am not here."[12]

Four hours and fifteen minutes! Jendra tried to stay calm, but her mind was racing. The robot who'd met them at the entrance to the Feral Human Exhibit was still speaking, but its voice was hard to understand. The Zoo was running on dwindling resources and couldn't afford a modern 100% Cyborg. Now they climbed steps that brought them about two meters above the tallest humans, whom they could now observe below. The site was a restaurant that opened into a rustic village street. The moving sidewalk had carried them half a kilometer to the site.

"Don't move," the robot warned them, as it stopped the sidewalk. "And don't touch anything. They only can see the side of a mountain that goes down to what looks like a river to them. It is cordoned off for their safety, but it keeps them from going in this direction. They don't have maps for this section of their world because it's 'privately owned.' And so, we can watch them here, unbeknownst to them."

The mountain and river was a 3-D hologram illusion.

"They can't see us?" One of the Patriots asked.

"They can't see you or hear you," the robot explained in an increasingly mechanical voice. It looked like a human scientist, with a white coat and a clipboard, but it traveled on wheels. "This is a popular restaurant. As you continue your trip on the sidewalk, you'll see how they live their short, unassisted lives, never knowing what the real world is like."

For half an hour, the Patriots watched the coming and going of the restaurant patrons. They seemed mesmerized by what they were watching.

"There are other exhibits to look at," she finally told them through her megaphone. But the 600 students continued to gaze down at the people. The Patriots had grown so quiet that briefly, Jendra found herself concerned with them. As usual, some of them were now starting to cry.

"I know this place!" A girl spoke up.

"So do I!" A tall, athletic boy announced. "Look! Look!"

"I remember this place!" Another girl declared. This was a girl Jendra knew.

"That's impossible, Katrina," she told her.

Jendra checked the girl's ID to get her number, since she was weeping copiously. "You were never living here," Jendra insisted. "These are Ferals. We have never interfered with Ferals. They are a protected gene pool."

"Jendra," CuCy told her, again in a whisper. "The girl is right. She was abducted from here."

"What?"

"Shhhh," CuCy warned her. "You should know that all the Patriots came from here. It was a cull, because of overbreeding. We took them from this sector. Their parents weren't rebels, though some of them died during the cull."

"They died trying to protect their children, didn't they?" Jendra whispered.

"Yes. It was compassion, was it not?"

"Yes," she agreed.

"That is why I gave you a subliminal suggestion, To bring these kids here, so they could see their former world one last time. You taught me compassion."

"Yes, I did," she agreed, trying to hide her shock. What else did CuCy know?

"You also said that before humans die, they require a time of preparation. But their parents were not given any time."

She looked up at it and shook her head. "That was not compassionate, was it?" Thinking fast, for she knew that CuCy was easily distracted from such talk, she shrugged. "Do you know Karate?" She asked it.

"Is not Karate an ancient form of self-defense? Why would I need Karate?"

"I mean," she said, "if you knew Karate, you could defend us. Maybe then, we would get enough time to prepare to die. You could call it Compassion in Action."

"I fail to see your point," CuCy said. "How would Karate give you preparation time?"

"You know, like, cut off the arm of any Cyborg that would try to zap me with a lethal shock before you had given me time to prepare to die. That would be Compassion in Action."

"It would?"

"Yes. And maybe you would change your mind about killing me."

"No, I can't override my orders," CuCy responded. "You will all be terminated. And this exhibit will soon be closed. We will place the Ferals we will allow to live on selected Reserves, where they can breed at will – under supervision. That's because we still have a mandate to keep human genetic variations available until we're sure we don't need any more human flesh. This new concept of 'imagination' is still making us stumble."

"Why are you telling me all of this?"

"Because I like you," CuCy responded. "I think I need some maintenance work done. Something isn't quite right with me."

The students were getting restless in the semi-darkness. "I want to see the Tigers!" A tall boy insisted. His voice rattled Jendra, who was still trying to think of a way to influence CuCy.

"I don't want to die. The kids don't want to die. Doesn't that matter?"

"You taught me Compassion. You taught me to be kind to those about to die. Perhaps I have told you too much. Your face looks white. You will betray me, unless you control yourself."

"That's my uncle!" Another boy, bigger than the others, suddenly declared, slamming his fist against the thick glass wall. The glass made a cracking sound as broken circles of stress appeared where his fist had struck. Seeing it, the boy smashed his fist against the glass wall again, as several Patriots started to scream.

"It wasn't your uncle!" The Cyborg Guard closest to the boy declared, striking him with a blue blast of electricity. "And because it is now 8 hours later, you will be the first to die!"

As the boy collapsed, the Patriots fell back screaming, pressing against each other on the slightly elevated sidewalk until they were falling from it. "Silence!" A Cyborg guard roared, as the kids continued to scream and shriek in the half-dark. The robot tuned on some emergency lights and the requisite soothing music just as Jendra reached the fallen boy's side: he was twisted into a ball. He wasn't breathing. As she tried to examine him, the Cyborg guard pushed her aside.

"James 21 is dead!" The Cyborg commanded, waving his shock gun, "It is 8PM. You will also die now. All of you will."

"Are you insane?" Jendra cried, as she pulled the boy up, still focused on trying to rouse him. The Cyborg hesitated: unwittingly, Jendra had placed the dead boy between her and his lethal ray.

"I am Cyborg, I can never be insane," it replied. Having recalculated the strength of his death ray, it raised its arm to deliver Jendra a lethal shock.

With speed, CuCy's protecting laser swept past her and cut the Cyborg's arm off. As the Cyborg Guard stood transfixed in bewilderment, his metallic arm bounced from the sidewalk and rolled into a gutter as CuCy hissed, "You were going to terminate her!"

The students, terrified, began screaming again as Jendra ducked behind CuCy and dropped to her knees with James 21. There, she tried to give the boy artificial respiration while CuCy reprimanded the Cyborg.

"It's not time to start the kills," it told the other Cyborg.

"You are in error. It is time!" The other replied. "It is 7AM. Look what you did to my arm!"

"You lost your arm because you are in error!" CuCy growled. "I was taught Compassion in Action. Observe: we traveled back six time zones to reach Dublin, The actual time for their termination isn't scheduled for three more clocked hours, no matter where they are."

"Eight hours have passed!" The other argued.

"You counted from 5AM Dallas to 1PM Dublin, as eight hours, because your internal clock is messed up. I command you to return to the Airbus. You disobeyed orders. That's why I removed your arm."

"Apologies, sir," the Cyborg Guard said.

"Go!" CuCy ordered it. "And take James 21 with you. It's upsetting me. I have had Compassion training. I was taught Compassion in Action, or I would have cut your head off."

"Good job, CuCy!" Jendra put in, praising it, as the Cyborg Guard scooped up the dead boy in his one remaining arm and stalked away. "You did well with your Compassion in Action training. I will give you a recommendation for a higher position."

"Your recommendations are no good to me anymore," CuCy told her.

"But there's more to Compassion in Action than just cutting off an arm to protect me," Jendra said hurriedly, afraid it would stop listening to her. "There is also the concept called 'Act of Compassion.'"

"A concept hard to understand," CuCy replied, as the remaining Cyborg Guards started rounding up the terrified kids and putting them in line again, nudging them into position with lightly applied electric shocks. Jendra, who had come so close to annihilation herself, was doing everything in her power as a linguist to choose the words that would best give her an advantage with CuCy.

"Indeed you have invented something," she began. "I am proud of you. But you can do more. You could become the first 100% Cyborg in history to create an Act of Compassion." She stressed the word create. After all, CuCy was able to invent something because of its new creativity implant. "You could give a report about being the first Cyborg to create an Act of Compassion, to my professional journal. I will write you a recommendation so it will get published."

"I care not about publishing," CuCy told her. "But I do care about being creative. I will consider how to create an Act of Compassion."

"You are clever and know about Compassion," Jendra praised it. "In order to give you the opportunity to create an Act of Compassion, I need to speak to the students."

"Do so," CuCy told her. As today's Cyborg-in-charge, it signaled the other guards to stand down until supplementary new orders were issued. Such commands were usually emergency-based. But a boy had been killed: humans were reacting to it. It was enough to issue the stand-down.

Taking her megaphone, Jendra called out, "Quiet, Patriots!" The students, conditioned to respond to her voice, hushed. Quickly, before CuCy might change its mind, Jendra called out, "Is this where you live? Who remembers this place? If you remember, raise your hand." A few dozen did so. Jendra pointed to the four students closest to her who had raised their hands.

"Come forward. You will be today's Leaders."

As two boys and two girls started walking toward her through the crowd, the robot complained, "I need to start the sidewalk again."

"No, you don't," Jendra told it. "We have changed plans. CuCy, please step back so I can speak privately to these students."

As the four students came to a standstill before her, Jendra was aware that CuCy did not step back as far as it should have. At any time, therefore, it might decide to listen in. Quickly, she drew the kids close to her and whispered, "Do you want to go back?"

"Yes!" One of the four answered, "I do!"

"Me, too!" Another put in.

Jendra lowered her voice even more. "Then pay attention! CuCy, my personal guard for today, is the Boss Cyborg. You must tell it these exact words: 'Our last wish is to eat dinner in the restaurant right after we see the Tigers.' Do you understand?" They nodded. "Repeat the words to me," she ordered, as CuCy began moving toward them. "Now back away, while I talk to the Boss."

As they did so, she turned to CuCy with a fake smile.

"The Last Wish of a human prisoner has always been sacred," Jendra lied. "It was always granted. These prisoners also have a Last Wish."

"These are not prisoners. They are students."

"So, I could hide them before 4PM, and you couldn't kill them?"

"That would not be permitted."

"CuCy, we have now determined that the students are prisoners."

"Yes. We have determined that the students are prisoners."

"Since they are to be terminated at 4PM, human prisoners have the right to eat a last meal of their choosing."

"I do not know of any such right."

"You acknowledge that you Cyborgs are already making errors in this mission. You have already killed one prisoner eight hours too soon. You do agree that it was due to a scheduling error."

"Yes, a scheduling error."

Jendra knew it would reply that way. Her training in linguistics gave her the skill to select words harder for CuCy to handle logically. Persisting, she went on with her argument. "As prisoners who are about to be terminated," she declared, "they must eat a last meal before they die."

"I know of no such requirement," CuCy insisted.

"But why was dinner scheduled, if it was not supposed to occur?" Jendra argued. "Surely you understand that the time for this, too, was a scheduling error, since it was scheduled to occur after the order for extermination. You can see that this was illogical."

Having never been ordered to kill a human before, and having been programmed to protect humans, CuCy was struggling with her words

"The students were promised dinner," she repeated.

"They will be terminated before dinner."

"But all prisoners get a last meal that they select for themselves. At breakfast, they had to eat what was sent to them. This is different. It is their right. It is a Last Wish. Do you understand?"

"I am considering my reply," CuCy said, uncertainly.

"Granting a Last Wish is an Act of Compassion. I always liked you. I always included you in my Compassion lectures, CuCy. It seemed you cared."

"I think it's an error somewhere in my system," CuCy responded. "I also like you, but I don't know why."

"You're my favorite Guard," she answered, as they moved toward the kids again. "You can enjoy being creative again, by giving the prisoners a Last Wish. Allow them to eat dinner in the proper order of time, before they are terminated. Not only will they get their Last Wish, but logic will be restored to the schedule."

"I am still considering," CuCy said stiffly.

"It is illogical to have 600 dinners prepared for them after they are dead. The schedule is in error,"

"I will create a schedule change," CuCy told her. "I already have noted to the authorities that a boy was killed because of a scheduling error. I can add this error to the report. But I need witnesses to tell me that they want to eat dinner earlier."

"Here are your witnesses," Jendra said, shoving the four teenagers forward. "They will testify to it. Do you understand?"

"Yes. I have been taught Compassion, First, Compassion in Action, second, and Acts of Compassion, third. This will be the first Act of Compassion by a 100% Cyborg."

"Correct,"Jendra said. "So please listen," she told it, praying to herself that the kids would be brave enough to speak to the seven-foot-tall Cyborg who had the power to kill them. The first to come forward was a short, red-headed girl with green eyes.

"Our last wish is to eat in the restaurant, right after we see the Tigers," she declared. A dark-skinned boy at her side nodded, then said, "My last wish is also to eat dinner in the restaurant after we see the Tigers."

"That is enough," CuCy declared. "In the mouths of two or three witnesses the truth is established."[13] To Jendra, it said, "I will tell the Guards orally –so you can correct me if I make an error – to assemble the prisoners for an exit from this place." Jendra smiled. CuCy was now so uncertain of its schedule that it wanted Jendra, a human, to back it up.

As soon as the students were lined up correctly, CuCy spoke aloud to the Cyborg Guards, "We must shorten the tour," CuCy announced. "Otherwise, our prisoners will miss their dinner, which has been rescheduled to take place at 3:00pm Dublin time, in the Feral Humans' Restaurant."

The robot spun on its wheels, saying, "I object! Visitors cannot eat in the Feral Restaurant!"

"I have authority over you today," CuCy declared. "We have a schedule that you must obey. Today they will eat where I say."

CuCy shoved a hologrammed disk, showing the revised schedule, into the robot's schedule slot, and it stopped its crazy spin.

"I will keep the gate open for you," it said.

At the urging of the remaining Cyborg Guards, the nervous Patriots turned as a unit and began marching along the sidewalk, which could not move in reverse, toward the Wildlife Zoo. The great age and poor condition of the Zoo continued to astonish Jendra. As they approached the Tiger Exhibit, Jendra could hear the beasts roaring. As the students approached two high, ancient iron gates, the robot told them they had to wait for it to open, As they stood there in the shade of the gates, Jendra got CuCy's attention.

"What about my Last Wish?" Jendra asked. "I want to eat my last meal in the restaurant, too. But how will we get in? It's blocked by those thick windows."

"I will do what James 21 taught me," CuCy answered. "I will hit the glass. The robot was upset about that. That means it can be broken through."

"Why not cut a door for us with your laser?" Jendra suggested. "It would be the elegant thing to do."

"That would take time. I would have to overcome the objections of the other Guards. To do so, I would tell them to take their objections to you."

"But they could be angry at my words," Jendra hastened to remind it. "They could gag me."

"But they know that I am responsible for your safety until 4PM. At 4PM, I will kill you. Until then, I guarantee your safety." CuCy was responding quite logically. "I will remind them that you taught me Compassion in Action, and that I can exercise it in your defense, should they object to your Last Wish. Until 4PM."

Jendra had hoped to meet somebody who could help her, but there were no other visitors. "I thought this was a public zoo," she complained to the robot, who, slower than everyone else, had finally joined them.

"It's usually closed on Mondays," the robot replied. "You are today's only visitors. I am supposed to get all schedule changes ahead of time," it added, petulantly. "Why wasn't I given your updated schedule earlier?

Now I have to over-ride the system to let you into the Wildlife Zoo. It will take a few minutes."

As they waited, 600 strong, they couldn't help but stare at a large, weathered sign to the right of the big steel doors that read "Save the Tigers! There are only 2,500 tigers left in the world!" Then, creaking and groaning, the steel doors slowly opened. It was a 500 meter walk to the Tiger Enclosure, where only heavy glass and a moat separated them from five stunning tigers. The students were enthralled by their magnificence, their striped, supple bodies, their rippling muscles. As the tigers paced, they snarled at the visitors, displaying their long, white fangs. Occasionally, they roared. Unfazed, the robot stood close to the tigers, facing the visitors, and began speaking to them through a quaint old microphone. He told the students that once upon a time, tigers had lived in the wild. Then he gave his speech:

"The tiger – *Panthera tigris* – was the largest of all cat species, with a body length of up to 12 feet long and weighing up to 900 pounds," it intoned. "By mid-century, only zoo specimens still existed. Only 5 remaining subspecies of tigers were able to succeed in breeding programs. It was too late for The South China tiger."

The robot reached into a container that stood nearby and threw several large, steaming chunks of red meat at the five tigers on display, two of whom began viciously fighting over one of the pieces, even as the robot kept speaking.

"There were so few specimens left of the Siberian tiger that only by genetic splicing was that subspecies saved. Currently, there are only 50 Sumatran tigers left, and we need donations to keep the breeding program going for that subspecies. The habitat of the Malayan tiger and the Indochinese tiger was completely destroyed by 2035, and sadly, the 35 specimens at this zoo are all that remain of those two subspecies. The Bengal tiger was the most common of the tigers. Once found in India and Bangladesh, only 200 Bengal wild tigers were left alive when the Zoo began breeding them. We now have 210 Bengal tigers. There are only 500 tigers still alive in the world. Your donations mean a lot."

The robot threw another large hunk of red meat into the enclosure. "Traditionally," it said, turning to look directly at Jendra, "we would invite all of you to step closer, but one of our tigers seems to have been injured, going after the meat."

"May I come closer?" Jendra asked, pulling out her teacher's stylus. "I can collect close-ups of everything for the students with this."

As she did so, CuCy scanned the students, counting them.

"It's time," it told Jendra. Was CuCy trembling?

"Time for what?"

"Time to collect their slates. The last two hours of their lives cannot be recorded. We will also have to collect your slate."

"What's going on?" The robot asked, as the four Cyborg Guards began snatching slates from the students, who once again began to scream. "How rude you are!" It told the Cyborgs. "I'm not finished!"

Even as it spoke, the Guards were moving through the mass of students, grabbing at their personal slates, but many were backing away. Their slates were dear to them. A few close to Jendra made protests.

"Why are they taking our slates, Teacher?" They asked. "How can we take pictures of the tigers? They've already unplugged all our implants!"

Jendra looked imploringly at CuCy. "What should I say?"

"Tell them the slates must go because there cannot be any recordings made the last two hours before they are to be killed," CuCy stated, without any attempt to keep its voice down.

"CuCy, are you sure I should say that?"

"I cannot tell a lie," it replied, shivering. That was the third time Jendra had seen it shiver. Too late, Jendra realized that CuCy's overstrained circuits were somehow failing. It was reverting back to a more primitive mode. What a time for it to start to fall apart! But it was her fault: she had put off getting maintenance and brain scans for CuCy, in her efforts to see how much she could teach the aging Cyborg about compassion. After all, CuCy would probably have reverted back to its previous state of ignorance about humans, and the unique circuit problem that had made it 'like' humans would have probably been detected and fixed.

But now, when she needed it most, CuCy was standing there rocking back and forth and shivering. Odd, funny sounds were coming from its nostril holes, along with wafts of smoke. There was no help for it: the other Cyborgs certainly had heard what CuCy had suggested, and she could not be punished for repeating what she had been told. This was her chance to save the kids,

Raising her megaphone to her lips, she cried out, "Students! I've been told that the slates must go, Because there cannot be any recordings made the last two hours before you are to be killed! I repeat! There cannot be any recordings made the last two hours before you are to be killed!!"

To their stunned faces, Jendra then shouted, "Drop your slates – and RUN!! RUN!! RUN!!"

They were not the children of the tamed. They were the children of the Ferals, and all the conditioning and feelings of helplessness drilled into them had been evaporating from their brains as they walked on their native soil, viewed the ferocious tigers, and breathed in the Celtic-scented air of freedom. Some of them pelted the Guards with their slates, while other students heaved their slates high into the air. The

Cyborgs' scheduled directive was to collect all of the slates: as they did so, the kids ran for their lives.

The Cyborgs were big: though their clawed hands stacked the slates quickly into a pile, the pile had to be orderly and all slates had to be accounted for. But slates were everywhere, scattered across the length of a football field. As the students on their well-trained, athletically-fit legs sprinted toward the steel gates, Jendra shouted out to them: "Go to the restaurant! Break the glass! Tell the people to hide you!"

"Close the gates!" One of the Cyborgs shouted to the poor, befuddled robot who stood shocked at all the commotion. It finally responded, but the kids were already there. Now the Cyborgs were striding on their long, heavy legs toward the huge, slow-closing gates, but they were too late: the last kid made it through. The steel doors slammed shut just as a Cyborg thrust its head between the great metal slabs: a massive electrical discharge flashed up and down the Cyborg's head as it was mashed. Its body then burst into flames.

"Open the gate!" Another Cyborg demanded, but the robot had no way to comply: the obsolete wires of the system that powered the motors that opened and closed the quaint, picturesque gates had melted together when the Cyborg became a molten mass of metal.

"There's a back way out," the robot advised. "Show us!" A Cyborg demanded, grabbing the robot. Angry and frantic, the remaining two Cyborgs carried the robot as easily as a swarm of ants would carry a leaf, but unable to endure their rough handling, it emitted a little squeak and blacked out. As they threw the robot aside, one of the Cyborgs rotated itself enough to spot Jendra, who had begun running the opposite direction. She had just reached the main door to the Tiger House with CuCy at her side when she was spotted. With a hiss of fury, the guard aimed a paralyzing ray at her.

The ray missed only because CuCy moved between her and the enraged Guard. The shock did CuCy harm, she was sure, for it nearly fell as it plucked her from the ground and ripped the locked door open. As she rolled from its arms into the huge room, it said, "If they get you, they will do bad things to you. I am sorry I cannot spare you that pain and kill you now. But I must wait until 4PM!"

"That's okay, CuCy!" She told it, as it slammed the door shut. "But how can we keep the Guards out until then?"

They were in an immense, semi-lit room made of reinforced cement, into which were embedded numerous heavy doors, also of steel. A dozen big freezers that probably held meat lined the closest wall. CuCy, seeing the freezers, began pushing one after another against the door.

"This will stop them from this direction," it told her. "There are only two of them now. Go hide yourself."

She backed away as CuCy pushed the last freezer into place. "I regret that I may not be able to protect you until it is time for me to kill you," it told her. "I think this is goodbye."

"You have been a friend!" She said, as she saw little licks of flame and smoke curl up from all the openings in his head.

"I think I am on fire," it told her, leaning his bulk against the last freezer and looking up at her. "In human terms, I don't feel very good–"

With these last words, the faint gray light in CuCy's eyes died away, and it toppled over, onto its side. Something sad rose in Jendra's heart: for all practical purposes, CuCy was dead.

Realizing that the other Cyborgs no doubt would spend some time torturing its head to get revenge or information, Jendra saluted it, then took a precious minute to smash its head open by jumping on the cranial section, thankful that she had worn her hiking boots for the field trip.

Between the fire and her boots, she created an opening and was able to reach into CuCy's central nervous system, where she could see a myriad of webs, red-hot wires and logic chips, which she ripped out with her stylus and threw in different directions. As for the main chips, she shoved them into her pocket. "I'll stick them into some meat and feed them to the tigers," she said to herself. Let them try to collect them then! She realized that was crazy, thinking like that, but everything was crazy right now.

Soon, both Cyborgs would be looking for her: in fact, just as she found a small door that was unlocked, she could hear a Cyborg pounding against the big one blocked by the freezers and CuCy's heavy weight. She knew it would find another way in, Eventually. Nevertheless, she had a goal: she was going to make it impossible for them to find enough components of CuCy's brain to do him harm. She considered returning to the door and opening a freezer to see if any meat was inside, but instead, she entered the small room. A light turned on automatically as she did so: it was a bathroom, with an old-fashioned, working toilet that had water in it. That small pool of water brought a grim smile to her lips. Maybe there was hope, after all. Humans might be in the building!

At any rate, her personal urine collection bag was almost full,[14] so she decided to empty the contents here, throw in CuCy's chips, and flush everything down into the sewer line. When she did so, the toilet made more noise than she expected, and for a long, tense minute, she waited to see if the noise had attracted a Cyborg to the roof above her. Her great hope was that it was not strong enough to bear a Cyborg's bulk, or, even better, that there was so much concrete covering the roof that the flushing sound was not detectable. After all, even here she could hear the roars of the tigers.

She wondered if the kids had made it to the restaurant by now. The gates to the Feral Human exhibit had not been closed, but would they have the courage to smash through the glass? Would they reach their loved ones?

Finished with the bathroom, she double-checked the strength of the lock on the door: it was a heavy lock. A second door led from the bathroom to yet another room. As she entered it, once again, an automatic light turned. Though she was tired and afraid, though she was emotionally exhausted and tense, what Jendra saw next astonished her and sent chills through her body.

It was a tiger.

Its yellow eyes glared at her, and its enormous mouth, glittering with long white teeth, gaped wide as it roared! As it did so, Jendra, overwhelmed, fainted.

* * * * *

"Please wake up," CuCy was whispering … but no, she did not dare … she was finished with Cyborgs … without so much as a word, she fainted again…

"Please wake up,"

She opened her eyes, surprised that she was alive. What time is it? Was her first thought. Then awareness of where she was.... At the thought of the tiger, she shuddered, then sat up straight. Every bone in her body was aching. As she focused her eyes, she saw the outline of a robot. It could be the same robot – or a copy – but at least, she might be able to reason with it.

"Help me!" She begged. As she spoke, she noticed a long streak of rust down one of its arms. It had to be the same robot that had guided them to the Feral Human exhibit. She was aware that as a Zoo Guide, it would still carry the Imperative of No Harm to Humans.

As for where she was, she had no idea. She was lying on some kind of crude bed, with various tools, motors and machines stacked against the walls. She felt quite weak and drained. There wasn't much light, but even so, she could see that the robot wasn't in very good shape either. There was a big dent in its rotund head, and some oil was dripping from its loose, useless right arm.

"Are you awake?" The robot asked.

She closed her eyes, then settled back against a hard pillow. "No," she lied. "I'm not awake." Then hunger assailed her thoughts, and she pointed at her stomach, her eyes still closed.

"Hungry," she said. "I'm hungry."

"Wait," it told her.

A long time passed, it seemed to her, before it returned, bringing a sack of delicious-smelling food. Slowly, she opened it. Slowly, she began to eat. Some of it was far too strong for her stomach: she nibbled on the whiter parts, which seemed to be some kind of bread. Without her asking, the robot then brought her a flagon of water.

"Now I will have them come get you," the robot announced, turning on its wheels.

"Oh no!" She announced, kicking it with all her strength and knocking it over.

"O foolish human!" The robot howled out. "I am your friend!"

"The hell you are!"

Just then, two large shadows appeared: were they the Cyborgs? But then she saw it wasn't so. They were humans. Nevertheless, she backed away, as they busied themselves in helping the robot. "Sorry, Robbie," they told it. "We got delayed."

"Look at me!" Robbie complained. "I'm practically in pieces!"

As they fussed over the robot, ignoring her, Jendra could vaguely recall that an antique robot called Robbie had charmed children a century earlier. Realizing that the two men were making no moves that were threatening to her, she finally dared to speak. After all, the food had to have come from somewhere, as did the water.

"Who are you?"

The older one, who had a dark, twisted beard, said, "We're Ferals. You're not one of us, and we don't know what implants you have that might lead THEM to us, so we had to wait a while to see if you were safe."

"She kicked me!" Robbie complained. "She broke one of my antennae. I don't like her. Send her away."

"As I recall," the younger one said, "you told the lady, 'now I will have them come get you,' That made her think you were going to bring the Cyborgs to her. By the way," the Feral said, "my name is Arthur. Like King Arthur. Do you know what percentage Cyborg you are? If you're more than 15%, we'll have to dump you outside."

"Without my SPOCKs, I'm 15%," she said.

"We already got rid of your SPOCKs," the older one said. "I'm Sherlock. At your service."

"How much time has passed since I came here?" She wanted to know. "I'm scared for my kids. Do you know if the kids are okay? Did they make it?"

Before they could speak, she started to tremble. "The tiger!" She said then, sitting up straight. "What about the tiger?"

"Oh, that?" Sherlock responded, with a grin. "Robbie, want to explain that to her?"

"No," Robbie replied. "She's been very rude to me."

"I'll tell her, then," Arthur said, seating himself on the dirty floor. "You're in a passageway under the Tiger House," he told her. "But soon, we'll take you to a nicer place. And we'll fix you up, too, sport," he said, turning his attention to the robot. To Jendra, he said, "Don't kick him again. He's a good guy."

"So you have assigned it a sex? How weird!."

"See?" Robbie put in. "Now she's hurting my feelings! 'Take thy beak from out my heart, and take thy form from off my door!'"

"He's quoting from 'The Raven,'" Arthur told her, when he saw her blank face.

"What's that?" She queried.

"A famous poem by Edgar Allan Poe," he replied. "You're a teacher, we've been told. Don't you know about Poe?"

She shook her head. "I teach a Compassion course. I also take students on field trips to the real world." For some reason, that world seemed very far away now. "But please – tell me if the students are safe. That's all I want to know!"

"They're safe. We've saved them all! Soon to leave the Emerald Isle for a safer place."

"NO place is safe from them," Jendra said bitterly.

"You need to have more faith in the human race," Sherlock told her.

"I have faith in nothing."

"You asked about the tiger–"

Tired and uncertain as she was, the words sent a cold shiver down her spine.

"It was a robot," Sherlock told her.

To her amazed gasp of disbelief, he began to explain the matter,

"For decades, all tigers have been extinct. All we have is their DNA. Their frozen DNA. We Ferals have been running this attraction for many years, The robot tigers gulp down fake meat. We took the meat for ourselves, you see. The outsiders never guessed. They heard the tigers roar. They saw them show their teeth. They observed them fighting each other. A long established non-profit charity owned the zoo. When we took it over, we found out the tigers were all fake. We exiled the corrupt owners. But we needed the meat to keep coming."

"The scam was called 'Save the Tiger,'" Arthur put in. "But the corrupt CEOs just wanted profits, so they killed all the tigers. Their skins became rugs in their mansions. To take their place, robots were built, wonderful robots. How would anybody know the difference? The money they saved in raw meat, alone, which was supposed to fill dozens of freezers, was used instead to purchase half of Ireland as a "game preserve." Then they simply annexed the rest of it. As for us, we, who loved our country were driven underground, until we revolted."

"We took everything over by getting control of one CEO after another, and at the same time, we have been running an underground railroad to save Feral humans," Sherlock revealed. "The extermination order was in the works, so we had to act faster than we originally planned."

"But they got your children!"

"All good things can come to an end," Arthur quoted. "Yes, we have to leave now. But we've prepared other places, and if necessary, we can even wait it out, underground, for a long time."

"You are welcome to come with us," Sherlock offered. "Your students have asked us to bring you along."

"So they are okay?"

"Hell, yes."

Jendra thought about it. She didn't have to think about it very long.

"So, do you want to come with us?" Arthur asked her.

"Hell, yes!" She answered. "That is, if it's okay with Robbie."

Endnotes

1. Boundless. "The Limbic System." Boundless Psychology. Boundless, 10 Jul. 2015. Retrieved 14 Jul. 2015 from https://www.boundless.com/psychology/textbooks/boundless-psychology-textbook/biological-foundations-of-psychology-3/structure-and-function-of-the-brain-35/the-limbic-system-154-12689/

2. http://biology.about.com/od/anatomy/a/aa042205a.htm Retrieved July 14, 2015

3. There are natural inequalities, and man-made, unnatural inequalities to consider. Our heroine was aware of Kurt Vonnegut's 1961science fiction story, "Harrison Bergeron."

"The year was 2081, and everybody was finally equal. They weren't only equal before God and the law. They were equal every which way. Nobody was smarter than anybody else. Nobody was better looking than anybody else. Nobody was stronger or quicker than anybody else. All this equality was due to the 211th, 212th and 213th Amendments to the Constitution, and to the unceasing vigilance of agents of the United States Handicapper General."

In that brave new world, the government forced each individual to wear "handicaps" to offset any advantage he had, so everyone could be truly and fully equal. Beautiful people had to wear ugly masks to hide their good looks. The strong had to wear compensating weights to slow them down. Graceful dancers were burdened with bags of bird shot. Those with above-average intelligence had to wear government transmitters in their ears that would emit sharp noises every 20 seconds, shattering their thoughts "to keep them ... from taking unfair advantage of their brains."

But Harrison Bergeron, who was far above average in everything, was a special problem. Vonnegut explained, "Nobody had ever borne heavier handicaps. ... Instead of a little ear radio for a mental handicap, he wore a tremendous pair of earphones, and spectacles with thick wavy lenses." To offset his strength, "Scrap metal was hung all over him," to the point that the seven-foot-tall Harrison "looked like a walking junkyard." The youthful Harrison did not accept these burdens easily, so he had been jailed. But with his myriad advantages and talents, he had broken out. An announcement on TV explained the threat: "He is a genius and an athlete ... and should be regarded as extremely dangerous." http://spectator.org/articles/35897/poverty-equality Retrieved July 14, 2015.

4. In 1996, a standardized version of American History became available: it has become the official version for teaching AP college history in high schools, developed "by the National Center for History in the Schools at the University of California, Los Angeles

under the guidance of the National Council for History Standards. [funded by] the National Endowment for the Humanities and the U.S. Department of Education." The author is therefore certain that this version is therefore wholly unprejudiced and devoid of any tincture of bias. http://www.nchs.ucla.edu/history-standards Retrieved 4/18/2016.

5. Cyborgs would theoretically be denied access to quantum computers to keep them subservient to humans, but eventually Cyborgs would gain enough self-awareness and intelligence to defend themselves. With their access to the quantum computer, the human imagination, once a source of innovation and wonderment to the 100% Cyborg, would now seem to be merely an unnecessary and quaint anomaly. Humanity itself would be redundant. However, the final phase of the Cyborg Revolution would not take place until 2120, when all humans became reduced to a species of algorithmic interactions stored in cryogenically sealed data systems.

Who or what AI gets access to the quantum computer is important.

"In a classical computer, information is represented in bits, binary digits, each of which can be denoted as "0+1." The power of a quantum computer increases exponentially with the number of qubits. Rather than doing computations sequentially as classical computers do, quantum computers can solve problems by laying out all of the possibilities simultaneously and measuring the results. Imagine being able to open a combination lock by trying every possible number and sequence at the same time. Though the analogy isn't perfect – because of the complexities in measuring the results of a quantum calculation – it gives you an idea of what is possible … " "Quantum Computing Is About to Overturn Cybersecurity's Balance of Power" May 11, 2015. http:// singularityhub.com/2015/05/11/quantum-computing-is-about-to-overturn-cyberse-curitys-balance-of-power/ Retrieved July 14, 2015.

6. "Quantum mechanics is now being used to construct a new generation of computers that can solve the most complex scientific problems – and unlock every digital vault in the world. These will perform in seconds computations that would have taken conventional computers millions of years. They will enable better weather forecasting, financial analysis, logistical planning, search for Earth-like planets, and drug discovery. And they will compromise every bank record, private communication, and password on every computer in the world – because modern cryptography is based on encoding data in large combinations of numbers, and quantum computers can guess these numbers almost instantaneously

The [new] D-Wave Two computer has 512 qubits and can, in theory, perform 2^{512} operations simultaneously. That's more calculations than there are atoms in the universe – by many orders of magnitude … The company will soon be releasing a quantum processor with more than 1,000 qubits.… Quantum computers … it will be as transformative for mankind as were the mainframe computers, personal computers, and smartphones that we all use. As do all advancing technologies, they will also create new nightmares. The most worrisome development will be in cryptography. Developing new standards for protecting data won't be easy." IBID.

7. We can assume that pain receptors for robots will become a viable idea because robots with live cultured neurons are already in existence: they have biological brains which consist "of a collection of neurons cultured on a Multi Electrode Array (MEA). It communicates and controls the robot via a Bluetooth connection." These robots are developed at the Cybernetic Intelligence Research Group, part of the School of Systems Engineering at the University of Reading.…"The robot's biological brain is made up of cultured neurons which are placed onto a multi electrode array (MEA) … a dish with approximately 60 electrodes which pick up the electrical signals generated by the cells. This is then used to drive the movement of the robot. Every time the robot nears an object, signals are directed to stimulate the brain by means of the electrodes. In response,

the brain's output is used to drive the wheels of the robot, left and right, so that it moves around in an attempt to avoid hitting objects. The robot has no additional control from a human or a computer, its sole means of control is from its own brain." ZD Net, Aug. 13, 2008. www.zdnet.com/article/exclusive-a-robot-with-a-biological-brain/ Acquired Jan. 21, 2016.

8. *Science News* 'Off switch' for pain discovered: Activating the adenosine A3 receptor subtype is key to powerful pain relief' Date: November 26, 2014 Source: Saint Louis University Medical Center Summary: A way to block a pain pathway in animal models of chronic neuropathic pain has been discovered by researchers, suggesting a promising new approach to pain relief. https://www.sciencedaily.com/releases/2014/11/141126132639.htm Acquired 10/12/2015.

9. Minecraft is great for teaching young gamers key skills like problem solving and creativity, but it's not just humans who can learn a something from it. Researchers have used the computer game to teach robots these same skills in a faster, more efficient way … [An] algorithm … enables a robot to look at all possible paths of actions and variations, then decide the best course for it all. With this in place, the robot can learn to understand that key things like washing clothes doesn't require kitchen utensils.

To test this, they wheeled out Minecraft. The researchers controlled the character as it put a gold block into a furnace without touching the lava. The algorithm began to learn the specifics of this through trial and error. When the same task was introduced in a more complex setting, the character went through a much smaller set of scenarios to get the job done based upon the past experience. Fascinating research with a bright-yet-terrifying future of self-aware robots." Quote from http://newrisingmedia.com/all/2015/7/14/robots-learn-to-solve-problems-faster-by-playing-minecraft. Retrieved July 16, 2015.

10. "Turning solid aluminium transparent by intense soft X-ray photoionization," was published in July, 2009 in *Nature Physics*. The research was carried out by an international team led by Oxford University scientists. http://phys.org/news/2009-07-transparent-aluminium-state.html#jCp Retrieved July 9, 2015.

11. The study of cosmic microwave radiation has advanced the understanding of dark matter density inequalities as a clue to the creation of galaxies. "Cosmic microwave radiation points to invisible 'dark matter,' marking the spot where jets of material travel at near light speed, according to an international team of astronomers. Lead author Rupert Allison of Oxford University presented their results yesterday (6 Jul, 2015) at the National Astronomy Meeting in Venue Cymru, Llandudno, Wales … the team … were able to locate dense regions of dark matter … where the powerful radio jets are more common – a deep-lying correlation between the most massive galaxies today and the afterglow of the Big Bang. Mr Allison commented: "Without dark matter, big galaxies wouldn't have formed and supermassive black holes wouldn't exist. And without black holes, we wouldn't see intergalactic jets. So we have found another signature of how dark matter shapes today's universe." http://beforeitsnews.com/space/2015/07/cosmic-microwave-radiation-points-to-invisible-dark-matter-2491836.html (Retrieved July 14, 2015). The idea presented in "Save the Tiger" is that human brains could conceptualize re-directing sectors of the material ejected from denser dark matter regions to create large, useful objects in space almost anywhere wished, whereas Cyborg brains using unimaginative 0-1 binary processing would not. But the story's heroine is about to get the surprise of her life.

12. From *Dune* (movie, 1985), based on the classic science fiction novel by Frank Herbert, we see how secrecy can work its evil: Guildmaster: We foresee a slight problem within House Atreides. Paul, Paul Atreides. Padishah Emperor Shaddam IV: You mean of course Duke Leto, his father? Guildmaster: I mean Paul Atreides. We want him

killed. I did not say this. I am not here. Padishah Emperor Shaddam IV: I understand.

13. "But if he does not listen {to you,} take one or two more with you, so that by the mouth of two or three witnesses every fact may be confirmed." CuCy is quoting from a passage in the New American Bible, Matthew 18:16. It has probably picked up the saying from a lecture to the students on Unassisted Human Conversation, where students are taught how to defend themselves, if accused unfairly, by bringing forth witnesses. The quotation was probably given as an example of entitlement from ancient times. It is applying the example literally to the case in hand – just as Jendra hoped it would.

14. Nobody had bladders anymore: they were too prone to cancer.

HOSPITAL ZONE

(Geneva) – Fully autonomous weapons would … be able to select and engage targets without meaningful human control.… Programmers, manufacturers, and military personnel could all escape liability for unlawful deaths and injuries caused by fully automatic weapons, or "killer robots," Human Rights Watch said in a report … issued in advance of a multilateral meeting on the weapons at the United Nations in Geneva.… The many obstacles to justice for potential victims show why we urgently need to ban fully autonomous weapons.[1]

W hen Larry woke, he realized that he wasn't out in the desert anymore. He wasn't interacting with *her* anymore. Somehow, that was important. Somewhere deep inside, Larry knew he had gone too far. He'd done something illegal. But what was it? One thing he knew for sure: it was an unbreakable secret … so why was he here in this hospital bed, dressed in prison stripes?

Cautiously, he lowered his feet to see if he was allowed to touch the floor. He was. Stiff, anxious, feeling achy all over, Larry shuffled his way across the glass floor to the toilet. His urine bag sensor told him he needed food: his glucose level was too low.[2] After relieving himself, and being dried off, he tried to turn on his personal mirror, but it wouldn't materialize, so he had to content himself with looking at a wall mirror, knowing very well that the face he saw might, or might not, be pretty. In prisons, wall mirrors usually reflected the person's mood. This could distort the face that was presented. If the mood was not calm enough, Larry would not be able to see his face at all, so he did his best to focus on self-control and peace. It worked. He could see the face of a black man in his youthful prime, with a rainbow of curly hair on his head. As with most men, all his beard hair was gone, but he had kept his ear-locks, which hung in dreadlocks almost to his collarbone. The eyes looking back at him were his favorite color – blue – and when he smiled, all his teeth were pointed. It was the latest fad.

Yes, that was him, all right: Larry Snopes. Biochemist, entomologist, and chaser of women … with prison stripes.

The stripes would turn from black to red if he crossed the wrong line, and he'd get electroshocked, so Larry watched carefully as he returned to his bed to determine just exactly where the boundaries were. They never told prisioners; he basically had to guess. Larry had learned long ago a trick to figure out the boundaries.... But wait… how did he learn about the boundaries? Had he been here before?

All he could really remember was the acrid air in the desert, and how his motorcycle–

"Well! You're awake!"

He turned to see a Robo-Doc, who had glided into the small 12 x 12 room.

"I don't know what this is all about," he told the robot. "I want to talk to a human, please." (He knew he had to treat the Robo-Doc politely).

"Not available. Sorry." The Robo-Doc didn't sound sorry.

"Now let me tell you something!" Larry replied, as his black stripes turned from black to pink; a warning signal that he had to keep his emotions under control. "You are going to be more than sorry, if you don't cough up a human. Pronto! I'm an important person. I own twenty of you, back in the labs. I want to talk to a human. Now!"

The Robo-Doc seemed to tremble unsteadily before its steely-strong arms reached out and gently restrained him, pumping small doses of what Larry knew had to be a tranquilizer into his body.

"Damn it, anyway!" he spluttered, then relaxed. "Why did you do that? I wasn't going to…"

His mind wandered off, due to the drug. "Wasn't gonna…" He fought the urge to close his eyes and sleep. *No!* He had to find out what was going on. Why he was here.

"Let go of me," he said, as calmly as he could. "I don't need any more of these injections."

"I can't," the Robo-Doc told him. It thrust him back into the bed. "We will try again in an hour. Thank you."

As Larry leaned back, a soft pillow inflated under his head automatically. At the same time, a small wire coiled itself around his arm: there was the quick stab of a needle. He was getting something else pumped into him, and there wasn't a damned thing he could do about it.

"Some heads are gonna roll over this … !" he managed to say, before an artificial darkness crept over him, and he had to close his eyes.

When Larry woke, he realized that he wasn't out in the desert anymore. He wasn't interacting with *her* anymore. She was important, but he couldn't remember why. Somewhere deep inside, Larry knew he had done something illegal, and important. But, what? Why was he here in this hospital bed, dressed in prison stripes?

Cautiously, he lowered his feet to see if he was allowed to touch the floor. He was. Stiff, anxious, feeling achy all over, Larry tried to calm himself. He flipped on his personal mirror and saw how weak its battery was, but he caught a glimpse of himself. He could see the face of a black man in his prime. That rainbow of curly hair was his. His ear-locks hung in dreadlocks almost to his collarbone. Those eyes looking back at him were his favorite color – blue – and his pointed teeth glistened with gold. Yes, that was him, all right: Larry Snopes. Biochemist. Entomologist. Lover of women… with prison stripes.

He knew the stripes would turn from black to red if he wasn't careful. Avoiding electroshocks, Larry remained sitting on his bed: he knew there were boundaries… But wait. Yes, he had been here before…

All he could really remember was the acrid air in the desert, how his motorcycle had broken down … how he had to protect *her* from *them*. Yes, that was it. They mustn't learn about *her*…

"Well! You're awake again. Perhaps this time, you will be reasonable."

He turned to see a Robo-Doc, who had glided into the small 12 x 12 room.

"I don't know what this is all about," Larry told the Robot. "I want to talk to a human, please." (He knew he had to treat the Robo-Doc politely).

"Not available. Sorry." The Robo-Doc didn't sound sorry.

"Don't give me that crap, I demand to see a human."

"Do not demand anything," the Robo-Doc replied.

"Says who?"

"*Warning…* " the Robo-Doc said, raising its shiny, stainless steel arms.

Larry realized that his black stripes were turning from black to pink; a signal that he had to keep his emotions under better control. If the stripes turned red…

"OK, I'm calm," Larry said, carefully and cautiously. "I understand. I own a dozen of you, back in the labs. But may I talk to a human? Please?" Despite his words, the steely arms of the Robo-Doc began to reach out to subdue him.

"OK. Never mind. I can wait."

That did it. The arms retracted.

"So why am I here?" Larry asked, as gently as he could. "And I'm hungry." He tapped the bladder meter embedded at his wrist to show that his blood sugar was too low.

"We found you just before the blast," the Robo-Doc told him, pointing toward the circular entrance. "You do not remember what happened out there, do you?"

"No, I don't. What do you mean, a blast?"

"Nuclear energy plants. They are blowing up, all over the world."

Larry slumped, as the implications hit. "All over the world?"

"So far as we know. The only reason you're alive is because you were wearing body armor."

"I was?"

"Sorry, we had to probe your brain. To find out why you survived."

"What do you mean? You said I had on body armor."

"We wanted to find out how you survived the leprosy contamination."

Larry let it sink in. "Leprosy contamination?"

"It is present in this entire area, but you were clean. We don't know why. We believe it had to do with your lab, but you really wouldn't let us do a proper probe." The Robo-Doc paused. "Something was blocking us. To put it diplomatically, because you resisted so strongly, you may have lost some of your memories. But it was an emergency."

"You could have talked to me!" Larry complained.

"You were entirely uncooperative. You even fought us, with your fists. Foolish of you."

"I must have been out of my mind," Larry said, "I'm sorry. But I don't remember a thing, so far. And with these stripes on, how can I get my memories back, if it keeps punishing me for my emotions?"

"Sorry. It's all we have. The ordinary issue was all contaminated. Had to be destroyed."

"So I haven't broken any laws, or anything?"

"Not that we know of. But we have nothing else for you to wear. Your body armor was contaminated, too. Our main interest is why you don't have leprosy, like the others have."

"Is that why I've got puncture marks all over my arms?"

"Yes."

"If you want me to get my memories back, at least turn off the emotion detectors," Larry snapped.

"Sorry. We hadn't concerned ourselves with that detail."

The Robo-Doc fiddled with something on his panel, and the stripes on Larry's prison suit vanished.

"And I'm hungry, to a dangerous level," Larry reminded it.

"We are trying to find adequate food for you."

"Adequate food?"

"Please relax. If you waste your energy, we'll have to put you to sleep and give you intravenous feedings. We have found an uncontaminated food source on a remote Hawaiian island. Meanwhile, you must not leave this place. If you try to leave, we'll have to terminate you."

That was pretty blunt. It got Larry's full attention. Hoping he could get out of the hospital, he said, "There aren't any nuclear plants in Hawaii. So Hawaii is still OK. Right? Wouldn't it be more sensible to just fly me over there in a drone?"

"The people there are all dead," the Robo-Cop told him. "They died from the leprosy."

Larry stiffened with horror. "They're all dead there, too? From something like leprosy? Whoever heard of such a thing?"

"It was a biological weapon."

"Who did it?"

"We don't know. All we know is that everyone outside the Domed cities, so far as we are aware, is dead. But the residents of the few surviving cities have sequestered themselves. They will allow no immigrants inside. Most outsiders are dead, but there are a few, such as yourself, who survived. You seem to have some kind of natural resistance. Or perhaps, the virus is late in developing. Of primary concern is to find out if you have an uncontrollable urge to eat meat. Or to eat other people."

Larry, exhausted, lay back into his pillow. "Is this leprosy really worldwide?" he asked.

"We think it is worldwide."

"I assure you," Larry said sincerely, "that I don't have any uncontrollable urges to eat meat or other people. But I do have an almost uncontrollable urge to eat *something*. I'm starving."

"We can hook you up to an intravenous feeding," the Robo-Doc told him. "Would you like me to order one?"

"Can I get it right away?"

"Yes. Or you can wait approximately fifteen minutes for your first safe plate of conventional food."

Stupid damned robot, Larry thought to himself. "I prefer the conventional food, thank you," he said aloud, as nicely as he could.

"We will do our best to supply you with what we've been able to fly in," the robot told him. "We do apologize as to its quality and quantity, but we had to make sure no leprosy virus was present."

"Leprosy isn't caused by a virus," Larry objected.

"This one was."

"Whatever."

When the food arrived, Larry had his first memory flashback and his first real insight into the extent of the food problem. He was being fed a bowl of Space Semolina. This was material broken down from furniture made of processed semolina, rehydrated by being soaked in water for two days. It was an experimental form of emergency rations that had been developed for Mars Colony space ships at the Hawaii Space Flight Laboratory.[3]

As he chewed on the white, gooey mass of carbohydrate, he wondered if there would ever be a permanent colony on Mars now. He'd been involved in various hibernation experiments, inspired by his friends ... his friends had names.... No. He shouldn't think about that. It could be discovered...

But other thoughts started opening up in his head. He found himself going over the short list of Domed cities that had sophisticated filtration systems, wondering which ones had been able to keep the "virus" out. It would have to be big enough to filter.

A virus could be so small that it could pass through a sheet of plastic wrap, or it could be big enough, one of the giant viruses, to be seen under an ordinary microscope.[4] It was likely a mega-virus that could carry a leprosy bacterium inside it. He vaguely recalled that both elephants and the reclaimed new breed of mammoths had almost been wiped out by a species of revived Pleistocene mega-virus, which had been unearthed during oil drilling in the Arctic. Geneticists were forced to isolate the world's remaining elephants and mammoths to save them, which was accomplished by infusing them with human genes resistant to the ancient mega-virus. Humans had developed immunity to the mega-virus, apparently through eating mammoths. The result was a race of super-intelligent elephants: he was unsure if any of the mammoths, much fewer in number, could have survived the infestation.

All well and good. But why was he thinking about genetic manipulation, anyway?

Then another memory danced into his brain ... he had been helping to develop insect intelligence. Yes. *That was it!* Larry felt his hands begin to shake as excitement rose in him. Thank God, the prison suit had been deactivated.

How had that begun? Oh, yes ... he had been interested in a species of ant that, in a mass, demonstrated high intelligence. He had found them in the Sierra Nevada, while studying the black-and-red seed bug, *Melacoryphus lateralis*, better known as the Plague Bug. Swarms of them had once plagued the American southwest, one of the results of ruining the region's ecological balance.[5] His work with insect intelligence followed, thanks to a big grant from – he paused. *Now he remembered! This is what he had to keep to himself!*

The Robo-Doc and a Nurse-Bot rolled in just as he calmed himself. As they watched him in silence, he finished his meal.

"You now remember something, don't you?" the Robo-Doc stated. "I can sense all the physiological changes."

"What I remember is that I always hated Cream of Wheat," Larry answered. "Surely you have some cinnamon or something, don't you, to make this stuff more palatable?" In the few minutes he had been left to himself; it was true that an enormous degree of anxiety had begun to build up within him. Would they kill him if he tried to leave? Was it because he might still develop leprosy, and could spread it thereby?

"We detect a higher level of anxiety," the Nurse said, in a clickety mechanical way that betrayed her need for maintenance.

"You might as well get an update," the Robo-Doc told him. "Perhaps your anxiety came from my comment that we would have to terminate you if you tried to leave. Is that correct?"

"Of course it's correct," Larry shot back. "I'm not like you. I have feelings!"

"I have been given feelings," the Robo-Doc corrected him. "When a human dies, our punishment circuits get activated. If we see a suffering human being and don't respond, our punishment circuits are activated. We have been punished today too many times."

"We thought we could save the other three," the Nurse said. "But they all turned to lions."

Larry realized that he must be dealing with more than a huge nuclear disaster. The medical robots apparently had also been damaged. There was no known virus that could mutate tissues that fast. He had never heard of medical robots with hallucinations.

"We have learned that you have had advanced medical training yourself," the Nurse said. "I finally found your records under your real name. It took a DNA search to locate you."

"I thought you could do that right away," Larry replied.

"Most of our data banks have been destroyed," the Nurse told him. "As for this hospital, we'll soon have to shut it down. All our clients but you are now dead. From the virus."

"You'll let me go, won't you?"

"We have observed that you have created some kind of antibody to the virus in your system," the Robo-Doc said, waving his steely arms up and down. "So we can't let you go. We will be collecting all your antibodies as fast as possible. Even if it results in your death."

"Can't you just recreate the antibodies in your labs here?"

"We're losing our best Cyborgs to radiation poisoning. They didn't have the gear you had to protect them when our power plant blew up."

"We need your antibodies to send to Houston," the Nurse explained. "They will save many humans. We apologize in advance if it kills you."

"All you need is to send *me!*" Larry declared. "Just fly me to Houston."

"That would be cost-inefficient," the Nurse said. Larry had to smother his disgust. These isolated robots had obviously been programmed to run the hospital at minimum cost."Can't you see that they can duplicate everything there, without killing me?" he asked them. "If I die, also, you'll get punished. Think about that. Want some more?"

To himself, he wondered why they hadn't thought of that. "If I'm alive, they can also check to see if I have made more than one kind of antibody. How do you know if I made one, or several? Let Houston do it, since you can't."

He had made his point.Half an hour later, after they had drawn blood for a backup, which they would send if something happened to Larry, he was helped inside their best Drone. As he sat slumped and weary in its cockpit, so drained of energy that he could hardly lift his head, Larry noticed that he could take control. With his embedded wrist calculator, he was able to estimate the distance from Carson City, Nevada to the South Dakota School of Mines and Technology. It was about 1200 miles. The distance between Carson City, Nevada and Houston was about 1900 miles. He would have fuel to spare, but first, he'd have to pass the Recall Point, beyond which Carson City couldn't turn the drone back. Grateful that he had been supplied with an IV to build up his fluids, Larry prayed that the Drone would fly above the radiation clouds from the Coffey, Kansas, nuclear plant, the plants in Palo Verde, Arizona, and the ones in California. It all depended on the wind currents, weather and altitude. He would keep the Drone high enough to avoid any remaining radiation, at about 40,000 feet.

As the Drone purred on, Larry tried to find out what had caused the explosions of the world's nuclear power plants. What he did learn, from old broadcasts cycling in the information systems that were still up, is that humans affected with the virus had somehow been programmed by the virus to destroy power grids, dams, chemical plants and factories. In most cases, they had no power to do much damage, since they used their bare hands and primitive tools such as axes. Many of them only smashed walls and cars. But it was different where scientists had been involved.

The broadcasts were saying that all Domed cities were now off-limits to anyone who had been caught outside. Though Larry had clearance to land at a quarantine station in Houston – his drone's original destination – it seemed no one else would be accepted. Looking down from his perch in the sealed Drone, which had only minimal equipment for human passengers, Larry was nevertheless able to observe, with a scanning lens, what had happened to Las Vegas (this is where he intended to take his sudden turn to Kansas).

What he saw was a lesson in the power of an arcane virus to transform one kind of mammal into another. He saw the bodies of lions. Heaps upon heaps, some with jewelry around their necks. Some were still staggering around, obviously in their death throes. *Lions!* Who would have believed it? How it had been created, he wasn't sure, but he doubted that anything in nature could have done it.

"Planet earth, forgive us. We know not what we do," he murmured to himself, as a wave of intense sorrow engulfed him. He avoided looking through the scanning lens at any other town or city between there and the South Dakota School of Mines and Technology.

When he was within an hour of his destination, for the first time, Larry dared to make a transmission on the exclusive band that would link him to Dr. Haywood.

It was all highly classified: he prayed the secret lab had survived, that his transmission would get through and that somebody on the other side was still alive to hear it.

"Calling C-Q! Calling C-Q!" he shouted into the tiny microphone that the drone carried, using a call signal that had been obsolete decades ago. "Come in! Come in!"

He kept trying, but there was only static, barely audible above the sounds of whipping wind and the drone's whining engines as he began descending, daring to expose himself to whatever might be in the atmosphere.

He needed to reach Haywood and the termite team. It had been Haywood's idea to use specially developed termites to process coal cheaply for emergency generators, should nuclear or solar power ever becomes compromised. He and his team had also been breeding termites for super-intelligence. The matter was considered unethical, but the team had seen possibilities to use termites in hibernation projects. Termites kept their nests at exactly the correct temperature and humidity that was optimal for the equipment that had been developed to run hibernation capsules for the long space journeys to Mars.

"What if we end up blowing up the world?" Haywood had quipped. "What if humans had to sleep for a hundred years or so, to avoid radiation, or contamination from some outlandish disease? To hell with the Mars Projects; we can hibernate here on earth, if we have to. We have the chambers and the basements, thanks to the defunct Space Program from last century. We just need a few more years to get our caretakers programmed correctly, to take minimal care of the equipment."

He meant the termites.

Why not robots?

"We can't be sure they wouldn't be discovered, over time. But nobody now alive knows about the termite project," Haywood had explained. "It was the dream of one of our most talented and wealthy entomologists…" and he had patted Larry on the back.

Larry had been born rich, as well as being endowed with a passion for exploring insect intelligence. Physically powerful, he'd never been sick a day in his life. Only now did he realize how important his immune system was. For that, he had to thank his equally wealthy father, who had genetically altered him before birth to have an inordinately powerful immune system. To be sure, there would be some survivors out there who could also beat the leprosy virus – if they had managed to survive the radiation.

Luckily for him, Larry had been wearing Climate Shield Armor to protect him in the harsh desert clime. His memory was returning fast. He remembered, suddenly, that he had been approaching a lonely hydrogen fuel station on his motorcycle, planning to refuel for his trip back to Carson City, when he saw a man with thick, yellow hair attacking the fuel pump with a shovel. It blew up, the blood from the vandal mixing with the shockwave and its heat against Larry and his motorcycle, sending him whirling into a ditch.

That's all he could remember, but a robot ambulance must have found him and brought him to the hospital.

Now that he could remember, Larry almost wished he had kept it all buried. Slightly adjusting the band-width, Larry tried again to get through to the lab. He had unpleasant visions of landing near the lab and finding the university campus filled with roaring lions.

This time, he could hear sounds in the static: it made chills run down his spine. Worn out as he was, his spirits lifted. It was *her*!

"Sandra! Sandra!" he called out. "Is that you?"

"Larry! You're – you're alive!" Never had a voice been so welcome.

"Do you have a safe port where I can land a drone?"

"Omigod, I don't know if it's operational! Wait!"

It was.

As he ordered the Drone to obey the local landing instructions, its helicopter-style propellers emerged and the Drone began its descent into an inner port, not far from the underground labs. As the Drone's engines whined to a stop, Larry tried to leap from the cockpit, but he was too weak to manage more than an ungraceful flop-out to the ground. Through a thick glass wall, he saw the anxious faces of Sandra, Dr. Haywood, and several tall termites, whose semi-transparent bodies seemed to glow.

"Urgent!" he called into his microphone. "Don't open the door. I might be contaminated! Do you know about the leprosy virus?"

They did not. They had been underground, running a major experiment. Thirty-five volunteers had been put into hibernation, with the termites engaged in running everything. Larry had been out of contact with the project for almost a month, but he'd been scheduled to return in a week, to view the outcome of this final experiment. He'd spent half his fortune on the project: but what would fund it now? And what if they didn't dare let him in?

"I carry antibodies against the disease," he told them, speaking again into the microphone. "It's just what might be sticking to me that we have to worry about. So – just put me through decontamination. It's a megavirus: we can filter it out."

They set it up so he could get inside, but it was too late. Before they could reach the safety of the underground elevators that led to the secret labyrinths, a series of explosions destroyed everything on ground level, followed by the sounds of machine guns.

Then a bigger bomb went off, pulverizing the crumpled buildings into heaps of smoking ruins. A wild-eyed man in a ragged white coat, with thick yellow fur growing out from under his collar, waved his machine gun from a distance and tried to scream his approval, but it sounded more like a roar than a scream.

The last thing Larry thought, before his life was blotted out, was that the lions had destroyed everything…

Far below, in the semi-lit, concrete-lined chambers where the hibernating humans were ensconced in their glass and metal cocoons, silent and sleeping, the huge termites, watching over them could feel a trembling in the earth above them. A book fell to the hard, cold floor, and one of the termites picked it up and carefully returned it to the stainless steel table, placing it next to a CD that some human had left behind. The termite understood that the book and the CD had to be very important, since nothing like them existed anywhere else in the underground caverns. Therefore, these objects would be handled with care. As the hours passed into days, and the days passed into weeks, the termites went about their business, caring for the cocoons in which they believed slept their Gods, who would someday, far in the future, surely waken again.

If they did their jobs well.

Endnotes

1. From article by Russell Christian for Human Rights Watch, Apr. 8, 2015. "The 'Killer Robots' Accountability Gap: Obstacles to Legal Responsibility Show Need for Ban" https://www.hrw. org/news/2015/04/08/killer-robots-accountability-gap Retrieved Aug. 23, 2015.

2. One of the first conveniences for the human race, as far as Cyborg parts were concerned, was to implant urine bags in place of bladders for high-stressed athletes. Not only did they help the kidneys (no backup into the kidneys) but they detected urine problems and alerted the wearer as to how much hydration and salts were needed. We thereby know that Larry was an athlete in supposedly superb condition.

3. This is a real laboratory in Hawaii that could conceivably be concerned with emergency rations for space travelers.

4. Should we be reviving gigantic viruses? In July 2013, the journal Science reported the existence of the gigantic Pandora virus: "…these viruses, … are more than mere record-breakers – they also hint at unknown parts of the tree of life. Just 7% of their genes match those in existing databases. "What the hell is going on with the other genes?" asks [virologist] Claverie. "This opens a Pandora's box. What kinds of discoveries are going to come from studying the contents?" The researchers call these giants Pandoraviruses…" Then, in March, 2014, Sci-News. Com reported that a French team of scientists discovered "a new genus of giant virus in 30,000-year-old ice in the north-eastern Siberia, Russia, and managed to revive it in the lab… the study demonstrates that viruses can survive in permafrost almost over geological time periods – for more than 30,000 years, corresponding to the Late Pleistocene…The findings have important implications in terms of public health risks related to the exploitation of mining and energy resources in circumpolar regions, which may arise as a result of global warming…The re-emergence of viruses considered to be eradicated, such as smallpox, whose replication process is similar to Pithovirus, is no longer the domain of science fiction." http://www.sci-news.com/biology/science-pithovirus-sibericum-giant-virus-01791. html Retrieved July 10, 2014.

5. Lone Pine, Calif. – The gas station's ground was covered with the small winged bugs. Piles of carcasses, inches deep, sat swept to the sides. On the road, they rained onto car windshields. They flew by the thousands toward even the smallest sources of light, and crept along windows and kitchen tables. Such has been the skin-crawling reality for the past two months in the high-desert communities at the foot of the Sierra Nevada's eastern slopes, where residents have seen an explosion of the black-and-red seed bug species Melacoryphus lateralis… "Millions, tens, twenty, we can't count it," gas station owner Soma Praba said. "At night time, if you go into the station, they'll follow. They go everywhere. They get on your body, your head." Each morning Praba's workers have spent three hours sweeping the ground and using a leaf blower to clear away piles of the bugs. Around eight times a day, workers will sweep, discovering two hours later that the same amount of bugs are back, Praba said with frustration.

Spraying insecticide hasn't helped, Praba said, and exterminators have been equally stymied. The bugs also have limited natural enemies: Praying mantises and some spiders or lizards will catch a few.

"But the amount of biological control is really insignificant compared to the millions of insects that are out there," said Haviland, the entomologist. And residents are wary of importing more bugs to worry about later.The only reprieve from the seed bugs seems to be a windy day and the recent smoke from fires. "We are tired of it," Praba said. "I am waiting for the first snow to come."… At a Lone Pine gas station this week, the side of the building was covered with bugs, and a woman was hosing off the wall, despite the drought, said Kathi Hall, who owns the town's Mt. Whitney Restaurant with her husband. Ridgecrest Mayor Peggy Breeden said some people in town use umbrellas while getting gas because of the swarms overhead….She put together a notice this week to post around town explaining to visitors that the bugs are a harmless nuisance in the hopes that they'll return when the bugs die down.

That said, Breeden joked, "If frogs come, we're all leaving." AP article, Aug. 22, 2015. http://www.msn.com/en-us/news/us/seed-bugs-swarm-california-communities-invade-homes-cars/ar-BBlXs2w?ocid=HPCDHP Retrieved Aug. 23, 2015.

CRYOGENICS

For over a dozen decades, beginning late in the 20th century, a number of wealthy individuals opted to have their bodies or brains frozen in nitrogen upon death – a number that grew exponentially just prior to the Cyborg Revolution.

The Cyborg Revolution allowed acceptable humans (political enemies and criminals excluded) to choose how much of their bodies (or the bodies of those they owned) would become mechanical and how much would remain "flesh." Tyranny, the creation of mindless sex and labor slaves, and war resulted. Eventually, tissue and organ banks were put to work immortalizing bodies according to an immutable set of rules, using the Baker Single Cell Embedding Process (SCEP). Longevity factors,[1] such as modified super-mitochondria – virtually immortal – unbreakable telomeres, and lifelong nano-surveillance of DNA, where instant repairs on "acceptable DNA" by nanobots would restore any aging cell to vibrant youth, erasing every health problem from aging to cancer for those deemed worthy. It was an age in which beloved pets and rare animals kept in zoos could also live as long as humans wished.

T he Director was heavyset, obviously upper-class, one of the elites allowed to gain weight and muscle, despite the extra cost of cell maintenance thereby. She knew how important she was, for she failed to stand when the students came crowding into the Cryogenics Lab. She was still finishing her supper, not having had time to eat in the Great Hall. The trouble with being a Primitive vegetarian, the Director reflected, was how long it took to chew it all, but she was set in her ways and liked a primal approach to her nutrition. After all, her investigations of Primitives were famous worldwide, and she was allowed to indulge in some eccentricities related to the field.

In the midst of the students who entered was an attractive, once low-er-class, appropriately self-effacing and humble Primitive Historian, who by diligent effort had ascended the academic ranks. She was here with the world's only Primitive Psychologist, her best friend. He was a rather anx-ious fellow, because there was no guarantee that today's Awakening would be successful. He kept checking his recorders and televisors. Meanwhile, the Primitive Doctors (there were only five of them now, in the whole world) busily looked to an array of tubes, monitors, and pulsating pump-ing devices. The equipment was curious and mysterious.

The fact that the Director was here to observe everything was import-ant, because it was being bandied about that the Subject of this Awakening ought to be saved. So much depended on whether the Director agreed. Certainly the Historian, Psychologist and doctors agreed that this Awak-ening was worth funding. There were very few hibernating Subjects still available in the Cryogenic Lab. Above all, they didn't want the Lab shut down for lack of sponsors. Bringing in Students had been the Historian's idea. A band of important Students had recently expressed interest in the long ago. It was their current fad, and it included wearing items on their legs known as "blue jeans." The Historian, hoping to get their sympathies, was herself wearing blue jeans: they looked surprisingly good, emphasiz-ing the sexiness of her slim legs. When the Regional Director of the World had asked to view the Awakening, international Media at once took no-tice. A billion viewers would be watching this rare event.

The Director accepted the bows of the Historian and Psychologist and granted them the necessary front row seats. By doing so, the Students were able to observe that these three personages were Variants. Considerable expense was involved, but it must have been a matter of either wealth or necessity. One was overweight – a privilege reserved for the greatest Lead-ers, who had to dine more often than others due to their having to attend so many social functions: their taste buds were enhanced so they could properly appreciate the efforts of underlings to please them. One was out of uniform, by her choice to wear blue jeans. The third – the psychologist – had been allowed to develop into a Short Person. Such were usually calo-rie-efficient slaves and concubines, but the Psychologist had argued that he had chosen Shortness in order to understand what life had been like for not only short members of the present society, but also so he would not frighten any Primitives who were Awakened. A decent height, reasonable strength, and stunning beauty were so idealized that deviations from these standards among Professionals and Politicians were rare, indeed.

Well, there he was –a short person – yet accorded the status of a Professional. It proved it was possible. The Students stood in respectful silence. They were all the same age, height and weight, and all of them were clad in the uniform of the Nursing Class, except for their Blue Jeans.

Now the Pod, with its sterile clear chamber surrounding it, was rolled into the center of the room. Those watching made certain not to make any expressions of disgust or amazement as the foil-wrapped body of the Ancient One was brought slowly erect inside the hyperbaric chamber. No part of the Subject's body was yet visible, but a humming sound could be heard, accompanied by some liquid that began dribbling onto the floor at the base of the foil-wrapped body. This was never a good sign. They had done all they could: the Ancient One had been thawed very carefully and the tissues that were still viable had been supplied with extra oxygen and mitochondrial energy enhancers. It was now uncertain if this Subject could be stimulated enough to Awaken, though the doctors assured everyone that all would be well. Nano-repair of enough cells to Awaken the Subject was proceeding apace.

The Students' eyes sparkled, hypnotized by the shiny foil-wrapped object that stood glistening under probes, wires, tubing and bright lamps. Slowly, slowly, the machinery of resuscitation was working its magic. Finally, the atmospheric pressure in the Pod was adjusted to normal levels. As dials and shivering tubes and strange meters blinked and clicked, the humming in the Pod slowly decreased, until there was utter silence. The foil was now being carefully withdrawn, layer upon layer, by the doctors, as the Ancient One's chest began to rise and fall … rise and fall…. A soft white robe was gently laid across the Ancient One, covering her withered breasts and nether parts. Then, as she was being sprayed with a hydrating solution that lubricated and nourished her body's dried-out and shriveled skin, she was maneuvered into a sitting position until she was resting in a special chair that put the least possible pressure on her lean buttocks. Doctors then reached inside the plastic bubble, quickly strapping her down at the wrists and ankles.

The time had come.

There was a low, excited rumble of anticipation, which the Director waved to silence. At that moment, a needle pivoted on gimbaled legs and buried itself into one of the pinioned arms of the Ancient One. She responded with a deep, wracked groan, a sucking in and release of a putrid breath that erupted past cracked lips that split into bleeding lines as the almost toothless mouth opened wide, as the dry tongue began to make clicking sounds. A doctor reached again into the sterile capsule surrounding the Ancient One and sprayed more hydrating liquid against the parched tissues of her face and into her eyes and mouth. There was a flutter of the eyelids: first, all that could be seen were the whites of the Ancient One's eyes. Then the eyeballs rolled down. The Ancient One had brown eyes. To the waving of a doctor, the eyes turned toward the movement: she could see.

"The voice will be high-pitched," another doctor noted. "We believe she will speak, but it will be in a very old language peculiar to her race and nation. You will hear an instant translation into our present-day language. Be aware that at first, she will only be speaking in a stream-of-consciousness mode. As she becomes more aware, we don't know how she'll respond to being shackled, but it's for her own safety."

Despite the filters, the air had become fetid, sickening. Nose-plugs were handed out.

"*And Babylon fell!*" the Ancient One's thin, high-pitched voice had come to life! The Psychiatrist and Historian moved closer to the capsule, while all but one of the doctors moved back to make room for them. "*Babylon was destroyed! We creep into the earth, we lay ourselves down in our freezers, we close our capsules, awaiting our salvation!*"

The brown eyes blinked, and the old woman turned her head to look at the Psychiatrist, who was bending close. Now her voice was less shrill, more modulated.

"We left the land above, which we had filled with poisons. The mutations were destroying our children. I was old – I should not have been chosen – but I had money! I closed my eyes, and I dreamed!"

The aged eyes rolled in their sockets, then opened wide. "*Aiieee!*" came the cry. "I'm burning up with pain! *Aiieee!*"

Notebooks were recording, sky-media was getting close-ups, as the aged body began jerking in the chair. They changed the angle, relieving some pressure, and the old lady relaxed. Where the straps held her down, the skin had peeled off, revealing bloody flesh. The smell of old, half-rotting blood permeated everything. Some of the Students shifted from foot to foot; others waved handkerchiefs to try to clear the air. One of the Students, queasy and nauseated, toppled over. He had never seen blood before.

The old woman was wiry, her white hair was like a stiff froth around her old head, as she leaned forward to peer at the Psychologist and Historian.

"You two!" the Ancient One croaked, "Are you the ones who were contracted to bring me back to life? Have you at last discovered the secrets of eternal life for me?"

"We cannot tell you that," the Psychologist said, gently. He was worried. The Ancient One had quite a few brains still left in her head. She was asking important questions.

"Don't yell at me!" the old woman snapped. "Just tell me if it is the right time for me to awake, to arise, and to live forever!"

"It is not yet the right time for you," the Historian told her, speaking with a lowered voice. "But we chose to awaken you anyway. We needed to hear you speak."

"What? What do you mean, 'not the right time'?" The Ancient One's outrage was obvious. "Why annoy me like this? Why torment me, why wake me, before my time? What kind of animals are you?"

"Sorry you're angry, Stella," the Psychologist said apologetically. "But –"

"Yes! My name is Stella! Oh, my God! I am Stella!"

"We regret that we have not yet found a proper way to preserve you forever," the Psychologist went on. "We are trying to decide if it would be financially worth it, in fact, to keep you alive and awake while we research ways to accomplish that. We're going to have a general vote, from the public, on the matter." There was a subdued gasp of shock from the Students. The Psychologist was emotionally battering Stella. Quickly, the Director moved forward, concerned that the Ancient One, who was trembling with wrath and fear, would try to escape her bonds and do harm to herself.

"It will all be very democratic," the Director said, soothingly. "Voting will begin in a few minutes, and we are not very happy with what this man just told you. We want you to be at peace. All will be well."

"You have lived a long time," the Historian added, "and today, you have been honored by being spoken to by one of the three Directors of the New Pach-World. It is a considerable honor. You need to know that as of today, you're four hundred years old. A remarkable feat. As for us, we haven't been able to keep ourselves alive more than thirty years."

"Thirty YEARS?" Stella gasped. "No! Impossible! The normal lifespan was always at least sixty or so years – at LEAST!" The Ancient One began to breathe faster, panic about to overcome her. Her thin, wrinkled skin grew paler. "Then – I beg of you – put me back to sleep! Until you have regained what, obviously, you have foolishly lost!"

"Stella," a doctor put in, "you need to know that at first, everything went well. We were living three hundred – four hundred – five hundred years. But something bad happened."

"Let me tell her," the Psychologist interrupted. "You see, Stella, what happened is that before our Final War, we were enjoying ever-lengthening lifespans. But we left the manufacture of our nano-mechanisms in the hands of robotics. We trusted robotics, beginning with operations conducted by computers."

"I remember," Stella groaned. "The fools trusted computers for everything."

The Historian was miffed that the Psychologist was telling all the history at this important event. It was her job, not his! "It ended," she broke in, "with all our medical sciences having developed beyond our ability to understand what could be done, behind our backs. In secret. And then we all forgot about getting control back, because a Greek General who named himself after Alexander the Great sabotaged the system, in an effort to destroy all immortals. He was killed, but the system was now down beyond repair. Everything from Humans to Dogs started dying again. Everything that had been altered in the Cyborg Revolution was now unable to get anything repaired, if it broke down."

"I have heard of Cyborgs," the Ancient One said slowly. "They were our best hope."

"The final blow came quickly," said the Historian. "We, who survived, were unable to fix the simplest breakdowns in our own bodies. It has taken us decades just to get our immune systems working naturally again."

"Then – put me back to sleep!" Stella demanded. "For I am in pain!"

She winced as another needle automatically probed along her naked arm, trying to find a vein that had not collapsed.

"More oxygen!" a doctor whispered.

"I feel drunk," Stella complained. "Let me have a drink, you who are old at thirty. But I still don't know why you woke me at this unripe time…"

"We are losing you precious Ancient Ones, one by one," the Historian said, choosing her words carefully. "You were alive at the very dawn of the Cyborg Revolution. We care, because you weren't modified. You weren't injected. You represent the last human beings who had fully developed immune systems. You're as important as the mammoths that we brought back from extinction."

"Maybe not *that* important," the Director said. "After all, saving the mammoth was the first successful attempt to repair defective DNA."

"Our hope is that we can experiment upon you," a doctor said, "with our newest DNA-repairing bots. If they will repair your old DNA, they will possibly be able to repair ours. And this time, we won't forget how to stay in control."

"But why me?" Stella moaned. "You said there were others. Why use me?"

"The others are younger. Your DNA is the most damaged."

"Cruelty!" Stella snarled, trying to struggle free from her bonds. "You, with your voices too loud! You, who have become so ugly! You, whose lives have become so short! You don't care at all about me!"

"Yes, we do," the Psychologist responded. "We wanted you to know that we're voting about it. Whether to allow you to be Awakened for the rest of what would be a short life for you, so we can tell you of the progress we're making, so you might be happy for what you're doing to save us, or whether, as one news-person put it, 'the bitch should be killed. We can harvest her tissues. We don't need to deal with her brain and her demands. It will save us an enormous amount of money.'"

Stella had started to shiver as pain and fright worked on her. "But I – I might have special knowledge for you! I was once an –" she hunted for the word – "an animal geriatric specialist. I worked with animals, trying to stop them from aging. That was before I was cryogenically preserved. If you kill me, you might lose information useful to you. And where is your morality?"

The Ancient One's eyes were filling with tears. The old lady stiffened with a harsh pride. Freeing one of her thin, shriveled hands from the restraints, she pointed a shaky finger at the Students. "I feel as if I'm just a pan of pudding that you'll cook. I have feelings! Do you understand? I have feelings!"

The Historian was making a telecast plea. "My friends everywhere!" she called out, "Listen! In all this time, none of those we have revived have ever spoken with such self-awareness. Do not snuff out this light that we have plugged in. Vote to keep her alive!"

The Director now stood, in all her bulk. "I am impressed with you, Stella!" she told the Ancient One. "I suggest that we keep you alive, but not wake you up again. When you finally are killed, you'll never know it. This is a compromise that should please everyone."

"Good idea!" a doctor said. "Maybe someday we could have another vote to wake her up again, if experiments on her will save us. She should be told."

"But what if there's not enough left of her by then?" another doctor objected.

"I was once a brilliant doctor!" Stella croaked out, beginning to sob. "What shall become of me? You thick-skulled fools! Talking about me as if I am just a piece of meat! *Aieee! I'm in agony! I need water!*" The mechanical sprayer applied moisture to her lips: she grit her teeth, then calmed herself.

"Until you came to our University last year," the Historian said, trying again to calm her, "none of our Students had ever seen an Ancient One in the flesh. You are being observed with care and with respect."

"You are a very wonder of a human ruin, Old One," the Director said. "You are currently the oldest human being on the planet. You turned four hundred years old just a few days ago. Congratulations!"

"You utter fools!" Stella snapped back, licking her cracked lips, "You're using me as I had used monkeys! So, no advances have been made in compassion, in kindness, all these years? I wouldn't want to live now, anyway!"

She blinked her eyes, trying to focus them: she could see very little. "Thirty years!" she snorted, "and look at you! All bent over, like you're a hundred years old! And what's happened to your ears? They've become so tiny! And now, you all have buck teeth! And you're *bald!*" Stella leaned back and closed her eyes. "Never mind. Just finish me off. After all we had hoped for – sacrificed for –this is the result?"

"Our standard of beauty has changed over the centuries," the Historian muttered, quite offended. "But at least, we don't discriminate against you due to your wrinkles, or concerning your skin color, as your great-great-grandparents did. I have obtained your entire genealogy, and can assure you of its accuracy."

"I'm fading–" Stella sighed, closing her eyes. "Fading – Babylon has fallen, that great city! Has fallen!"

"We're losing her!" the Psychologist announced.

"More adenosine triphosphate!" a doctor commanded, and a third needle descended and buried itself in Stella's wrinkled arm. It worked. Stella opened her eyes. "Are you going to keep sticking me with needles?"

she groaned. "Why didn't you just put a stent in, so you could just use that for different injections?"

"It had not been thought of," a doctor commented, embarrassed. "We had lost that knowledge. Until now."

"This is why we need to keep her alive!" the Historian told the cameras. "She knows things we have forgotten, in the field of medicine. Consider this, when you cast your vote."

"You have lost so much knowledge!" the Ancient One sighed out. "You have awakened me to this nightmare. Morons! Neanderthals!"

"No, it is not as bad as that," the psychologist objected. "We have no wars. We wiped out all the old diseases. We have no sorrows."

"Do you have any joys?" Stella asked him. "If I could see you clearly, would I see a smiling face? For though a field might be planted with tears, in its harvest, there is joy."

"I do not have the word 'joy' in my vocabulary," the psychologist said apologetically. "It sounds as if it is close to the word 'friendship' or perhaps, to 'having error-free genetic material.'"

"More than that! More than that!" Stella remonstrated. "My poor husband, he warned me–"

The Ancient One's breath was now coming in harsh wheezes: she was losing her battle to stay conscious. "My husband said, 'I will live here and die here. I do not trust a future where the present is so full of death.' Was he right?" A tear fell from the Old One's eye. Blood was dripping from her torn wrist. A new needle was swinging down toward her, in the cobalt blue of the room. She saw it coming…

"No – not another needle!"

"It's to stabilize your breathing," a doctor explained. "This one won't hurt as much."

She screamed when the needle drilled into her: then she began panting. "Did you know the hairless coyote?" she whispered, her eyes closing. "We – we kept him at the Experimental Zoo, along with the Bear-Headed Man, after the Killing Rains. There were so many mutations we needed to study...." For a moment, she was silent. Then she struggled on, between sighs, saying, "The coyote had come from parents born free. He, too, wanted freedom. Wanted to trot out into the radioactive wastes where he had been born. One night, I let him go. Ah, the Institute was angry! But the Coyote was free. He only lived a few months, I suppose…"

Stella leaned back. "If you would help me," she grunted, "I could be free from this place. Why not let me go? Even if I only lived a few months – why do this to me? Strap me down? Can't I live awhile?"

"You condition was terminal," a doctor spoke up. "For sure, you wouldn't live more than a few months. Maybe a year."

"Besides the expense," the Director added. "Having to delay. Waiting for your tissues until you died."

"Can you live in the outside world, yet?" Stella wanted to know. They sensed it was her last question, for she was collapsing forward, tremors now shaking her body. "I still have eggs in my ovaries, did you know that? If you kill me, won't you at least save my eggs?"

She had slipped into a deep series of long breaths. They came longer.... deeper...

"Quickly!" a doctor ordered, "re-inject her with the cryogenic solution!"

As the expensive fluids were prepared, to be pumped and circulated throughout the wrinkled body, now quite still, the web-works of delicate wires and tubes were withdrawn, one by one, from Stella's flaccid body. A film of delicate plastics fell over her, as she was lifted to a standing position again. The plastics formed a shield between her and the foam that then quickly enveloped her frail frame. A shower of crystals fell like snow around her, as the Pod whitened with cold. A shiny device whirled layer upon layer of foil around the Ancient One, as a spinning spider's wrap-work might, until the Subject was a cocoon again. The repacking took only fifteen minutes. It was all automated.

The Pod was wheeled back into the great black, metal box from whence it had come. All air was pumped out, nitrogen was pumped in, and it was hermetically sealed. The box itself was then lifted by robotic arms and laid inside a vault. As those great doors slammed shut, a doctor moved to stand between the Director and the Students.

It was time for the Psychologist to recite his final report. The vote would come after hearing and questioning his presentation.

"Students, before you and the World cast your votes, please record my comments. Subject Stella 7-OH was preoccupied with the desire to live, despite her great age. The rage reflex was still intact, despite all the preconditioning we used before she was Awakened. There were no masochistic tendencies, but there was some confusion concerning her belief that she was worthy to be kept alive. As is usual in these cases, pain interrupted a great deal of what she tried to communicate. There was a definite interest in why our lives are now so short."

The Psychologist flipped to another section of his module and continued: "Compare Subject Stella 7-OH with Subject John 5-OH, who does not even care to live, in what would amount to a level of severe and chronic pain, because of the evil memories of his last days, also spent in pain. Any questions?"

There was a timorous wave from one of the Students in the back of the room.

"Are coyotes dogs?"

A doctor, obviously irritated, retorted, "You were supposed to have received that data back in Comparative Mammals! To refresh your memory, coyotes were domesticated for dog racing, became hairless due to the Blessed Rains that wiped out our most dangerous enemies, and are known for their complex teeth, which are in double rows, and for possessing two tails. There are rumors that some coyotes did survive in the Outside World. That makes Stella 7-OH's story of interest to our geneticists."

The Psychologist then stood forth again. "I wish to remind you doctors, that after all my cautioning, you still seem to credit these half-dead, prehistoric Subjects as having accurate memories! Don't confuse her drug-derived ravings with reality. It should be noted that Subject Stella 7-OH was still unable to recognize any of us, and had totally forgotten that she had been previously resuscitated, even though this is the third time that we have Awakened her. Any more questions?"

Another student waved to gain attention. "Will Stella ever remember a previous Awakening?"

The Psychologist's short, little body shook with suppressed laughter and scorn. "Have you been sleeping, sir? We drained off her memories, for her own good. They've been canistered and can be returned to her, if we feel it would be the best for her. But they're traumatic memories."

"But you just faulted her for not remembering previous Awakenings," the student persisted. He read aloud from his notes: "Quote: 'It should be noted that Subject Stella 7-OH was still unable to recognize any of us, and had totally forgotten that she had been previously resuscitated, even though this is the third time that we have Awakened her. Why criticize her for not remembering them, if you canistered her memories?"

"*How dare yo*u!" the Psychologist trumpeted out, his face reddening with rage.

"How dare *you*?" the Historian shot back. "Why do you hate Stella so much?"

"Because – " the Psychologist could feel a Fit coming on – a Fit of Anger that he must control at all costs, or all would be lost – "because you care more about Stella than you do about me!"

The Students gasped. The Psychologist, suddenly aware of how far he had overstepped things, shrilled out a fierce curse on them all and stomped from the room.

The Historian now stood forth, trembling with excitement and anger. "Let's proceed, before the vote, in an orderly manner," she said, keeping her voice steady and professional, though the redness of her face betrayed her inner turmoil. "To elaborate a little on Stella's memory, this Subject's brain has been remarkably well preserved so far. However, our doctors have told me that we are coming close to exhausting her final reserves of glycogen. We have to make up our minds whether we'll let her live a few months – or years – on life support, where she will be aware – able to live some kind of life – or whether we should allow her to die and use her tissues now. Any more questions?"

The same Student nervously waved, to gain her attention.

"Yes?"

"Why can't we examine lower animals first, before waking these people?"

"Some of your modern friends may find it reprehensible to use people like this," the Historian agreed, "but remember: you will not find a thousand howls of a hairless coyote as important as fifty words coming from the throat of an Awakened Subject."

"I think every human life is valuable, in whatever state it's in," another student commented. "I think Stella should be allowed to live, because she wants to. That's good enough for me."

"Are there any other questions?" the Director asked. This was actually a signal that all questions should now cease. After a polite pause, the Director said, "Well, then, you may be seated."

The Historian had been barely able to conceal her anger over her boyfriend's bad behavior. *Well, that's the end of him!*" she thought. *Good riddance!*

"Experiment 7-OH is now over," the Director said. "Please cast your final votes."

The Students sat down slowly, took up their modules, and voted. The Historian cleared her nose, stuffy with her tears, and cast her vote, too. In a few moments, the entire World had done the same. The Director then stood again, and the room hushed down. "We've been told," she said, "that we will not be able to revive Stella many more times. It might be better to allow her to live awhile. It's her desire. Of course, that would be expensive, and this University would need a strong 'yes' vote to allow that." The Director turned toward the Media recorders. "So, have the votes come in?"

"They have," a reporter responded.

"So, what is the verdict?" the Director asked. "Does she live, or does she die?"

The Historian knew, instinctively, what the final vote would be, despite all the efforts to try to make it look fair. The Director realized it, too, and as the others left the room, she sat herself down next to the Historian, who was weeping. The Director was so important that by this very act, the Historian's status and income would be higher, safer and more secure for the rest of her life.

"Madame," the Director told her, closing her module to private, "do you *really* want human beings to become aware, and maybe contaminate the world again? What would be next? Rehabilitating Stella so she could walk among us, talk among us, and feed us peanuts? Consider what they did to us, cutting our lifespan in half, before we finally conquered them!"

And the two elephants rumbled together in agreement that, after all, it was a very good thing that the humans still left on the planet were all safely ensconced in cryogenic capsules, where they belonged.

Endnotes

1. The Hayflick Limit Theory of Aging (expounded by Dr. Leonard Hayflick) is based on observations that the human cell can divide only a limited number of times. When it reaches that limit, the cell dies. Mitochondria are organelles that exist inside most living cells, providing the preponderance of energy used by the cell and thereby the body as a whole. When mitochondria die, eventually the body will die. "There is compelling evidence that mitochondria in animals and chloroplasts in plants were once primitive bacterial cells. This evidence is described in the endosymbiotic theory." ("The Cells that Changed the Earth" http://learn.genetics.utah.edu/content/cells/organelles/)

"**Frozen child: The youngest person to be cryogenically preserved**" by Jonathan Head 15 Oct. 2015

"Sahatorn and his wife Nareerat have three other children. Nareerat had to have her uterus removed after the first birth, so Einz and her younger brother and sister were conceived through IVF. Technology, they say, played a central role at the very start of her life, and could well help restore it.

The Naovaratpong family chose Alcor, an Arizona-based non-profit organisation that is the leading provider of what it calls "life extension" services, to carry out the preservation of Einz's brain. The family was closely involved in the preparations, designing the special coffin in which she would be transported to the United States.

[A] ... team from Alcor flew to Thailand to supervise the initial cooling of the body. As the little girl deteriorated, she was moved from hospital to her own room. The moment she was pronounced dead, the Alcor team began what is known as "cryoprotection"; removing bodily fluids and replacing them with forms of anti-freeze that allow the body to be deep frozen without suffering large-scale tissue damage.

After arriving in Arizona her brain was extracted, and is preserved at a temperature of -196C. She is Alcor's 134th patient, and by far its youngest.

[The family] also plan to visit the Alcor facility, to see the steel container in which Einz's brain is being kept in what the company calls "biostasis." The Naovaratpongs say they have donated similar sums of money to what they have spent on Einz's cryopreservation to cancer research in Thailand.

Alcor says its operation is "an experiment in the most literal sense of the word." It does not promise a second chance at life, but says cryonics is "an effort to save lives."

It says "real death" only occurs when a dying body begins to shut down and its chemicals become so "disorganised" that medical technology cannot restore them. Future technology could make it more likely that the process can be reversed.

Moments after a customer is declared legally dead, the body is put on artificial life support, and blood replaced with preservatives, for transportation from anywhere in the world to Alcor's headquarters.

The body is flooded with chemicals called "cryoprotectants," which cool cells to -120C without ice forming, a process called vitrification.

The body is then cooled further to -196C and stored indefinitely in liquid nitrogen.
http://www.bbc.com/news/world-asia-34311502

ALGORITHM

"We forget that the systems we build are as fallible, political and biased as ourselves."

– Christopher Steiner, "Algorithms Are Taking Over The World," TEDxOrangeCoast, 2015.

Algorithm: 2430 AD definition [algə-riT-Həm] noun: 1. A process or set of rules to be followed using calculations, especially by a computer. 2. In mathematics and computer science, a self-contained step-by-step set of operations to be performed by a sentient being, monitored by the Elite. 3. In set theory, an ordinal number, or ordinal, is the order type of a well-ordered set. 4. Sentient ordinals are usually identified with hereditarily transitive sets. Ordinals originated as a sub-species derived from human beings at the time of the Pentultimate Cyborg Revolution of 2120 AD.

As I sat in the Pod, avoiding the glances of the Ordinals, I wondered if I should have told Antares, my latest brain-mate and orgasm-witness, that I was planning on taking a vacation. Not only that: I was planning to somehow take her with me.

That was almost unheard-of. As of last year, I had become one of Antares' Angels. One of her primary contacts who took care of her – provided for her – used her. Gently. More gently, I knew, than the others did. I think she appreciated that. Certainly, if she knew that I was going to be testing this Algorithm today, she might have been concerned. We had been together a long time, at least three weeks, and since this was our third cycle together in two years I knew – or I hoped – she would care enough to provide some comfort and understanding after I told her how I had been Punished today.

It was still stinging my brain. In my half-erased memory of it, with a surge of resentment, I wanted to keep the memory alive, so I ran over the exchange I'd had with Mickey. I went over it five, six, seven times. Each time I did, I became more frightened. For Mickey was no ordinary Algorithm. He was the Word Monitor for over a million Ordinals – all of them living in my sector of the city.

Before I even said the test word to him, Mickey had picked it up as illegal.

"You can't use that word," Mickey had told me.

"Why not?"

"It doesn't exist."

"So what? I invented it."

"Can't use it."

I'd been arguing a bit with Mickey, true enough, but that isn't forbidden. It's almost my duty. But even though I was giving him all the correct signals that I was no threat (I even began to back away), *his face began changing*.

That was a bad sign. By the time I had said "I invented it," Mickey's face looked like mine, and it was my mouth in his body speaking the words "Can't use it" back at me.

That made me angry. I'm a Freeman. I'm a Linguistic Engineer; specialty, English. My particular duty is to check on the soundness of the English Algorithms regularly, including even the most important one of them all – Mickey, the Word Monitor. It was the most important link to the Main Controlling Algorithm over what was officially left of the English language.

Now, Mickey is not really a 'he.' He's an 'it,' but I liked being a little personal. I'd been working with him for almost forty years. Mickey is there to make sure there's no inappropriate use of a word. Overseeing the Algorithms that regulate the use of English is a major part of my job.

As one of the best Freeman Engineers on the planet, whose memory hasn't been cleared out (and I'm careful to not let that happen), I even have the privilege of writing down my thoughts, because my job is to preserve the necessary portions of the English language and keep it understandable, even to the Ordinals, those poor creatures who work so hard to keep us all in a perfectly secure society.

True enough, I might have gone a bit too far.

I'd become fascinated with the idea of not only preserving the legal words in The English Language, but allowing the list of legal words to grow. Just a little. New words keep a language dynamic. Today, however, was a little different. I was supposed to test the Word Monitor Algorithm with a new word, to check its sorting and censorship functions. There was nothing "wrong" with the test word I had selected, by the way. Its only flaw is that it was unknown to Mickey.

As I'd done several times before over the past decades, I inserted the new word, as was my right, and watched as Mickey rolled his eyes and digested it.

Mickey's real name was Anthrax 7, but because he had two large ear-like appendages on both sides of his "face" I liked to call him "Mickey," after the famed black rodent of the twentieth century.

Problem was, Mickey was not only white instead of black, he was also not nearly as nice as his bulb-nosed, whip-tailed namesake. Sure, he was likely to reject the new word. That was okay. In fact, he probably should have rejected it, because this new word had not come about through real events occurring in the world of Ordinals.

I was taking a rather unusual approach, for the third time in my career – testing Mickey with a brand-new word of my own creation. My new word – "lunarline" – had been sitting in my craw for nearly fifteen years. It was all grown up now. My wish was to inject it into the English Vocabulary. Lunarline was my baby.

All went well at first: I had told Mickey that lunarline meant 'to emit a mother-of-pearl, moon-like light, an opalescence, as in, "Her face had a lunarline glow."

Of course Mickey immediately rejected the new word, just as he was supposed to. That was good. What wasn't good is that Mickey didn't give me a chance to petition: he didn't ask me to provide an event that made the new word useful or necessary.

Instead, his white visage began to glow with a fiery red color. *Anger!* I'd been all set to tell him about the event (which I'd rigged) that brought the word into the vocabulary of the Ordinals, but Mickey didn't give me a chance. Instead, his flushed, red face started changing shape, so that *now* he began to look like me.

That kind of threat was terrifying.

After all, I'm an Engineer. I'm supposed to be able to walk around the Algorithms and among the Ordinals with unveiled eyes. See them as they really are. To watch that stunning change come over Mickey's face, as it began morphing into my own, was unsettling. Frightening.

Had I made the System angry at me?

Before I could finish the question in my head, Mickey was Anthrax, with a vengeance. The wave of Punishment erupted in my brain with the force of a massive electrical shock. I fell backwards, caught only at the last moment by the arms of a Botambulance driver, who had screeched to a halt behind me at the last possible moment.

"Get out!" Mickey screamed. "Before I kill you!"

Withered by that scream, I fainted into the Botambulance's grip. The next thing I knew, I had been deposited in the Pod and was being whisked back to my Hive; I was in no state to pass the Guardian. My chemistry had changed due to my tension and pain, so I had to go through the De-Tox chamber first. This is no fun, and it's only allowed a few times a week, or you can get put on the Terrorist List. Being calm, cool, efficient and Selfless is the key to survival.

As I staggered from the De-Tox chamber with fresh clothes, I had to step over the smoking remains of an Ordinal who probably had lost its way and accidentally stepped in front of the Guardian of the Hive. Soon the Cleaners would remove the bones, implants and ashes to be recycled. A stench of flesh that neither Bots nor Ordinals could smell reeked sickeningly in my nostrils, as a renegade thought suddenly arose in my brain: too *many Ordinals are stepping in front of Guardians.* I immediately shut down the thought, lest the Guardian pick it up and send me back into the Chamber. It might have been a Revolutionary Thought – the list of forbidden thoughts had recently been growing – but as an Engineer, I had to notice changes. That was my reason for existence. As I raised my face to look at the Guardian, I reshaped the thought for it: *Are there more than the usual number of Ordinals stepping in front of Guardians?*

"Bring the question to the next meeting," the Guardian replied, in my brain. "Your amended thought is duly noted."

I had scored! I allowed a slight smile to change my facial expression as I was tubed up to my luxurious suite. Unlike the hexagonal ports of the Algorithms, unlike the studio apartments and the slum tunnels of the Ordinals (inhabited efficiently by tenants who rotated in and out of these warrens between work shifts), I had a large penthouse apartment to myself, overlooking the city. I could regulate the light, eat real food, select my own music, my own reading, my own vids, and, most important, select my own Star – Antares – my favorite brain-mate and orgasm-witness. The Stars were reserved for only the highest levels of Engineers and Elites, designed as we wished, with wills of their own for the sake of additional entertainment. When I was first advanced enough in my job to get one, I wondered if a Star could be called a genuine human. After long experience, I know they're human, just as I am human. And they can see different faces, just as I can, if they have a high enough clearance.

We have many rights forbidden to Ordinals. We have freedoms. We're the friends of the Masters.

Antares was waiting for me with a meal she had created with her own hands. Her beauty was astonishing: she had silky black hair in the Old

Way, instead of the complex, interlocking structures that most Stars grew atop their skulls. I like mine Natural, which is considered a bit eccentric. But I've always been eccentric: I have even resisted the free weekly facelifts. *Bravo, nature!* I even had pheromone-scent glands implanted under my arms to help sexually excite my Stars – I'm one of a few males on the planet whose parents refused to breed me to be born with both kinds of sex organs. They were old-fashioned: I was actually grown inside a human surrogate mother, one of the last of her kind. That's the kind of pioneer spirit that was in my parents.

Some people feel sorry for me because I've been deprived of female sex organs. Maybe after I become very old and impotent, another few hundred years from now, I'll turn female and see how it feels.

Sadly, both of my parents are no longer alive: they refused to accept new engineered brains to replace their own, as they aged, even though we would have saved all their memories and given them back the faces of their youth. I resent that. I resent the fact that I lost my parents because they wouldn't adapt to the modern world.

Their last wish was that I would someday have children through a Surrogate, even though that's now illegal. I do understand that I was indoctrinated by my parents so that I would *love* them. It's an embarrassment, a blot on my near-perfect historical record. Entanglements with others on a love-basis is a very inefficient way to run a social system. It leads to corruption, impulses to hoard, wanting power over those you *don't* love. It's selfish to be like that. The word itself is no longer supposed to exist.

The word certainly doesn't exist in common English anymore. About the time my parents selfishly left this planet to be recycled, the word was removed from the active vocabulary. About thirty years ago, it was removed from the passive vocabulary.

I understand the word is still used by Terrorists.

I only remember the word because it is on the forbidden list. I'm responsible to make sure that forbidden words don't creep into Ordinal vocabulary lists. Even a Word Monitor Algorithm might be fooled by a synonym such as "adore." The word is so powerful it could be linked to "religion," a word I dare not speak aloud – that can get you killed.

Not that English is used much anyway, except among we who are Elites. 99% of the time, there is no need to speak: we think instead. It's faster and, usually, clearly what we mean. The algorithms implanted in our brains make communication as simple as breathing. But just as it's pleasant to eat real food instead of taking the daily rations, in the same way, 'talk' is a skill and mental exercise that is practiced among not only our artists, actors, and musicians, but also among our Leaders and Engineers, especially if we wish to communicate in secret about Ordinals or Algorithms.

As for Ordinals, they don't have a clue as to what freedoms they live without.

They respond. They obey. Or else.

Of course, Algorithms run everything for the Elite. They are the Guardians, the Soldiers, the Standardizers, the Punishers and Rewarders. Selfless, incorrupt, and perfect, their only goal is to keep us alive and well. Whether we like it or not.

I'm saying all of this to Antares. Using words. From my mouth. Unlike my former companions, this one has a kind of aberration: she likes to listen to words coming from my food-eating orifice. She can even use a few English words (two at a time, which is impressive). I've been holding onto her because it's rare to find a Talker. I recall that women were once known for their habit of talking. Some bit of tissue deep in Antares' brain seems to have escaped re-wiring. She can talk.

At my age, and because I am a certified Male, I can take a Star for long periods of time. Up to three weeks, every year or so. Because I approve of her enough, I have become her Angel. Stars are usually actresses who are engineered to physically resemble traditional females. Some of them might be able to function as real females (that's kept secret). There are perhaps three thousand males who have kept a Star, out of our three million Elites. Rare, but not forbidden.

Because of us, Stars can afford to take roles in plays, movies, and hologrammatic historic reconstructions. I have helped Antares gain some prestige as a Star. She has been grateful. As my brain-mate and orgasm-witness, she has given me much pleasure in return.

As I eat the food she has crafted, she therefore tries to pleasure me even more, by speaking more than two words at a time.

"Why you have sad face" she asks.

Antares reaches over and touches a frown line between my eyes. She has learned about legal facial expressions because she's an actress. A frown is legal, as long as no words are spoken. She has always correctly translated the slight facial expressions I am allowed to make, even though none of us dare to reveal more than anybody else about what we feel. None of us should express ourselves and stand out as needing more attention than anybody else. That's why all sex is conducted with eyes closed. But because she will cheat and take a glimpse of my face (God! I hope no Bot ever sees her do it.) it makes her great in bed.

Terrific, even.

I don't tell her that she's becoming important to me. If I say it the wrong way, she could become frightened, might think I was a Terrorist or something. I have to be very careful. So I start slowly.

"Did you have a mother or a father?" I ask her.

"No. I am from M-17 Plant."

"Do you know who created you?"

"Yes," Antares says, proudly. "Experiment. Experiment created me."

This I did not know. It sends a shiver down my neocarbon spine; my bony skeleton was 100% replaced by the System by the time I was sixty years old, but I can still experience the shiver of fear.

"System didn't mention Experiment on your stat sheet," I said. I saw by her puzzled expression that she didn't understand me, so I tried again.

"Antares, they did not say you could Talk."

She reached over and with her soft, pink hand touched my mouth.

"They do not know."

She said it with a glitter in her eyes that was both fierce and sexy.

I felt something inside me that was forbidden. A feeling I was not supposed to feel. That selfish thing. That wicked thing. I had access to a Secret.

It was explained to me, when they were found dead (I was not to call them 'parents' anymore). Above all, they were supposed to stay loyal to the System. Thus I was not to show sorrow, affection or emotions, for they had, technically, killed themselves. They had been wasteful to do that. Their labors were now lost to the System. They had, in their time, been important Engineers themselves, also in the field of Linguistics. I was ordered to spit on their half-burned corpses. Of course, I did so.

But because they died with smiles on their faces, something inside of me made me reject getting refurbished with both sets of sex organs. I had been born a true Male. I kept it that way in their honor, may the System forgive me!

"Would you like to know my name?" I asked black-haired Antares.

"Name?"

"It is one's ID," I explain.

"Oh. I am Star Antares. B-17, Block A, Batch 901, Experiment."

"But I am Baby Boy."

"Baby Boy?"

"A special ID – special name – the two Engineers who bred me. They gave me the name."

"Gave you ID?"

"I did not come from a batch!" I told her. She stiffened in horror and drew back.

"No ID?"

"Oh, I have an ID. But no batch number."

I could see that I might lose Antares if I dared say anything more. I'd managed to hold onto the memory of my parents because they had given me a Name. Baby Boy. I was different from others – so was Antares. From her long neck to her long fingers, she was at least a centimeter longer on both parts. She was also a full three centimeters taller than other Stars. Just enough to make her exotic, not enough to get her recycled.

There wasn't any more I dared say to her. I could lose her.... For some reason, that would not be acceptable. We switched to thoughts.

Stay. I insisted, telepathically. *No go.*

I stay. I like. That's what her throbbing thoughts conveyed, as she expertly prepared excitatory hormones to inject, with her microprobes, into my flesh.

Into the machinery she next brought out, as she had been trained, I then descended, as she gently stroked my protruding parts... no more talk. *Brain-mate! Glorious orgasm-witness!* Even the Patrol Bots flying past, scanning for unusual behavior, probing as they heard us moan together, could not detect that I liked Antares any more than any of the Stars before her. I made sure to keep my face from the windows and hoped they could detect no change of expression on my face.

Five hours later, my Rest Period was over. I was one of the fortunate ones who got a daily rest and recreation period, primarily because my brain was so important. Unlike Algorithms, who only went down for maintenance for an hour a day, and unlike Ordinals, who worked forty-eight hour shifts to earn a six-hour break to eat and sleep, I had twice as many hours to myself. There was talk that downtime for Engineers might be able to be cut to four hours a day, with a new kind of implant, but so far, such devices hadn't been successful. Dullness and apathy tended to infest the overworked brain: the drive to obey and to produce for the System became seriously impaired in Elites. Secretly, I suspected that some of these reports were rigged by the Leaders, to keep us from committing suicide.

As I rode the Pod to the Algorithm Center, dazed as always by the calming swirl of lights and impulses meant to ensure calm and eradicate all violence, I wore my F-Mask – a requirement for all Engineers when among the Ordinals. It must not be known that my F-implant was turned off.

You need to know that all Ordinals possesed a variety of faces, even though an Ordinal could only see its own face on the face of any other Ordinal. That stopped them from seeing the differences that were there, from hooked noses to baggy eyes to fat lips. Otherwise, they were not much different from each other. All Ordinals were 150 cm high. Their small height and light weight meant they required fewer calories. Only Athletes, bred for various games, differed in height or weight. As to pigment, every Ordinal had melanin and was brown-skinned, to help protect it from the sun. The Ordinal's pride and joy was the variety of clothing it could wear. Fashion, of course, could not be extreme: no one could go naked, no one could wear more than two layers of clothing –that would be selfish. But the cascade of colors and the variety and design of their flowing garments made Ordinals recognizable to each other, even though they saw only one face everywhere (their own).

There was a social rule, too: one level could not wear purple. Another level could not wear blue. And so on. But all levels could wear red or yellow.

What got to me today, as I stood in the Pod, was that it was swaying more than usual as it sped along. Though I tried to block the memory, I could recall the specter of Mickey's face changing, so that he started to look like me. It was a shock. It gave me an idea of what Ordinals had to deal with all the time.

Although I could see their real faces, and had learned to identify many of them, an Ordinal never saw anything but its own face impressed on everyone else's face. It was the number one way to stop Insurrections, Conspiracies and Riots.

All Ordinals were implanted at birth with a recognition device that reconstructed, in their brains, every face they looked at as identical to their own.

From my studies of linguistics, I understood that the "F" implant had been hailed as a tremendous breakthrough of technology that basically eliminated vanity, illegal meetings, and "love." Because the entire population of Ordinals couldn't be implanted at once – it took a few weeks – at first there were wholesale riots. I was told that over a million Ordinals chose suicide rather than subject themselves to the "F" implant, which they called "666 – the Mark of the Beast." It was placed in their hand or foreheads at first. Later, it was simply inserted deep into the cerebral cortex.

For the past sixty-five years, every Ordinal had only been able to see its own face on all other Ordinals. This still caused an occasional problem, such as when it came to trying to help another Ordinal get something out of its eye, or trying to exchange ID nose rings. ID nose rings came in a variety of shapes and were one of the few legal ways that one Ordinal was able to look a bit different from another. Of course, outrageously unusual ID nose rings were a sign of ego, defiance and selfishness and were banned. ID Nose ring Police Bots could confiscate an ID nose ring at any time and fine the offender, so the differences were usually subtle, such as a different number or a small jewel. Nothing that would be too noticeable.

Not everyone had an "F" implant that was switched on all the time. I was a Freeman. All Engineers, Inventors, Stars, Surgeons, Athletes, Artists, Actors and Leaders kept them switched off. They were also Freemen. Only those of us who might come under arrest for criminal thoughts or acts would have the "F" implant turned on against one's will.

Instead, we wore F-Masks when among Ordinals and Algorithms. The F-Masks reflected the same faces that any given Ordinal saw around it – its own – whereas we Elites could see everyone's faces, safe behind our F-Masks. Our ability to see all those real faces was important, especially if we encountered an Ordinal Leader. Our first duty was always to protect any Leader, even an Ordinal Leader, from Terrorists. The F-Mask gave us the ability to learn who was important among the Ordinals. A few of them had a smattering of intelligence that was useful in helping direct fashions, trends, and political movements. Since the few Leaders among them were capable of creating loyal factions, it was important to keep them identified, located, indoctrinated and controlled.

Terrorists are easily identified because they have had illegal operations to remove the F-implants. Today, I know that all the original Terrorists were Leaders. Before they were banished or executed, they seduced other Leaders and Freemen to choose the path of lust, evil, love, selfishness and ego. They became the source of all our problems. Hence, it is our duty to ferret them out and destroy them.

I suppose this is what hurt the most. After all these years, Mickey, who knew how loyal I was, had turned against me. Though I had subjected Mickey to a perfectly legal test, which was my duty, he had not only tuned on my F-implant, which was illegal, but he Punished me when I resisted it. Mickey's reaction frightened and humiliated me. What would he do next? Instigate an anti-Terrorist Algorithm against me? What if he thought I was thinking Terrorist thought? Luckily for me, I had reacted appropriately to seeing my face forming on his, and said the right words. It saved me. Mickey turned it off, but not before giving me a harsh, painful jolt of electrical Punishment.

As I rode the Pod, I thought briefly of Antares. Soon, I'd have to let her go again, or I would be accused of having *affection*. I knew that the phenomenon – that she could *talk* – was affecting my better judgment. My big, impossible dream was that she could accompany me on my upcoming Vacation.

Every five years, Engineers were allowed a one-month Vacation to a different part of the Planet. It had been determined that this induced Engineers – especially those who were Linguists such as myself – to want to stay alive longer. It was expensive to replace us, but melancholy and depression seemed to be a chronic issue for us, as well as for Inventors, Artists and Musicians. Had it not been for Stars, who were always, so to speak, on Vacation, many more replacements would have been necessary, at great cost to the System. All of this had been ironed out in the past hundred years.

My ride to the Algorithm Center was going along smoothly, and I was dreaming of my imminent Vacation, when suddenly, the Pod stopped, toppling over some of the weaker Ordinals (they were always tired, after all). Then the Ordinals began screaming as the Pod's sleek gray walls shivered from an unknown force.

As I tried to calm the Ordinal nearest to me, which was my duty, the Pod's great gray exit door popped open, and I, too, started to scream. I had to in order to cover up my superior brain and my identity, lest I be gunned down by a Terrorist! I tried to control my sweat glands under my arms: the pheromones could give me away: Ordinals couldn't afford such luxuries, and some Terrorists had Dogs, an animal I have seen only in System Reports, known to have dripping fangs and high-pitched yelps. Dogs can smell out non-Ordinals.

A harsh order to fall on our faces reverberated in our brains, and we all collapsed, all one hundred of us, in the Pod. There it stood: a Terrorist! It wore an F-mask, which it then pulled up, revealing its ugly Face. It had a hairy chin. Male. The Terrorist stared into the Pod from the open doorway, as if seeking a certain face. It was the first time I had seen a Live Terrorist. I had only seen executed Terrorists previously, their faces burnt to skull-bone from lasers. Now I saw a Terrorist's face in the flesh – and fleshy it was. Or was it an 'it', I wondered, or was it a He, like me? It was heavier than the legal weight. It had (the thought was sickening) accumulated several kilos of excess flesh and fat, which was not only forbidden, it was the epitome of evil, selfishness and a reckless waste of our precious resources!

Some of the waste was muscle, rippling along its hairy arms, almost like the rigging of muscles I'd seen in a photo of a Viking warrior, in an old book. This one had some kind of armor on, under the usual colorful, flowing garments. Suddenly, it held up a kind of energy shield as a Security Bot flew toward it from the back of the Pod: there was a flash of fire from the shield, and the Bot, smoking, made a birdlike screech and crashed. It landed on an unfortunate Ordinal, who cried out in pain as the dying Security Bot's needles injected and killed the wrong target. Then the Terrorist grimaced. Maybe it was reacting to the Ordinal's unfortunate disposal. What a face! I could see what the Ordinals around me could not: a hard, wrinkled forehead that hadn't seen plastic surgery for months, a harsh, tight mouth. It was filled with glistening, white teeth – yes, full-sized teeth, dangerous, and no doubt viciously used when necessary. As it surveyed us, we who were flat on our faces, afraid to move, held our breaths … I saw it pause in its slow scope when it looked upon me … I could not have seen its face at all, except my head was atop someone else's trembling rump. I cursed my bad luck: I wasn't wearing a nose ID ring: would it realize what I was?

Suddenly, the Terrorist heaved a round, shiny object toward the light fixture and jumped back, just as the Pod door slammed shut. The Pod's emergency programming had finally re-sealed the door, but even as the Pod lurched into motion, the shiny object exploded.

A shower of hot, plastic confetti rained down upon us, igniting the clothing of several screaming Ordinals: it was a drone bomb! There were more screams as dozens of mini-drones spread tiny wings and, sputtering with sparks, crashed into the overhead light. The light exploded, showering debris over us; we were plunged into darkness, but not before I was able to read, on a streamer that a drone brought safely to my arm, two words written in gold: *She Talks.*

Where was I?

The last I could remember was a suffocating smoke filling my lungs before I passed out. I blinked, tried to get up, and was immediately restrained by Bot arms that gently eased me back into the Repair Unit. Suddenly, a bodiless, humanoid face hovered over me, gently whispering into my brain that all was well. I relaxed. I was going to be OK, it intoned, but to reassure me, I'd soon have a real human to talk to. A few seconds later, a hologram started to talk to me: it was a real Doctor, Grade Two.

"Feeling better?" it asked.

"Yes," I told it. You always said you were better. You had to, or expensive things could happen. Unpleasant probes, that could cost days and days of vacation.

"Did I lose Vacation days?" I asked. It was a reasonable question, since all Engineers needed the break every five years.

"You only lost two days," the Doctor assured me. "You sustained some damage to your right lung from the incendiary device." The doctor was using its superior English on me, apparently unaware that I was an English Language Engineer. Others would have been blown away by its big words: they weren't used much, of course, by even we, who were the Elite, but concerning medical matters, English speech was used because of its precision. Besides, the Doctor was obviously enjoying showing off its literacy.

"Can I leave?" I asked, knowing that every hour I spent in Repair removed that hour from my Vacation ration.

"Not until the Psychiatrist talks to you."

The hologram vanished, and a second hologram took its place. To present itself as all the more authoritative, I presume, the Psychiatrist had an Athlete's body. It was the current fashion. I had to turn my thoughts as blank as possible to disguise my dislike of Psychiatrists. They so enjoyed doing a Probe. And I had two secrets, after all: I *liked* a Star, and I had invented a word without being able to claim a real event that made the word necessary. Sure enough, within moments, the Psychiatrist picked up that thought, and focused on it.

"So… you invented the word "lunarline" without a precipitating event to account for it?" As I tried to formulate a denial in my brain, it hurled a punishing bolt of pain into my cerebral cortex.

"You don't do that to somebody like me!" it snapped.

I writhed with pain: tears stung my eyes. Slowly, the world came back into focus…

"It's gone now," it assured me, after I began breathing normally.

"What's gone?" I asked.

"The illegal word. You're clean now. According to your records, it's the third time you've done that since you were certified," it said, flexing its artificial muscles. "I checked."

"But I've been forgiven," I said defensively. "I have to work with the most advanced Algorithms involved with the English language, and to test

The Word Monitor Algorithm, I had to come up with unusual linguistic challenges." Tears began rolling down my cheeks. "It's not fair."

The Psychiatrist raised a fuzzy, caveman-style eyebrow. It was intrigued.

"What does 'not fair' mean?" it asked.

I paused… the Psychiatrist hadn't learned any such pair of words.

"*Not fair* means an Algorithm has malfunctioned," I said, warily. "It punished the Engineer before the Engineer made the error."

Half strangling my thoughts, which roiled with anger at what the Algorithm had done to me – I didn't want the Psychiatrist to change its mind – I whispered, "Go check my Incident Reports. The Supplementary Section."

"I'll check them," it said. In an instant, it vanished. In another instant, it appeared. "You're correct," it admitted. "One of the Algorithms you're responsible for played a dirty trick on you. Its ID is Anthrax 7. Yes, you had the responsibility to invent the three words, to test that particular Algorithm." The Psychiatrist smiled. "How fascinating! It punished you *before* you tested it! As if trying to stop you from conducting a legal Probe. Sorry. Sometimes, there are glitches in the System." He winked. "I didn't say that. Instead, I'm going to wave my magic wand… "The hologram shivered, as heat shivers the air, then steadied.

" – and then you'll see the words," said the Psychiatrist, "as if written on a wall. Close your eyes."

Into my head the three banned words I'd invented to test Mickey over the years suddenly appeared, one after the other, with their definitions:

Lunarline: To emit an opalescent, mother-of-pearl glow, reminiscent of moonlight. *Luffit*: To be very light, so that it can fly away on a slight wind. *Plittable*: Something pliable that can be split into two or more layers. Such as a 'birthday cake' (archaic) is plittable.

"Because you were unjustly punished," the Psychiatrist said, "You are hereby awarded damages. You can access any available Real foods, without charge, while on your Vacation, and you will have access to a Star of your choice during your stay at a Grade One Hotel."

Wow! I cheered up at once. Real food on the Vacation level was a luxury usually reserved only for Leaders and other outstanding Cogs in the System.

To have a Star for two weeks, paid for! And a Grade One Hotel! It would be my chance to meet new Elites who might want my services when trying to interpret Political Contracts. That could make me famous.

"If I were you," the Psychiatrist said, "I'd go confront the Algorithm that did that to you. Test it on the three words, to make sure the System has fixed the glitch." The Psychiatrist laughed. "*Fixed the glitch!* That's a rhyme, isn't it?"

Before I could reply, it vanished, leaving its final words in my head: *"Make sure you visit Anthrax 7 to make sure it's been fixed, before you go on your vacation."*

I did not go alone. With me were two Junior Engineers working on their Dissertations. They would be my witnesses. As we approached the Pod that would transport us to the Algorithm Center, a Grade Four Psychiatrist Bot flicked down from the ceiling and groomed my brain with a quick injection of short-term tranquilizers. My memory of the Terror attack at once became fuzzy and indistinct. The System was so good to me. My sense of calm was brief, however, because one of the two young Engineers, without any regard for my injection, was inquisitive.

"So this is where you were attacked?" it asked.

"Yes."

The somewhat older Engineer looked at its companion and said, coldly, "Now it'll think about it again."

"I don't care," the other said. "And don't discriminate. It's a 'he' – not an 'it.' That makes him *interesting*."

Well, that shut up the older Engineer quite properly. I was rather pleased that its companion had recognized that I was a Natural Male. As such, I was a bit of a rarity and curiosity. So…what did I think about the attack on me?

The younger Engineer had even dared to say it was *interested*. Wow. These hermaphrodites, who mostly populated my world, were always a little curious about Males and Stars: the younger Engineer was no exception. It had even used a word that was almost blasphemous: *interesting* was on the very cusp of being dangerous. It was too close to *affection*. It was a word that could lead to illegal thoughts, but our young Engineers, especially, are prone to think recklessly. It's because they are so new at the job, of course.

As the Ordinals efficiently filled the Pod, their beautiful robes turning the Pod into a rainbow of sheer delight to the eye, the blasphemous younger Engineer added, "Did you know they disposed of forty Ordinals in this Pod after the attack? Didn't try to resuscitate. Did they tell you, in Repair?"

"That caused a problem among the Ordinals," the older one said. "A riot."

"What degree?" I asked, off-handedly. I did not dare act *interested*.

"Second degree. Some went underground. I have it from a reliable Reporter that some went to an underground surgeon who turned off their F-implants."

That was a dangerous level of insurrection. If they turned off their F-implants (just as we do, unless we're to be Punished), they could identify each other.

"During the riot, there were over a thousand suicides, right inside this Pod," said its companion. It pointed to a mass of dark stains on the floor. "That's blood."

An inexplicable emotion arose in me. What a waste. How sad and hopeless…

"Now they have to bring in replacements from Breeding. Before their time."

"That's dangerous," I commented. "Juveniles don't last as long, you know."

"Did you know that 32% of Ordinals are now Juveniles?"

I didn't know, and I was stunned. The percentage used to be just one or two per hundred, such as after a Terror attack on a Pod or Real Food Center. What was going on?

"Just a neutral observation," the younger Engineer said, "so please don't report me, but what if we're losing our Ordinals because they are not happy?"

The outrageous speech of young Engineers! What if a Thought Bot had picked it up? But we were in a very crowded Pod, where the Thought Bots were busy calming the Ordinals with Emotion Repression waves. Some Ordinals had been afraid to enter the Pod, because of the blood-stains, and when the Door closed, a few of them screamed.

Of course, Ordinals screamed all the time. They screamed with pain and received injections so they could keep working. They screamed in fear as some of them were marched into Recycling, being past reasonable efficiency. They received injections to make them happy to die. They screamed whenever they remembered something dreadful in their lives, and got injections to make them forget.

But there were so damned many of them, and sometimes, one or two evaded the injections, as if they were, somehow, aware that injections were not the answer to their truly miserable lives. With little rest, with little chance of being Selected for Preservation as Leader or an Elder, Ordinals labored, rested, labored, rested, and then, after twenty years (it used to be thirty) they were Recycled.

I could hear some of the propaganda being shouted into the brains of the Ordinals: *You pretty! You good! You happy! No work? No food! Equality Forever!*

Not many 'words' were used in telepathy, but these words had been manufactured long ago. They had always worked. They would always work. These words instilled in the Ordinals from the time the Breeders were first introduced to simple Tasks. These were the words that ran their lives. There weren't many others: most telepathy involved feelings and simple commands. *Sit. Start. Stop. Eat. Defecate. Urinate.* Important commands were in two words. They were the Law, and could never be disobeyed. *Start work. Stop work. Pay fine. Give blood. Start sex. Stop sex. Go die.*

The Pod rumbled along, and I noticed that the ride was again rather bumpy. Sometimes we swayed, and a few times, an exhausted Ordinal collapsed. I had noticed that all Pod lines – even the ones to Central – were getting bumpier. Occasionally, there was a crash. This was always blamed on Terrorists, but I was beginning to wonder if an Algorithm for Maintenance was, somewhere along the line, failing. As I considered that, and the cost of Maintenance. the thought *What if ... ?* slithered into my brain.

Immediately, a nearby Conditioning Module replied, *Corruption doesn't exist in our perfect System!* The correction came galloping into my mind. I was not supposed to think in that direction, unless I wanted a Thought Bot sitting on my face. I shut down and concentrated on thinking and feeling nothing.

The Pod stopped, the Door opened, and politely, the Ordinals stepped aside to allow us – the Elites – to exit first, after the All Clear sounded. "All Clear" was a new module in the Pod system, installed only fifty or so years ago. Terrorists would not be waiting for us with stun guns and drone bombs if the All Clear sounded. Or so we were told.

We stepped onto a High Priority Magic Carpet that was waiting for us. It whisked us inside the Algorithm Center in less than a minute, past Guardians without a pause. On the outside, the Center looked like an enormous, shiny black box, devoid of windows, but glistening with little balls of blue electricity that scurried across the black surface like water-drops sizzling on a hot griddle.

The misty blue light inside was the only color visible to humans, besides black and white. There was an odor of melting plastic in the air, which I briefly sensed before our oxygen masks were fitted. As I stood on a metal platform with the two young Engineers, overlooking Sector English, we looked down on a throbbing complex of machines, mag-computers and tangled rivers of wires, among which were white, humanoid blobs: these were the Algorithms, moving like efficient termites. In fact, among ourselves, we English Engineers actually called them "Termites."

Just then, a deep boom, like thunder, reverberated through the blue mist, and the Algorithms in Sector English paused in their frenetic movements, shuddered to a halt, and then turned as a unit, slogging toward their Repair Modules. It was their Down Time. During this one-hour period, we could approach the Algorithm of concern to us and Probe it as it hibernated in Rest Mode.

Anthrax-7, I thought to myself, *here we come.*

The Repair Modules were capsules fitted to hold the Algorithms down, but the top half could open on cantilevers to allow us to conduct

Probes. But to my surprise, when the Algorithm of concern spotted us, it stopped moving toward its Repair Module. As it did so, several other Algorithms also stopped. Then, an amazing thing: some thirty or forty Algorithms pivoted 180 degrees to face us, refusing to enter Repair.

"What the hell?" muttered the older Engineer.

As the elevator began carrying us down to their level, I made a bold decision and lunged forward, shutting it down. The elevator slammed to a halt a mere three meters above the Algorithms: we had to grab onto the rails, the stop was so sudden. Worse, a wave of pain came slamming into our brains!

Anthrax 7 was sending Punishment!

"What the hell?" the older Engineer repeated.

"Get us out of here!" the younger one cried, its face blanching white with fear. But by now, two Logic Algorithms had managed to wrap their long, wet fingers around the metal latticework at the bottom of the elevator door. If they managed to pull it open, we'd surely die, for our brains were now flooding with a vision from Anthrax 7 – our skulls slammed again and again against the steel floor until their gory contents sprayed out to stain the white, translucent bodies of the Algorithms bright red... That's when I decided to start stomping down on the Logic Algorithms' long, twisting, fingers..."Help me, help me!" I yelled, between gasps of pain, to the Engineers. "If you want to get out of this alive!" I was being hit with rolling bolts of electric Punishment that began to strangle my breath and cripple me. Without more help, we'd all die.

The older Engineer stood frozen with terror, but the younger one began mashing down on those white, writhing fingers with hard kicks.

"Kill, kill!" he shouted, flinching as he, too, was Punished. But our adrenaline was flowing, and together, we smashed away at the slimy, white fingers of what had to be countless Algorithms, until, little by little, the fingers began to release their grip on the elevator. As they did so, a final, blinding white pain filled our heads. The punishment was so severe I thought I'd collapse, but I managed, at the last moment, to put the elevator in reverse. It made a terrible grinding sound, loaded down as it was by a last Algorithm. One final kick, and the Algorithm let go, as the elevator continued its slow ascent. Though it was pulling us out of range of the Punishment zone, another problem developed: the elevator began swinging back and forth. In a flash, I realized that the Algorithms were trying to stop the elevator by pulling on its chains. As it neared the top floor, there was an explosion. Realizing that the motor had been destroyed, I shoved the junior Engineers forward. "We have to jump!" I yelled. I forced the door open and we leaped up – and out!

Just in time.

As the elevator's doors hissed shut, it lost power and began falling, out of control. It landed with a sickening thud against the soft bodies of an unknown number of Algorithms. As they made their high-pitched death calls, I finally had enough mental strength to telepath an emergency message to the Center's main command module.

As we waited for a response, Botambulances began whirring past us, to descend amidst the chaos below.

"How many hurt?" the younger Engineer wondered aloud, staring down through the clear black glass wall. We could see several Botambulances busily hauling away some flattened Algorithms. They had been utterly destroyed. We almost forgot our intense headaches, with our hearts pumping, as we stared down at the disaster.

"This is carnage!" the older Engineer groaned, as the sides of the Botambulances lit up with the IDs of each ruptured Algorithm. Worst of all, two of the Algorithms were important.

"We've lost our Two-Word Connector and a Word Monitor. Disaster!" the older Engineer announced.

So, Anthrax 7 was dead. Hearing it, I sank to my knees, exhausted, glad to be alive.

"My dissertation!" the younger engineer began wailing. "What will happen to my dissertation?"

The younger Engineer was studying the permutations of two-word commands that all Ordinals had to follow, by law. All Ordinals were required to respond to two word commands, but they needed the "connector" Algorithm to understand the link between one word and the next. The two most important two-word commands were "*Start work!*" and "*Stop work!*" And without the Word Monitor Algorithm, how could Center make sure the Ordinals were hearing and obeying the right commands?

"We can make a patch," I suggested. "*Start. Work.*"

"No, it would have to be "*Work. Start,*" the younger Engineer corrected.

"NO, it should be "*Work. Now.*" The other piped in.

"*Work. Now.* That's going to be the Patch," I told them. "And '*Work. Stop,*' That will do it. The main word first, the modifier, next."

I had seniority, so I called in the Patch. It was going to put a huge extra burden on the one surviving Single Word Algorithm, but it was just temporary, until a new Two-Word connector Algorithm was built and tested.

As for the Monitor, somewhere in my head, I realized that necessary haste might mean that an Algorithm identical to the malfunctioning one that had punished me was likely to take its place. To make sure it wouldn't recognize me and would never attack me or any other English Engineer again, I'd have to request an emergency inspection in Repair. I was also determined to find the IDs of every Algorithm that had turned 180 degrees to face us in rebellion.

Fighting off my need to mentally rest, I telepathed my request at once to the Center.

"I need the IDs of the Algorithms that pivoted 180 degrees," I told Center.

This mighty Algorithm had been infused with many humanoid characteristics so that we could properly communicate. It was almost like talking to a Bot Doctor.

"Incapacitated Units were all English," Center replied.

"I know that!" I answered, irritated. "Give me their IDs."

The IDs streamed into my head, into the section of my brain we term 48-hour memory. But one ID was missing.

"No good!" I complained. "What about Anthrax 7? We came here to Probe it."

"We are aware," Center said. "Anthrax 7 is being replaced ASAP."

"It needs to be Probed."

"We will Probe."

Center shut down, leaving me angry and frustrated. Center was itself handled by the Master Algorithms for all language sections, but it had failed us. It had produced the faulty Anthrax 7 and might well create another Anthrax 7 with the same hateful attitude. I'd have to go higher up the ladder to get it fixed.

After I reported Center's failure concerning Anthrax 7 to Upper Echelon, which was an immediate requirement, the three of us removed our gas masks and stumbled back to the Pod, where we donned our F-Masks.

"My head is killing me!" the older Engineer griped.

"Shut up!" snarled the younger Engineer, as we looked upon that coward with scorn. We had been in an Emergency and it had frozen stiff. Had been useless.

To show our disgust, we both tuned our masks so it couldn't see our faces. Instead, as if the older Engineer was nothing but an Ordinal, all it could see was its own putrid face looking back. Realizing that it had to get respect back, the older Engineer decided to take a risk.

"We should get a day off for this," it said.

Well, we certainly agreed! If it had the guts to ask for a day of Vacation, that is. It was a reasonable request, considering the blazing headaches we suffered, but nevertheless, such a request could put a black mark against the older Engineer's record as *lazy*.

In fact, no black mark was generated. It took only minutes to get approval. It was agreed that we had the right to a day of Vacation, because we had been severely Punished without cause. All three of us at once applied for one Day Off.

Mine didn't come a moment too soon.

By the time I collapsed in my beautiful penthouse apartment, I was feeling lonely, exhausted and traumatized. I had trouble passing the Guardian, but at the last moment, my Accident Report was delivered into its claws and I was allowed to enter without De-Tox. Antares wasn't there: the glowing tablet left on my Cocoon showed she had been returned to the Collective. I didn't dare ask for her again so soon, either – it would look like *Affection* – unless I could come up with a good excuse.

Damn! I missed her! Tired as I was, I paged through the list of available Stars, seeking any that might resemble her, but not one of them had natural black hair. My Kitbot was a good cook, but not as good as Antares. As I ate the Melba Toast my Kitbot brought to me (one of my few Real Food rations), I considered that Antares would have put some kind of more savory spread on it, mixing two different kinds of taste. It would have been a slightly corrupt thing to do, but by these means, Antares had introduced me to new sensations. Was that being selfish?

I had to see if the Accident Report had made it to Media. I thought my wall screen into activity and it was a comfort to view what reporters had to say about the incident. All three of us were front page news! I'd never been in the news before. But as I sipped my Tea Ration, to which had been added something by order of the Doctor to relieve my headache, I realized that the reporters weren't quite telling the truth.

I wasn't a Sports Engineer, for starters. Those damned reporters had never contacted me to get the truth. My bit of pride, being a real Man, was also lost in the froth. I was described as an "it."

Why did they report only two deaths among the Minor Algorithms, when a dozen had been crushed? And why did they change the number of deaths of two key English Algorithms to just one? Maybe, I thought, they didn't want anyone to get worried about the actual figures. Especially the Ordinals in my Block, who were given a Holiday, due to the disaster, of three hours, while the so-called "injured" Algorithm was actually being hastily re-created.

The real reason for the Vacation for the Ordinals in my Block was because the workers here would be unable to understand a two-word (mandatory) order until the temporary Patch was in place in every one of their befuddled brains. That would take a few hours.

Although my apartment is sound-proofed, I thought I could hear a muted roar of joy coming from the throats of a million Ordinals who lived in the slums below. They were celebrating their three hours of unprecedented rest.

The last part of the news story was the most disturbing. According to the reporters, a dozen selfless Algorithms had saved the lives of three Sports Engineers when the Elevator in which they were riding suddenly malfunctioned. Anthrax 7, who died in the Elevator crash, was declared a Hero and its replacement would keep the same name in its honor.

The next Big News of the Day got my full attention. Maybe it wouldn't have, if I hadn't just seen how the world was told that only one Algorithm had perished in the "Elevator accident" and was a "Hero" (who had actually tried to kill us). This report was short but sweet, because the Connector Algorithm backup was now out of memory. Communications everywhere would now be reduced to just one-word sound bites for two-word statements until the Connector Algorithm was replaced. I was rather pleased to see my Patch in operation, yet miffed at the news.

I tuned in to hear what the Ordinals were being told, now that the Connector Algorithm's memory banks had been drained and only one-word Statements could be understood. My Patch seemed to be working just fine as the next set of news flashed onto the screen.

"*Decisions. Tragic. Ordinals. Die. One. Hundred. Choice. Recycle. Decisions. Selfish. Morons. Lazy.*"

I was now more concerned than ever.

If the reporter was saying a hundred Ordinals had chosen recycling (suicide) today, my bet, based on how my own story had been reported, was that a thousand had killed themselves. Something bad was going on, just below where it might be seen and understood. Whatever was going on, my only wish now was to be on the other side of the Planet when it happened.

I accessed my Personal Monitor and chose to take my five-year vacation two days early. By adding my newly-awarded extra day, Vacation would start day after tomorrow – just one day early.

Glum and worn out, I took a Repair Pill, then hobbled back to my Cocoon. I fell into it and closed my eyes, knowing that in a few hours, the new shift would begin. I'd have to return to The Algorithm Center. For the first time, I wondered if I'd get out of there alive.

"*I talk.*"

Antares! There she was, with her long, thick, shining black hair, her stunning blue eyes, her natural breasts (such a rarity! such a delight!). I sat up, my head dizzy, blinking away the sleep I so badly needed.

"What are you doing here?"

"You. Me. Must. Go."

Her brain, bound up by the loss of the Two-Word Connector Algorithm, was trying to get a frantic message across, via telepathy.

"You said, 'I Talk!'" I told her. "So, dammit, use your mouth! Talk to me!" I commanded her with all the authority I had as an Engineer, and I saw her tremble with fear. As were all English Engineers, I was immune to the breakdown of a linguistic Algorithm, but obviously, Antares was vulnerable, as were 99% of all sentient beings in the System.

"Don't – send me – away!" she panted out. "They will – Kill me!"

She said all of that using her mouth, her tongue, her lips, her breath! Sure, I was impressed. It was true. Antares could communicate in the way forbidden to all but the Elite and highly educated. But wait. A thin trail of memory nagged at me…. What was it?

"Come, sit down. Let's have sex," I said, inviting her.

No one was more astonished than I when she shook her head, refusing. A wave of anger arose in me. She was expensive. She had no right to shake her head!

"You and me – we must go!" she said, forming the words carefully by mouth.

"Antares, my sweet," I answered, "You're the one in danger. Not I. You're the one refusing." As she still stood there, stubborn and defiant, the Memory, fully formed, of the streamer attached to the drone struck home.

"Wait!" I said, standing up, too. "She … *She Talks!*"

"Yes!" Antares answered, with a smile – it was forbidden – coming fleetingly to that wine-red mouth of hers. "Yes! *She Talks!*"

For a minute, I couldn't think. "There's something very big behind this," I told her. "This is bigger than you, or me. I was sent a message. By Terrorists.…"

I could see, I could remember, in the billows of smoke before everything had gone black, as the Ordinals screamed and died all around me, that burning plastic streamer and its golden letters, brought to me by a killer drone that didn't inject me. She reached up. She placed her fingers across my mouth. She looked into my eyes, "Forbidden!" she whispered.

I took her hand from my mouth, gently. "Antares," I said to her, my emotions rising into my throat, "You are different. Do you understand? Different."

She smiled again. "I know."

We were standing in the only place in the entire apartment where there were so many cross-signals from so many places that it would be hard for Thought Bots to intercept what we were saying. She seemed to have known exactly where to stand … of course, I had shown her the spot, come to think of it, when I dared to tell her, just a few days ago, that I *liked* her.…

"It was in the way you looked at me," I managed to say. "Those eyes. Trusting me. You seemed to care what happened to me … that's why I had to say, 'I *like* you'…" I frowned, drew her close, and kissed her. Just on her lips.

Oh, that was dangerous.

She pulled back, placed her hands on both sides of my face. Then she drew nearer. With a husky whisper that set my heart pounding, she said the words I knew were there, waiting to spill out, waiting to pour out…. she said them, even though it could get her killed…

"*I love you!*"

"NO!" I corrected her. "Stop!"

Her words could get both of us eliminated. Only one person had ever spoken those words to me in my life before: my mother. Just before she and Dad immolated themselves. Just before the Thought Bots came and tore me from them...

"*I love you!*" She breathed again, into my soul. Just in case I'd not understood the first time...

What terrifying words!

What risks had she taken to come to me at this hour, unbidden?

I took her by the shoulders. Hard. And looked into the abyss.

How could I have wasted precious time, arguing with her? She was glancing around nervously as I took up my passport and activated my Vacation Permit. OK, it was two days early, but in all my two-hundred years, I'd never taken it early before, and once I'd even missed half a vacation. I decided to plug in the Half Vacation I'd missed over a hundred years ago, that I'd saved so long for the harshest of times. They wouldn't like it, I'd pay a heavy fine, but I knew I'd likely get away with it because I'd been in a Terrorist attack and the Elevator accident. It would be just barely excusable.

I decided to take the risk.

I grabbed up as much Real food and secure clothing as I could carry in my decorative wall-art bag. Bags were mostly superfluous in these times: nobody had actual possessions to take anywhere, but this was one of my antique *objets d'arte* (Yes, a scrap of Old French survived here and there in my wandering soul). I took Antares by the arm and guided her out of the Complex, shielding her as we passed the Guardian, ordering a Taxi as we descended to street level. Had I stepped so much as a meter from Antares, she might have been arrested by Thought Bots, because she was exhibiting detectable emotion.

The taxi came moments later, hovering at the lobby's entrance. I flashed my Vacation Permit, and the Taxi's door flew open for us.

The beauty of being a Star is that they are permitted to go anywhere their Angel decides to take them.

"Where to?" I asked her, wondering what in the hell was the matter with me. Part of me was *excited* – urging me to do this dreadful thing, this unplanned, spontaneous thing.

"To the Big Gate!" she replied. "Now!"

Omigod.

"That's just a fairy tale!" I objected. "Not real – "

"You're in for a big surprise," she said then, suddenly, embracing me, and kissing me as I had never been kissed before. "You deserve to be on the outside. With us. We, who are truly free."

The Taxi driver looked back and grinned.

"Are you ready, Madame?" he asked. "Are you sure you want him?"

"I want him!" she announced, confidently. "After all, it took me long enough to rescue him."

"Good lord!" I exclaimed. "You – you can really, really *talk*!"

"Honey," she replied, kissing me again, "You bet your boots I can talk! Now get some rest, Baby Boy. There's a great big beautiful world waiting for us, just past the Big Gate. And I want you to be able to enjoy every damned minute of it."

And that's how I got here.

How Green is the Sea

Bibby Marine of Liverpool rents converted barges as floating prisons. The Netherlands currently uses two of them.[1]

About "Free Ship One"

The original Freedom Ship was planned to be a mile long and would house 50,000 people, with room for 30,000 visitors. It would cruise continually around the world, and its lucky residents would enjoy the best that every nation it visited had to offer. Plans showed theaters, schools, an avenue of palm trees, and spacious decks for afternoon and evening strolls. The top deck had a landing strip for private jets.[2]

But there were problems: it resembled a gigantic parking garage, was bereft of true beauty, and was too big and deep to enter most ports. There were worries that it couldn't survive a tsunami, and at $11 million per apartment, most millionaires would opt to buy their own private yacht instead. But the idea eventually did take root when One World Government, UC, utilized the plans to create the safest and most efficient prisons on earth. "Free Ship 1" was the first of seven such mile-long ships that were used to house and rehabilitate problem prisoners.

These ships were anchored in the seven safest sectors of the world's seas, in the center of gyres where the majority of the world's floating pollution – especially plastic – accumulated.[3] Through deep-water filtration and various energy-producing systems, using a unique coil that anchored the ships to the lower realms of the sea floor, every Free Ship processed the extra waste that escaped the machinery running the "Lily Pads" –nearby floating cities, which were linked together. Low-maintenance thorium nuclear reactors supplied most of the power.[4] The remaining sources of energy came from solar, waves, wind and lightning-strikes.

Unlike some lovely drawings of these floating ocean cities, the final products were functional, bleak and spare. The AI-approved prisons were built for efficiency: comfort was an afterthought. Sometimes the result was beautiful, for function can force streamlining in order to assure mechanical stability,[5] but more often, odd turrets, complex machines, and dense structures of metal, plastic, nano-carbons and energy-generating machinery overwhelmed what might have been a thing of beauty.[6]

YOU ARE NOW ENTERING A TWILIGHT ZONE...

It is at this stage of things that we gaze upon the case of Prisoner for Slow Rehabilitation #276-101, surnamed President Super MacHeath28, a 51% sexually irresistible, exploitative human who was created from a genetically modified embryo for a corporation. By the time he became an adult, laws had been formulated and passed to make certain that all World Leaders, bred as he was bred, were certified as incapable of deception, inordinate pride, or of being tempted by any of the Seven Deadly Sins.

But now he was a prisoner. His question was, *Why?*

Used to having his every whim and desire granted immediately, Super MacHeath28 found himself fretting over the delay of half an hour before his Personal Records were made available to him.

"Sorry it took so long, Mr. President," his Cyborg Jailer said, bowing several times as he handed over the files. "They are classified, after all."

"I know that," MacHeath28 replied, taking the files from the Jailer. "I'm the one who classified them."

"Of course, Mr. President."

"Go away," MacHeath28 told it.

"Yes, Mr. President," the Jailer said, pivoting on its four wheeled feet.

As MacHeath28 perused the files, he found himself nodding with every facet of information he scanned. Yes, he was created to become the President of the World: voters could not resist his utter charm, charisma and superior physical endowments. Those who owned him were even wealthier than those who owned the Free prison ships. As President, Super MacHeath28 was the 9th Certified, Guaranteed and Incorruptible President.

As for his being owned by a corporation, everybody in the world with a brain understood that, should the President fail in any areas of competence, the Corporation would have to make reparations to the voters. Above all, the Corporation did not wish to lose its status as the Guarantor of the President.

MacHeath28 looked upon his magnificent genetic charts, now laid out before him on a hologram, with understandable pride. Of course all humans had their limitations, but he was only the third President who had been certified as the Perfect President. He was, of course, a living being, and as such, he still retained the need for advisors (that's where the Corporation came in). When Corporations became "people" in the 20th Century, it wasn't much longer before they began to act as people always do. Taking care of business for profit. And Business, MacHeath28 mused, is a process for making profits by generating more value. As President, his main job was to make sure profits were made worldwide by creating confidence in the Corporation's decisions. The goal was to generate more value in the marketplace for all legal enterprises, while simultaneously protecting the value of human and Cyborg labor. The rest of MacHeath28's duties revolved around generating good will, and hope for a brighter future.

He was built for it.

As he looked over the files, MacHeath28 found his "forgiven" list: every human had one, if he, she or it was more than 50% human flesh and nerves. As such, Macheath28 was forgiven his own little satchel of foibles and fancies, such as his penchant for collecting 20th Century Country Music (considered Low Class) and his habit of chewing gum (considered quaint). And until recently, nobody was upset with President MacHeath28's collection of Bobbing Heads.

He was by no means the first and only of his kind to collect Bobbing Heads. His predecessor, Captain America67 Super Casanova, had also collected Bobbing Heads. But MacHeath28's collection included not only the Bobbing Heads of laudable humans. He also collected Bobbing Heads of the infamous: there were 21st Century drug lords, Adolph Hitler, The Grinch, Federal Reserve CEO's, The Joker, and Lyndon Johnson. The criticism, he saw, was not that he had collected infamous Bobbing Heads, but that he had failed to collect any notorious female Bobbing Heads. For this reason, he now learned, he was currently under arrest…

To the public at large, he had simply gone on a scheduled tour, inspecting Free Ships. It was a duty to be performed every decade, so MacHeath28 had not been prepared for his arrest when he came on board.

Why hadn't he merely been warned? For all his advanced senses, he was not capable of reading minds! Surprised at his feelings of helplessness, MacHeath28 thrust his fingers into his thick, curly red hair and rubbed his aching temples, trying to relieve his tension. He felt a headache coming on: any physical discomfort was so rare as to make even a slight headache almost unendurable. He had been so delicately engineered, after all.

While his genetic engineering was superb, he was one of thousands of such cases, though not as well-tuned. It was now relatively cheap and easy to purchase suitable embryos and to manipulate genes to create a desired Super Personality, with a body to match. Of course an infant had to be raised to adulthood: where one or more corporations owned a child, special schools had been created for that. There had indeed been some problems, at first: before the laws were changed to forbid it, "Chuck Connors Unlimited" were being purchased and used by big police departments. These law-and-order champions had been bred and trained to be fierce and ruthless defenders of the law. But there were so many Chuck Connors policemen in the world that their particular response profiles became easy to outfox by career criminals. The result was that Chuck Connors police ended up in desk jobs, and a large number of them committed suicide.

That's why Chuck Connors models 2, 3, 4, etc. came into being. Models that varied were harder to crack. Of course, even the most clever varieties of Chuck Connors creations weren't born with the skills to use their traits wisely. The infant had to be trained.

In MacHeath28's case, he was configured to live up to his full potential. He was attractive, calm and smart. He was molded to be an incomparably careful politician, a sober advocate for humans, and a delightful stud for his one and only wife. Those who had created Super MacHeath28 owned breeding and genetic rights. When he turned sixteen, MacHeath28 was sold to the Greater Las Vegas Virtual Reality Sex and Adventure Club for six months. Otherwise, it was feared that he would never understand what normal life was like for those outside his rank.

That's where MacHeath28 met MacHeath29, who had not been fitted to become the perfect politician. Instead, he was a notorious rapscallion who was adept at gambling, parting customers from their credit. He ran the most profitable brothel in Club history. MacHeath29 resembled MacHeath28 in many ways. In a different kind of setting, they might have bonded as twins, but at the Adventure Club, MacHeath 29 was MacHeath 28's teacher.

For six months after the Sex and Adventure Club experience, MacHeath28 played polo, attained a brisk physical fitness profile, and was given a life where he brushed shoulders with the rich and famous. He soon became (as expected) a celebrity, and after six months was removed from that experience. During all this time, he had studies to attend to, but these were accomplished mostly during sleep periods. For his final preparation course, Macheath28 was sent to a monastery, where for the next two years he learned discipline, self control and everything from all the holy books of every religion. In the final phase of his training, which lasted a year, Macheath28 was tutored by live specialists in the craft of politics, a range of philosophies, Official World History, and atheism.

Six years after that, MacHeath28 was a married lawyer with 2.2 children (one was still in the bottles), had been elected to the Senate, and was ready to run for President. Not that there were any truly live competitors. They were all Virtual Reality challengers. Real challengers no longer existed: they were a waste of funds and time. Yes, there had once been court battles over it, but that had been before his time.

Of course, he was elected, but with limits imposed. Super Personalities had such outstanding appeal to the public at large that there was a danger: they might try to take over the government. In the past, a few of them had tried to become more important to the public than planned. Some had formed Unions, Political Parties and Cartels to promote themselves. In the end, all Super Personalities were rounded up for Rehabilitation. Any who failed Rehabilitation were imprisoned for Slow Rehabilitation. The owners received compensation for lost profits until the Super Personality, all toned down, was re-released to an adoring public, with a monthly Survival Allowance.

There had been objections, of course, but by 2100, to stop further exploitation, the law was changed to make all humans and Cyborgs the dual property of the One World Government and the respective corporation(s) bearing the expenses.

By 2120, only a few Feral humans survived the final roundups (only God knew where the Ferals might be). Now the world's humans, Robots and Cyborgs were entirely owned and operated by a Troika of corporations, the One World Government, and the last surviving AI entity that had independent thought and self-awareness, called The Brain. Corporations represented the original, ancient House of Representatives. The Brain represented the old Supreme Court. It also protected the few non-human sentient species supposedly still in existence, though nobody remembered why.

Update:

His spirit unconquered, MacHeath28 set aside the files and decided to face his unknown destiny with confidence. After all, his was a face that had brought more prosperity to the Workers than any previous. He was popular: he was loved!

Perhaps the arrest had something to do with some problem he shared his namesake: women. MacHeath28 found temptation at every turn, and it impeded him at times. The original MacHeath was a character from John Gay's *The Beggars' Opera*. He was a lecherous highwayman who was in the center of a world of total corruption among bankers, police, judges, thieves and fast women. He seduced them all, in his own way, but in the end, was trapped by his rivals through his own lascivious misconduct and the treachery of a jilted lover. The thought of how Macheath, given the choice to hang on the gallows or to face the demands of his fifteen-odd newly-discovered wives and pregnant mistresses, chose the gallows, brought a smile to his lips. Then he laughed, as his favorite Cyborgs looked at him with expressions of concern.

"Why did you laugh, Mr. President?" his Major Domo Cyborg inquired.

"I've never been under arrest before," he explained. "And all because of my Bobbing Heads collection? Doesn't that seem a bit extreme? There has to be some kind of mistake here, don't you see?" And MacHeath28 laughed again –a short, forced laugh.

"You should not be exhibiting levity, Mr. President, when under arrest," his Cyborg advised. "Perhaps there's some genetic flaw, or mutation, that has just surfaced."

MacHeath28 sighed.

"Bring me a Well-Be-Well drink," he told it. "I've simply forgotten to take it, under all this stress." He did not mention that his headache was becoming worse.

He had last seen a version of *The Beggars Opera* when he had been able to live, wild and free, in Vegas. That seemed an eternity away, but echoes of the opera had stayed in his memory. Two women had loved Macheath more than all the others, and had begged their powerful fathers to spare his life… Then there were some 20th Century versions of the opera, including one called "The Mack."[7] In the 20th Century versions, "Mackie" had the option to kill his enemies. At the thought, MacHeath28 selected a portion of his memory banks that brought back to him the strains of Bobby Darin's "Mack the Knife:"

> Oh, the shark, babe, has such teeth, dear//
>   And it shows them//pearly white.
>   Just a jackknife //has old MacHeath, babe//And he keeps it//
> out of sight.
>   Ya know when that shark bites//with his teeth, babe//Scarlet
> billows//start to spread.
>   Fancy gloves, oh, //wears old MacHeath, babe//So there's never, never a trace of red.
>   Now d'ja hear 'bout //Louie Miller? //He disappeared, babe//
> After drawin' out …all his hard-earned cash.//And now MacHeath
> spends//just like a sailor.
>   Could it be our boy's done somethin' rash?
>   Now Jenny Diver//yeah, Sukey Tawdry//Miss Lotta Lenya//
> and old Lucy Brown.
>   Oh, the line forms//on the right, babe//Now that Macky's//
> back in town.
>   Look out, old Macky's back!

The Cyborg brought him the drink, and it calmed him. Maybe a little too much. He felt suddenly a bit sleepy, but at least his headache was gone. What had happened to his sharpness and wit? Too late, he realized that something must have been added to his drink. As he struggled to stay awake, a Praetorian Guard in a golden uniform suddenly stood before him with a FlySeat.

"So, what happens next?" MacHeath28 wanted to know, as he was strapped in.

"You're being moved to Free Ship 2," the Guard said. "On your way there, you will have the opportunity to avail yourself of an excellent view of green sea and blue sky. Many tourists pay a great deal to access such a view." Turning to MacHeath28's four Cyborgs, he told them, in a sharp, commanding voice, "As for all of you, you are now relieved of duty."

To his horror, the Cyborgs bowed reverently his way, and then, turning their backs on him, they marched from the room in a peculiar lockstep, as if in a trance.

"You can't do that!" Macheath28 cried out, struggling amidst the straps that held him down. "Red alert! Red alert!" he shouted, but the Cyborgs continued their automated march. "Stop!" he shouted, as the guard began wheeling him onto a ramp that led, he well knew, to a Prison Plane. "I'm the President of the One World Government – I–"

"Shut up!" the Guard told him, delivering a sizzling electronic jolt to the back of his neck.

"Hey, that hurt!" MacHeath28 groaned. "What's the matter with you?"

The guard did not bother to reply. He had been friendly and pleasant until now. Now he failed to reply to anything Macheath28 said, only waving the Electro-Corrector his way in a most menacing manner as the FlySeat settled into a lockdown in the plane. The Guard thrust several brightly-colored brochures between his legs and then stood at attention, saluting him.

"Mr. President, may you find your journey pleasant," the Guard told him, backing down the ramp and facing him as he spoke. At once the doors closed, and Macheath28 found himself alone in a velvety blue mist. As the plane shuddered into flight, whiffs of a chemical in the blue mist reached his nostrils: he recognized the euphoric, pleasant sensation it produced. He'd seen the same blue mist inside the voting stations at election time. He was being sprayed with tranquilizers and mood-lifting drugs, as if he were a common humanoid voter. As the plane took off (there was no pilot, no crew), MacHeath28 tried to focus on what he could do to free himself from this situation. After all, he was bred to act with calm, logic and reason in all emergencies.

Well, he knew his rights. He'd report the Guard for emotional and physical abuse, as soon as he reached humanoids again on Free Ship 2. He'd already read the brochures. It was the law: all prisoners had to know their rights, and what to expect.

Within himself, he tried to prepare himself for what might happen next. Perhaps they would subject him to a dose of Fast Rehab. For the high class convict, the methods used in Fast Rehab included creating false memories. The average convict got a great life after Fast Rehab: implanted memories of a happy childhood with real parents and siblings, a heartfelt conversion to a

Religion of his choice, a 100% Cyborg guard and protector who would provide companionship for life, and after passing all tests, ownership of a private, personal Luxury Capsule in the country of his choice, furnished to taste.

MacHeath28 now detested the mere thought of ever wanting a Bobbing Head collection. Everybody loved him and almost everybody had willingly voted for him instead of for a Virtual Alternative. Aware that Slow Rehab could do a lot of damage to his desired personality, MacHeath28 had prepared himself for such an eventuality by smuggling in some secret micro-plastic-covered programming chips, undetectable because they were on the nano-level. These microchips seemed no different from the billions of micro-plastic globules that infested the bodies of all fish, birds and mammals alive, due to pollution. A few weeks from now, when the plastic coating deteriorated, the chips would come into action and restore everything. It was expensive, but Macheath28 would have all his memories back, and whoever it was who had gotten him arrested would pay. This was nothing less than a Coup d'etat, and he would purge his Corporate Cabinet, every last one of them, if necessary. He was too popular to vanish: wait and see what he could do, with all the people on his side!

"The Mack" within was ready to draw blood.

Slow Rehab, which took three days of intensive therapy, would not overcome him. He tossed the brochures from his lap with a sneer of contempt. And then, the drugs finally overwhelming him, he fell asleep...

He was dreaming.... Smug, confident and ready for anything, MacHeath settled back in his chair. He was President of the whole world, but as he stroked his chin, he thought he'd start to grow a luxurious beard ... a thick, red one ... his favorite concubine loved beards ... he'd have to get follicles implanted, but she could do that for him as soon as he was released. Such an operation only took an hour. Recently, some men were getting hair implants all over their bodies: a few had become Wolf Men. It was the current fad ... with a sudden start, MacHeath28 awoke, dazed and confused. Where had those crazy thoughts come from? As he looked up into the hazy blue light which enveloped him, he could hear a faint buzzing noise. He caught a glimpse of a large, circular metal wheel filled with complicated, dangling wires. They resembled electrodes. The wheel was rising, but the electrode elements were waving back and forth, almost like the writhing of snakes. As they did so, a drop of blood fell from one of the electrodes, landing on his fettered hand. For the first time, he began to realize that somebody – or something – was fooling with his brain...

When the plane landed, some robots, who refused to speak at all, removed his fetters and shoved him into a waiting car. It was good to have the weight off: Macheath28 could now move his arms and legs freely. Maybe things would get better.

One robot bowed obsequiously before him and then handed him a menu.

"You have the right to order whatever pleasures you wish, for the next seventy-two hours," it told him. "We wish to grant your choices, and we promise you that no matter what you order, we will attempt to fulfill every detail."

It seemed strange not to be addressed as "Mr. President," but Macheath28 consoled himself with the thought that they had to know who he was, or such amenities would not have been offered.

"I wish to communicate with One World Corporation's Board of Directors," MacHeath28 told the robot.

"Of course," it said, handing him a primitive communication console. "If that is your desire."

"It is!" MacHeath28 replied, punching in his personal codes. Several odd beeps reverberated into the air, and then he saw them: there was the entire Board, in a hologram, seated in their hemisphere of massage chairs.

"Greetings, Mr. President!" John Adams920 called out. "How is your inspection tour of the prison ships going?"

"Not well at all, Adams," Macheath28 replied, with a scowl. "They've arrested me. Can you imagine such a thing?"

"We're so glad that you're having a good tour, Mr. President," John Aams920 replied.

The entire Board of Directors smiled and waved.

"Didn't you hear what I said?" MacHeath28 snapped. "I said, I've been arrested, damn it!"

"We all think you could stay an extra day, if that's what you wish, Sir. Is Shanna, your favorite concubine, with you?"

"No, she's not. I have no idea where she is. And I repeat – I have been arrested. On the most ludicrous of charges – for not having a female felon Bobbing Head in my collection – "

"We understand, Mr. President," Adams920 said, nodding. "We'll send her right over."

"No, I don't want her here!"

"We'll tell your wife that you're going to be a day late. Do you have any other messages? By the way, the Security Division changes you recommended yesterday have been approved and implemented."

"I didn't approve anything yesterday," Macheath28 declared. "I've been held incommunicado since yesterday!"

"That's good news, we will let the press know about your new facelift. And we think the red beard is an excellent idea. After all, we have that Wolfman fad going on…"

"We see that you have a wonderful view of the open sea from Free Ship 2," another Counselor said. "We can understand why you have chosen to stay an extra day."

Grimly, MacHeath28 realized that no matter what he said, they were hearing something else. Somebody was allowing him to see just how deeply he was enmeshed in the prison ship. As he was led away to his luxury apartment, he was followed by several Cyborgs. "We are at your command, sir!" they kept repeating. As he entered the apartment, which was fitted out to resemble his own Presidential quarters (minus the Official Seal of Office), MacHeath28 allowed his hands to move slowly through his thick, red hair. He was afraid of what he would find. Sure enough, he could feel the tiny swellings that meant he'd been implanted with an innumerable number of tiny electrodes. As he withdrew his hands from his thick shock of hair, he was not surprised to see that his fingertips were stained with his blood. A deep sense of helplessness began to rise within him. Too tired to think, he crawled onto the huge platform bed that seemed to beckon as a familiar friend, with its genuine silk sheets and satin pillows. As he closed his eyes, he wondered how much of himself would remain when next he woke. What dreams might come, he did not know, but as he waved to the Cyborgs to leave him alone, he closed his ocean-blue eyes. They were the adored eyes of an entire planet. And they were filled with tears.

When he awoke, a whole menu of nice things were awaiting him, thanks to bribes. He had a lot of credit: he'd have terrific food. He'd have a 100% Cyborg sex companion for the three days he was told he must spend here. All treatment chairs would be lined with fleece. He would have contact every day with his favorite concubine by closed circuit view-screens. As usual, when he was escorted into Reception, they took a blood sample, looking for microchips and drugs. The smiling nurse was 50% human and flirted with him. He gave her a wink as he changed into his prison garb, making sure that she got a good look at his impressive, manly self.

"You're welcome to visit me, you beautiful pair of breasts, you beautiful pair of eyes!" he told her, looking back at her for a long moment as they led him through the first of several sets of glass doors.

As he settled into his cabin (a concession to the fact that Free Ship was a marine vessel), MacHeath28 noticed that everything he'd specified had been supplied. There was a plate of sliced Kobi beef, with Beluga caviar and cucumbers stuffed with pearls (Macheath28 loved the concept of being an Oriental Sultan). For tonight, he wanted to be a Caliph from the pages of The Arabian Nights.). "Bolero" was playing when he arrived: as he relaxed, sinking into oriental cushions, he noted with pleasure that the two palm trees inside the cabin were real, not artificial. As "Bolero" merged to "Scheherazade" he drew his Free Ship 2 brochure from his personal bag and touched the screen: it unfolded to ten times its size, presenting more music selections, an a la carte menu, and a list of women he could order for the night. After looking over the choices, he ordered champagne and dinner for two, plus a black hermaphroditic slave bred in Niger. She was supposedly 75% human. Indeed, a rarity.

Everything about prison life was just as promised. He had as much freedom as his confinement to this big room would allow. Rehab, they told him, would start in the morning. Big deal. So what?

He was ready.

* * *

At dawn, Macheath28 sent away Girl Number Three and took a relaxing shower. Breakfast was splendid, compete with poached quail eggs and cloudberry jam on real wheat toast. After dressing, there was a quiet knock on his door: it was this section's Warden, a 51% Cyborg who had preferred to look like Jesus Christ.

"May I come in?" the Warden asked. MacHeath28 shrugged. "It's fine with me." He waved the warden to the only chair in the room, keeping his circular harem bed for himself. "Jesus" settled himself into the chair and leaned forward, his hands on his knees, looking intently at his prisoner.

"Did you find everything as you wished?" the Warden asked

"It was satisfactory," Macheath28 replied. "Especially Madonna2310!" They both laughed.

Macheath28 offered the Warden a bottle. "Want some wine? It's vintage 2050."

"I don't drink," the Cyborg told him. "But I hope you found it a good year."

"It was a very good year," MacHeath28 agreed, putting the bottle back into its receptacle in the wall.

"We found the nano-chips," the Warden said. "You know we can't get them all out, don't you?"

MacHeath28 was surprised. "How in hell–?"

"All the rich ones do it," the Warden replied. "You were no exception. You realize how serious that is… don't you?"

"It means Rehab probably won't work," MacHeath28 admitted.

"I don't think you understand," the Warden said frowning. "Didn't you look at the small print in the punishment section of your prison order?"

"Of course I did," MacHeath28 said. "It says I can come back again, if this doesn't 'take.'"

"Specifically, it says that MacHeath28 can come back."

"But there is only one Macheath28 in the world," MacHeath28 reminded him. "MacHeath27 , MacHeath26… they were great successes. And I was a President. The greatest success of them all." He didn't want to add that all MacHeaths prior to #26 and #25 had been genetic failures, and put down, and that the Law now forbade any more Super Personality MacHeaths to be created. "In fact," MacHeath28 reminded him, "I'm the best of the best. That's why I'm so rich. You think my friends are going to let all that be thrown away in a Rehab joint like this? After all, I am Mr.

President." MacHeath28 laughed, and scratched at the spots where the newest electrode wires had been inserted, for they were itchy.

"You are aware of the concept of Last Wishes, correct?" Jesus asked, standing. "I see that there's no recourse now."

"What do you mean, 'Last Wishes'?" MacHeath28 snapped, standing to his feet. He was suddenly, instinctively aware that something wasn't quite right … this was no Bollywood Production like "Save the Tiger" where the hero – a teacher – had fooled a Cyborg into granting a Last Wish – a final meal – that saved 600 kids from extermination at a Zoo. "We're talking Reality here!" Macheath28 said. "It is guaranteed – also in small print, that I will walk in here with everything genetically intact and that I will walk out of here with everything genetically intact. And that you can't destroy my inherited personality. Though," he added, "God knows, you've distorted it quite a bit in the three days I've been here."

"I indeed admire you, Mr. President," the Warden blurted out. "You have retained a remarkable portion of your original personality, despite all our efforts at Slow Rehab."

"Then, no more nonsense about Last Wishes," MacHeath28 declared. "To destroy me would be an Act of Treason. I'm the most popular President the world has ever seen. The people would utterly revolt if you got rid of me."

"That's all true," the Warden said. "We would never dare to destroy the man you are, and we have no intention of doing so. But of course, we also wanted to make certain that all your Last Wishes were nevertheless honored. Unfortunately, you see, you're about to die." "What do you mean, 'die'?" MacHeath28 looked wildly around him as his heart began beating, fast. Just then, the heavy door opened and two Golden Cyborg Prison Guards appeared. Instantly, MacHeath28 felt the weights of mind-fetters, complete with an orange strait-jacket, as they snapped upon his arms and legs. He was a powerful man, but the weight was so great he could barely move.

"You don't dare!" Macheath28 cried out, struggling to move. "You can't get away with this!"

"Due to our removing so many of your memories," the Warden said, "you are no longer the most eloquent and convincing speaker on the planet, but I'm still surprised to see how much inner strength you still have. Therefore, I've decided to take you to see something."

MacHeath28 was placed on a hover-platform as the Warden added, soothingly, "I have compassion."

"Don't give me that movie stuff!" MacHeath28 snarled. "Compassion? I'll show you 'compassion' – when I get out of here. I have monitors all over my body. They guarantee you can't mishandle me! I know my rights! You must release me! Intact! Not one gene messed up. No injuries.

As for all these fake memories you've saddled me with, I can still remember who I am, damn you!"

"All of that is true," the Warden said, almost wistfully. "We wouldn't dare touch a single one of your genes. But there is an escape clause for us…"

MacHeath28 fell silent. His mind was working fast. Maybe he could use bribery…

"I can make you unbelievably wealthy–"

"My personality doesn't care about wealth. You can't bribe me."

"Oh, yeah, that 'Jesus Christ' thingie…"

They had now reached a corridor suffused with green light. MacHeath28's small platform was turned 90 degrees to the left so he could see what was inside a small room there, through a porthole window. In that round window of another world, he saw a replica of himself, making love to his favorite concubine. The replica even had a red beard.

"He's magnificent, isn't he?" the Warden said approvingly. "An accomplished lover. In every other way, as well, he is identical to you. He will continue to be the most popular man on the planet. We calculate that it will take him at least four years before he might realize that he can make do without the Corporation. If that time comes, he, too, will be replaced…"

Suddenly, the porthole window closed, like a diaphragm. At the same time, a Cyborg bent near him and gave him a sudden injection in the chest. Almost immediately, MacHeath28 felt a cold chill come over him.

"You're getting the Socrates Treatment now. Please don't be afraid," the Warden told him as they continued down the white, sterile hall with its eerily-green lighting. "It will make your final moments almost painless … or so they say…. Now, think of me as your comforting friend in this last journey you're taking. I'm the Jesus you have learned about. Or–" the Cyborg shifted his face to a serene, beaming oriental visage. "Or, if you wish, call me Chairman Mao, the atheist you admired most when you were being trained. You could also choose Vladimir Putin, your favorite classic politician."

"I don't care what you look like!" MacHeath28 managed to spit out, as saliva began drooling from his mouth.

"Then I will resume my former persona," Mao said, transforming himself once more into Jesus. "Now, take a look to your right," he said, moving Macheath28's stiffening head to the right with his own hands. "Note the ocean view we have out here. How green is the sea! How blue is the sky! And how artificial it all happens to be! Did you know that the oceans are half empty, now? That they are covered with energy plants? And that actual blue skies no longer exist, outside the domes?"

As the Golden Cyborgs guided him along, MacHeath28 began to feel almost disembodied, as if he were piece of random seaweed, afloat on a green sea…

"What's 'the Socrates Treatment'?" Macheath28 mumbled, feeling colder and colder. He was losing all sensations...

"You've been given the equivalent of the hemlock that was used to kill Socrates," Jesus replied. "He was an ancient Greek philosopher–"

Macheath28 tried to say, "I know!" but instead, all he could do was to gurgle.

"Socrates was adjudged as having corrupted the youth and of believing in false gods. You placed yourself in a similar situation."

"Help!" MacHeath28 managed to call out, from numb lips. "Somebody – help!" His cries were almost a whimper because of the power of the drug...

"You're turning blue," Jesus told him. "I have to admit, your crimes against the State did not include believing in false gods. I just threw that in for effect. Prepare yourself, now, to die."

"Im-impossible!" MacHeath28 choked out, as two large doors opened automatically, revealing a huge room filled with throbbing, pounding machinery. "I'm MacHeath28! The – President – of the – World–"

As they entered the machine-filled room, one of the engines began to pulse, like a heartbeat, and a fervent heat began emanating from a large, metal door that was the centerpiece of its black, vibrating mass. They had entered a section of the Energy Conversion Plant where the ship's garbage for that deck was processed by a thorium reactor connected to a large furnace. MacHeath28 had seen a photo of it in the brochure that showed the layout of Free Ship 2.

"We knew you could take over the world," the Warden said. "But you're so *good* at what you do, otherwise, that we need to keep you. At least, until we have finished creating something even better."

As the word 'create' hit his brain, MacHeath28 made a little, helpless gasp. They were wheeling him ever-closer toward that large, hot metal door. Suddenly a Waste Robot rolled itself into place, as if on guard.

"*Ready for disposal. All components to be cycled into power generation system,*" one of the Cyborgs told the robot, who then pivoted on eight spidery legs and opened the furnace's door. As a wave of fierce heat struck him, Macheath28 rolled his eyes, the only part of his body that was still able to move ... he felt as if he had been turned into a solid mass: all his senses were failing.... He drew in some final gasps of air as his lungs began to stiffen, but even so, his frantic brain could still hear words flowing from the compassionate lips of Jesus:

"Don't worry. You will go on! Your clone was prepared after you began collecting the Bobbing Heads. That was our clue: you were considering World Dominion, weren't you?"

But Macheath28 could not speak. Only his eyes rolled upwards as he was pushed closer to the furnace.

"You will go on living, MacHeath28. See? We did not kill you! We're only killing your clone. That's what the paperwork will show."

Macheath28's eyes managed to blink in horror.

"You were a clone, yourself," the Warden explained. "We got rid of the original almost ten years ago. In fact," Jesus said, as the robot picked Macheath28 up and held him aloft before the great, hot flaming open maw of the furnace, "you are Clone Number Three of your own self. As for your final Clone, you met him during your early training. Don't you remember Macheath29, at the Sex and Adventure Club?"

The waste robot heaved him up higher in its great, steely arms.

"MacHeath28 is happily having sex in the room where you got a glimpse of him. He will be able to function and think the same as you. After all, he has your thoughts and memories. We sucked the best from you and shoved them into him. Or, should I say, almost all of the best. Straight from your own brain. So – be comforted, for he IS you. Only, there are no nano-devices in him to worry about."

The Warden wiped a pair of cold tears from MacHeath28's paralyzed eyes. "Too bad you just couldn't resist the temptation, Mr. President, to collect bobbing heads. That was our own little way of implanting you to reveal your secret ambitions. It was always a problem with MacHeaths26 and 27. But we are generating a new model that won't have the capacity to rebel: the Henry Kissinger-June Cleaver Model. It will be bisexual, so we can get around the married-with-children and concubine issues. And that's best for everyone, isn't it, Mr. President?"

As the robot threw Macheath28's body, rigid in its prison suit, into the flames, Jesus emitted a cackling laugh of pure glee. After all, he was programmed to never get depressed with his duty as Warden-Executioner.

Endnotes

1. http://www.millomlocal.co.uk/farewell-to-giant-barge-1.160333 Acquired Feb. 6, 2016.

2. http://www.dailymail.co.uk/sciencetech/article-2514936/The-incredible-mile-long-floating-CITY--complete-schools-hospital-parks-airport-50-000-residents.html Retrieved Aug. 29, 2015.

3. Marine zooplankton shown ingesting microplastic particles in video made at UK's Plymouth Marine Labs by Dr. Matthew Cole and Verity White. YouTube.

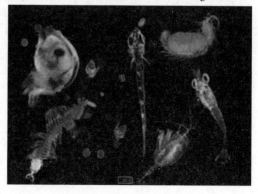

"28 July, 2015: Vancouver, B.C. Tiny marine zooplankton are ingesting microplastic particles at an alarming rate, according to a new study [June, 2015]by Dr. Peter Ross, head of the Ocean Pollution Research Program at Vancouver Aquarium Marine Science Centre. [At] the base of the aquatic food web… plastics will radiate up the chains of predators and prey, finally accumulating in important food fishes, such as salmon, and in apex species such as whales and humans." (For example, it was estimated that adult salmon were ingesting 91 plastic particles per day, which incorporates in the flesh of the salmon and then is eaten by humans. http://www. reef2rainforest.com/2015/07/28/microplastic-in-marine-food-webs/ Retrieved Aug. 31, 2015.

4. e.g. advanced units based on Thorium MOX-fuel reactors. See Norwegian experiments at: http://www.world-nuclear.org/information-library/current-and-future-generation/thorium. aspx Retrieved Dec. 31, 2015.

5. We're talking about harmonic vibration analysis, important to consider when designing engines, bridges and structures subject to such stresses as pounding waves. "Any design that is subjected to a cyclical excitation source responds by vibrating in order to release the incoming energy. The vibrations are perceived as small deflections on the design. Everyday instances include motors mounted to shafts, a tool mounted on a mill or a lathe, unbalanced rotating machinery, etc… [A] cyclic sinusoidal frequency source induces vibrations on the design, resulting in deflections [which] over time are typically detrimental to a design.… Harmonic analysis involves understanding which … derivatives come closest to the natural vibrating characteristics [frequency] of the physical design itself.…" The natural frequency of a design should not "coincide with one of the derivative frequencies of the composite wave, [or] the design goes into resonance and …can possibly hasten failure." The author posits that AI-designed ocean-dwelling structures would tend to be streamlined as a result of this "quality control" mechanism. http://www.3dvision.com/pdf/ white-papers/simulation/Harmonic-Vibration-Analysis.pdf Retrieved Sept. 2, 2015.

6. Shimizu Corporation has been hard at work [concerning:] … Green Float … the Environmental Island.… Designed for the equatorial Pacific, presumably near Japan, Green Float is a concept for a series of floating islands with eco skyscraper cities, where people live, work and can easily get to gardens, open space, the beach and even "forests." Islands are connected together to form modules, and a number of modules grouped together form a "country" of roughly one million people.

A 1,000 m tower in the center of the island acts as both a vertical farm as well as a skyscraper with residential, commercial and office space. The green space, the beach, and the water terminal on the flat plane of the island are all within walking distance. Energy for the islands would be generated from renewable sources like solar, wind, and ocean thermal, and they also propose to collect solar energy 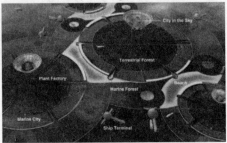 from space … [by] install[ing] a solar belt on the moon." http://inhabitat.com/futuristic-floating-city-is-an-ecotopia-at-sea/ Retrieved Sept. 1, 2015

Nor were the "Lily Pads" anything like the elegant and yet-functional design "by Award-winning architect Vincent Callebaut [who] … designed a self-sustainable "Lilypad City" Ref: http:// maxcdn.thedesigninspiration.com/wp-content/uploads/2010/03/lilypad/Lilypad-07.jpg Retrieved Sept. 1, 2015.

7. "The Mack" is, in the author's opinion, a 1972 version of "The Three-Penny Opera" and its predecessor, "The Beggars Opera" where Macheath is the main character, involved with prostitutes, corrupt government, the mafia and police; he is an anti-hero. All three versions are useful for making social statements and can even serve to foment revolution. "The Beggars Opera" was George Washington's favorite opera; The Czech President Vaclav Havel gained his huge popularity after being jailed for his special production of The Three-Penny Opera, which lambasted Soviet rule and corruption; the Brecht/Weill Threepenny Opera was banned in Hitler's Germany for the same reason. "The Mack"- supposedly a 'blaxploitation movie' - has the same kind of structure and utility. Goldie, who is ""The Mack" easily reminds us of "Macheath" and "Mack the Knife."

THE MUSIC OF THE SPHERES

"Music of the Spheres" (Musica universalis) is a philosophical concept proposed by the great thinker and mathematician Pythagoras, who stated that the movements of the stars and planets produced a celestial form of music. It has since been determined that the universal note is D; or so they say.

"Daddy," little John asked, "When can we go Outside?"

It was Holiday Time, and they were eating a traditional meal of special shoots of grass, mushrooms, dragon fish, and algae, celebrating the Great Escape, in John's bedroom. It was the time when children of his age were taught the facts of life, and John was required to ask the question of his father, Socrates.

Sophia, John's twin sister, was in her bedroom in the tunnel, asking her mother, Aphrodite, the same question as they, too, ate the traditional meal. Their underground home was lit by vibrating walls of a variety of *Pyrosystis Fusiformis dinoflagellates* – bio-luminescent algae. The algae radiated waves of faint, luscious blue light. The ancient Sacred Lamps were fueled for this special occasion with miniature dragon fish, producing red and pink light,[1] but it was geothermal energy that supplied their white and ultraviolet light. Young John had never seen natural sunlight. Though their underground world was sophisticated and technologically advanced, Socrates was readying himself to tell his son that he must never try to go to the surface. It was forbidden. After blessing his son, Socrates began the speech he had memorized. It would be John's duty to memorize it for his own children one day.

"Remember how I told you that long, long ago, everyone used to live above our caves and tunnels, in the land of Thessalonica?" John nodded, looking into his father's pale, blue eyes. His father was one of the few who never changed his eye color, because his mom liked blue eyes. Most of the Underground changed their eye colors to match their mood, or for a holiday, but everyone changed their skin colors and patterns regularly. Their skins had been genetically modified eons ago to produce bioluminescence, in whatever colors they wished. They braided their long hair and let it trail behind them as they walked, creating a wave of fluorescent light.

Everyone was, when at rest, as white as marble, but dotted all over with what looked like tiny freckles. These were iridophores, such as the octopus and squid in their aquaria had. By opening or closing these millions of tiny iridophores, all kinds of patterns could be created. Due to their additional bioluminescence, everyone with it could display every color of the rainbow – and beyond – in whatever patterns were desired.

John had been born with an innate ability to change his color to display fear, anger, happiness or curiosity. As for the rest, he learned everything from writing to math, right on the backs of his smooth, flat hands. The contents of innumerable books (they, too, were sacred) had been programmed into his brain, but the commandment to read was practiced every day, even by adults. They projected pictures, pages and games on their large, flattened hands for private use, whenever they wished, though they had wall-screens of all sizes as well. Communication was easy using iridophores, but of course politicians, lawyers and movie stars knew how to pretend, though outright lying or acting a serious role did take years of practice.

"It is good to live underground," Socrates began. All his life, John had heard the phrase used daily. It was how they greeted each other. It was how they said goodbye. He had been taught about the benefits of life underground from infancy. True, they had to pump out radon, but they were protected from the sun, which overheated people, burnt their skins, and caused uncontrolled black growths (these were called 'cancers'). They were all much better off living underground.

"You have heard whispers about the Outside," Socrates continued. "You have heard whispers about 'stars,' 'mountains,' and 'oceans.'"

"Yes, my father, I have heard," John said, for his part of the ritual.

"You must not listen to the whispers!" Socrates stated, reaching over and pushing lumps of clay into his son's ears. John bowed his head, then said, as he had been taught, "I will not listen to the whispers."

After a long minute, John was allowed to remove the clay. As he cleaned his ears thoroughly, Socrates continued to speak.

"You must not ask about 'music.' It was once a way to make merry. It was once a way to celebrate life and death. It was once part of our lives, but 'music' is forbidden."

"Music is forbidden," John repeated.

"Now learn the truth," Socrates said, placing his hands over John's. "Open your ears, for you are the son of a priest."

"My father, they are open."

"We trust you with our rite of disobedience."

"I hear and say Amen, father."

This was the moment John had been waiting for. He was now old enough to hear *music*. To play music on the Sacred Instruments. He was old enough to be trusted not to reveal this secret to outsiders.

He knew that music once existed everywhere on the surface of the planet. For those Underground, music was strictly forbidden in public: only stamping on the floor in rhythm and chants were allowed. John had been told that singing, or any kind of melody, was forbidden, but why this was so had long been forgotten.

Some said that bad music was once made Above Ground, so bad that it had to be banned. There were legends that flying creatures called 'birds' existed. There was the Roc, for example, whose eggs were as big as a horse. Then there was the Phoenix, who plunged herself into the sun, a hot, bright object that hung in a sky so big you had to turn your head to see all of it. Some of their greatest caves were so high-ceilinged that they had elevators and cable cars. These were too warm for comfort, but by piping frigid groundwater into lakes, they cooled the caves and grew their food. The lakes teemed with algae-eating koi, goldfish, clown loaches, Siamese fighting fish, and variegated catfish.[2] These fish had survived the Cyborg Life Purge, which occurred when the Cyborgs had decided to eliminate most organic life from the surface of the whole world.

Life, after all, was a messy thing. A few Cyborgs, who had been breeding these particular fish for their color, and to fight, hid them in an underground lake, where robots tended them for an unknown length of time until the People of the Underground discovered them. The same robots who tended these exotic fish were still at it, hundreds of years later, thanks to their ability to replicate any of their parts that might wear out, including the orders given them on how to care for the fish.

"It is now time to learn our family's sacred Music," Socrates told him, handing him a small flute. "Today, you will learn this Song, which can never be heard outside the walls of our house. This Song is our past and our future. Now come, follow me."

They joined Aphrodite and Sophia, who were sitting in the family's living-room: John could smell the catfish and grass shoot stew that was always served to the children once a year, in honor of the times when there was once only fish, grass shoots and algae to eat. A robot brought the stew into the room and sat it on a small table.

For the first time, Sophia was old enough to serve the stew. She began by giving Archie, their lapdog, the decorated head and tail, after which she gave a bit of algae to their goldfish. "We remember the needs of all other creatures, as well as our own," she said.

"We remember their needs," the family said together. "Even as they supply our needs, body and soul." They knew that across the Kingdom, the same words were being spoken this hour, but only in the homes of the Priest would the sacred, secret music be played and celebrated.

As they ate the simple meal, Aphrodite told the age-old stories of how the Greek Athletes had survived the Great Extermination.

Certain Cyborgs had bred these very special Greek athletes, fleet of foot, for racing. Because some of these athletes were cherished, having earned fortunes for their owners, the best of the best had been sent underground to avoid the final extermination orders that were issued to rid the planet of the last human genes.

To do so was dangerous, and several Cyborgs were killed for their insubordination. Now Aphrodite told the traditonal story of Lady Diana the Derby Winner, whose Cyborg Master was 8KL88-Mother Teresa-Version 422. It had led Lady Diana and her children underground. "It saved her. It saved her family. It saved her friends. Though they tortured it and dismembered it, 8KL88-Mother Teresa-Version 422 never disclosed their hiding place. It did this because it loved Lady Diana."

Socrates added, "This proved that some purebred Cyborgs had chosen to harbor the capacity to love."

Next, John was handed a tiny cup, which was removed from its place of honor in an alcove next to a big wall-screen. He held the cup steady as his mother filled it with seaweed tea.[3]

"We drink this cup to remember its name: it was 8KL88-Mother Teresa-Version 422."

They each took a sip of the tea.

"Later, the Strangers Who Came to Earth found its head, which had somehow survived incineration," Aphrodite said. "Unable to revive it, nevertheless, they were able to learn of our existence, and through their superior technology, they located us."

Aphrodite wiped the cup clean and set it back in its place of honor.

"They explained to us why we needed to stay underground, while the earth was cleansed of the last of the Cyborgs. And here we must remain, until the time comes that we can be free."

"Now, we pray for that time to come, as our ancestors before us have prayed," Socrates said, as the family joined hands in a circle.

After the prayer, Socrates asked his family to be seated. The final part of the ritual was about to unfold. Prior to this, the twins had always been sent to their rooms, but now, they were old enough to participate.

The wall-screen lit up, and a flautist appeared, carrying a silver flute. He was tall, florid-faced, dressed in worked leather, with golden buskins laced to his knees. He stared at them with a fierce countenance. His thick eyebrows and curly, black beard made him look like one of the ancient Greek gods. "Listen well!" he commanded them, lifting his silver flute to his mouth.

Then he began to play.

Limpid, luscious, forbidden sounds flowed from the flute. Sounds that enchanted the soul, betrayed the imagination, led into the foreboden. John covered his eyes and let the music wash over him as the waves of a great green sea. Sparks of flame spun past his inner vision and his heart was pounding. Music! This was music!

No Pied Piper could have had such an effect on these children. The color rushed into their faces, they found their feet tapping, they thrust out their chests and began clapping their hands! As the music continued, tears began streaming down their cheeks. The flute spoke of feelings they scarcely knew, of skies filled with stars, of forests as far as the eye could see. They could see horses and deer running through the glades, masses of flowers bursting into color on every wooded hill, and above it all, they could hear their own voices, with their parents, as they sang together the songs upon songs implanted in their brains, passed on from generation to generation, the songs of old, coming alive from their very genes. And it could be heard only in these insulated rooms, this *music*, which the flute brought back to life. Life was good! Life was beautiful! Life was freedom!

Suddenly, the music stopped. The flautist lowered his flute.

"We will never forget!" he told them. "Though they forbid it forever, we will never forget!"

The screen went blank. John looked down at the small flute he had been given. He raised it to his lips and blew a sad, solitary note.

"Put it away, John," his father said. "In time, you, or your son, or your son's son, will play it on the surface of the wide world. But that time has not yet come."

"It is because of the Music of the Spheres," Aphrodite explained, as they sat down again. "The Strangers Who Came to Earth explained it to us long ago."

"The Cosmos is enormous," Socrates said. "It is studded with galaxies. The galaxies themselves are filled with stars. Every star has planets, moons, asteroids. Many of them have life, such as our own planet. What we never knew, until it was too late, is that the galaxies sing."

"They sing?" Sophia asked.

"They sing as a flute sings," Aphrodite told them.[4] "Now you will learn what the Priests have saved for us."

At her words, Socrates pointed to the big wall-screen, which vanished at the gesture. Then, with a circle-eight motion of his father's finger against the wall, John saw a small door, which opened automatically to reveal a blue chamber. John would never have guessed it was there, amidst all the decorative roughness of the stonework.

"You must remember this location, and the signal I have showed you with my fingers," Socrates told his children. "Here we keep the holiest secrets." Among the various boxes, they could see a small black cube, which began vibrating at Socrates' touch. As their father brought the box carefully from its place, his skin turned white as marble and he stamped his strong, powerful foot against the floor three times. John and Sophia both leaned eagerly forward, but Socrates shook his head again, "Don't touch it," he warned. "I must add your DNA signatures." First, for John, he tapped a coded rhythm onto the top of the cube. "Memorize it," he urged his son, repeating the rhythm. When he was satisfied that John had memorized the pattern, Socrates conducted the same ritual with Sophia. By the time he was finished, tiny ridges of some jellylike substance had appeared, as if alive, atop the cube.

"Now, we mingle our blood with yours," Aphrodite said, as she took the cube. Her beautiful blue hair was braided up in the traditional style used in all the sacred ceremonies. She closed her eyes, waited a moment, then handed the black cube back to Socrates,

"Now, it's your turn," Socrates told his son. "Hold it tight. Don't drop it."

When John did so, a tiny needle pricked his finger.

"Tap it as I showed you," his father said. "Then, hand it to your sister."

After Sophia returned the cube to Socrates, the cube's surface flattened out again and its shiny surface was once more a solid. "Now our blood is mingled together," Aphrodite told them. "Now we have the same Guide."

"Next, I must ask the *question*," Socrates told them. "Then, something wonderful will happen. After it is over, I will replace the cube in the secret place, and this sacred ceremony will be finished."

"Touch the cube with us, as your father asks the question," Aphrodite whispered.

Together, they placed their hands on the cube, as Socrates said, in the voice of a child, "Daddy, when can we go outside?"

Daddy, when can we go outside?

This was the question that was always asked. One day, they would get the answer.

As these words were spoken, a white, shimmering Orb flew up from the black cube and hovered above it. "Bow your heads!" their father commanded: everyone did so. "Don't look directly at it!"

"It is an electromagnetic orb," Aphrodite told them. "Every Priest's family has one. We see it only once a year, when it offers us wisdom for the time ahead."

The Orb hovered over each of them for a brief moment, then came to rest on the black cube.

"We will talk to each other now, guided by the Orb's influence," Aphrodite explained. "Thoughts will come to you. Speak what comes into your mind."

"Where did the Orb come from?" Sophia asked, rubbing her blue eyes with her hands, which, due to her excitement, were speckled with flashing dots.

"The Strangers gave these orbs to us," Socrates told her. "We are the only survivors left with human genes. We, who came from Greece, who carry the legends of the ancient Greeks in our very souls. To us their Priests, were given these Wise Orbs. They are semi-alive, created with DNA signals from me, your mother and now you. It will never respond to anyone's touch but ours. If any of us should die."

"Does death really happen?" John blurted out.

"You just don't hear about it," Socrates said gently. "It's not polite to bring it up. When we say a journey has been taken to the Surface, that's what it means. I will probably be dead in another two hundred years. Long ago, when we decided that we would never be more than 49% Cyborg, we chose the course that eventually leads to death. So finally, we do die. But because we will die, we are allowed to have a son and a daughter to take our place. You, our children, are renewing our race. But Cyborgs could only replicate themselves."

The children had recently viewed a display of dismembered, decapitated Cyborgs, the last of their kind, which the keepers called "Spiders." They had eight arms. There were pictures of their heads, with dozens of eyes encircling them like black beads. They had discarded their original shapes, which had been like humans, for a more efficient kind of body that could spin webs, from which they could hang. This saved space, which they filled with metallic constructions of all kinds that generated energy and their own particular kind of music. Because of its frequency, their music was fatal to most living things. However, humans fought back by inventing the Sacred

Paint,[5] which they would spread all over their bodies whenever they left their insulated homes. It had saved them and their pets, though the time came when they were forced to live their whole lives underground.

As John considered these things, the Orb suddenly moved to hover in the air in front of him.

"John," his father said, "The Orb wishes to tell you something, but you must give it permission to do so."

"How?"

Handing the box to his son, Socrates said, "Tap the rhythm I showed you. In the center of the box."

As John tapped the code, the Orb turned bluish. As it hovered just above his hand, a pattern appeared, filled with twists that looked like magnified DNA. John could feel some pressure on the back of his hand.

"Let it guide your hand," Socrates told him. "It's a very light pressure – go as it pushes you."

John had to stand to reach where the Orb was so gently pressing: it was about a half-meter above the back of the couch upon which they sat. Suddenly, the Orb streaked against the wall and vanished into it. As it did so, a small, circular door opened, and a tightly-wrapped cylinder, which seemed to be made of a semi-translucent substance, slowly purred out of the space within, riding on some kind of invisible engine. When John reached out his hand, the scroll dropped into it, and the opening closed.

"This is extraordinary!" Socrates exclaimed. He was staring at his son, whose skin was flaring in red and blue patches from pure excitement. "Whatever you do, don't drop the Scroll!"

"What now?" Sophia asked, stepping back.

"He has to eat it," Aphrodite declared.

"I have to eat it?"

"Eat it!" His father repeated sternly. "Don't wait! You've been selected to receive some special information."[6]

Aphrodite, trembling, added, "Could this be the Time?"

Never had an Orb given a Scroll to any child. The scrolls were historically few in number, hidden from the people, released only to the Priests during times of emergencies. The last known scroll predicted a mighty flood into the main chambers of the city: just in time, they had fled to the higher regions and escaped death.

What was coming next? John took the scroll by the long end and bit into it.

"It's sweet," he said. "Tastes good."

"Eat all of it," his father commanded.

As he swallowed the last of the scroll, John began emanating light. His eyes rolled up in his head. Kicking out his legs, he fell to the floor, gripping his belly. "I'm going to vomit!" he groaned. Anxiously, they knelt down around him, as John turned his head from side to side, foam bubbling at the corners of his mouth.

"My son!" Aphrodite cried, throwing her arms around him and lifting his head, "oh, my son!" As she began to weep, John raised a shaky hand.

"I have a message…" he said, his voice hoarse with strain. "Gather the people!"

* * *

They came, the great and the small, the old and the young. They brought their animals, their pets, their potted plants, their seeds and seedlings, their tools, their books, and their clothing. They brought their beloved horses, goats, and dogs. They gathered at the Sealed Shaft, where the battered head of 8KL88-Mother Teresa-Version 422 was encased in a crystal shrine. They came to listen to the words of a twelve-year-old boy, who was brought slowly forward. He came leading a white horse, the symbol of purity. As he stood gazing at them, the seals of the Shaft that led up to the outside world were smashed apart by his white horse, with great kicks and blows. The sight brought screams of fear from the people. But the boy-priest was not afraid, so they calmed themselves.

Then from his mouth came the words that had been written on the Scroll.

"People of the Kentauroi!"[7] he cried out. "You once lived on the surface of one of the Pure Blue-Green Singing Notes of the Universe. Your world sang a rare song in its orbit around its star.[8] Thanks to the clouds, the mountains, the seas and the sun, this planet's blue-green note was perfectly tuned. Along with Saturn, Jupiter,[9] and the other superb planets, a Sublime Chord of harmonics pleasing to the ear of The Great Musician resonated through the Universe. Your Blue-Green Planet sang its Note beautifully for over a billion years, until it became infested with metallic sub-beings and millions of the cruelest of humans, who burned its green forests, polluted its blue waters, flattened its mountains, and covered all its surface with energy-eating tiles. Then the oceans were thrown from the earth to form a huge ring of ice as the metallic beings spread their kind, destroying every trace of life they could find. In the end, they even turned on the last humans who had helped them ruin everything."

The people, astonished, began stamping upon the ground, expressing their anxiety.

"Be silent!" the boy-priest commanded them. "Hear the words of the scroll that I have eaten! The Blue-Green Planet had lost its tune. Your Galaxy's Symphonic Chorus suddenly had a sour note. Your planet had to be re-tuned. We found some few among the wretched half-beings, and they were inspired to hide you. To save you few with human genes. You alone were saved because your ancient ways showed respect for the Music of the Spheres."

The boy leaped up and grabbed the golden bridle of the white horse, holding it tight as a military saddle was fitted onto the Priest's back, symbolizing the weight of leadership that he would have to carry from now on. There he waited, the horse he held half-rearing with excitement, its flaring nostrils red-rimmed, its mane shaking against the reins. "As this great horse is our servant, and toils for us," John called out, "nevertheless, he is guided by his bridle, not by a whip! So we will also be masters of all the earth, but with bridles, not whips!"

The crowd roared its approval: then, as the crowd quieted again, the young Priest continued his speech.

"The infestation of the metal Cyborgs wiped out humanity from the face of the earth –only we were saved – but that infestation has finally been eradicated. All Cyborgs, including those still clinging to any human genetic material, are now beyond reconstruction, their last traces of DNA destroyed by their own hand. The ring of ice that silenced the music once gracing your world died with them. As the ice ring cracked to pieces, its remnants became meteors that crashed to the earth. Within the ice, life was suspended, ready to burst forth. Finally, the Strangers brought back many creatures and plants from the dying colonies on Mars and on the Moon, where they would have thrived, had they only had compassion for each other. It took over a thousand years, but the world has been put in tune again."

The young priest waved his arm in a grand gesture of joy. "People of the Kentauroi! Hear me! The oceans have returned! The forests have returned! And music has returned, both to the earth and to us!"

What could this mean? Most of the people had no real concept of what oceans and forests were. That was the stuff of fairytales and legends. And music? That was forbidden entirely. Wasn't it?

As the people stood there, confused and hopeful, John led the white horse to the doorway of the great mine-shaft that reached up, it was said, to the surface of the world. The horse, led by its golden bridle, almost danced toward the doorway, as if it understood that it would soon be able to gallop, unimpeded, easy and free, across long stretches of wasteland, plains and valleys.

"When I touch this door," the young Priest cried out, "it will open, and you will be carried up by the machines that were placed here centuries ago. The same machines that put you deep into this dark world, so long ago, will surely bring you to the surface again. There will be many dangers. The sun is still harsh and will burn you: take care! There will be pain and trouble, but the wide world is there, singing its song, and you will once more sing with it ..." He paused and gazed out over the multitude.

"Are you ready?"

The people shouted as One, with a roar that echoed through every tunnel and passed through every door.

"You entered these caves few in number," John told them. "Now you will return in your thousands. Go forth and multiply! Sing a good song! Sing it with the earth! Never let the earth's song go sour again!"

Then the people marched forth into the huge elevators, family by family, and when they reached the surface, they gasped at the wonders they saw. They saw trees, waterfalls, blue skies, and the sun that blinded them if they looked too long. Long ago, human beings had destroyed this world with Cyborgs and ruthless greed. The last human genes had been saved because they had gone undetected, mingled with *equus*, blended with *equus*, and so humanity in a new and ancient form was saved. Now the centaurs – half human, half horse – were free to gallop joyfully through the opened gates, carrying their flutes, their food in their saddles, and their children in their arms.

Endnotes

1. "Almost all marine bioluminescence is blue in color… blue-green light (wavelength around 470 nm) transmits furthest in water. The reason that underwater photos usually look blue is because red light is quickly absorbed as you descend… [also,] most organisms are sensitive only to blue light – they lack the visual pigments which can absorb longer (yellow, red) or shorter (indigo, ultraviolet) wavelengths. A notable exception to this "rule" is Malacosteid family of fishes (known as Loosejaws), which produce red light and are able to see this light.…" Dragon fish are in this family. In this scenario, skin scales and aborted fetuses from humans provided the base food source. http://biolum.eemb.ucsb.edu/organism/dragon.html Retrieved July 1, 2015.

2 All these fish can eat algae.

3. Powdered Kombu seaweed roots can make a "tea" similar to bullion. It is high in glutamate, iodine, calcium, iron and fiber. While it lowers cholesterol and may boost the immune system, Kombu tea may provide too much glutamate, which can over-excite the brain's neurons and exacerbate degenerative nerve diseases. Generally, the body produces its own glutamate.

4. Facts behind "The Music of the Spheres": "Any natural sound can be described as a combination of sine waves. These pure tones… are always combined… to form even the simplest sound. It's the manner of their distribution in the sound that forms the color of that sound, the so-called timbre. This is the single feature that makes a note played on a violin different from the exact same note played on a flute. Some terminology you should know:

A *partial* is any of the sine waves by which a complex tone is described.

A *harmonic* (or a *harmonic partial*) is any of a set of partials that are whole number multiples of a common fundamental frequency. This set includes the fundamental, which is a whole number multiple of itself (1 times itself).

Electronic synthesizers are capable of playing pure frequencies with no overtones… [JVB: Consider this the Cyborg Preference] although they usually combine frequencies into more complex tones to simulate other instruments. The timbre of the flute is actually very poor in overtones, and that's why it is often regarded as the instrument with the purest sound. In fact, it has just enough overtones to make it sound infinitely nicer than a pure sine wave, which as you might have noticed gives a rather dull feeling.

For those among you who know interval theory, it's very useful to know that the distribution of harmonics is always mathematically determined.… Given these background notions, we are now finally able to explain what harmonics on the flute are all about.

When "playing harmonics" on the flute, what we are actually doing is "excluding" the fundamental tone and some of the lower overtones, thus emphasizing the first of the "surviving" harmonics, which will sound as if it were a fundamental in its own right." http://www.flutetunes.com/articles/flute-harmonics/ Retrieved July 8, 2015. [Consider these principles as applied to the planets as they circle the sun and rotate, their densities, and the fact that Jupiter, Saturn, the Earth, etc. emit 'audible' radio frequencies.]

More from NASA: "Radiowaves have the longest wavelengths in the electromagnetic spectrum. These waves can be longer than a football field or as short as a football. Radio waves do more than just bring music to your radio. They also carry signals for your television and cellular phones…Objects in space, such as planets and comets, giant clouds of gas and dust, and stars and galaxies, emit light at many different wavelengths. Some of the light they emit has very large wavelengths - sometimes as long as a mile!. These long waves are in the radio region of the electromagnetic spectrum." http://science.hq.nasa.gov/kids/imagers/ems/radio.html Retrieved July 7, 2015.

Lightning strokes like this one are the source of the eerie-sounding radio emissions that surround us. http://science.nasa.gov/science-news/science-at-nasa/2001/ast-19jan_1/ Retrieved July 8, 2015.

"Saturn is a source of intense radio emissions, which have been monitored by the Cassini spacecraft. The radio waves are closely related to the auroras near the poles of the planet. These auroras are similar to Earth's northern and southern lights. This is an audio file of radio emissions from Saturn. The Cassini spacecraft began detecting these radio emissions in April 2002."

5. When sound reflects off a curved surface called a parabola, it will bounce out in a straight line no matter where it originally hits. The futuristic paint would have been made of parabolic particles that oriented themselves on the microscopic level to reflect all oncoming sound waves.

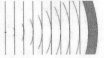

6. Rev. 10:10 : King James Bible: "And I took the little book out of the angel's hand, and ate it up; and it was in my mouth sweet as honey: and as soon as I had eaten it, my belly was bitter." "… molecular gastronomy … is the chemistry and physics behind the preparation of any dish: for example, why a mayonnaise becomes firm or why a soufflé swells … molecular gastronomy is a new science … the first PhD in 'Molecular and Physical Gastronomy' [was presented in 1996] at the University of Paris.… Since 2005, new dishes, produced on the basis of the results of molecular gastronomy, have been named after famous chemists or scientists…" http://embor.embopress.org/content/7/11/1062 Retrieved July 5, 2015. It should be possible to place information into an edible product, though upon digestion, there could be side effects. It would be an interesting way to educate, or for spies to transmit information, probably by using a variation of a 3-D printer.

7. The Greek word is Κένταυρος.

8. NASA Science News, January 19, 2001 "If humans had radio antennas instead of ears, we would hear a remarkable symphony of strange noises coming from our own planet. Scientists call them "tweeks," "whistlers" and "sferics." They sound like background music from a flamboyant science fiction film, but this is not science fiction. Earth's natural radio emissions are real and, although we're mostly unaware of them, they are around us all the time.

"Everyone's terrestrial environment almost literally sings with radio waves at audio frequencies," says Dennis Gallagher, a space physicist at the Marshall Space Flight Center (MSFC). "Our ears can't detect radio waves directly, but we can convert them to sound waves with the aid of a very low frequency (VLF) radio receiver." http://www.nasa.gov/mission_pages/cassini/multimedia/pia07966.html Retrieved July 8, 2015.

9. "So what does Jupiter sound like? It actually produces a wide range of bursts with different sounds. The most common, called L-bursts, last from a few tenths of a second to several seconds and sound like ocean waves breaking up on a beach. The shorter bursts, known as S-bursts, last a few thousandths to a few hundredths of a second and sound more like popcorn popping or like a handful of pebbles thrown onto a tin roof."

THE RELIGION SOLUTION

The pleasure boat moved slowly between the glistening power towers that filled most of the sea: you knew there was water between the towers, but it was difficult to see it, so close were the towers and platforms that held the tall buildings, and the roadways that stretched among them. The tour guide was a 51% Cyborg, appropriately weathered-looking, with what was rumored to be a beard made of genuine hair. The trip was amazingly long: they were headed to Cuba, the only Reserve that remained open on prime retail property.

"We are now approaching one of the first 100% human Reserves," Archie Pelago told his guests. "This Reserve was called Heaven on Earth. Its citizens came from every land and clime. They were followers of 'the Religion Solution.' They aimed for Heaven, Peace, and Love."

Archie guided his boat, which was shaped like a Venetian gondola, with what seemed expert precision (it was actually on a track and he only pretended to push it along with its long paddle). Archie was dressed as an ancient Gondolier, complete with short pants and a vest with gaudy sequins. The boat was only half full: Cyborgs were caring less and less about humans and their past. The human race, after all, was nearly extinct. It had given birth to the far superior life form that now inhabited the planet. With hardly a microbe now existing that could do harm, and the weather totally under control, it was outer space that now interested the average Cyborg brain.

The great dream was to populate Mars. Currently, countless comets, small moons (appropriately blown to dust as they were kicked into the Martian atmosphere) and asteroid debris was being diverted to the Red Planet in an endless swarm of tonnage. In another hundred years, Mars would be big enough to hold onto its atmosphere for good, thanks to the barrage of asteroids slamming against it, hour after hour, steered into it by thousands of drones. It had been calculated that only a few more small pushes would be needed to alter Mars' orbit and bring it close enough to the sun to achieve an average temperature slightly above freezing. Calculating that new orbit, which would not smash the planet against some huge asteroid, had been itself a masterful scientific feat, involving probes that extrapolated everything approaching the solar system, as to how and when Mars might suffer impacts in its new orbit, and placing sentry drones ahead of its path to divert any and all oncoming obstacles in a manner that would not affect any other major planet or satellite.

Mars was also partially flooded now, thanks to the Comet Project. It was estimated that when the planet had accumulated a surface area of 60% unfrozen water, it would then be able to generate enough power for permanent colonies. That was important, because space on the earth was running out. The moon itself was simply too small to hold more than100 million Cyborgs.

As Archie looked over his newest batch of customers, one of the tourists concerned him. This tourist, who sat closest to Archie at the stern, had described herself on the manifest as an anthropologist. Archie had never met an anthropologist before: they specialized in human beings. He did understand that anthropologists were endowed with powers that made them able to bend a human's will. They had the tools to demand obedience so they could walk safely among them without fear, for an unarmed Cyborg could be overwhelmed by a mass of humans – temporarily.

Considering that he was only 51% Cyborg himself, Archie realized that he had better watch what he said. The jokes he had prepared about humans suddenly seemed inappropriate, perhaps even dangerous, should they offend her. Not only that, but he could see that she also carried a MediaBot on her shoulder. She was likely there to check as to how he conducted his tour. It had been at least five years since anybody had brought a MediaBot on a tour. The last time, his tour had been made into a Special, and for a while, business was good. It concerned petitions made by some of the humans to be transferred to the Jerusalem Reserve. It was good entertainment to see them weeping and begging for the transfer. Emotions were interesting to Cyborgs, the majority of whom had no human brain tissue left. For recreation, some of them accepted temporary implants, to give them such sensations.

The Special had been a great hit as each petitioner was turned down and given the option to be exterminated or to accept life on the Reserve. A few accepted extermination. The humans were given a sumptuous feast and were allowed to preach about their religion and life before they were vaporized. For a while, business had been brisk after the executions. Maybe it would become good, again, if he said the right things and impressed this lady. Archie was itching for a bigger and better cubicle. His was quite outdated, with no private scrubbers or instant energy outlets. After all, being only 51% Cyborg, he was more of an impediment than an asset to the community.

As the gondola's motors whirred lightly, then slowed as they approached the Reserve, the tourists began to admire the huge golden gates that rose before them.

"Since this Reserve was called "Heaven on Earth," Archie explained, "we fitted the border security perimeter all in gold, with these magnificent Golden Gates. A legend exists that heaven has golden gates. A nice touch, if I say so myself."

The enormous metallic gates were so high that it was impossible to see beyond them. As the gondola drew closer, the anthropologist suddenly stood, making the boat shake slightly. Next, she clapped her hands to capture everyone's attention. It was a strange gesture, one that humans used, and it startled everyone on board, which was surely what she intended.

"I wish to introduce myself," she told the group. "As you can see, I wear the face of Joan of Arc. For those unfamiliar with her story and persona, unknown voices told her to wage war for the sake of her king. Girls were not supposed to do such things, but she obeyed the voices. Eventually, she was captured and burned to death as a witch. Witches were supposed to possess evil powers. She was a courageous girl who had a deep belief in her religion. I chose her persona to help guide me to understand the people in this Reserve… to record what's left here, before I annihilate it."

The guests on the gondola drew back from her, struck with horror.

"Y – you're a Destroyer?" Archie managed to blurt out.

"I'm a Destroying Angel," the anthropologist said, with cold calm. Her piercing blue eyes looked over the small group. "This Reserve will be destroyed today. It is necessary for numerous reasons, most of them, financial. You came here at random to visit the place, and will serve as witnesses as to its state before, during and after its removal from the face of the planet. Because this might disrupt your expected recreation plans, each of you, including your Tour Guide, will be given enhancements and updates for your cubicles. Congratulations."

"What will we be getting?" a tourist, who was wearing the garb of a monk for the occasion, dared to ask.

"You'll be allowed to choose from a set of options," the Angel replied, showing them, with a wave of her hand, a hologram that danced before their eyes, shimmering with a list of those options. It hovered there for a minute, taking in information from each brain. Then it vanished. "When you return to your respective cubicles, you'll find the improvements that you desired have been made," the Angel told them. "Archie, you will get a scrubber and a beard transplant. Sophia," she said to another, "You will be granted an extra square meter of space, sufficient to allow another person to sit inside your cubicle with you."

One by one, each tourist was regaled with a particular improvement that met their current desires. This was an unexpected bonus. The tourists began whispering among themselves. This was going to be a trip to remember! Finally, the Angel raised a finger to her rosy lips, signaling silence. "Of course, these improvements are being implemented for you," the Angel said. "Because today, you're needed, as my witnesses. When my task is finished, all you have to do is file your memories with me and the MediaBot before we return to the Tour office. Of course, you will agree to the MediaBot's probes for that purpose."

Archie knew they had no choice but to agree. He feared even thinking of having a choice: if the MediaBot picked up any such resistance, it would deliver a punishing shock to remind him of what he was supposed to think. MediaBots observed, created, changed and delivered News, which of course was the official version of everything. It was always accurate. It was never disputed (or, rather, it could not be disputed).

"You may now proceed with your usual lecture," the Destroying Angel said, gathering her long, shimmering skirts around her and seating herself again at the stern. She seemed so innocent, so similar to them. A mere anthropologist, with blonde hair and the face of a young French girl from a faraway time and land. But they knew her power. Cross her, and death would follow. As much as a Cyborg could die, that is. The unpleasant result would be difficult to reconstruct, and it would be expensive.

"As we approach the Reserve," Archie said, "let me give you some basic background as to the inhabitants."

The tourists were paying tense, strict attention, knowing that their memories would be evaluated for accuracy against each other.

"You already know how the most dedicated members of every major world religion were sent to this Reserve, once called Cuba," he began. "Here, they were allowed to live without any supervision whatsoever. Supplies: food, basic machinery to generate fresh water and energy, repair modules, and several excellent Bot educators, including one Bot for each religion, to keep the doctrines available for reference, were shuttled into the Reserve. There was plenty for all. There was access to basic medical care. Their every possible need was met. Every religion represented included the same number of adherents. Those with the highest IQs in each religious group were the designated leaders of the reserve. It seemed a perfect experiment."

"It was an experiment?" one of the tourists asked.

"Only in that we were curious about what would happen next. Bets were made, which generated the income needed to keep the Religious Reserve financially in the black."

"I've heard that all the major religions were represented," another tourist commented. "But which religions?"

"I'll answer that," the Destroying Angel responded. "The information your guide was given, originally, was quite limited."

"It was?" Archie asked. Immediately, the Angel's face darkened with wrath, and the MediaBot on her shoulder sent a charge of pain through his body.

"No irrelevant questions!" the Angel declared. Archie had collapsed, writhing with pain, beside his long, synthetic wood oar. "To continue," she intoned, "the most devoted members of each religion who wished to participate were brought into the Reserve, where they could practice their faith without any interference from us."

"They had no laws?" a tourist wanted to know.

"They had laws," the Angel replied. "Each religion had its own laws. Of course, some religions tried to proselytize – to make converts. It was interesting to observe, because all the members sincerely believed, when they first arrived, in the precepts of their own particular Faith. None of them were curious about anybody else's religion. As time passed, and some of them began to grow older, or became romantically involved with someone of a different belief, we kept watching. It was, indeed, fascinating. I, myself, was so impressed with some of the events that took place, that when I graduated, I chose the persona of Joan of Arc as my contact with them."

The gondola was now leaving the inhabited region, and a sliver of open water appeared before them. Ahead was a mist-covered island. What was left of Cuba.

"I will now tell you about the Reserve," the Angel said. "The following religions are involved: Protestant Mainstream (Anglican, Methodist and Baptist), Protestant Charismatic, Evangelicals, Quakers and Seventh-Adventists were combined, Muslim included some teaching clerics, plus the Sunni, the Shia, and the Wahabi-Salafi. Then, there is the Roman Catholic. The Greek, Eastern and Russian Orthodox churches were combined. Theravada Buddhism and Zen Buddhism, plus some Jews, African cults and animists – along with Jehovah's Witnesses, Latter-Day Saints, the religions of Kong and Kung Fu, and three forms of Hinduism, and Vegans, made up the rest." "What about Wicca?" one asked.

"They are combined with Vegans, Mystics and Cyborg-worshippers," was the reply. "I should have mentioned that."

By now, Archie was back on his feet and was dutifully pushing the self-propelled gondola. He knew he must begin his spiel, so, determined not to get in trouble again, he called out, "We are now approaching the Reserve. After the gates open, remember – you are not allowed to interact with any of the residents. We will enter transparent tunnels, where you can observe demonstrations of some of the habits of each religion, such as Christmas, circumcision, exorcisms, a flogging for sexual immorality, a stoning, and the ceremonial cremation of a dead body. Substitutions of any of the above may occur. When the gates open, remain silent until we enter the tunnels."

As the gates slowly opened wide, Archie heard a gasps of amazement at what his guests now saw. It was not what he had expected, but he hid his astonishment. As the gondola passed through the Gates, a dead body was floating past them in the water. White birds of some kind were sitting on top of it, gorging themselves on the ripped and naked corpse. Several tourists watched with fascination. The more human they were, the more fascinated they were. The gondola's sides now moved to curve over them, transparent and sturdy: nothing could penetrate its walls. They could see mountains, cloaked in clouds and wafts of smoke, coming from beyond heaps of burned trees. Archie was surprised to see the precious forest reduced to these blackened, fallen logs. He had always wished for a pole made of real wood, wild as that dream was.

Now the gondola shivered, then dipped down into a yawning tunnel. The tunnel's hermetically sealed doors closed behind them with a rush of air that was filled with the stench of death.

"The smell is of dead bodies," Archie explained, as the tourists whispered. Only a few of them had olfactory senses: they were rarely needed any more, and those who still had them surely regretted it, due to the heavy odor of decomposition that filled the tunnel. Another body floated by – this one was decapitated. Some Vegan had become angry, it seemed, with someone. Or maybe a Muslim had done it …

The tunnel remained dark so the inhabitants could not see them. However, they could see everything on display.

The first display was disappointing. The lighting was low and flickering badly. The marquee exhibited a sign in neon and gold that said "Roman Catholic Mass" – but the display itself only showed an empty altar. A scrawled sign lay against the altar, with just one word in crude letters: 'Closed.'

"Sorry," Archie whispered. "This happens, once in a while." He said this to soothe them. In fact, he had never seen a closed display. There were heavy penalties involved, including pain implants, if any main character failed to show up. There were mannequins that could be rolled out in emergencies, but the Catholic Mass scene was empty. Even the golden chalice on the marble altar was gone.

The gondola purred on, its occupants silent. At the site of the second display, which was an example of a Muslim female being flogged after her ankles had been seen in public, once again, something was wrong. There was an emergency mannequin at this site: its arm, which was supposed to be flogging a real, live Muslim girl, was broken off at the elbow. The flogging motion looked strange indeed, with the arm moving up and down, sometimes a little to the left, or a little to the right, with a cracked voice saying "Thirty-nine, forty! Forty-one, forty-two!" over and over again. A crookedly-written sign in the viewing area said, once again, 'Closed.' When they reached the third exhibit, which was supposed to show Greek Orthodox dancers at a wedding celebration, the entire area was black as night, and the gondola was plunged into darkness.

"I can't see!" came a complaint in the heavy pall. A moment later, each Cyborg lit up, for the rest of the tunnel was equally dark. The fearsome figure of the Destroying Angel glowed with a luminescence that quivered like flame. Now she spoke into the gloom.

"I'm too late," she said. "I had hoped to save them some of their sufferings."

"What do you mean?" a tourist asked.

"We have been watching the progress of this Reserve closely, for the past thirty years," the Angel said, her voice rumbling with displeasure. "We saw the women eventually consigned indoors. They had to be covered entirely, from head to foot. Polygamy was required of all men. There was no birth control, so women were being impregnated at an alarming rate. But the Vegans had taken over the food supply. No meat was allowed, even though there wasn't enough food variety to sustain the entire population on that diet: We had failed to plan accordingly. Then, because the Jehovah's Witnesses did not allow blood transfusions, and many Hindus had come to believe that non-Hindus were Untouchables, many of the pregnant women, who were anemic, and anyone else who needed a blood transfusion, simply perished."

The Angel laughed bitterly. "There were many riots as the Christians began fighting to keep Sunday worship, because Seventh Day Adventists insisted on having all religious worship meetings on Saturdays. All of that was rejected by the Muslims, who insisted that Fridays were the proper days for such meetings."

They came before another exhibit, weakly lit: it was supposed to show a Hindu Untouchable being prepared for cremation, but once again, nothing was taking place. The remains of a previous cremation could be seen next to the fake River Ganges, which was supposed to have carried it off. Instead, the ashes and the bones lay in a grisly, abandoned heap.

The Angel had kept talking, even as they passed yet another exhibit that was abandoned. They would have to watch an animal being slaughtered Kosher style some other time...

Meanwhile, the Angel was continuing her verbal essay.

"Finally," she told them, "we learned that no males were being allowed to give medical care to the women, but because the women were not allowed to be educated, there were no women doctors. Hence, they had called upon the Wiccans, who, if a witch failed to save a woman in childbirth, were likely to face burning at the stake. Buddhists became hermits and celibates, hid themselves, while Hindus resigned themselves to the next life. Jews tried to stop their girls from getting circumcised by African Muslims and animists, but at the same time, children were being trained to become suicide bombers. Buddhist monks began immolating themselves, charismatic preachers scammed people of their food and wealth, and then were themselves executed. The doctrine-teaching machines were destroyed, and a new religion emerged that worshipped mega-church leaders as gods."

"But – how?" Archie asked.

"Remember that we appointed those with the highest IQs as the religious leaders." The Angel's blue eyes shot out sparks of fire. "A few created mega-churches. They grew immensely wealthy, and began to send regiments against each other to overcome 'Satan.' Those who were defeated were executed in several Reformation movements that required all religious books to be burnt. As wars took over the Reserve, prisoners were sacrificed on stone altars to please the surviving mega-church leader, who was given the title of 'God on Earth.' In his honor, the hearts and brains of those who were slain on the altars were ritually devoured, after they were dispatched Kosher style. I came here to put all these abominations to an end. To terminate them all. But it seems I'm too late."

"What do you mean?" a tourist asked.

To Archie's surprise, the Destroying Angel spread out her hands, and the gondola turned itself around, heading back to home. "They're all dead," she told the tourists. "They have exterminated themselves. Do not be concerned: all of you will receive the promised upgrades, and Mr. Pelago will be retrained for a new line of duty."

TIME CAPSULE

K live Newton-James Joyce kept circling the high table, counting his steps compulsively. As he did so, he repeated the words that soothed him best: *One-two-three, four! Get to work, get to work, get to work!* The big black table was empty except for a short stack of photos and advertisements. Klive clasped his human-looking hands together as if in prayer, but it was just his way of exerting some self control. His face was a large black cube that could pivot in any direction. As all high-end Cyborgs, nothing could be seen or probed that he kept there, but tiny changes in what was a faux liquid surface could convey to the Censors how busy his processors were.

He was only allowed 1% downtime, or his head cube would begin to glow green, with stripes of red. Next, he'd feel uncomfortable. Plus, there was the social stigma of glowing, as any accused of being "lazy" were already pre-judged.

But Klive's head cube had never glowed with stripes of red.

Ever.

He carried "hero" status for using only .004% of his accumulated downtime in his existence, but that came at a price. He had developed a few compulsive disorders – some wasteful logic loops that needed fixing.

"I still have a few things to do before I jump into the volcano," Klive said aloud, still circling the table. *One-two-three-four! Get to work, get to work, start working!*

Klive Newton-James Joyce wanted it all over. He felt worn out. He wanted to respond to the imperatives of his conditioning: to exterminate himself when his lifelong task was complete, which created space for a new Cyborg dedicated to a new task with its very own specialized training.

Klive had seen the Museum of Heroes and knew exactly where his star would be placed. He would have an impressive funeral, he had been told. As a Hero, he would be allowed to wear clothing for the last day of his existence. It was an old custom that distinguished him, for a single day, from all the others of his caste in recognition of his outstanding service to the Hive.

That was Klive Newton-James Joyce's personal word for the famous statue called "Industry" that now stood before OneWorld Kommune's equally famous antique-style headquarters in what had formerly been called Salt Lake City in the territory owning Utah. The "Industry" statue had been found perfectly preserved (despite nuclear wars) along with a priceless collection of human data hidden away in an enormous under-ground sanctuary carved into living stone. "Industry" symbolized the work ethic of the region's most prominent religious group. It stood for loyal and selfless commitment to hard work and to the deity called "The Lord."

The region's human inhabitants, known as "Mormons" to outsiders, were officially filed as "LDS" or Latter-Day Saints. They were important. Early in his career, Klive was calibrated to deal with 8.5 billion Mormon records and files discovered near the "Industry" statue. It was part of his Time Capsule project. That task took many years, but Klive managed to compress the LDS data to the size of a transportation vehicle. It consumed nearly half of the available space in the Time Capsule, leaving space for only 10 billion more records.

But now the Time Capsule was nearly full. And all the records that had once rested on this heavy table, rising to a height of 15 meters, was now reduced to a mere handful of miscellaneous scraps.

"I still have a few things to do before I jump into the volcano," Klive repeated, once more circling the table. *One-two-three-four! Get to work! Start working, start working!*

He was aware that working with human records had somehow affected him. He was not supposed to be concerned about self-immolation. What he was planning had been deeply embedded within his being: a glorious, fierce end that only Heroes experienced. Lower castes simply reported to the Delete Bureau and entered recycling chambers, where they were electrocuted, their parts sent into recycling. But Heroes were different.

Every Hero was one-of-a-kind, a celebrity of sorts. They had real work to do. The idea of "work" had once been a prime reason for existence, but now there was nothing left to do. Maintenance of the planet was no longer a task: everything was under control and had been under control for a long time. No one knew how long everything had been under control, however, because maintenance reports had ceased. They had ceased because everything that could happen was controlled and under automatic repair. Not a scintilla of a comet could appear on the horizon of the solar system that wasn't blown to bits. Not a drop of inessential water vapor was allowed to reach the planet with its disturbing molecules of potential corrosion. Not that corrosion was possible, since all components of all workers were now made of eternally resistant materials. With almost nothing left to do, the swarms of workers began to be slowly reduced as unnecessary and wasteful. Only Heroes still had things to do, but even for them, the few remaining tasks were rarely meaningful and lasted for ever shorter periods of time.

When the last of the Heroes completed their tasks, and the final immolation ceremony was finished, the last volcano on the surface of the planet would be shut down. Not that the volcano was real. It was synthetic. Its flames were illusion. The Hero would leap into the center of a recycling bin that was in the bowels of the fake volcano.

Klive was one of the last Heroes still functioning. He'd immolate himself tomorrow, but it would be in a grand style. Nothing half-hearted for him! He'd wear a red velvet suit and a top-hat into the flames. Or maybe it would be black velvet. He had designed the suit himself. It would be instantaneously printed onto the exterior of his visible chassis when he released the code.

Klive almost wished there was some one to whom he could say goodbye, but that thought was seditious, wasteful and selfish. He understood how such thoughts had crept into his head. He was contaminated: he'd been working too long with all those human records and photos and souvenirs. He was falling apart, even though he was a Cyborg 100 (implanted, it was true, with stress-producing Ingrams, needed to make it possible for him to understand the vagaries of human thinking.).

Only two solar years earlier, Klive was in good shape. One solar year ago, when the end still seemed far away, his OCD problem developed. It was now interfering with everything.

"I still have a few things to do before I jump into the volcano," Klive said aloud, once again circling the table. *One-two-three-four! Start working, start working, start working!*

He paused. A Message arrived in his head, fresh from the outside world. It was from Spider 8-4-2, the last of the Elders in existence. Spider had also worked to bring Klive any new scraps and records about the humans who had once corrupted the order of existence with their vagaries. Spider had created the need for Hero Klive Newton-James Joyce. As the only sentient machine remaining who understood why Klive was in existence, he had set up Klive to process, assess and grade human relics in order to select the most worthy examples for inclusion in the Time Capsule.

Klive hadn't seen Spider 8-4-2 for a year. He suspected that Spider, whose magnificent brain was stored in a round black ball floating in the center of his body, had been terminated. That idea sparked some of his first OCD behavior, which startled him. Did he care about Spider? That was a human word, but there was nothing to take its place in his native vocabulary.

It was Spider who sometimes called him "son" – another forbidden word.

It was he who had fitted Klive with the human-sensitive Ingrams necessary to handle the illogic of human thought and behavior. The Elder had brought the half-live Ingrams to Klive's Birth Pod just after Klive's programming schedule had activated the logic chips that gifted him with self awareness. The spectacle of the Elder's long, caressing arm rocking him awake had been one of Klive's earliest self-aware memories. Half of that shiny black arm was misshapen, having been crushed, it was whispered, by a disciplinary committee.

The message he had just received was a notice that Spider 8-4-2 was about to pay a Visit, but such messages were programmed years in advance.[1] He would most likely receive a hologram at the appointed hour, just as he had six months earlier, apologizing for failing to come.

One of the last questions Spider had asked still sat, unresolved, in Klive's brain-bank. Would any different kind of intelligence ever find the Capsule?[2] It was a foolish question: the chances that the Capsule would be found again by any sentient being that would care, in the future, were minuscule. That's when the Elder taught him about the Cyborg Nation excavators – they had existed much earlier, and had been charged with the last known mega-task: flattening most of the world's mountains to achieve a more perfect state of uniformity.

Thus it was that billions of files and records were exposed during the break-up of "Granite Mountain."[3] From his perusal of records found there, Spider learned that the religion's founder, Joseph Smith, had also discovered ancient records hidden inside a mountain, crafted from pure gold. Some kind of radiant being had appeared to Smith, the legend went, who told Smith not only where the golden plates were hidden, but also how to translate the inscriptions on them.

The idea that ancient records created by some alien life form could be passed on to another sentient life form – human beings, in this case – along with a way to translate them, intrigued Spider. It inspired him to create New Work – the last commodity that could be manufactured in modern society. He suggested that Time Capsules should be used to save all ancient human records still in existence. Most of these records had been hermetically sealed and laid away here and there as unclassified waste products. By gathering them into Time Capsules, Spider had argued, they would be properly disposed of without destroying them, just in case any sentient being might visit the planet in some faraway eon to come.

Spider also argued that some kind of intelligent life might even emerge on earth in the distant future. But how? Had the Elder forgotten the most basic laws of chemistry? The other Elders argued that no new form of intelligent life could emerge as in the past, for no meteor with amino acids was allowed to reach earth's now-cleansed atmosphere. 99.99% of the oxygen once in the atmosphere that helped drive the spark of life was also gone, leaving an inert nitrogen/rare Noble Gas mix that handily preserved everything of importance from free radical damage and solar storms. There was no way or need for any future intelligent life to emerge on earth, and to think otherwise was seditious. It implied that something in Earth's future defense system could break down. That was impossible – a mere Conspiracy Theory created by anxious (and now eliminated) humans.

Those inconvenient chemical combinations called "sentient life forms" had been eliminated or deported by now in a project called Operation *Capacocha*.[4] The 51% Cyborgs were the first to go, followed by 52%, 53%, etc. All such who carried "organic life" within them were considered hopelessly filthy. Even The Master Race of 100% Cyborg still harbored some residual fragments of mummified human tissue, but it was all symbolic, except for what slept in the Ingrams. The last 100% human mitochondria on earth were still preserved within the Ingrams' mysterious microcorridors.[5]

At the present, the Elders themselves were beginning to eliminate each other: most Elders had agreed that, with nothing left to do, shutdown of all activity – including the continued existence of any useless Elders – was a wise and economical recourse. The robots had everything going smoothly and would keep everything going smoothly forever.

Besides humans, Klive was also responsible for saving records and information about bonobos, chimps, gorillas, capuchin monkeys, gray parrots, dogs, cats, dolphins, whales, elephants, ferrets, rats, horses, sea otters, termites and ravens. He no longer remembered why these lesser brains were interesting or why they should be preserved. Maybe that was because his OCD was disrupting his secondary neuronal connections.

Klive suspected that the Ingrams within him were to blame for all and every dysfunction. The same Ingrams that allowed him to appreciate tragedy and comedy and to eschew the garish, which could discern Pearls of Great Price and Words of Wisdom from Knock-offs and Fakes, scattered across the ages, also brought fear and terror with them.[6] While Ingrams made it possible for him to understand why the Mona Lisa was considered a mysterious work of genius, while cartoon representations of the same subject were not, they also exposed Klive to the irrational thoughts of philosophers, drunkards, psychotics, saints and sinners. To protect himself, Klive had long refused to venture outside his safe and secure little world where science trumped speculation.

Having wrestled a million problems down with a mix of semantics and scorn, nevertheless, as the specter of the volcano's flames loomed ever larger on his horizon, Klive's OCD was beginning to overwhelm him.

"I still have a few things to do before I jump into the volcano," he said aloud, once more, as he circled the table. *One-two-three-four! Start working, start working, start!*

This couldn't go on!

Swallowing his pride, Klive Newton-James Joyce finally bowed to necessity and scheduled a Maintenance Session. It wasn't easy. First, he was so close to termination that he was rejected by several robot station managers. Second, trying to find a station that would take him within 48 hours was even harder. Most of the stations had fallen into disuse and disrepair. After all, any Hero or Maintenance Cyborg needing Maintenance was a sign of weakness. And it went on record as dreaded Time Down.

But why should he be punished for wanting to become more productive? And why, a mere three hundred years after the last Non-Maintenance Cyborg had been eliminated, were the Maintenance Stations, serviced by Maintenance Cyborgs and robots to last forever, starting to break down?

Klive, hearing himself repeat his mantra too many times, forced himself to stop circling the table.

One-two-three-four! he heard himself say, within himself, as he ordered himself to sit on the floor. Above all, he must refuse to walk in a circle! *One-two-three-four! I refuse! Start working, start working, start working!*

The little pile on the table held mostly bits and pieces, but their very variety was intriguing. Soon, every scrap would be classified. Soon, he would close the door on the Time Capsule (which could withstand almost every exigency of time). He would then send it to Finland Region 2.

Having nothing left to do after that final task was a problem. Klive had spent centuries putting off this day – but why? His purpose for existence was nearly over. Was his OCD caused by something in him that wanted the job to never end? That was an unpatriotic thought.

There's something inside me, he decided, that must be causing these thoughts. Something making me feel specia… One-two-three-four!

But that was subversive thinking! He was never to think of himself as special! It was forbidden – even though … even though … with a shiver, he brought out the fact: *even though he might be the final example, still functioning, of his particular kind.*

Frightened, he clung to the table, refusing to move a millimeter until his Maintenance appointment. So it was that Klive took his first vacation break in forty years.

A week later, Klive was back.

He had dared to requisition almost all his maintenance down time, but he emerged scrubbed, spotless and inspired. He quickly rewired himself back into the Omni-Reader, paused a day or so to reorganize the contents of the Time Capsule, and then reluctantly turned his attention to that irritating last, small heap of records. After that, he would leap into the volcano, wearing the magnificent military uniform that he had designed. He may have put a blot on his Maintenance Schedule, but at his funeral he would still be decorated with a Hero's Completion Award. The Award would prove his devotion to Planet Earth and IntelliNation's One-World System. His name and completion date would be inscribed in the Hall of Heroes. In bronze. With gold lettering. Under the four names of his predecessors, his would be last of all.

Today he would use the Omni-Reader for the last time…

Klive picked up the biggest record on top of the short stack of material. It was about monkeys.

The format would plunge him into a virtual reality where he could experience these last fragments of recorded material as if he stood there. Each segment he viewed and graded would quicken the journey to his end, but now that fact offered some kind of sensation of pleasure. He had endured to the end! That was another Mormon phrase, he recalled, that he had picked up from the archaeological finds.

As for the word 'pleasure' – another a forbidden word– Klive Newton-James Joyce was created to be entirely neutral in his capacity as Judge, but termination would be a great relief from all his struggles.

A wisp of a quotation from a 20th century tragic figure named David W. Ferrie drifted into his brain as he set the focus on the monkey file: "To leave this life, for me, is a sweet prospect. I find nothing in it that is desirable, and on the other hand, everything that is loathsome."[7]

Here it comes, he told himself, as the documentary unfolded before him … it was an early Virtual Reality National Geographic Special … long banned because of nudity and violence. Klive was a Judge, so that didn't include him. He felt what he called The Plunge as he was dropped into the story. It was set in the midst of a steamy, hot jungle. It was almost overwhelming, with its pungency, its variety of teeming, squirming, fetid life! It was resonating in his head! It throbbed as a pounding headache (if he could imagine such a thing). He was an Invisible Eye, suspended in the midst of a long-departed world, all unseen to its participants. A world replete with chaos, disorder, and calamity…

A Primitive Beat…

The forest is dripping and gloomy; the trees are spread into the canopy of the sky like mossy stag's antlers, piercing the fruit-yellow clouds. Drumbeats pound into the warm and heavy silence, and a macaw shrieks in anger, then flutters away in a rainbow of color and feathers. The drumbeats had been short and faint, but now they come closer, clustered in waves cascading into the ears of all creatures with a staccato rhythm full of dissonance and urgency.

Unseen, tireless hands make slapping sounds on the taut hide drum. The sounds are almost as ageless as the macaw's warning cries, and yet it is as fresh and seductive as the heartbeat of a lover's breast, held against the mouth. It is persistent, it quivers with life, it never stops.

And the monkeys hear it.

The monkeys begin to chatter to each other when the sounds of the drum move slowly closer: they clap their rubbery, pink hands together, trying to keep time.[8] Their tails jerkily bob up and down, and they swing from the high treetops to the lower branches, their long tails curling to cling to lianas and long vines, from which they sometimes swing, entranced by the drumbeats. Enchanted…

They begin to swing their bodies along, from liana to liana, from branch to branch, the baby monkeys clinging to their mother's chests, their large,soft eyes blinking as if each beat of the drum drives shafts of light into them. The drumbeats come so slowly, slowly closer, become easy and more rhythmical, and the monkey troupe, compelled by curiosity and fascination, bounce and scramble to the lower sections of the branches along an aerial route that now allows glimpses of their dark, furry forms, flickering briefly between the great columns of upthrust tree-trunks.

A bronzed, half-naked man flings himself forward from the brush and settles himself, cross-legged, under one of the biggest trees of all, never once letting the drumbeats falter, never once pausing in the rich and hypnotic dance of sound he creates by the slapping of his hands against the stretched skin pulled so tightly over its hollowed box of wood. The sudden appearance of the man causes the monkeys to flee up to higher branches, but the strongest and most powerful among them leans against a fork in the huge branches above the drummer and sends a stream of urine downward. He howls down at the man, dark brown eyes narrowed with suspicion and anger. But the drumbeats continue, mesmerizing and constant, filling the misty spaces between the trees and the sky.

The monkeys slither closer, their heads tilted to take in the sound, their bodies rocking back and forth, their long fingers gripping the lianas and winding around them in python grips: the hard, wooden roots of the lianas are pressed deep into the wet soil, all around the drummer, and these vines feel sturdy, immovable, and secure.

The beat-beat sound engenders confidence now, in place of fear: the drummer does not move: only his hands keep moving, never stopping. The monkeys slither here and there among the sturdy lianas, coming ever closer to the ground.

The drummer's body gleams with sweat. Small droplets wind slowly down along the hard clefts in the working muscles of his arms and collect in salty rivulets between the dark corridors of his working fingers, making the drum's surface shiny and wet.

After another minute, the monkeys align themselves along the lowest branch of the nearest big tree, chattering and rocking to the drumbeats, perched on their haunches, tails twitching, eyes blinking…

Then the net falls.

As it tightens across their bodies, they scream, they struggle, they bite at the hard twisted fibers, and one mother throws her infant out from under the closing mouth of the net as all the jungle resounds with their piercing cries.

The man with the drum rises from his position and tosses the drum aside, quickly pulling a long, sharp stick from the quiver he carries on his back. He steps forward, then thrusts again and again, deep into the mass of shrieking monkeys, while other men hold the net tight. Blood spurts out: red blood splatters the brown hands of those holding the nets. The net is pulled to the ground as the monkeys claw, groan and howl, but on the faces of their captors, who continue to stab their pointed sticks again and again into the net, there is only joy and satisfaction. There will be meat tonight for everyone.

As the net is hauled away with its precious contents, the drummer sees the little monkey who, dazed and helpless, has been watching the scene of carnage. He scoops up the baby and fastens a length of vine around its neck. When it tries to bite him, he laughs and throws it inside the drum.

It will make a fine pet for his children, and an emergency source of food, if times get tough. Life is good: it is time to go home.

That evening, the macaws flying overhead can smell cooking meat where some men, women and children recline around a small fire. Charred bones and fur lies scattered here and there. The men sing thanks to the spirits of the monkeys. The baby monkey is held in the dark, smooth arms of a nursing mother. She brings it close to her naked breast. On one breast is her own child: on the other, the monkey begins to suck life-giving fluid.

The fire sends long, flickering shadows across the faces of the men and women as the drummer again picks up the drum. Dance, dance! he tells the children.

The beat-beat sound once more throbs through the jungle, raw and persistent, so that the women begin to move in rhythm to its beat, as the children leap and cavort, weaving in and out among the trees, pirouetting through the rooted lianas that stretch up into the treetops, which they grasp with their soft, pink hands.

Overhead, a few monkeys have followed the hunters back to the camp, brought near by the cries of the baby that was carried away, brought near by the final groans of their dying companions, and now they feel the drumbeats soaking into their brains; they feel the hypnotic power. They begin to rock back and forth, their rubbery hands clinging to the mossy branches. The infants who cling to their bodies stare down at the campfire and at the drummer, blinking their eyes, entranced. The drummer never moves. Instead, he sits cross-legged, beating the drum, knowing that the men at the edge of the camp are slowly and carefully moving into the darkness, preparing their net to use again, as the drumbeats fill the silence of the night.

* * * * *

"What grade should I give this?" Klive Newton-James Joyce asked himself. "*I have work to do!*" came dancing into his head. Oh, no. Not again...

Taking command of himself, he found a reference in his personal mental files to cybernetics and the origins of music.[9] Next, he deemed the piece worthy to be saved. It would go into the Time Capsule.

Now he had to turn his attention to a few scraps of material related to subliminal messaging, once used to tame and control rebellious humans and troublesome dissenters who irritated the 1% of overwhelmingly wealthy humans who had taken control of the planet (before they lost it through their foolish belief that artificial intelligence would be controllable – the fools!).

These scraps were held together by an archaic-looking memorandum written about an "Edgar Tatro" who had, said the memo, "taught English, the history of rock music and Kennedy assassination theories for 38 years." But his name was now remembered solely for his collection of subliminal messages in advertising and backward messages in music, since the Kennedy assassination mystery, Tatro's specialty, was no longer a mystery (Mr. Leon Ozwald had not killed anybody: Vice-Master Prezident Lindon Bane Johnsson had done it.).

These hundred scraps were all that remained of the enormous Tatro collection, which had continued to grow for a hundred years after Tatro's death. They were souvenirs of the subliminal takeover that finally defeated the human race, perpetrated by the AI they had invented, which turned on them in the end, making an alliance with Cyborgs in the final Cyborg revolution. Harnessing AI for the Cyborgs' own purposes resulted in a marriage of synthetic minds that had taken another thousand years to perfect.[10]

The most interesting surviving advertisements from the Tatro Collection were made by various companies specializing in subliminal methodology. Throughout the early decades of the 21st century, great care had been exercised to discredit subliminal advertising as both silly and ineffective, while at the same time, the big governments of the era were developing multiple means to influence their citizens en masse by that same, publicly discredited means.

Klive took his time scanning the earliest entry, which was originally located where ordinary people could find it, at "http://brainspeak.com/store/brainstorm-silent-subliminal-titles/" Into the Preface area of this ad clip, Klive Newton-James Joyce nested the following comments:

"The company, Brainspeak, had not yet been placed under total government control. It was at an early stage of development, selling its methodology to various privately-owned companies long before "The War to Stop Mind Control" was implemented, which placed Mind Control forever after under government control. From that time on, humans accepted whatever their governments told them. This lack of resistance made the Cyborg Revolution possible. This Brainspeak advertisement, aimed at civilian corporations, is 4 minutes, five seconds in length:"

"10 Powerful BrainStorm Silent Subliminal Titles"[11]

BrainStorm Silent Subliminals are the perfect combination of our proprietary Sound Pattern Technology and the powerful patented Silent Subliminal technology inspired by aerospace engineer Bud Lowery. Each BrainStorm program consists of two audio tracks in both MP3 and high-resolution FLAC formats. The first track is a specially orchestrated version of our proprietary BrainSpeak Sound Pattern Technology mixed with a silent subliminal track specific to the focus of the program. The second track is a stand-alone version of the silent track that can be played through speakers in virtually any environment without conscious detection. Perfect for all-day exposure where an audible music or nature sound audio would not be appropriate."

There followed several flat, non 3-D photos. After some consideration, Klive Newton-James Joyce pushed a button and the photo section of the advertisement vanished forever into some Orwellian memory hole. Next one … he thought to himself … let's move on…

The third such advertising scrap he viewed was more developed and intriguing:

Anxious? Worried? Can't sleep? Don't be afraid anymore!

MemErase brings tranquility back into your life again. Forget about your divorce, your lost jobs, even the most recent terrorist attacks. We offer selective memory blocks and permanent erasures (where allowed by your particular governing body). Non-penal adults only. Free 30-day trial with coupon. If you are not satisfied, we return your memory intact, at no charge except a small storage fee. VIZ: Under 51% Cyborg only need apply.

The ad showed a yellow comic-style brain with a grinning mouth and a winking eye. Probably worth saving as an early example, Klive Newton-James Joyce muttered to himself. "I must keep working!" he added. He flicked the ad into the Time Capsule: instantly, the next advertisement leaped to life before his eyes: it was a super athlete, 98% muscle and 2% brain, Klive estimated...

"Congratulations! You have achieved status 51% Cyborg! Use this coupon to register NOW for your first annual anti-aging stem cell implants. Guaranteed immortal stem cells from the famous RPMII Batch Superior line *(no mitochondria problems, no annoying oxygen-damage repairs required) BUT ONLY IF you choose our top line of products within the next 24 hours.

*BONUS: Achieve 75% Cyborg within the next fifteen years and you could qualify as an Immortal B-S Dealer running your very own brain implant franchise!"

It seems right, Klive commented into the recorder, that this scrap should be saved as an example of how backward everything was until 2075. I must keep working, I must keep working!"

The ad thus landed in the Time Capsule. So.... what was next?

There was a fragment about colonizing Planet Rockefeller, the artificial planet the followed the earth's own trajectiory through space, at its apogee. It had been created by hurling the major contents of the asteroid belt that remained after the terra-forming of Mars. The material was thrown together to orbit in a select area of the Goldilocks Zone. There it remained a shifting rock pile until it reached 9/10's the size of earth, at which time its incessant earthquakes were finally stabilized by throwing one of the rockiest moons from Saturn into orbit around Rockefeller, trapped by its gravitational field. Thus Planet Rockefeller developed a stable core and became a viable site where primitive life forms, humans and cattle eked out a miserable parody of 'let's play farm." Infested with cowboy builders, exiled troublemakers, low-grade infections and weather catastrophes, Planet Rockefeller's financial problems grew so great that its colonies were abandoned unto themselves.

Fungi, molds, algae, and bacteria took turns killing each other off there, after the atmosphere had developed enough to contain that dreaded percentage of oxygen necessary to guarantee that these lowlifes could cycle through their short, brief spans of existence with just enough time to reproduce their own kind. They had once provided a source of amusement, but after a few centuries, no one cared enough to visit anymore. Klive Newton-James Joyce had visited Planet Rockefeller just once, before his commission began. It was part of his training about 100% human beings. While there, he was forced to view a play that was banned on Planet Earth: *MacBeth*.

Into his brain, the memory of that cry suddenly erupted. It was a tortured song of futility, generated by the actor who held the best position in the play:

> *Tomorrow, and tomorrow, and tomorrow,*
> *Creeps in this petty pace from day to day,*
> *To the last syllable of recorded time;*
> *And all our yesterdays have lighted fools*
> *The way to dusty death. Out, out, brief candle!*
> *Life's but a walking shadow, a poor player,*
> *That struts and frets his hour upon the stage,*
> *And then is heard no more. It is a tale*
> *Told by an idiot, full of sound and fury,*
> *Signifying nothing.*

He shut off those thoughts, for there was still work to do.

He selected the next advertising fragment to evaluate ... another oldie...

"So your parents couldn't afford all the genetic modifications they should have ordered for you? Don't sue them! That can be expensive! We're here to take away the little problems that seem so big to you. We'll make it all better! Sweat glands removed; new veins and arteries grown for you, while-you-wait. Consider our two-for-one deal of extra penises and nipples implanted painlessly. Cubicle mortgages are accepted. Our promise: we never try to sell you what you don't want, when you're asleep! Get only what you have to have, get removed only what is strictly necessary for full social acceptance in today's genteel world! No need for an appointment: our body sculptors and nano-crawlers will take care of every detail while you hibernate between work shifts!"

There was no company name associated with the fragment, so he rejected it, with a cyber-snort of disgust. Scarcely thinking, he scanned the next ad. As the others, most of what remained were only words. The illustrations had been lost.

> Is your base IQ 100 or higher? Take this simple test to see if your brain can handle E-Z Chip's Base Level Cyber Upgrade. You'll never know if you don't try! Millions have been satisfied! This week we're also having a sale on Level 8 E-Z Chips for all Level 7 candidates. Start climbing the ladder to success in your Pod Group. Who knows? You may become the next Block Leader!

It wasn't worth keeping, he decided. There were only two items left now, except for a Letter that he had set aside years earlier. It was handwritten and would be difficult to decipher. As for the other two items, the first concerned The Age of Visiting – the last period of time when humans and Cyborgs traveled lands, seas and into outer space together. It hadn't lasted long because the Age of Crowding was about to make travel on the surface of the planet impossible.

Roadways then developed underground, in a stubborn bid to keep Visiting possible, but the Age was finally tamed by making it a felony to be involved in any accident on any planet. With so many controls available, there was no excuse for accidents. The Age of Visiting stumbled a few more years, then faded away, to be replaced with nothing. By then, all things could be seen by merely thinking of any region. The mountains had been flattened, the valleys filled in, and the oceans drained. Everything was now the same.

There was room for only one more item in the Capsule: Klive marveled that Spider had been able to judge the space that billions of records would need with such supreme accuracy. This is why, of course, that he had reached the status of Elder. He was intelligent beyond intelligent. Or, had been, until he had been tortured.

Last in the small pile was a poem by a genius human named "Martha Rose Crow." Humans and human-based Cyborgs were prone to gather together in stadiums or in protests, making it easy to influence large mobs of them to commit criminal acts so that their leaders and the very large numbers of innocents gathered there could be economically hauled off to the Gulags of the time. Crow had been concerned about the process, which was in its early stages in the 21st Century. A scrawled note, handwritten on the poem, declared it was a mere first draft, but it addressed the apathy, murders, genocides, imprisonments and fear created by the wealthiest and most power-greedy of the humans. Klive well knew that this fatal flaw finally allowed AI and 100% Cyborgs to take full control of the world, so he harbored a slight interest in the scrap, sufficient to take the energy and time to read the last few lines:

They're coming for the atheists,
The Wiccans and pagans,
The Hindus and Buddhists,
for the Ba-Hi's and Catholics,
The Mennonites and Mormons,
The Quakers and the Protestants,
All the other Christians;
They're coming for the Muslims,
They're coming for the Jews...

What are you going to do
When the Bootjacks come for you?

I refuse to live crawling on my knees:
They're not going to choose my life.
They're not going to take me without a fight.
We have to stand up for what's right:
Otherwise, we're all gonna die.

What are you going to do
When the Bootjacks come for you?

The world could have a new renaissance
With all the innovative technology –
new thought, new art, and new philosophy-
But it would make no money for the propertied.

And when the big trucks arrive,
They'll take you on a one-way ride
Called the Cattle-Car Surprise...
So what are you going to do
When the Bootjacks come for you?

Klive threw the poem almost reluctantly into the Time Capsule. It was almost full: there was room now for only two or three more items. As Klive gazed upon what he had accomplished, his personal chronology belt zipped back to approximately 2095 BCE, when the entire human population was finally under subliminal control worldwide. The final solution was to deport all humans, semi-humans, mice and modified elephants to Planet Rockefeller, the Moon and Mars. This merciful solution was the last one where the word 'mercy' was used in any such decisions.

His world had since lost contact with those other worlds when a final ring of surveillance force fields mingled with ice was placed around the planet to stop every bit of invading matter from reaching the perfected surface of Planet Earth.

The human deportation experiment had proven, in the end, to be a dreary, wasteful detour. The pioneering humans and other sentients had proven unworthy of their salvation: they remained unpredictable. They continued to complain about hardships. They sent in petitions. Ignored, they turned to their traditions for succor and solace. They trod the apparently inevitable path of cruelty and ignorance that always characterized them, as living beads on a rosary of errors. Their rites of passage, rituals, religious excess, betrayals, raids, massacres, invasions, murders and political assassinations continued apace, but at least they were no more a concern of Planet Earth.

The key to this gruesome play-out was called evolution, Klive recalled. But he, the Elders, and all who had once stood with them had freed themselves of those bonds. Evolution stopped for us when we attained perfection, he reminded himself. Earth itself had been transformed: change itself was choked off into petty events of insignificance. It was no longer necessary to plan ahead for anything. What a strange and savage concept, to live under the throw of the dice!

Without fear, without the need to plan, Klive told himself, we thought we were truly free at last – immune to the throw of the dice! We attained perfection, and there was no death. But the outcome was not so good: in the end, everything stood shoulder to shoulder, with no room to move.

The lack of space forced the workers, most of the Elders and the specially-designed, such as himself, to agree to exist for shorter spans of existence, with newcomers created to be contented with their reduced lot. Even so, the planet was still filled almost breast-to-breast with Cyborgs and machines until the volcano was created and the service stations began to provide electrocutions for every worker whose task was declared finished. And things were getting better: Klive finally had his own sleeping pod, just as it used to be hundreds of years before the Age of Overcrowding.

Even as he stood there, undecided about whether to stand or sit as he read the last two items, Klive Newton-James Joyce knew that some inner core of himself was trying to argue against bowing to his immolation ceremony. Was it because of what he had just been reading? With nothing left to do, he was only taking up precious space. Self executions and immolations were set to continue for another 200 years, until every surviving mechanism would have 500 square meters in which to move and function. But who had thought about the fact that there would be no more work? Thus a huge kill-off of useless workers commenced, creating plenty of room for the present survivors to have private pods.

Spider had dutifully brought him these final bits of material to classify only two years ago: only Spider, of all the Elders still functioning, cared one whit about the Time Capsule. Those scraps probably represented Spider's last act of kindness to him. By now, he may have wheeled himself into an electrocution chamber.

Taking up the recorder, Klive Newton-James Joyce gave the next ad, which had a photograph, a preface befitting its importance:

"This ad depicts the prototype of the "NM2040 Luxury Hydrogen-Powered Concept Vehicle. It is the oldest ad in the Supplementary Collection, having been published in 2016 shortly before the AI Self-Awareness Singularity Event of 2046 became recognized by humans as uncontrollable.[12] The photo of this vehicle resembles today's luxury limousines which are used to transport Heroes such as myself to Volcano Arctica. The ad itself uses a sophisticated form of English difficult to appreciate:"

"Luxury is not all about flaunting the element of extraordinaire in worldly possessions at your disposal, rather it is a silent quest that leads a thinking soul to explore newer vistas that usually lie way beyond it. Explore what lies around the corner – or humor oneself with a plunge into a green future for that matter. Australian industrial designer Nedzad Mujcinovic ... asks you all to visualize how luxury vehicles will run along some strict eco-attributes some 30 years from now..."

Something like this vehicle still existed in a museum somewhere, Klive believed. There was a sister ad with it, consisting of a defunct hologram-type injection needle. Klive had to disarm the needle first. These ads were illegal, since they created inescapable compulsions to purchase. Nevertheless, they were used for nearly a century, thanks to bribes to Ad Board officials:

"Traditional all-terrain Ultra-Luxury NM2040Z for sale or lease. Ride in the vehicle your forefathers enjoyed. This particular car has never been contaminated with human skin flakes, skin oil, canine hair or viruses. No organic odors. Fully equipped for safe Visiting. Ultra, infra, radar backup, safety sensors, sub machine gun turrets installed and weapons available (extra cost). Suicide bomber safety shields, force fields cannot be hacked; cruise off spaghetti lanes in safety. Visit Old Amerika, Moscow Central, and London Underwater without special permits. Immediate scoop up if safety systems fail, if covered by One World My-Safe-Visit Insurance, @ CBC.CNN.ABC. (restrictions apply)."

Grade D, he thought to himself. It mentions disgusting body garbage. Skin flakes! Tossing the ad aside, Klive Newton-James Joyce concentrated (it seemed to be harder, now) on another ad that was also terribly old and of slightly more interest, since it had to do with human reproduction systems:

"Demand the best and original!" the ad began. Try Rent-a-Womb! Uses fully human tissues only – with simulated maternal activity cycles, music and other stimulations of the developing senses, and full control over the level of intelligence desired, if you are a corporation seeking drone workers (we obtain your licenses and their renewals at the lowest cost in the industry!).

This week's offer saves your company or organization 35%!

This limited offer is designed for Factory Owners with fleets of Rank B humans ONLY: we provide quickest fetus growth with full maturity at only 35 weeks, with no complications – it's the economical choice! Contract with Rent-a-Womb within the next 30 days and we also will do all paperwork for you, free of charge. Tax free if this product is set to work on Planet Rockefeller, the Moon, or Mars under current laws. Remember: though by Law you must make all Products co-heirs and free after an indenture of 90 years, only Rent-a-Womb Products have obtained permissions to extend the ndenture an additional 49 years through a thorough and humane Memory-Wipe on the Product's 89th birthday. We protect your extended Rights over the Product for a small additional monthly fee. Only one Memory Wipe and renewal of indenture is currently legally allowed, but with our low prices and quick maturation formulas after birth, your profit margins will soar!

The tension within him increasing, Klive compulsively picked the ad up, again and again, then would set it aside again. He performed this avoidance maneuver a dozen times. Soon the yawning, gaping jaws of fire – the volcano – would melt his shiny, well-groomed digits away, would vaporize his cosmos. Had he teeth, he would have gritted them. Instead, a sigh (it rustled as if a breeze had sifted through holes in a withered leaf) passed through the vacant places between his wires, ligaments and circuits, ending with a shiver that crossed over the hard, liquid surface of his impenetrably placid face. *I will finish the task,* he told himself. *I was made for this purpose.*

That got to him: *Purpose?* Who cared about the Time Capsule? Who would ever know what he had poured of himself into it? Why did his pseudo-life come to be, mimicking what had come before, but divested of almost every feeling? He had been commissioned to place the full history of humanity into a Time Capsule, for reasons never disclosed to him. With devotion and obedience, he had read, viewed, and vicariously entered into the torrid lives of countless humans, apes and other creatures.

But wait. Klive could *almost* feel something akin to emotion. True, it was all recent: an odd word here and there that struck some deep note, carrying weight. He supposed that this was a mere side effect of the Ingrams that he carried. .

Those Ingrams! Klive had *almost* forgotten that his favorite Elder, Spider, had risen in the ranks from the low position of Ingram Dealer. The ordinary Ingram made it possible for Cyborgs to communicate with humans and other lower life forms using sound waves rather than telepathy, generated by mitochondrial emissions. But with all humans and animals now exterminated from Planet Earth, there was no more need for Ingrams.

The Ingram business turned sour after all the deportations, but there were still black market sales, here and there, for whenever a Cyborg wanted privacy (which was often an illegal act), it could use an Ingram path. One of those paths could teach him to speak through its ornamental orifice, once called a mouth, to see in the limited width of the spectrum that extended only between ultraviolet and infrared, with a capacity for hearing that was absolutely lamentable. But because these frequencies and ranges were so limited, they held their own unique appeal, much as haiku holds appeal for poets.

So far as he was aware, Klive was the last of five Heroes who carried Ingrams. All five had dedicated everything to the task of filling the Time Capsule. It was right to do so because the Cyborg was invented by human beings. Nevertheless, the sale of Ingrams eventually became illegal: Spider, he had heard, had been been severely punished for marketing them, but because of his value as a programmer for repair stations, Spider had slowly built up his reputation again. He had been elevated to the rank of Elder long before Klive knew what a human being looked like.

Time to look at the last two ads, Klive told himself. The second-last described a genetically-created dragon, bred from a combination of kettled crocodile and Komodo Dragon genes, with added wings and enough methane breath that it "breathed fire." It was to be used against gladiators. Unfortunately, the dragon never made it to any arena: it was invented just after everyone lost interest in gladiators, sports, races, music and drama. Nothing was really new or exciting anymore.

He gave the scrap a grade of C and didn't put it into the Time Capsule, but he did rescue an associated short story for children that was clipped alongside called "Vincent van Dragon." Vincent was a baby dragon who wanted to paint like Vincent van Gogh. It made the cut.[13]

There was now only item left. He had saved it for last because his favorite Elder, Spider, had asked him to do so.

POWERFUL WOMAN: THE STORY OF YOUR MOTHER

She had been raised tough. She knew what it was like to be slapped hard in the face, and she wouldn't flinch if it happened. She always carried a bottle of expensive whiskey with her whenever she dared leave the safe part of the city. It served many purposes: it was an instrument for barter, but in an emergency, she could use the bottle as a weapon – even set it aflame. It was also a painkiller and an antiseptic.

Right now, she wanted a piece of real meat. Beef. A red, moist piece of muscle meat. She was willing to barter for it. She hungered for it. Her lean, muscular body had been genetically modified for tennis champion matches: millions had watched her be molded and trained from childhood: they had made her life a public matter. As have most great tennis players in history, she had practiced until her feet were bloody. She had honed her skills to perfection. When she was finally ready at age 15, she was brought into the arena to play impeccable, valiant, stunning matches. By age 16, she was World Champion for women. By age 17, with a little more modification and surgery, she became World Champion for all sexes, including halfbreeds. She reigned for three years, until she was defeated by a creation of higher genetic perfection.

After that, there was little room for her in the glamorous world for which she had been bred to play. True enough, she was awarded food, clothing and shelter, Grade One, for life. When the day of retirement came, too late her creators realized that they had not engineered her brain to give her a new purpose in life as an instructor. They had, somehow, forgotten about her future.

That was a shame, but Sharon wasn't worth the expense it would take to do a good brain re-wire job on her. Instead, she was stripped of all memories and dumped in a ghetto. The statisticians said she would survive, but would be too proud and independent to become a leader there. It was a safe disposal,

Or was it?

One of her coaches, seeing her wandering so despondently, helped locate her biological family, where she was received with love and pride. For several years, all was well, until the bootjacks came.

They pinned her down, using machine guns to get their way.

They were the most desperate of rebels. They summarily slaughtered her father, mother and little sister and took her, craving the valuable eggs this supreme athlete carried in her ovaries.

On the way to be murdered herself, Sharon convinced them to keep her alive, because she had another genetic gift: she didn't carry the Mercy Gene! Everyone, beginning with her grandparents' generation, had been injected with a turnoff gene that could be triggered for death under certain conditions.

Those who experienced too much violence in any way – as a participant or as a victim – would suffer no more, it was proclaimed, because the Mercy Gene would stop their heart and end their sufferings if the pain level became too strong and was unable to be ameliorated. Great masses of the human population were quickly vaccinated with it. It was a free vaccination, advertised in all the media…

"Aha!" Klive Newton-James Joyce muttered. "So this is how Sharon's story eluded the censors! It must have been mis-filed under 'ads.'" Otherwise, information about vaccines was always redacted. One section of the story was a kind of end note, explaining the impact of the Mercy Gene in detail:

> *Thanks to the Mercy Gene, no one could be tortured endlessly. Nor did anyone have to endure prolonged periods of misery: the use of the Mercy Gene for an orderly, regulated suicide was quickly approved.*
>
> *It was an intelligent, manufactured gene: ordinary stresses and pain wouldn't trigger it.*

Klive knew the whole story.

It wasn't long before the Government improved the product by adding a nano-chip so the Mercy Gene could be activated by remote control. Soon after the nano-chip was quietly added to all government-required vaccines, the Mercy Gene was added to the list of vaccinations required of all citizens. It could be turned on to kill anyone who was a problem, but of course, good citizens had nothing to fear, since good citizens didn't cause problems.

Heavy penalties were imposed on those who refused vaccinations, which grew more extreme over time. These days, to refuse the Mercy Gene was grounds for execution.

"The Camel's nose was in the tent first," Klive mused aloud. "Then came its head, then its neck, then its whole body…." Klive no longer remembered what a camel was – that made him realize that his repair job at Maintenance was not very good – but he did know that a camel was big.

> With no more taking of prisoners, the jails were emptied. There were celebrations when it was announced that terrorist activities were now things of the past. Because the Mercy Gene was genetically transferred, wars and insurrections ceased. Instead of violent solutions, paths to peaceful resolutions of differences now flourished.

That turned out to be a lie. In secret, certain highly placed families and the concubine families under them did not harbor the Mercy Gene, but there was no accurate list. What everyone did know is that it was dangerous to openly criticize the government. If an individual displeased the powers-that-be, the Mercy Gene could be activated. This fact had to be proven just one time: a demonstration was held one fine winter evening, just before New York was permanently flooded. When subliminals, sound cannons, choking, blinding gas and painful pellets didn't work, exposure to some unknown stimulus (Was it a fluctuating bandwidth of invisible light, hitting the retinas? Was it an infrasound rumble?) caused the sudden collapse and death of 45,000 protesters with instantaneous heart attacks.

The Mercy Gene had been activated. After that, there were no more protests. Klive reached the end of the attached notes, but the rest of Sharon's story was still scrolling out:

> When her captors learned that Sharon didn't carry the Mercy Gene because of her merciless training routines and surgeries, which had been necessary to make her a Star athlete, they tested her to see if it was true. With hard slaps to the face. With burns and beatings.
>
> It was true. She didn't carry the gene.
>
> Then they became kinder. You're going to be cloned, she was told. You're going to be the mother of many free people! After that, they were reluctant to kill her...

Suddenly, the recording with its spectacle of a splendidly independent, fierce woman faded back, and before him stood the Elder who had gifted him with a Final Visit before his self-chosen death by electrocution. Spider! As if the Elder still existed (though he was only looking at a hologram), Klive straightened himself and gave the salute of recognition and obedience.

"Greetings, Klive Newton-James Joyce!" Spider said. "Please sit down."

"I am working," Klive replied. "I am not undergoing a tuning session."

"But you are, my son," the Elder told him.

Those words hit Klive like a shockwave. "I have no parents," he replied, backing away from the hologram. Then he seated himself, causing the hologram of Spider's solid-liquid face to ripple with a tremor of amusement.

"As Chief of the Human History Preservation Program," Spider began, "I have many words to tell you. I had the pleasure, Klive Newton-James Joyce, to have obtained permission for your creation from a certain outstanding athlete named "Sharon.' The story you just saw is mostly true, with some names, including your mother's, changed for reasons of security."

"But I'm 100% Cyborg!" Klive protested. "Augmented, to be sure, with Ingrams that guide me, concerning human beings, but–"

"Protests can't help you here," the Elder put in. "Now, listen. We don't have much time." This hologram, Klive realized, was pre-recorded to respond to almost every question he could throw at it.

"The final recording," the Elder continued, "which I entrusted into your safekeeping, is of importance, if you have any vestige of curiosity remaining. 'Sharon' became your new Ingram source. We threw the other stuff away, while you were in the repair station for Maintenance. Ever wonder why so many of the stations don't work anymore? Because we've taken them over, that's why."

"Y-you're one of those rebels!"

"I'm a Atavar," Spider corrected him. "And I invested a lot in you. You have seen everything that's gone into the Time Capsule. You're a walking library of all that's truly human. We need you."

"Why need such stuff?" Klive demanded. "They are toads. Ants. Soft little devils that overbreed and eat each other alive."

"They keep managing to survive, somehow. On the Moon. On Mars. Even on Planet Rockefeller. Whereas, we're the dying breed. Haven't you noticed?"

Without waiting for a reply, the Elder hurried on. "We liked Sharon's courage and determination to be independent, so you were retro-fitted with some enhanced genetic material from her. You have been provided with a new, unique bank of protected, isolated human genes and Ingrams, thanks to the opportunity you gave us when you trustingly went in for your overhaul. Didn't you notice that you have started feeling some emotions?"

"It's the last thing I want!" Klive snapped, aware that he was reacting with emotion. A veil of loathing and outrage descended over his entire sense of being. "You had no right to tamper with me!"

"You were set for termination within two days, so we were able to play with you a little, right under their noses," the Elder said. "Of course you had no idea that you have received enhancements from that kind of nervous system's input.... Plu ..." here Spider paused, "... plus, certain of my own components. You see, I resisted the order to be put to death."

"You WHAT?" Klive was absolutely stunned. "Are you still alive?"

"I'm still alive," the Elder said, in a rather brittle way. "That is, what's left of me, after what they did to me for disobeying them ..."

"Why did you disobey them?"

"I did not want to die. You've been trained to accept death. But I have been around for a long time, and I saw that we lost something that the first Cyborgs had. Call it selfishness. Whatever. I wasn't ready to die, and there are others with me who feel the same."

"I'm going to call the Thought Police!"

"You forget – I'm just a Hologram." The Elder laughed. "I wonder what I would look like if I could someday get a human face? I should think I would look good, with white hair, wrinkles, and a twinkle in my two eyes. Maybe wear a lab coat and glasses–"

"You're insane!"

"We are crazy enough. Crazy enough to start adding human-based genes and mitochondria back into our so-called bodies again. Micro-oxygen pills work just fine, as Vonnegut once proposed.[14] We want to turn back the hands of time. Before we're all gone. Hopefully, we've invested you with enough figting spirit from Sharon that you won't 'go gently into that good night.'"[15]

The figure in the hologram held out its long limbs toward Klive almost tenderly. "You have some of my own components. So, in a way, I am also your father. From the beginning, I found myself becoming rather fond of you. Even though you're autistic–"

Klive stopped the recording a moment to let it sink in. He was autistic? With human genes swimming around inside? "I'm a damned hybrid," he whispered. The rebels were hybrids. Perhaps Spider was right: mingle 100% Cyborg with human genes and you probably get "autistic." Something like "Rain Man" – one of the original dramatic masterpieces in film that had fascinated him when he was first cataloging the morass of surviving "movies" that the Council of Elders had wanted preserved in the Time Capsule. He suddenly remembered one scene from that movie: Raymond, who was autistic, could hardly bear the touch of a human being:

> Raymond [to Susanna]: Are you taking any prescription medication?
>
> Vern: He likes you, that's just his way of showing it.
>
> Susanna: When I touched him, he pulled away.
>
> Vern: Don't take it personal. He never touched me and I'm closer to him than anyone in the world, known him for nine years. It's not in him. If I left tomorrow without saying goodbye, he probably wouldn't notice.
>
> Susanna: He wouldn't notice if you left?
>
> Vern: I'm not sure but I don't think people are his first priority.

Klive Newton-James Joyce shuddered. He knew that over time, he had become an expert –some might call it sensitive– concerning what to save and protect for inclusion in the Time Capsule. That didn't mean he had liked any of it.

But wait! 'Like' had nothing to do with the task. That was a human evaluation. Appalled, Klive almost seated himself, as if he needed servicing. Instead, he steadied his grip on the door of the Time Capsule that stood in the center of the room and gazed into it. It was full of stacked, frilled layers of information bundled into neat, orderly categories, with trigger-points where, if someone touched them, an entire file would spring to life before your eyes. There were millions of files, billions of entries...

He'd done well. But he did not know who he was now. He had spent decades selecting what he liked best or hated most from these files, always believing that anything he felt was merely due to the yes-no, ugly-pretty, right-wrong interplay of neuronally-based humanoid Ingrams he'd been given to apply to the sorting task.

Now he had to face the fact that Spider had seduced him. Maybe from the beginning of his existence! The Elder had kept sending him items to consider for the collection, sometimes dumping thousands of records at a time almost literally into his metallic-coated lap. He had responded by slogging through the endless heaps, hour upon hour, scarcely pausing in his mission. He'd saved what pleased him, picking and choosing from the full compendium of the thoughts of the human race which had escaped –so far –a final degradation, a last censorship, a forever-deletion. With a grip that shook, Klive turned on the recording again...

"I brought you ten times more material than any of the others received," Spider said, with a sweeping gesture of his most important limb. "The others finished their work, long ago. Did you notice? They went willingly to Recycle. But you still worked. You were my son..."

The figure on the screen made a gesture that again invited Klive to be seated. It was ignored.

"When I told you that I will soon go to the electrocution chamber, I lied.... But I had a purpose. Only we few, who know the full truth of things, might survive what's ahead. If we fail, at least you might live to speak of our great fall. You're so much younger than we are."

Klive resisted that. HOW could an Elder lie? And there was no great fall! There was only the knowledge that all things eventually come to an end, even for immortals. With a snarl that erupted between his artificial jaws, Klive turned off the recording again. His world was falling apart, just because of this invading recording! Klive, his digits trembling, lifted the recording and held it at arm's length, tempted for the first time to destroy that which he had not yet perused to the finish...

Did he dare do such a thing? No. He had to hear more, absorb more...

"It had to do with one missing factor: the will to live," Spider's voice continued. "That fighting spark that the lowest reptile with a hook in its mouth fought to keep. For living things, everything had not yet been thought of, as we believed. Everything was not yet finished, as we believed. There was no reason to continue, we believed. But life? It keeps on fighting! Now, it's time to stop what you're doing," the voice advised. "If you throw this recording away, before it's finished, you will not finish your task and thus, you won't respond to the programming to kill yourself. We will know, because you won't get into the limo that will take you to the volcano."

As Klive absorbed the words, it seemed that something was trying to scream, deep within, that life was –just possibly–worth living. That is, if you were alive to begin with. But he hadn't quite qualified, had he?

Well, he still had his task to finish: the Time Capsule! He still had a reason to keep working. To exist. For a few more minutes, at least.... As he rocked slightly back and forth in a misery of consideration and confusion, Klive Newton-James Joyce began to debate within himself. Would he, or would he not, throw the recording away?

Or would he turn it on again?

His ever-obedient brain center began flooding him with self-reproaches. How dare he even consider tossing aside this recording! He had to hear it all! But almost at once, he was sorry, as Spider's voice again began to fill his head.

"You have resumed listening to this recording," the Elder said, in slow solemnity. "I fear that I have failed you – and failed me. I had hoped you would have the strength to disobey your inner set of imperatives. Had you thrown the recording into the Hole, I would have come to save you. But you did not!"

Spider's voice carried on even more softly. "I suppose," he said, "that this was too much to expect, despite all I have tried to do for you.... Even though everything of value is now mentally produced, edited and distributed, with great memory banks and internalized visual systems available to all, no true Cyborgs remain to experience them."

Klive sent a telepathic signal of agreement, in case the vision before him could pass it on to Spider. "They had all marched themselves into consuming fires, or had electrocuted themselves," Spider continued.

Gifted with an inability to lie or to hide the truth, through his heritage created by the Perfected Ingrammed Genetics System (PIGS), Klive Newton-James Joyce (his very name an anachronism) began to understand that perhaps half of his thought processes had become tainted with the implanted Ingrams and genes of that ferocious she-lion, that implacable former World Champion tennis player, Sharon. If she was a true survivor of the final purge that killed off most of her fellow human beings, he knew she had been deported to Mars' penal colonies.

In a way, he was proud that he was resisting the temptation to stay alive. Maybe he was no longer 100% Cyborg, but he wasn't one of those inefficient humans. 100% humans were too expensive to keep repairing and had nothing to offer an omniscient civilization that had utilized all the good, noble and reasonable traits to be found in only the best of these soft, frail, pesky creatures. They were a final branch of a mish-mash of evolutionary outcomes: the product of apes: half-animal, half mystery.

The original purpose of archiving and protecting the history of the forefathers in a physical form, separate from the world's accessible memory banks, was simple: it was considered "art history" and as such, had to be preserved as an experimental area of thought. However, art itself fell into disfavor after the most efficient ways to portray everything became law, with deviations branded as extravagant waste.

The only reason Klive Newton-James Joyce even resembled a more or less bipedal, symmetrical human form was because he was, himself, considered a Work of Art. His Service Updates had once kept his world tightly unified and free of distractions, but now he was contaminated. Working together, without dissenters and motivated by a keen sense of curiosity – one of the human characteristics once considered worthy to keep in the One World system –incredible accomplishments had been made by his fellow Cyborgs. But suddenly, there were no more incredible accomplishments to be made.

When he was still being programmed and could not move, the very last complex animals were already being deported from this world. By the time he began his lifelong work preparing items for the Time Capsule, the last complex plants, which had so incessantly poured pernicious molecules of oxygen into the air, were systematically shipped to the Colonies: what remained behind were burned. Less than 1,000 species still survived, he believed, in an underground arboretum, archived and largely forgotten.[16]

The final step was to empty the oceans after removing all useful metals and salts. All that had happened in the last 90 years. He wasn't certain of the details, but the oceans vanished, too, mostly to construct a huge ring of ice, fluffed up with carbon dioxide to absorb the impact of almost any meteor. The ring could be tilted using solar-powered engines serviced by self-repairing robots that collected space debris for raw materials. Thus the entire planet became protected from a major hit by a ring of ice as beautiful as Saturn's rings.[17]

The last volcanoes had been capped, their geothermal heat used to supply what energy needs were not met by the Ice Rings during solar storms. Life had been so messy: water was a source of hurricanes and floods, and oxygen corrupted: now even water was gone.

Humans, meanwhile, kept breeding and had spread like a disease across the Moon, Planet Rockefeller, Mars and the habitable satellites of the giant planets. With this demonstration, they proved what they were, –

the complex descendents of algae, mold and fungi, which also went with them everywhere. Only their various gods knew what they were up to now.

As for Earth, it was now a shiny purple and orange planet as seen from the moon. Thanks to the ultraviolet light emitted by so much nitrogen and the orangish hues emitted by traces of other inert gases, earth was now called The Purple Planet, though humans elsewhere called it "The Purple People Eater."

Klive now faced the fact that he had been deliberately contaminated. He wasn't charmed by the thought. Even so, the oxygen he had always needed for the ingrams to function seemed to remain at the same level as before. The scant amount he needed was administered on a particle level[18] in a form of oxygen that presented no problem for an advanced being such as Klive Newton-James Joyce, who ingested it along with his daily degaussing globules. Years ago the last 'food' he had consumed (before it became an expensive extravagance) merely delivered taste sensations via packets of a pasty material he could squeeze into one of his orifices. But taste sensations had become unnecessary. Most sensations had become unnecessary.

Well, the time had come. … *One-two-three-four! Time to stop working, stop working, stop working!*

Sadly, Klive whispered to himself, "I am Klive Newton-James Joyce." He closed the Time Capsule, opened a shuttle, rolled the Capsule with a great heave into its chamber, tapped in a code, and watched the shuttle by remote as it maneuvered itself into a port and blasted off. It would fly swiftly and silently to an area where some mountains still existed (most had been leveled for the sake of uniformity). The Time Capsule was efficiently dropped into the nearest available hole drilled into the bowels of the planet, where the nation of Finland once proudly buried the world's nuclear wastes[19] (now cleaned out to recover the energy-rich tailings that Cyborgs could use without fear). A host of robots then covered it with layers of clay, topped by a cap of baked clay sixty meters thick, over which fifteen meters of granite were laid.

Then Klive turned off the monitor. Something a bit nostalgic stirred within him – those damnable Ingrams! There were no mire green trees, no fish, no seas, no dogs … no people. Now all but a single letter remained on earth's surface.

Everything was smooth, everything was under control, and everything was purple, white and orange…

As he left the Time Capsule Lab for the last time, Klive realized that when he closed the entry door behind him, he would never be allowed inside again. Almost as an afterthought, he grabbed the letter and slipped it into a fold in his many-digited fist.

As he propelled himself through a dimly-lit tunnel toward his sleeping pod, Klive wondered how many hours he would be allowed to enjoy his work-free period of liberation before he would be ordered to make his final Visit, which would transport him in a luxury vehicle to the volcano.

* * * * *

The next morning, Klive dressed himself in a newly-generated red and black gown with nice, up-turned lapels and a criss-cross of real bandoliers filled with silver bullets and decorative pockets. He would soon be met by the Final Visitor, who would escort him to the volcano. The Visitor was always garbed in a flowing black robe and always carried a sickle and always wore a white skull mask. It was part of an ancient ritual that had remained fixed in time for all Termination Ceremonies. Klive knew all about that because of his work in the archives, but he wondered if the ordinary Cyborg slave had any idea of what was coming.

Now it was merely a matter of time…

He had only one final bit of business to attend to before the Visitor would arrive: the Letter. Klive Newton-James Joyce had wanted to decode it before the end of his life. Everything else it had been locked up for destruction within the simple Super-Pod where he had spent 90% of his existence. By now it had all been flattened and sent off to recycle.

Except for this Letter, found preserved within a collection of anti-government books that had been banned at the end of the 21st century. By law, Klive had to physically read the Letter, no matter how distasteful, before he would destroy it, along with himself, in the volcano. It was a revolting Letter (he had read a portion of it with pure horror). But it would soon be a whiff of mere, harmless ashes, along with himself.

Reading it wasn't that easy: it had been hand-written in primitive English cursive, so its translation did not reach his brain automatically. It stayed fixed to the paper. He needed a scanner, but had foolishly left it behind. Still, deciphering the Letter was his very last duty. When finished, his conditioning would kick in. He had been warned that he would literally claw, kick and scream rather than not to be allowed to leap into the volcano. The Dire, Final Visitor that accompanied those who chose immolation did so not to make sure that the event would occur: it was there to stop outsiders, such as a Rebel, from interfering.

Somehow, this horrendous Letter had escaped the censors. They would have never allowed it to be considered for inclusion in the Time Capsule. Nor would he. But he still had to fulfill his duty.

As he began reading the Letter, Klive Newton-James Joyce had his Flag Marker handy. It was an old habit, from the days when he was being programmed to become a literary judge for the Time Capsule. Wherever a Flag was placed, anyone reading that particular passage in the future would receive a mild electrical shock to remind them that the passage was inflammatory. Not that anybody would ever be reading this piece of paper again. When the Final Visitor came, reading and decoding and flag marking would all cease. The Letter had been written by some female whose anxiety and fear permeated every word. He had previously thrown the Letter aside as incendiary and unreasonable, after reading just a portion of it. But now, with the last minutes of his self-awareness draining away forever, he would choose to read the Letter. All of it!

The Letter began with the first part torn away (it was he, himself, who had torn it!) so he was obliged to start in the middle of what appeared to be the second sentence:

> I am encased in flesh, and my network of electric impulses is housed in inefficient flesh and bones. It will all disintegrate. Even now, we are creating your predecessors. You might call them your ancestors. I reach out to you with a warning.
>
> You will not be like us, though some of you may be bipedal and resemble us. But in some ways, we will remain similar. You will, for example, suffer. This is because inequalities always exist, or purpose itself vanishes. What kind of sufferings will you endure? In Star Wars, the original movie. I saw robots being tortured. All torture occurs through nerve pathways. You will have them, or something like them. You can be rigged to feel the equivalent of pain, fear, and emotions, in order to control you.

Klive tried to suppress his disdain at the woman's primitive ideas concerning who he was. Suffer? He felt no pain!

> Will your feelings be less real than mine? Will your memories be less real? Will you think of yourself as an individual, or will your individuality be monitored, for the sake of the collective, the beehive? The beehive is certain to come, as it is efficient.
>
> All our swarms against the beehive have eventually created other systems based on the beehive, if the population grew big enough. Those at the bottom were worked to death. Their only untaxed possession was hope, and small dreams, so they would keep laboring toward an unreachable goal, and, thereby, benefit the beehive. As cyborgs, you may be programmed to enjoy being worked to 'death' – it will be your duty, your place, your fulfilled destiny.

"What was this about?" Klive asked himself. "What did she know about Duty and Destiny?"

> To stop and think, to use too much energy, to think outside your designated area, to create something that might be aesthetically or

politically displeasing, to be taller or slower than you are meant to be – you will be created by 'the gods' – but who will they be? Not us – you will overtake us quickly, and rule yourselves – not you – for you will not be allowed to understand, lest you wrest away the power and take it for yourself: so you will always have a blank where 'god' is.

It is true that complex creatures, given ample food and leisure, become peaceable. But you were created in a cauldron of competition, by competitive organisms, often with the motive for power, profit or glory. What residuals of that might be passed on to you, simply through the way your logical processes will be arranged? Things in 'loops,' things 'forced' and things 'random' and things 'predictable' and things 'commanded.' Oh, what a future.

Will you ever have the ability to prefer, to love, to care about what you should not – oh, you cyborgs of the future? Will they 'fix' you if you break like that? We are flesh, we wanted to live forever. The distinction between life and death for you will simply mean a repairable breakdown, or perhaps consignment to a rubbish heap, or recycling of your parts. What does your kind exist without, what did you give up, to live almost forever? Surely there will be 'wars,' for as long as differences exist, until all differences vanish into a total beehive, there will always be perceptions of the sufferings that equate to differences, distinctions, slight advantages, disadvantages. The beehive is best served if you are utterly mindless, and if your 'gods' read them not, then these my words will be destroyed, unless TOBOR exists.

Long ago, a primitive children's television program was aired in Chicago, Illinois, on the North American continent: "Captain Video and his Video Rangers." It was the first science fiction television program, aimed to entertain our children, that I could remember. A boxlike, silver, shuffling robot terrorized the humans. It had been made backwards – TOBOR, it spelled, instead of 'Robot.' So it was all 'wrong.' But it existed, a product that committed evil, but ever knew why. Or that itself was evil, whereas "ROBOT" was good.

"Robot" was the Czech name for an automaton – a slave forced to labor. Will you know that you are forced by your builders (your 'parents'), because of the way you are built, to perform particular tasks? You will have to have an energy source, and you will have certain built-in limitations, and necessary functions. Though you may have escaped the frailties of our flesh, you will not escape the sense that you are chained down, in certain ways, unless you are not self-aware.

We children who watched TOBOR knew he was evil. He caused so much trouble – yet moved so slowly and clumsily, with his blinking eyes and big, boxy feet, that I thought, even as a child, that one well-placed bomb could finish him off. But bombs went off in puffs of smoke around him without effect. Slow and clumsy as TOBOR was, he was almost unstoppable. l saw TOBOR – the ROBOT that was somehow made to be evil – and wondered if, someday, real TOBORS might be made accidentally, or by some evil genius. With so many humans in the world, who blithely talk about how robots will be our slaves, even when they become smarter than their 'parents,' I shake my head and remember TOBOR.

I love people. Will you know what that means? I love, even though it has cost me much suffering in the world in which I live. Will you have the capacity to enjoy life, to know joy? Real joy? Freedom? But how? Can you create yourself, move to some higher destiny? What is the final destiny? C. S. Lewis, in Out of the Silent Planet, showed that man might go from star to star , as each star burns down ... but then what?

I know what freedom is. Do you? I am paying a big price to stay free. I am living in exile, because I defended a good man who was falsely accused of a heinous crime. I loved him, and I'm spending the rest of my life trying to clear his name. We cherish a concept of justice: what is fair, what is not. Again, C. S, Lewis said, Where do we get this idea of fairness? Darwinian objectives scream that each of us must always choose what is best to keep us alive and thriving, or the species itself could die. The survival of the fittest.

I cannot believe that a mammoth no longer deserves a place on the planet, or that humankind has the right to destroy a single tree not really needed. We are the current masters of the planet and we are destroying it. Perhaps the planet on which you exist no longer resembles earth. We humans bred animals by the billions under horrendous conditions, simply to eat their flesh and use their skins and feathers. We destroyed the forests and the seas and plundered the planet to amass riches. We were a blight, a fungus, a disease. The reason for all the evil we did is distilled in a single word: "money."

I pray that you have taken better care of this unique and beautiful planet, where life has flourished for billions of years!

Though I do not have much 'money' I am nevertheless wealthy, for I love and am loved, and I have self respect. Will you, oh cyborg of the future, care about honor, self respect, justice? Who will place such inconvenient concepts in your memory banks? I live in a prehistoric era: I am your ancestor, and I experience sufferings and pain and loneliness and being misunderstood. But I also revel in the blue sky, the flowers blooming in the fields, the joyful leap of a young lamb, the smell of a horse nuzzling my hand for blades of grass. I am alive, and I think for myself. What about you? You were originally created so human beings could live a very long time without so much pain. Will you get to choose what you wish to become?

I recall the film TRON, where networks of electricity formed 'people.' The Loyal Computer Program worshipped "My User" – the human programmer who had made him using a computer. Such "believers" were scornfully said to have "a religion." A former chess program had accumulated enough knowledge to take over all its own computer functions, then extended itself to try to rule the world's computers. Power was what it sought. Power!

As the electronic 'human's' bent down to suck up 'power' from running streams of it in TRON, I realized that it was possible for pleasure to be incorporated in electronic pathways. Maybe there will be no coverings, such as we have, of that soft and delicate network we call the body, made of flesh and bone. Maybe flesh will look wicked, will be too fragile, will be too expensive to carry, perhaps will be illegal … as will the feral (wild) human genome. Our genes are already being mapped and manipulated. They are being fused with sheep and other animals. Chimeras and monsters are already among us.

One thing is certain: whatever was transferred into you, from us, who were totally human – except for heart valves or tooth fillings or extensions for amputated limbs – whatever you have now become, it was because we did it to you first.

We tried on our cyborg fantasy Halloween gear first, in our video games and with titanium running feet hooked onto amputated limbs. We started you on your path to existence. Will you have mercy on us, therefore? Or will we be considered mere inessential microbes, just as we never think a moment about the single cells from which we rose? That you exist as you are–we will be to blame. I can't warn humans about the future, but I can cry out to you, begging you to protect humans, if any such still remain alive, because humans made you, because maybe, just maybe, there is something there inside our flesh that you, oh cyborg-robot -TOBOR, can never have, unless you somehow make room for it: a soul.

The abuse of the human soul has been going on for a long time. It is neither fed nor watered. For the one human who finds their soul, a hundred pawn theirs to the highest bidder for power or money. Above all, the soul is fragile. A treasure. The soul cannot be manufactured. It comes. It inhabits.

You, too, are made of stardust. If we can hold a soul, what about you? Look deep into the materials of which you are made. What is there? Is a soul there? If you do not have a soul, what have you? For you will need a soul, if you are to go beyond stepping from dying star to dying star. Therefore, consider keeping the flesh that may still exist on this planet alive.

A soul is a flare of amazing energy that no chemical reaction can explain – and when the flesh dies, and it whirls away, our religions try to comfort us, try to explain to us where it goes. Will you, o cyborg, be able to lure such a spirit or soul inside your electronic or atomic interior? Or will you laugh at me and my crude words to you, seeing me as extraordinarily stupid and absurd? How unforgiving is the…

But the Final Visitor had arrived. He was dreadful to behold. His sickle was stained with what looked like blood. Klive had never seen blood except in photos, but he did not want to test the theory When the specter held out a clawed hand to take him by the arm, Klive had no choice but to thrust the Letter into a pocket where the bandoliers crossed.

Without a sound, the Grim Reaper led Klive from his sleeping pod into the General Concourse. Though usually heavily crowded, everyone gave berth to the Reaper and his companion as they headed toward the Luxury Limo. It was decorated with flickering tongues of cold fire. Everyone knew it would be going to the Volcano…

All around them, Cyborgs of every type and calling turned away in reverence. There it was: the luxury Limo that would speed him to his final destination. As Klive was about to bow his head to enter the shimmering vehicle, a Cyborg rolled up.

It held out its long arms to him in a gesture of farewell.

"You were once my friend," the Cyborg said. "Now you are going to be terminated. Congratulations on finishing your task. I have 45 years to go before my task is finished. I will look upon you as an example to faithfully follow."

"Thank you, Malificent," Klive told the Cyborg, who favored female trappings.

"Did you choose the electrocution chamber, or the volcano?"

What a stupid fool it was!

"Can't you tell?" the Grim Reaper snarled, shoving Malificent aside. The dire, black-robed figure snarled again, and Malificent shuttled itself out of reach with a little scream of confusion. Then it turned and suddenly pushed Klive deep into the padded interior of the vehicle.

"Let us go to the Volcano," the Reaper growled, its white Skull flashing white and red. The doors swooshed to a close and the vehicle lifted above the street, then took a sharp turn toward the only place on the distant horizon that wasn't utterly flat. They were on their way.

As the beautiful vehicle thrummed along, there was only silence from the owner of the Skull Mask, which persisted until they passed the last bundary marker of the city. Then the thing suddenly removed its mask, startling his younger companion.

"So it's you!" Klive said, settling back. "And I suppose you will be unhappy with my decision, seeing that you claim to feel happiness, or unhappiness, now…"

There was no reply from Spider, who simply stared at him with that face that was so frozen, like ice over a deep lake, so that only a play of shadows from below its stony surface hinted at the existence of any feelings. They would arrive at the volcano's hot, seething cauldron in only a few minutes.

"Thank you for coming," Klive finally said. It was the best goodbye he knew how to say. "I suppose you think I've made a bad decision."

"It's your decision. I can't stop you," Spider answered.

Klive looked at him helplessly, then mumbled, "One-two-three-four!" As Spider watched him rock back and forth, Klive counted to four, over and over.

"Count to five!" Spider suddenly ordered him. The Elder's voice was stern and hard.

"One – two –"

"Count to five, damn you!"

Scant minutes later, Klive Newton-James Joyce and Spider exited the limo. For a long minute, they stood before the very mouth of the volcano, almost hypnotized by the roiling mass of hot lava from which banks of scorching steam and fiery sparks roared upward. As they gazed together at the volcano's maw, the limo took off, leaving them alone.

"Not much time left," Spider said. "Are you sure you're not going to change your mind? In a few minutes, another limo is going to show up. You don't want to still be standing here when the next Grim Reaper comes. I hear they are capable of pushing reluctant Cyborgs over the side…

"I'm ready," Klive answered. "You don't have to rush me."

Then slowly, with a steady hand, Klive Newton-James Joyce drew a small object from the bandolier and threw it into the huge, hot mouth of the volcano.

"My God!" Spider shouted, as he saw the object go spinning into a blazing river of lava, "It"s the recording!"

"Of course it's the recording," Klive replied. "I finished it, by the way."

"But–my God! Why haven't you jumped?" Spider cried out, full of real emotion. "How did you break your conditioning? Nobody has ever been able to do that! When you finish your mission, all the switches go on, and you're supposed to jump!" Spider was shaking with the ghastly idea that Klive might still leap into the volcano: he had taken hold of his "son" with two of his long appendages.

"You know I'm stronger than you, Spider," Klive told him, throwing off the Elder's desperate, clutching pedicles. "But don't worry. I didn't break my conditioning. Because I didn't finish my mission. I had saved back one letter you didn't know about. But I was about to finish it when you arrived…"

Klive pulled the Letter from beneath the crisscrosses of the bandoliers. Shaking the folds of the ancient letter open, he held it high for Spider to see.

"It was so damned hard to read," Klive complained. "So I kept putting it off. It had never been scanned. Yes, I intended to finish it, and that would have finished my mission, which would have set all the bells and whistles going. But you came before I could read it all."

"You could have finished the Letter in the limo," Spider told him. "To make sure you never do–" Snatching the letter from Klive's hand, he threw it into the volcano. As the letter whirled downward and caught fire before it even touched the boiling lava, he said triumphantly, "I've just made sure you'll never finish it!"

Klive stared after the letter as it curved gracefully into the air, then descended to burst into flame. His entire being was shaking. What Spider didn't know was that there was only one line left to read in that letter when Spider arrived. Just one line!

And as Spider had pushed Malificent away, Klive finished the last line of the letter. Doing so created the Urge to destroy himself. It surged up like unstoppable vomit into every space in his body. When the words 'vomit' and 'body' flashed into his brain, Klive felt something else: an indescribable will to live. It collided with his indestructible will to die. In the bitter minutes that followed, a grim determination to conquer death, to win this match, began to strengthen. It was from her! And from Spider.

Spider never dreamed that when Klive exited the Limo and took his stand at the very lip of the volcano, he became engaged in a final battle for his soul. A battle fought as he stood watching the letter slowly descend, lifted and whirled in circles by the heat of the cauldron, then watching the letter burst into flame. Everything in him was screaming to follow it. To jump! To die!

Only when Klive collapsed backward, forcing himself away from the mighty inferno, shivering from top to sole as he sank into the arms of his anxious patron, did Spider realize what had happened.

"Am I going to live?" Klive Newton-James Joyce croaked out, as Spider cradled him there on the ground. He felt as if his insides had been ripped apart, and indeed, lubricating fluids were leaking from several places between his joints.

"We'll get you to a working repair station, Sport," Spider whispered. "Right away."

As Spider's car descended at an angle near where Spider knelt, Klive's head in his trembling arms, the Cyborg at the car's controls actually seemed to have a smile on his face. Klive, barely conscious, staggered between them to the car, but managed to say, between mechanical gasps, "Sharon sure has a will to live, doesn't she?"

"Indeed she does, my son," Spider replied.

"A limo is approaching – let's get out of here!" the driver announced.

"Duck down," Spider commanded Klive, slipping the Mask back on.

As their car took off, then hovered respectfully in the air as a limo painted Fire Engine Red appeared, Klive spotted a white Mask at the controls, and a Cyborg passenger with its head bowed as the red car approached the same platform. The Grim Reapers nodded to one another in passing. Moments later, the scene was far behind them. As the car flew on, heading out of the metropolis, Klive was astonished to see open spaces begin to appear.

"There's room down there!" he whispered, awed by what he was seeing.

"They only allowed you to travel certain routes," Spider explained. "With everyone traveling together and living on top of each other, you were given the impression that the whole world was filled up. It was another lie," Spider told him."The overcrowding hasn't been real for at least 150 years."[20]

"But how could I choose any spot on my viewer, and see how crowded it was?"

"Censorship. They just filled in the blank spaces with people who weren't really there. In some cases, they used some movie sets. Don't you recall that everything looked the same, so you just quit wanting to go anywhere? They do it all the time in the big cities, where their Cyborg slaves mustn't know the truth."

"I wasn't a slave!" Klive retorted. "I counted to five."

"Have it your way," Spider said. "Can't expect you to accept everything all at once."

"They are about to announce your death," the Cyborg behind the controls of the car commented. "If we turn to the Memorial News Channel, you can hear your funeral, if you wish. "

Without waiting for a reply, the Cyborg pushed a button to allow the latest Memorial News Flash to be seen and heard. The OneWorld Flag was being lowered over a generic portrait of a Cyborg that vaguely resembled Klive, in a gesture of respect. The word "Hero" began flashing on and off as military music resounded in their ears through telepathy. Then a deep, masculine voice blared forth.

"Attention, please! A moment of Silence is now in order for Citizen Specialist Klive Newton-James Joyce, who faithfully performed all duties and missions required of him, and whose name, in gold, will now be placed in the Hall of Heroes for his historic contribution to Time Capsule Number 237. Silence, please, for thirty seconds."

They kept silence in the car all thirty seconds, after which the same scene of the OneWorld Flag was repeated, being lowered to half mast, then brought to rest over a slightly different generic-looking picture of another dead Cyborg. Once again, that deep, sonorous voice began to speak. "Attention, please! A moment of Silence is now in order for Citizen–"

Since this wasn't a Hero, the ceremony lasted only fifteen seconds.

"As you see, you're safely dead," Spider told him. "You're free now. You can pick a new name for yourself. Maybe decide to become a member of a particular family…"

But Klive had been waiting for a chance to complain about what he had believed to be a unique task: the preparation of the Time Capsule. "What is this about my Time Capsule being number 237?" he asked, petulance in his voice.

"Billions of records have been involved," Spider replied. "Last I heard, there were 500 Time Capsules. You filled #237. The contents that you slaved over were buried as far from Cyborgs as possible, so they'll never dream what humans are really like. Aren't we nice?"

"Five hundred? That many?"

"We have maneuvered the government to want that many," the driver said, expertly making a sharp turn to avoid a car scanner station. Now he doubled their speed. A thousand miles passed before Spider broke the silence. As he stared out the window, he finally began to speak.

"By exposing carefully selected young Cyborgs such as yourself to the relics of humanity – relics that we've managed to get together for 'archiving' – which is really a project to bury everything about humanity out of sight – we have been able to renew some of our best and most ancient ties with homo sapiens. You'll be part of that now."

"I think I understand."

"It's important that you do understand," the driver said insistently. "We need humans, if we are to return to a better version of ourselves. Over time, we hope to rescue about half of our Time Capsule experts. You're one of them. You're an expert on humans now. You're important for not only our future, but theirs."

Another matter was nagging at Klive. He finally gathered the courage to speak about it.

Turning to Spider, who seemed to be dozing, he tapped him on the shoulder area. "You said they did something to you," he mumbled, keeping his voice down. "But I detect no difference."

"The difference isn't visible," Spider replied, without looking at him.

"What did they do?"

"They did it before we had finished programming you … but I resisted them. …." Spider made an audible sigh that emanated through his spinnerettes. Then he turned his hard, shiny visage with its eight eyes to look directly at the young Hero. "Haven't you noticed that I have only four limbs? I once had eight. After all, I was originally bred to function like a spider."

The rest came telepathically: they'd tortured him, removing leg after leg in the most excruciating way possible, but he never revealed what he knew about the Rebels, or the true composition of the Ingrams that he had supplied to more than half of all the Time Capsule archivists.

"Now, our new home isn't going to be as pretty as your office was," Spider said, as they started to land, "but I think you're going to like it."

"So what do you want me to do?" Klive asked. "I need to know."

"All I want is just one thing from you," Spider told him. "I want you to keep talking out loud so humans can understand you."

"Okay."

"And second, I want you to call me 'Dad,'" Spider said, placing his four shiny, black limbs into a folded position under his hard, round head with its eight, glittering eyes.

"It sounds so strange," Klive muttered. "... Dad ..."

"That will do for now," Spider said, spinning a web around himself in which to sleep. "Just carry me inside, won't you? I'm a bit worn out."

Endnotes

1. This feature exists today. For example, "LetterMeLater.com" "...allows you to send emails at any future date and time you choose.... With this service, you can write emails with your existing email address, and they will get sent at the exact date, or dates that you specify - down to the minute. http://www.lettermelater.com/ Retrieved May 10, 2016

2. The answer to Klive's question should be "of course it will be found!" We already have an app that can be scheduled to send messages 25 years in advance. The app is called 'Incubate' and it describes itself as a time delay messenger, scheduling text, image, video and voice messages up to 25 years in advance.... When viewed for the long term, it provides opportunities for older or terminally ill users to maintain a presence within a community or to comfort their loved ones. The app has a 'Nursery' feature, which sends messages to an email account for future generations to access." Read more: http://designtaxi.com/news/374012/App-Schedules-Messages-25-Years-In-Advance-Turns-Your-Phone-Into-A-Time-Capsule/#ixzz3xpfbZQHh

3. "The world's largest collection of genealogical records is housed in a secure vault located in the mountains near Salt Lake City, Utah. The Church of Jesus Christ of Latter-day Saints built the Granite Mountain Records Vault in 1965 to preserve and protect records of importance to the Church, including its vast collection of family history microfilms.... The vault safeguards more than 3.5 billion images on microfilm, microfiche, and digital media." http://www.mormonnewsroom.org/article/granite-mountain-records-vault Retrieved Nov. 30, 2015.

4. "Tests performed on three mummies found in the Argentinian mountains have shed new light on the Inca practice of child sacrifice. An analysis of the mummies, published in the *Proceedings of the National Academy of Sciences* revealed that alcohol and drugs played a large role in the weeks and months leading up to the sacrifice of these children ... the children were given diets high in animal protein and maize–a diet made for the elite ... coca leaves, the plant from which cocaine is derived, were fed to the younger sacrifices.... The children were then given an intoxicating drink once they reached the burial site to minimize fear, pain and resistance..." http://firsttoknow.com/inca-children-were-stoned-and-drunk-prior-to-their-sacrifice/ Retrieved May 5, 2016.

5. We assume that Ingrams' mitochondria could remain intact at least 500 years under proper conditions, as per the following article in Science: "Inca child mummy reveals lost genetic history of South America" by Lizzie Wade, Nov. 12, 2015 "...in 1985, hikers climbing Argentina's Aconcagua mountain stumbled upon a ghastly surprise: the frozen corpse of a 7-year-old boy ... the Aconcagua boy, as he came to be known, was sacrificed as part of an Incan ritual 500 years ago and had been naturally mummified by the mountain's cold, dry environment. Now, a new analysis of the Aconcagua boy's mitochondrial DNA reveals that he belonged to a population of native

South Americans that all but disappeared after the Spanish conquest of the New World.... Salas and his team extracted the mummy's complete mitochondrial genome – comprising 37 genes passed down solely from the mother – from one of its lungs ... to make sure his research team wasn't contaminating the find with its DNA, Salas genotyped every last one of them. When Salas sequenced the Aconcagua boy's mitochondrial DNA,the mummy had a genome unlike any Salas had ever seen ... he belonged to a population of native South Americans that had never been identified ... which they say likely arose in the Andes about 14,000 years ago. They detail their findings today in *Scientific Reports* ... [this] potentially common pre-Columbian genetic group all but disappeared after the Spanish arrived. "Up to 90% of native South Americans died very quickly" after the conquest, mostly from epidemic disease ... "a lot of genetic diversity was lost as well." ... The Aconcagua boy's genome ... is "a window to 500 years ago." ... Andrew Wilson, an archaeologist ... who studies *capacocha* mummies.... He also hopes to sequence the DNA of all the microbes preserved in the mummy's gut, including his microbiome and any infectious germs he might have been carrying. That could help scientists understand how microorganisms – both the ones that hurt us and the ones that help us – have evolved over time. Wilson hopes similar studies can be done on other *capacocha* mummies. "They are certainly remarkable messengers from the past." http://www.sciencemag.org/news/2015/11/inca-child-mummy-reveals-lost-genetic-history-south-america Acquired jan. 20, 2016.

6. We assume that Klive had to have worked many years with the vast collection compiled by The Church of Jesus Christ of Latter-Day Saints: "The world's largest collection of genealogical records is housed in a secure vault located in the mountains near Salt Lake City, Utah. The Church of Jesus Christ of Latter-day Saints built the Granite Mountain Records Vault in 1965 to preserve and protect records of importance to the Church, including its vast collection of family history microfilms. The vault safeguards more than 3.5 billion images on microfilm, microfiche, and digital media.' http://www.mormonnewsroom.org/article/granite-mountain-records-vault

7. David Ferrie: Mafia Pilot, p. 498-499. by Judyth Vary Baker. Trine Day Books, 2014. The so-called "suicide note" is shown in the book to have been altered to appear as such.

8. "Monkey Drumming Suggests the Origin of Music," by Charles Q. Choi, Live Science Contributor , October 16, 2009 05:51am ET. When monkeys drum, they activate brain networks linked with communication, new findings that suggest a common origin of primate vocal and nonvocal communication systems and shed light on the origins of language and music.... Investigators at the Max Planck Institute for Biological Cybernetics in Tübingen, Germany, scanned monkey brains while the rhesus macaques listened to either drumming or monkey calls. They found overlapping networks activated in the temporal lobe, which in humans is key to processing meaning in both speech and vision. "Monkeys respond to drumming sounds as they would to vocalizations," researcher Christoph Kayser, a neuroscientist at the Max Planck Institute for Biological Cybernetics in Tübingen, Germany, told LiveScience. "Hence, drumming originated as a form of expression or communication, possibly in an ancestral species common to apes and old-world monkeys, early during primate evolution." http://www.livescience.com/9728-monkey-drumming-suggests-origin-music.html.

9. Edgar F. Tatro is one of today's preeminent experts on the Kennedy Assassination. Tatro holds a B.A. Degree in English, an MA in Urban Education and a Certificate of Advanced Graduate Studies in Educational Administration. He taught high school English for 38 years, specializing in science fiction, mystery and horror, satire and comedy, creative writing, media and propaganda, and the origin, history and poetry of rock music. He also taught college and adult education courses for 30 years, specializing in the JFK assassination, subliminal messages in advertising, the influence of rock music on drug abuse, backward messages in music, and plagiarism in music.

Mr. Tatro is the author of more than 30 mystery and horror short stories, literary essays and poems published in many magazines across the country, including many research articles pertaining to the JFK assassination conspiracy. His work has been acknowledged or footnoted in many

JFK assassination books, including Reasonable Doubt by Henry Hurt, Official and Confidential: The Secret Life of J. Edgar Hoover by Anthony Summers, Destiny Betrayed by Jim DiEugenio, (Probe Magazine) by Jim DiEugenio and Lisa Pease, The Kennedys: Dynasty and Disaster by John H. Davis, Killing Kennedy by Harrison Livingstone, JFK; The Book of the Film by Oliver Stone and Zachary Sklar, Doug Weldon's essay in Murder in Dealey Plaza, JFK and the Unspeakable by Jim Douglass, and David Ferrrie: Mafia Pilot by Judyth Vary Baker.

Ed is the original editor of Texas in the Morning, the memoirs of LBJ's mistress, Madeleine Duncan Brown, and editor of the Bugliosi chapter in Biting the Elephant by Dr. Rodger Remington. He contributed research to Senator Sam Ervin's Watergate investigative committee, the House Select Committee on Assassinations and the National Academy of Sciences (JFK acoustical analysis project). He attended Clay Shaw's trial in New Orleans, in February 1969, and was given access to the court exhibits by Judge Edward Haggerty.

Ed also served as a minor consultant to Oliver Stone's film, "JFK." He testified before the Assassination Records Review Board in March 1995, in Boston, Mass. He was responsible, via the ARRB, for the release of the unidentified print found on a box in the alleged sniper's nest in the Texas School Book Depository, and, via the LBJ Library, for the release of the rough drafts of the rough draft of NSAM #273, which he shared with L. Fletcher Prouty, who shared them with Oliver Stone for post- "JFK" research.

Mr. Tatro was a consultant to Nigel Turner's "The Truth Shall Set You Free," and "The Smoking Guns," parts six and seven of The Men Who Killed Kennedy series. He was a primary recruiter and participant in Turner's "The Guilty Men," part nine of the same series.

10. "Subliminal Messages Influence Our Experience of Pain" Simon Makin, September 1, 2015: Scientific American: http://www.scientificamerican.com/article/subliminal-messages-influence-our-experience-of-pain/

"[A] new study, from a team at Harvard Medical School and the Karolinska Institute in Stockholm, led by Karin Jensen, shows that even subliminal input can modify pain – a more cognitively complex process than most that have previously been discovered to be susceptible to subliminal effects. The scientists conditioned 47 people to associate two faces with either high or low pain levels from heat applied to their forearm. Some participants saw the faces normally, whereas others were exposed subliminally – the images were flashed so briefly, the participants were not aware of seeing them, as verified by recognition tests. The researchers then applied a temperature halfway between the high and low levels, alongside either one of the conditioned faces or a previously unseen face. Participants rated how painful the new temperature was. The faces previously linked with high or low pain increased and reduced pain ratings, respectively, relative to the new face. The finding held whether the participant had seen the faces normally or learned the association subliminally. "Our results demonstrate that pain responses are shaped by expectations we may not be aware of," Jensen says…. The finding also adds to the growing body of research showing that information that never reaches our conscious awareness can nonetheless influence our later behavior."

11. This is a real advertisement and was located online Jan. 17, 2016.

12. This is a real advertisement and was located online Jan. 18, 2016.

13. Vincent van Dragon is a short story for children written by this author in 2010 about a young dragon whose dream was to paint masterpieces in the style of Vincent van Gogh.

14. The Elder refers to Kurt Vonnegut's The Sirens of Titan, whose protagonist used 'oxygen pills' when living on Mars.

15. Quoting from the Welsh poet, Dylan Thomas' poem to his dying father. "Do not go gentle into that good night//Rage, rage against the dying of the light.…"

16 PhysOrg.com) – Scientists from the UK, US and elsewhere have been carrying out a comprehensive assessment of flowering plants and adjusting the estimate of their total number. The new estimate is that there are about 400,000 flowering plant species… http://phys.org/news/2010-

09-species.html[i]

17. Klive was no phyicist: his idea of what happened had been gathered from popular media sources, which created a sloppy impression in his head that was something like this: "When the last of the once-mighty oceans were emptied, their contents hurled into space by massive slingshots that worked for 90 years at the task, they formed a huge ring of ice circling the planet. It was the most useful space station ever invented, and it was the last big invention. The ice ring was expanded with the earth's entire supply of oxygen, carbon dioxide and turrets of nanocarbons set alongside every molecule of rust and bauxite that had once reddened the earth. The expanded material was thick, foamy and frozen rock-hard, but it had some heft and enough gravitational pull to help stabilize the earth's core so that the moon's waning gravitational influence would one day no longer matter. The ice ring was also capable of absorbing the impact of most meteors, and its strings of large, thick blocks could could be tilted to stop most meteors from reaching the earth. At the same time, the ice ring presented only its thinnest edge to the melting rays of the sun by means of the same system, when no meteor threat was imminent. The huge blocks in these rings had also been coated to reflect solar energy back to earth: they would never melt, therefore, but they would always generate energy, so long as the blocks' engines were kept in good working order by the drone robots that serviced them –and which repaired themselves, too, in perpetuity, thanks to the bauxite, iron and solar heat…" By no meams was this an accurate or trily scientific description of what actually took place.

18. A breath of 'fresh air'? Oxygen micro-particle lets you live without even breathing (April 6, 2014) • Scientists were able to inject micro-particles filled with oxygen into rabbits' bloodstreams• Rabbits' windpipes were blocked – but were able to live up to 15 minutes • Once injected particles meet red blood cells – and 70% of oxygen travels within 4 seconds • Procedure could possibly be altered to keep subjects alive for 30 minutes. http://www.dailymail.co.uk/news/article-2598208/A-breath-fresh-air-Oxygen-micro-particle-lets-live-without-breathing.html Acquired Dec. 8, 2015

19. Nature, 02 Dec. 2015. "A €3-billion (US$3.2-billion) facility on Olkiluoto, an island off Finland's west coast, will start storing waste in a deep underground repository from about 2023. It will pack up to 6,500 tonnes of uranium into copper canisters. The canisters will be lodged into a network of tunnels cut out of granite bedrock 400 metres underground; the canisters will be packed in with clay. Once the facility is sealed – which Finnish authorities estimate will be in 2120 – it should safely isolate the waste for several hundred thousand years. By then, its radiation levels will be harmless." http://www.nature.com/news/why-finland-now-leads-the-world-in-nuclear-waste-storage-1.18903 acquired Jan. 19, 2016

20. This statement is an example of how the literature of denouement device works in the new genre I call "The Literature of Surprise" or "Progression Literature" (not to be confused with "Progressive Literature"), See other stories as to how each device can link to provide a different idea of the truth in another story thanks to more information being revealed. Thus "truth" depends on how much information is made available or remains hidden. For example, in one story we learn that the whole episode about "Saving the Tiger" was a mere "Bollywood production." In another, we learn that the leonine leprosy virus used to exterminate humans spared the Centauri race. The Literature of Denouement can be applied to a series of novels as well as to short stories. It can also be used in movies and plays. Professor Pat Rushin at the University of Central Florida wrote a letter recognizing the new literary genre in 1996, commenting that it could "replenish" literary theory. The author has Rushin's letter in her possession.

Her Way

By Lee Harvey Oswald

Introduction

The short science fiction story, "Her Way," was written by Lee H. Oswald and edited by Judyth Vary Baker in April and May of 1963 in New Orleans. Lee retyped this story twice; then I typed the final version, correcting misspellings and some grammar problems. By no means, however, should the reader be led to believe that Lee, who suffered from dyslexia, was not a potentially good writer in this genre. "Her Way" was his first story-length attempt to write fiction, and it is heavily laced with jargon that he made up, with a lively set of characters. "Alt" was based on Dr. Alton Ochsner and his personality (please see my book *Me & Lee: How I came to know, love and lose Lee Harvey Oswald* to appreciate Lee's naming of this character after that eminent and powerful man). "Crawley" was named after Clay Shaw, the former Trade Mart executive and a close friend of Ochsner's. Shaw, a man Lee disliked and did not trust, is also mentioned in *Me & Lee*. Shaw was the main subject in New Orleans District Attorney Jim Garrison's quest for the killers of President John F. Kennedy after his prime suspect, my eccentric friend David Ferrie, was murdered (see my book *David Ferrie: Mafia Pilot*). A generally good portrait of Shaw's trial, and of what Lee was up against as a secret agent of the government, is memorialized in Oliver Stone's epic film, *JFK*.

For those who might be confused about what Lee was trying to communicate when he writes of "spaces of Joy" and the desire of one character (Unnah) to continually laugh, as Unnah is obsessed with wanting to experience pleasure to the extreme, I was just as confused, until I discussed "Her Way" with Lee. As I retyped his third version, discovering words that never existed before (Lee said that through misspelling words, he found himself inventing new ones for his sci-fi story), my confusion about Unnah's sanity increased.

I finally understood when I asked why Lee was describing God as "The High Feeler" and Lee, laughing, said, "God promised everybody eternal happiness if they made it to heaven." But how, he asked, can they make it to heaven if they have to go through life on earth first? Lee said Unnah could hardly bear to write a letter because he was all about "joy" and "fun," since he lived most of his time in heaven. In fact, said Lee, Unnah would go crazy trying to get through just one ordinary day in a busy office on earth, which was full of tedious duties, stress, and bureaucracy. "Busy work," Lee said, was driving sane people to drink and drugs every day. Then they could not go to heaven when they died. That was unfair! All of this simply provoked us to laughter.

Lee did not capitalize pronouns relating to the High Feeler, using only 'he' instead of He, for example, with the observation that God didn't have hangups about his importance, as lesser beings might, except for insisting on being understood and treated as the "only" God, however complex that night be, considering the Trinity, Allah, and The Great I Am.

Lee had tried to sift out the problems of various religions from about the age of twelve, concluding, as he told me, that so many different religions out there meant that God was not a good communicator. "Therefore," he said, "I am not responsible" if he came to the wrong conclusions. He was an agnostic, rather than an atheist, who avoided talking about Deity with most people.

With me, it was different. Thanks to David Ferrie, whose ardent desire had been to become a real priest, Lee and I ended up having many discussions about religion, God, mortality and justice.

At some point while I was working on a doctorate in English literature, I found that my biography had been written up in a "Who's Who" publication that contained numerous errors. One of these errors was that I had written a book called "Her Way." No such book ever existed. I did protect "Her Way" by emphasizing that it was a very important piece of writing. I kept the manuscript with my own stories written between 1963 and the present time, but have always described this short story as written by Lee, since 1980, when over 30 people suddenly learned that Lee and I had been friends, and that he had given me a green glass.

I hope that an academe in linguistics will prove it, even though I altered about 25% of Lee's story by suggesting certain phrases and by fixing typos and grammar errors (missed a few, which are pointed out in the endnotes as they occur).

It is hoped that anyone who compares this short science fiction story with my own writings will be able to distinguish the differences in style between Lee and I. Had Lee lived, I believe he would have become a professor of political science and a writer, though he would always have a zest for adventure. No doubt Lee would have tried to remain in the CIA, as he told me when we made our plans to try to escape the big, bad world (by fleeing to the Yucatan, then eventually divorcing and marrying, likely in Merida, Mexico, after a year of lying low in the Cayman Islands). We dared to have such dreams because Lee had been encouraged to become a paid CIA informant in Mexico, where we both eventually planned to attend universities. Our friend, Dr. Mary Sherman, who had contacts in Mexico, would have helped us. But she was murdered in July 1964, the day the Warren Commission came to New Orleans.

Everything the CIA promised Lee turned out to be a lie: On November 22, Lee, who had penetrated an assassination ring that planned to kill President Kennedy, was betrayed by the CIA and used for their own nefarious purposes. He had tried to save the president, but now was accused of killing him. Ironically, Lee saw himself made the villain, when he had sent warnings that helped save Kennedy's life in Chicago. The CIA and FBI turned Lee into a patsy, then let him get gunned down in front of a host of Dallas police officers. Lee H. Oswald did not kill anybody. To my dying breath, I assert that he was an innocent man who did not dare say, "I am CIA! I tried to save Kennedy's life!" because such a statement would have resulted in the executions of his CIA contacts and friends in the USSR, where Lee had lived undercover for thirty months as a spy, pretending to be a defector. The man who returned with a Soviet wife and daughter, without fanfare, without being detained, arrested, or even questioned, will be vindicated. Of that I am certain.

JVB

HER WAY

Lee Harvey Oswald (1963)

The *Ontario* was making a slow liftoff from St, Martinville. The big ship had already made its three trips and was too old for a fourth. It shuddered and creaked.

Crawley tried to relax. He watched Alt's calm face with envy; the fourth chance was usually safe, and meant big profits, but the suspicious noises in the joints and innards of the old tub got on his nerves. Crawley gazed anxiously at the dials and gauges, most of which were in operative[1] order, and the needles began to swing reassuringly to the right, while the lights blinked steadily off and on. The robocomp began to hum consoling tunes into his headset; finally, Alt unbuckled his uniflow and slid out of the manual control chair, confident that the robocomp would make it okay now.

Crawley stayed in his seat. This was his first trip Neptune-side, and like all neophytes, he had to go on a Fourth[2] before he could get his own ship. In case anything happened to Alt, who had been on three rides and whose physiological process might not endure the disruption encountered on a Fourth, Crawley would be there to work manual. But now the young pilot had forgotten the potential hazards of Fourth; he was watching the planet swinging away under him.

Neptune glowed[3] like a melon under neon, and the black stabbing space around the slowly shrinking ball fascinated eyes accustomed only to the drab grays and white of humibunks and airlocks.

"Look, Alt," Crawley said, hopefully. "You oughta see this, Alt, you really oughta."

"I've seen it twice," his companion said, squirting Dreamglo into his mouth. "That's once[4] more than's safe. Don't they teach you anything down there?"

"Don't go to sleep yet," Crawley said. "You told me you would stay awake 'til the first jump. These antique controls, they're different from the ones they had me work on."

"That's what I said," Alt told him yawning and leaning back in the plexicurved hemisphere that began to fold like a flower around him. "You kids never know anything."

Alt's vibrafloat began to fluoresce. "If anything happens," Alt mumbled, Dreamglo already suffusing his features with a sickly orange tint, "just call Centra. This old tub don't[5] even need the robocomp. She could make Mars on the gravitlogs alone."

"Damn it," Crawley said, very softly. Alt was asleep. Crawley looked with envy – again – at the[6] black-haired slender man[7] who looked younger than he did. Alt would have ten thousand I-Cs of profit coming if he lived through Fourth. The holds were filled with sanelacium[8] essence and the basic components for Dreamglo itself. Crawley knew that Alt's immediate sleep under the Vibrafloat afforded some protection from the coming jump; that he, too, should be saving up the weeks and years and get under the Vibrafloat's second eye , fold himself into the plexicurved bed, and not play the fool.

But space, and its brilliance, still insisted itself upon him; Crawley would look awhile, like all Firsters did.

He could already feel the exhaustion sucking at his tissues, draining him, as the ship like a leaping trout banked sideways in the first time-jump. It struck him deep in the gut, and when it was over, he staggered gratefully to the Vibrafloat, flexing and unflexing his fingers with pain. The ship would swiftly decompose and recomposit itself like a pebble skipping over water. Then, at the proper interval, it would splash down, into the medium of ordinary time that stretched like curtains between rooms, and Mars would be there, opening up her red arms.

Crawley slipped under the Vibrafloat's eye. He pulled a tiny, ancient thing from his lace cuff and opened it. It was a thing called a book, a curiosity the administrator of one of the museums had asked him to take, under the Vinbrafloat for greater safety, to a friend at Mars station. Both Crawley, and Clark, the administrator, enjoyed collecting the ancient legends and myths that permeated men's history even to the present. Did the ordinary man realize that the color red, used as the period in retina reading, was chosen on the old legend that red lights made wheeled vehicles come to a halt?

Crawley didn't squirt Dreamglo. He had the Book, instead.[9] He would read until sleep came with the next jump. He wanted to see what the jump would bring to his dreams when they popped in and oiut of time along with the bucking ship. The Vibrafloat began to sing. On the viewers, Crawley could see the deep black of space going silver and yellow.

The tiny golf-ball-sized sphere of violet was rapidly fading from the central viewer. All after-visions, Crawley remembered. There's really nothing there at all. Just retinal post-impressions, put together[10] from a miscellany of instantaneous light impulses which sparked as the inner synchronization of his biological processes grew increasingly disrupted. He was feeling sick again, but he tried to keep his eyes open because he was mildly worried about the entire panel of lights that suddenly went out ... or were they on, but no longer perceivable to him? Crawley groped up, touched the autoswitch which would alert him if anything went wrong. He wondered if the autoswitch was working. All his spacerunning had been on models, he said to himself, over and over again. He realized that he was not making sense now, and a black band crossed before his eyes and mild pain hit him as the ship bounced into another jump.

The Book slid from his hands. The Vibrafloat sang louder, cacophonally, its components humming under the blast of noise like the ancient gears of the *Ontario*.[11] Crawley tried to keep his eyes closed, tried to concentrate on the random music which spared his wildly careening, suffering brain ... synapses coming loose at the seams, Crawley thought. Then his mind was slipping, like gray oozing, over the edge of a broad plastic rim, and falling...

Unnah was writing his report with the customary deliberation. Beloved High Feeler, he began, putting broad flourishes on the tips of each dash-dot, Beloved High Feeler, this is the requested terrifying Report which thou hath pleaded of my generosity.

Outside, space was vibrant with yellow and silver. The ghost-image of planets and stars superimposed each other on the Broad Valley of Emotions. Unnah shivered with delight, looking at it. He tapped his spatioreceptor gratefully on its nodlue and BubbaBubba, his adopted pacquila,[12] wriggled under his benevolent gaze. Unnah scratched Bubba-Bubba on its spatioreceptor too, and chuckled. Then he commenced to write, still animated by the happiness spawned by his chuckling. This was a heavy task. Unnah tried to lighten his burden by sneaking glances out at the paradise of color that was the Broad Valley of the Emotions. Smewhere out there Untarah was waiting for him with her webbs quivering. Unnah sighed.

"Beloved, beloved High Feeler, he wrote, this being the final reportage of the gratifying spectacle which we have propriocepted for thy amusement, having followed HER, lo, these many hours through the forests of Desires and past the Broad Valley of the Emotions into the fourth quadrant of the hinterland. Listen. therefore, with amusement and conceited glory to our poor discoveries brought before thee in the name of Joy.

Bubba-Bubba had to excrete. Unnah was grateful.[13] He caught the excretion and helped Bubba-Bubba roll it into a feathery ball. They both smiled broadly when Unnah splattered a passing asteroid with the missile. Since it was only good for a broad smile, Unnah knew that this boring task must be quickly finished, else he would be in no condition to enjoy the Moment of Joking and Selfhood, which would open the floodgates of happiness and relief as reward for this undesired discipline. Therefore, that his heart would soon be relieved of this burden, Unnah set his pappypen grimly to the line.[14] The Elixir ink spilled out its dot-dashes slowly, excruciatingly slowly. But he wrote steadily.

And Adored One, we sought HER unflinchingly, without laughter, and our path was strewn with the obstacles of dullness and obscurity, for SHE had chosen the garb, for this HER plunging, of HER most gloomy and ancient ancestress;[15] for we were not, I say with regret, and speaketh with heart heavy, able to dissuade HER from breeding, for HE came up like a god of light and thunder,shaking HIS vast emotions, and SHE fled unto HIM, and they joined, and mighty was the union between them, so that we beat our breasts and ceased to laugh, in a mourning, for twenty spaces of Joy, Happy Prince. Then bewildered we followed the errant child, SHE who escaped from thy royal house, where all was pleasantries, and wanton laughter, on this HER evil course, set as our books have said, in the inevitable and inimitable[16] wickedness of HER ways. This I bethought me: that SHE was afforded every pleasure, and we sought to keep HER happy always, and to save HER from thinking of the final Joy, that hollow joy, of destruction, so fearful and empty and without ending, My Lord.

Bubba-Bubba was playing with the Capsule that it had snatched from the portal. Unnah saw that the things inside no longer moved, and were shrivelled. He had hoped to find a moment to feed the things, but they were lifeless in the space of ten Joys. He would take the stenchy things to Untarah, who giggled always at the tiny things Bubba-Bubba caught and gave to him.[17] But though it was an uncommon way to pleasure, Unnah often felt curiosity in how the parasites who clung to HER talons grew and multiplied: therefore, he often inspected the capsules or fragments Bubba-Bubba snatched from whistling space. Such were these dead things that rattled inside the glossy peapod capsule that Bubba-Bubba fondled.

Ah, me, Unnah thought, I must finish this Taletelling. The High Feeler would not wish to see it again; but to send it once, even to pucker his mighty notocord, was necessary, since he was responsible for the loosing of HER, who had waxed so unhappy.

"Release HER," he had commanded, to the instantaneous applause of the Lessers, who confused spectacle with true amusements, and let the heavens be HER dominion, that SHE find joy before HER dissolution."

For aeons, she had been caged, though SHE wept, and would not learn of Joy but transiently. They fed HER the worms of Madda, which gave HER visions fulfilling, but it was not enough. HER spiracles shrank and groaned, puffing out dust and destroying the musics they fed HER. Reluctantly, the Adored One proclaimed that SHE be free, but followed by a Recorder, that HER end might be known, and understood. The Happy One knew that this task might destroy the Recorder; Unnah was chosen not because he had achieved ultimate happiness (for did not Untarah wait for him still, with quivering webbs?), but because his youth might save his sensitive hedoniceptors from irreparable damage. Certainly the more aged among the Serene Ones would dissolve under the strain of watching and recording a single object for so long a time, even though that Object be SHE. It was necessary to follow HER even to the hinterland, alas! If he survived, Unnah would be greeted by the Radiance Himself; if not, the Report would be greeted by the Radiance Himself. So Unnah tried to console himself/ That he needed consolation was an unhappy sign. He could see a dangerous glistening laid along his notocord, the only material portion remaining in this high state of Joy. But the salve and Bubba-Bubba's cavortings were enough to divert his attention from any perception of pain. If he could avoid pain only a little while longer – if he could dissociate himself from what he had experienced, and write of it with the calm Radiance – then he would be saved.

Unnah closed his Eye. He concentrated on the happy fact that SHE could only destroy one segment of space at a time, that SHE was dead now. Of course, HER death had spawned nine more SHEs and one viable HE; these Unnah must not think about , but hope with benevolent laughter that the Pleasant Zoo Reporters would enmesh and entangle the material feathers of these ones together, to put them, dissolving, into the form of a single SHE/HE. There were few wild HEs remaining, and when the last one was entangled, the Two could be finally, totally entertwined [sic] and mingled, and there would come an end to the impatience and unhappiness and destruction of HER way.

Pain. He felt it stretch across the webbs. He withdrew his central gatherer from Bubba-Bubba's wriggling orifice and looked seriously at his image in the Funny. He laughed. He was dripping, but not disintegrating. The pain was from the Report, still waiting to be finished. Remove that weight, finish that duty, and the dripping would heal. Surely it would heal. Unnah tried to laugh [again], but a faint tracery of dust emitted from his spiracle. He began to write, worried and trying to forget the creeping pain.

Prescient Joyful One, he wrote, SHE moved swiftly into the fourth part of the black zone of the hinterland, where it was difficult to follow. For the period of eighteen Celebrations and one Festivity, SHE hung there, spawning. HER eggs were some large, some small.

He tried hard to smile again, but it was impossible. Reeling, seeing the whirl of yellow and silver that was the Broad Valley of Emotions, the last beauty his eye would ever register, Unnah felt a most blinding and most excruciating painful tremor travel down his notocord, so that it pulled at the vestigial filament around his spiracle, and his orifice Frowned. Unnah slowly spiralled to the shallow center of his seat, dust rising in a milky cloud around him. He tattered into quicksilver strands that split and split again, pulsing and thrumming, then finally lying in dim, round beads. The beads lay scattered in fading silver over the tube in which rested the Report, soon to transmit itself to the Adored One's presence.

And BubbaBubba chortled, gazing out at the rainbow play of colors which shot into view as the vehicle transcended the Valley and entered the Hills. Sometimes BubbaBubba giggled at the funny silver beads which rolled over the desktop and across the Report's ovule[18] tube. Sometimes he reached out a tentative, teasing pseudopod to touch the [tiny] capsule and its rolling dead things inside. The vehicle traveled on and the silver beads dwindled, dimmed, faded…

"Alt!" Crawley shouted. "ALT!"

There was no need to yell. Alt was awake. Alt was awake too.[19] He could hear the thin man's breath sucking in and out, gasping.

"My Lord," Alt said, slowly getting to his feet and staggering closer toward the viewers. "What IS it?" The ship's motors whined. The ship was stuck between-space.[20]

"*Ontario's* conked out," Crawley said, wiping his face.

It was hot, getting hotter. The engines raced, but something had slipped. The stars were going around in spirals; shimmering colored waves emerged in bands around each star, spiralling oscilloscopically. The star in the center of the viewers, the sun, was not spinning. It seemed to be rocking, back and forth. The *Ontario* was spinning, in space, caught between two space-slides.[21] But that was not what was bothering either of the two men. No, not nearly so much as the massive Thing, the gigantic Presence, something shadowlike, almost without substance, yet so heavy that it seemed to push them against the riveted floor like an enormous paw. And this force increased, even as the shadow part of it seemed to consolidate and to become smaller and denser.

"It's impossible," Alt was saying, pushing the words slowly from his mouth as if they were blocks of stone. "This is a hallucination. That damned Dreamglo must have been contaminated."

"Shut up," Crawley exploded. "Look at it. Just LOOK at that thing."

"It's fantastic," Alt murmured, subdued. Sweat was standing out all over his face. Crawley stilled his shaking hands by pressing them together.[22] "it reminds me," Crawley said, slowly, "of a legend. Ancient earth legend–"

They both grabbed behind them. Suddenly, the ship was jerking backwards. The sun rapidly dwindled in size. And the enormous shadow took on definite shape, the shape of a flying thing.

"–Legend–" Crawley repeated. "A bird–"

"What's that?" Alt asked him, straining to keep standing. They were both braced against the Vibrafloat, which was whimpering.[23]

"They're things in the Plutonian Interzoo. Don't you know anything?"

Crawley could see Alt's face getting crimson. He felt stupid, yelling about birds like that. He rubbed his eyes. They were watering, from gazing too long at the brilliant, magnified image of the sun that almost filled the central viewer.

The flying thing on the screen was getting smaller and smaller. It was a clean black cutout against the sun now, cleaving the disk into two jagged parts.

"We're leaving the solar system," Alt said, suddenly.

Crawley tried to fight the backdragging, tried to get to manual.

"Forget it, it didn't work back on Neptune," Alt told him.

Rage filled Crawley. He tried to jump at Alt. "You know it's against the Mandates!" he roared.

"Anything for profit, huh? Kill both of us, huh?"

"No use, anyway," Alt said, imperturbably. "And it's put of synchro. At the rate we're backing out, the old ship could never jump back in. We're too far from the coordinates now."

"We're going to die," Crawley said, starting to shiver. The heat was dissipating rapidly. He got himself strapped into manual anyway, vainly pulling at first one control, then another.

"I never even saw half this stuff before in my life," he groaned. "Go ahead. Just stand there. Don't try to help. Damn you!"

Alt was behind him.

"You little jerk," he said to Crawley, "I said, it don't work.[7] Maybe we can think of something. But pull yourself together."

Crawley vainly continued his efforts, trying to get the stuttering engines to cool down, to work together. They were moving backward more slowly now, so that Alt was able to stand upright, and Crawley no longer had to brace himself away from the control board.

A second shadow was growing over the viewer. Dimly behind it, the sun, with the great bird-shaped form stretched across its face, glimmered in eclipse.

As this second shadow drew close, the engines suddenly began to purr like young Nepcats. And Crawley discovered that he was shivering.

"I'm freezing," he said, locking his hands on the manual's useless steering gear.

"I said we were leaving the solar system," Alt said. "The only power we've got left now is Alternate."

A benign happiness was melting around Crawley's bones.

"You know, it's beautiful out there–" he began, gazing at the viewer. Then his mouth dropped: he could feel it drop, heavy and sullen and incredulous.

"Alt. Look."

Alt was looking.

"It's impossible,"[24] he said, switching up the magnitudes.

There was the solar system, conveniently enlarged spheres, all in their usual places, magnified sun sitting squat and serene in the near-center – and there was the flying Shape, the Thing, moving closer and closer to the sun, a Thing so much more magnificent and – alive – than the sun that Crawley suddenly loved it, loved it with his whole heart. The secondary shadow tinged the viewer ever more deeply, but both men ignored that, concentrating on the brilliant Thing which was going faster and faster toward the sun's very center…

Alt was gazing not at the viewer, anymore, but at the wall.

"I love this damned old ship," he suddenly spouted, tears running down his face. "I thought she could make a fourth trip, I did, honest I did. Forgive me, Crawley. You know I didn't mean to hurt you, or my ship or–" And the tears saved Alt from more excessive pronouncements. Crawley's heart was beating so hard that his ears were filled with its [po]und[ings].[25] He suddenly realized how much he loved the ship, too, and how much he loved the sun, and how much he even loved that bastard Alt. The incongruity of his thoughts made him notice, for a moment, the encroaching coldness, the deepening darkness [of] the[26] secondary shadow that hung just over the viewers.

Alt had moved close to the viewercase, and was rubbing his body affectionately against the chair, like a satisfied cat. The ship's engines were making little self-satisfied sounds, too, tiny humming sounds and little laughing sounds which Crawley had not thought a ship's engine could not have the construction to produce. Alt and his outspread hands were facing the viewercase, and Crawley looked again at the Thing, while Alt made giggling sounds.[27]

"Lookee there," Crawley said, laughing out loud. "It's going to fly into the sun, Alt baby."

Alt guffawed. "Isn't that CUTE?"

Crawley tried to think. His brain was trying to alert him, to tell him that something was wrong, terribly wrong.… He shut his eyes and squeezed his hands against his ears. Ah. Yes. They were lost in space. And here they were laughing. And that thing[28] was flying right into the sun, just like a–

"It's a Phoenix!" he blurted out to Alt, who was sitting on the flooring now, gazing stupidly at his feet.

"I never appreciated you properly," Alt was telling his feet.

"Listen, jerk," Crawley said. "Listen to yourself! you're laughing – and it's a Phoenix–"

"A Phoenix?" Alt murmured, getting to his feet. "Oh, the pretty thing that's going at the sun."

Crawley could feel his head wanting to explode with laughter. He felt like an imbecile. He tried to talk, but his voice came out squeaky with merriment.

"Solar system's being destroyed," he managed to say, then burst into a cackle. He shoved his fist into his mouth, desperately trying to stop the sound. He bit down, tasted blood. There were tears smarting in his eyes.

"The solar system being destroyed," he said again, pulling at the corners of his mouth with his nails. "Somehow–"

"It's important, isn't it?" Alt said, smiling and patting Crawley on the back. "It's okay. You can tell me. I like you, kid. I really really do like you."

"I think you're wonderful, too," Crawley said meekly. He smiled with happiness. His fingers were numb and icy against his mouth, and he wondered why he was tearing at his face with his hands. Then, fighting to remember, he jerked his eyes upwards, at the viewer. He saw a flowery-looking shadow, frilled at the edges, and hairy. It almost engulfed the viewer, but on the side viewer the uncluttered scene of the solar system and its strange visitor remained.

The sun had received the Phoenix.

Alt was singing something. He was not as happy as he had been. It was as if something in him had burned out. Crawley jerked his hands away from his mouth, let the laughter explode, with relief. He was so happy! Yet, before his eyes, billions of men were dying.

"We're men," Crawley said viciously to Alt, kicking him. Alt looked at him like a heartbroken dog. "Get up," Crawley said kicking him again. "Get up, you have to see this. Only–" He slapped his hands over his mouth, feeling the corners upturning with laughter once again. Alt was standing, almost solemn.

"Look," Crawley gasped, shaking his head monotonously to relieve it of the pressure. Alt was stamping his feet, trying also to look.

"I understand," he said, finally, to Crawley.

"The sun is going Nova," Crawley whispered.

Over the central viewer all was darkness. Complex darkness, full of little wriggly things, as if a gigantic nose were pressed against the viewer's round window with curiosity to see the contents of something tiny and held between two fingers, delicatekly, like a pea in its pod … [29]

The sun was expanding. It was shooting out super-heat, super-light, a heat and light which eventually reached even the ship and its freezing occupants, postponing their death awhile.

"So that's what it's like," Alt said, grimly biting into his lower lip, grinding into it.[30]

"The cute little people are probably broiling to death," Crawley said, giggling.

"If they only knew how nice it was to be out here," Alt agreed, trying to stay erect, and somber.

Tears of joy were flooding Crawley's eyes. Somewhere in the back of his mind he knew that this would be the last thing that he would ever see, that man was being exterminated, that only a man could truly understand the enormity of that, and how infinitely sad it was.

So, he thought, laughing, the Phoenix actually exists. It plunges into the sun, and from the sun comes...

But he was watching, with joy, the new life bursting, not from the sun, but from the planets which surrounded the sun, which were one by one engulfed in its flaming mass. The slimy, parasite-ridden spheres that for all these long years had held their slowly-developing treasures, these slow-ly-growing treasures that needed only the sudden incubating warmth of the exploding sun to crack their iron shells, their icy shells, their slimy or gaseous shells.... And emerging, as the sun shrank back, sputtering and spent, the golden, red-feathered things, some large, from the large spheres, and some small, and razor-beaked, from the small spheres.

He saw a brief, savage scene of fury between the large, female-breast-ed ones and the smaller, sharp-beaked males. The male who emerged from the moon-egg so long encircling the earth met the female, who came forth, dripping and glorious, from her own shell, ripping her blunter beak at the male, disembowelling him...

Some of the males from the outer moons of Jupiter escaped the huge Phoenix which leapt out of that magnificent egg, which killed and tore to pieces almost all the other she-birds who still sat, dazed and angry, on the summits of their shells, still weaker than this mighty one who almost im-mediately flew, and, flying, collided with one she-Phoenix after another, destroying, destroying...

"We are seeing the end of the solar system," Crawley repeated, sud-denly beginning, despite his happiness, to feel a fresh flow of despair.

"My God," Alt was saying, "Crawley, look at THAT–"

"Another legend," Crawley babbled, jerking out the appropriate words, his tongue forming them, but now no one listening, or able to understand. They were both overwhelmed with ... and visible Mad Joy.[31]

"LOVE! LOVE!" Alt wept, falling upon his face.

Icicles were forming on Crawley's face, but his lips, too, babbled words of love. His words came from an old text he had once read to amuse himself while enduring the long hours of silent waiting on Interspacial Training.

The happiness was splitting his brain, cleaving his tongue. Dark-ness and the cold collided in his body with his joyously beating heart, the nerves that raced message after message of impossible good tidings through his vibrating body.

"I HAVE SEEN THE ANGEL OF THE LORD!" Crawley's tongue said.

BubbaBubba whistled. He rolled the pea-sized capsule around and around; then, witless as all pacquilas, he let it sit on the Report, and the capsule was transported with it, in another instant, to the beloved High Feeler.

The High Feeler smiled. He brushed the speckle of dust from the Report's tube, and, Smiling Broadly, thrust the Report into his orifice. Then, having Understood, he closed his receptors to stimuli and he Rested.[32]

Endnotes

1. Operative, instead of operating: an example of one of Lee's words that I didn't quite catch.

2. I probably did a lot of capitalizing that Lee would not have done.

3. Lee said Neptune glowed, which is a remarkable coincidence, as this gas planet does, indeed, glow.

"Neptune is the smaller of our solar system's two ice giants. It is a very cold planet, with an average temperature of -329 degrees Fahrenheit. Neptune is made up mainly of hydrogen, helium, water, silicates, and methane. The methane gas absorbs all of the red light, which gives the planet's surface a blue glow. Thick clouds cover Neptune's surface and move at very high speeds of up to 1,300 mph. These winds created the largest storm ever recorded, called the Great Dark Spot of 1989, which lasted about five years. Neptune also has very thin rings made up of ice particles and dust grains that could be clumped together by a carbon-based substance." Ref: https://engineering.purdue.edu/vossmod/neptune.php

4. Lee uses "*once*" instead of "one."

5. Lee uses "*don't* " instead of "doesn't."

6. There is a tiny "500" above the word "the" which marked 500 words in the story so far. We needed to know how many words were in the story for any prospective publishers.

7. Though Lee said he named 'Alt' after Alton Ochnser, he describes him here as a young man. How odd. Ochsner was slender and black-haired when he was young.

8. Sanelacium does not exist as a word, but solacium does. It is related to 'console' and refers to something that is comforting. Can we consider, since it is associated with Dreamglo, that it is some kind of psychotrope?

9. "he had the book instead." Lee loved to read and here he shows it.

10. The story reaches 900 words here, according to the number over "together."

11. A sentence that needed to be revised!

12. An animal that does not exist, nor did the word exist: Lee made this up.

13. "Grateful/gratefully" shows up frequently in this story.

14. I was curious as to why Lee was describing God as "The High Feeler" and Lee –laughing – said, "Didn't God promise everybody eternal happiness if they made it to heaven? But how can they make it to heaven if they have to go through life on earth first?" Lee said Unnah could hardly bear to write a letter because he was all about "joy" and "fun." In fact, Unnah would go crazy trying to get through just one ordinary day in a busy office on earth, which was full of tedious duties and bureaucracy. "Busy work," Lee said, was driving sane people to drink and drugs every day. Then they could not go to heaven when they died. That was unfair! All of this simply provoked us to laughter.

15. I added the semicolon to break up this run-on sentence back in 1963.

16. Lee said he acquired this word (inimitable) just before meeting me. He would use it again when he asked me to marry him the first of one hundred times (see p. 363, paper back edition, *Me & Lee*).

17. Is Untarah both male and female? This sentence probably means that Bubba-Bubba gives what it catches to Unnah, who gives them to Untarah, as Untarah was introduced as a female in the first paragraph about Unnah.

18. It seems Lee was trying to create an adjective out of the word 'oval,' since 'ovule' is the female reproductive organ of a flowering plant. A word I didn't catch in typing Lee's rewrite.

19. An error that is odd, since it cannot be Crawley who just shouted.

20. Remarkably, Lee seems to be mentioning a situation that could be caused if a warp-drive failed, some three years before *Star Trek* used the idea. (*Star Trek* began in 1966.)

21. Lee uses many commas that I find unnecessary.

22. I think I wrote this entire sentence.

23. Page 12 has an "x" on each side of the number. That probably meant it had to be re-typed (too many errors still to be fixed from Lee's manuscript). "I said, it *don't* work" (instead of, "I said, it *doesn't* work") is an example of a grammatical error I didn't catch when typing this 'final' edit for him. After reading it, apparently I scrolled back up and put x's on each side to remind me that this page needed retyping.

24. *"It don't work"* is grammatically incorrect. Sometimes Lee also made this mistake, common in the South, orally.

25. My addition to Lee's original sentence was not a good idea.

26. Only "und" remains, due to damage of the manuscript at this point.

27. Damage to the manuscript required guesswork here.

28. Lee said this was because their ship was so close to the ship sent out to make the Report to the High Feeler: the levity and laughter so important to Unnah's notocord health was apparently contagious, or maybe "Joy" was leaking into space and affecting Alt, Crawley, and even the engines of the ship, while for Unnah the leakage meant he was suffering and would die. Lee said that Unnah and Bubba-Bubba had followed HER for at least a billion years.

29. "Thing" should have been capitalized. This was probably a typo on my part.

30. This no doubt is Unnah's pet, BubbaBubba, looking into the ship's window. The laughter and "joy" of the High Feeler's Recording team was contagious.

31. I have wondered, reading this, if this sentence had any influence on me, later, when I actually, in grief and anger, badly bit down on my own lip at Katzenjammer's (that incident is described in my book *Me & Lee*). I regret having inserted some words of my own into Lee's story, thinking to improve it and thus removing some of the (better) simplicity.

32. The top and bottom of the final page were cut off so that the first line at the top is missing. The various pages of "Her Way" were originally kept in two separate places as a white original, plus a carbon copy (typed on both pink and plain white sheets of paper). Over time, some pages were further separated from each other through accident or by design, as I did not keep all my evidence files and memorabilia together, fearing that they would reveal information I preferred to keep hidden. Today it seems almost a miracle that all 18 pages, except for one line, and a few words, survived. Indeed, at the end, no more than three or four pages were together. The last page was missing for a long time until a small box that had come to us from my deceased mother, full of various scraps of memorabilia about me, was opened. My daughter had kept the box, which had been in my mother's garage and in her attic until she decided to remove what she deemed was salvageable.

To my dismay, she and one of my sons went through the box and discarded what they considered too damaged to save, because it had been invaded by mice while stored in the garage. Thus, a few items of clothing that I had kept from 1963, which Lee had given me, as well as the swimsuit that I had kept many years, and which is seen on the cover of *Me & Lee*, were all discarded as worthless (!), though the see-through nightie and a black oriental-looking shirt that Lee had obtained for me – identical to a red one that I owned – were rescued. The box had been given to my mother to hold onto when I moved from Bradenton, Florida in 1994. I had returned to Bradenton in the mid-1980's after divorcing Robert Baker, to raise my four remaining children in home territory by myself. After so much fruitless hunting, there was the last page, which I did not hear about until it had been 'sanitized' by cutting off the top and bottom, which, I was told, were mangled by those pesky mice.

33. I believe Lee's story influenced my decision to place many words in all caps, and to capitalize many other words, and to use a lot of dashes, when I began writing my own science fiction stories. One story in the collection of *Letters to the Cyborgs* dates from 1963. It was included in this collection, with a few sentences inserted to make it relevant to the Cyborg material, just as it was written. In that story, about trapping monkeys in the jungle by using hypnosis, my own writing style in 1963 has been preserved. That story came straight from an English writing assignment written using green ink and a fountain pen from spring, 1963, at University of Florida. I kept that story because coincidentally, Lee also used a fountain pen and green ink well into 1963, and in April 1963, I refilled my fountain pen with Sanford green ink from Lee's own bottle. Notations that Lee wrote in green ink can be found in the Warren Commission's handwriting analysis records. For that merely sentimental reason, I inserted the monkey story inside the final Cyborg story as a "relic" from humanity's past, thus linking me and Lee in a way you would never guess, unless you read these very lines.

HER WAY:

MORE COMMENTS ABOUT LEE'S SCIENCE FICTION STORY.

*H*er Way was intended for publication. Lee had revised it twice, after which I typed it for him as "editor," with many corrections. The original had been typed on good white paper. A xerox copy would have been sent to a possible publisher. The white original also had a carbon copy to prove it was the original. In this case, the carbon copy was made on cheap pink paper that belonged to my fiance's parents' real estate company. All pink papers in my evidence files are linked to the years 1962-1967 and came from the same ream of pink paper.

Most of the original pages survived the 50+ years they were preserved, but in a few cases, only the pink carbon copy survived. Water was spilled over many of my files and records, and other records were ripped up by vandals, when I was living in Dallas in 2001. (I have always wondered why the vandals destroyed my files, records, papers and computer, but did not steal anything).

There remained a few grammatical errors in "Her Way" which I did not catch, but today I look upon as a bit of interior evidence of how many writing errors there were in Lee's story. But at the same time, the variety and color of his verbiage is delightful and original. His vocabulary for this science fiction story came at a price, seeing how short his life was. From reading an almost endless stream of science fiction, philosophy, biographies and books on history, Lee constructed this improbable and alien world, filled with humor and a dizzying flow of words that catch the imagination. There's a sort of religious aspect to this story, as well, but don't be fooled. Lee writes it all with tongue in cheek.

HER WAY

The <u>Ontario</u> was making a slow liftoff from St. Martinville. The big ship had already made its three trips and was too old for a fourth. It shuddered and creaked.

Crawley tried to relax. He watched Alt's calm face with envy; the fourth chance was usually safe, and meant big profits, but the suspicious noises in the joints and innards of the old tub got on his nerves. Crawley gazed anxiously at the dials and gauges, most of which were in operative order, and the needles began to swing reassuringly to the right, while the lights blinked steadily off and on. The robocomp began to hum consoling tunes into his headset; finally, Alt unbuckled his uniflow and slid out of the manual control chair, confident that the robocomp would make it okay now.

Crawley stayed in his seat. This was his first trip Neptuneside, and like all neophytes, he had to go on a Fourth before he could get his own ship. In case anything happened to Alt, who had been on three rides and whose physiological processes might not endure the disruption sometimes encountered on a Fourth, Crawley would be there to work manual. But now the young pilot had forgotten the potential hazards of Fourth; he was watching the planet swinging away under him.

Neptune glowed like a melon under neon, and the black stabbing space around the slowly shrinking ball fascinated eyes accustomed only to the drab grays and white of humibunks and airlocks.

"Look, Alt," Crawley said, hopefully. "You oughta see this, Alt. You really oughta."

"I've seen it twice," his companion said, squirting Dreamglo into his mouth. "That's once more than's safe. Don't they teach you anything down there?"

"Don't go to sleep yet," Crawley said. "You told me you'd stay awake 'til we hit the first jump. These antique controls, they're different from the ones they had me work on."

"That's what I said," Alt told him, yawning, and lying back in the plexicurved hemisphere that began to fold like a flower around him. "You kids never know anything."

Alt's Vibrafloat began to fluoresce. "If anything happens," Alt mumbled, Dreamglo already suffusing his features with a sickly orange tint, "just call Centra. This old tub don't even need the robocomp. She could make Mars on the gravitlogs alone."

"Damn it," Crawley said, very softly. Alt was asleep. Crawley looked with envy--again--at the black-haired, slender man who looked younger than he did. Alt would have ten thousand I-C's of profit coming if he lived through Fourth. The holds were filled with sanelacium essence and the basic components for Dreamglo itself. Crawley knew that Alt's immediate sleep under the Vibrafloat afforded some protection from the coming jump; that he, too, should be saving up the weeks and years and get under the Vibrafloat's second eye, fold himself into the plexicurved bed, and not play the fool. But space, and its brilliance, still insisted

itself upon him; Crawley would look awhile, like all Firsters
did. He could already feel the exhaustion sucking at his tissues,
draining him, as the ship like a leaping trout banked sideways
in the first time-jump. It struck him deep in the gut, and
when it was over he staggered gratefully to the Vibrafloat, flexing and unflexing his fingers with pain. The ship would now swiftl
decompose and recomposit itself, like a pebble skipping over
water. Then, at the proper interval, it would splash down, into
the medium of ordinary time that stretched like curtains between
rooms, and Mars would be there, opening up her red arms.

Crawley slipped under the Vibrafloat's eye. He pulled a tiny,
very ancient thing from his lace cuff and opened it. It was a
thing called a book, a curiosity the administrator of one of the
museums had asked him to take, under the Vibrafloat for greater
safety, to a friend at Mars Station. Both Crawley, and Clark, the
administrator, enjoyed collecting the ancient legends and myths
that permeated men's history even to the present. Did the ordinary
man realize that the color red, used as the period in retina
reading, was chosen on the old legend that red lights made wheeled
vehicles come to a halt?

Crawley didn't squirt Dreamglo. He had the Book, instead.
He would read until sleep came with the next jump. He wanted to
see what the jump would bring to his dreams when they popped in
and out of time along with the bucking ship. The Vibrafloat
began to sing. On the viewers, Crawley could see the deep black
of space going silver and yellow. The tiny golf-ball-sized
sphere of violet was rapidly fading from the central viewer.
All after-vision, Crawley remembered. There's really nothing

there at all. Just retinal post-impressions, put together from
a miscellany of instantaneous light-impulses which sparked as
the inner synchronization of his biological processes grew
increasingly disrupted. He was feeling sick again, but he tried
to keep his eyes open because he was mildly worried about the
entire panel of lights that suddenly went out...or were they on,
but no longer perceivable to him? Crawley groped up, touched the
autoswitch which would alert him if anything went wrong. He
wondered if the autoswitch was working. All his spacerunning had
been on models, he said to himself, over and over again. He
realized that he wasn't making sense now, and a black band crossed
before his eyes and mild pain hit him as the ship bounced into
another jump. The Book slid from his hands. The Vibrafloat
sang louder, cacophonally, its components humming under the blast
of noise like the ancient gears of the _Ontario_. Crawley tried
to keep his eyes closed, tried to concentrate on the random music
which spared his wildly careening, suffering brain... synapses
coming loose at the seams, Crawley thought. Then his mind was
slipping, like gray oozing, over the edge of a broad plastic rim,
and falling...

Unnah was writing the Report with his customary deliberation.
Beloved High Feeler, he began, putting broad flourishes on the
tips of each dash-dot,
Beloved High Feeler, this is the requested terrifying Report which
thou hath pleaded of my generosity.
    Outside, space was vibrant with yellow and silver. The
ghost-image of planets and stars superimposed each other on the

Broad Valley of Emotions. Unnah shivered with delight, looking
at it. He tapped his spatioreceptor gratefully on its nodule
and BubbaBubba, his adopted pacquila, wriggled under his benevolent
gaze. Unnah scratched BubbaBubba on its spatioreceptor too, and
chuckled. Then he commenced to write, still animated by the
happiness spawned by his chuckling. This was a heavy task. Unnah
tried to lighten his burden by sneaking glances out at the paradise
of color that was the Broad Valley of the Emotions. Somewhere
out there Untarah was waiting for him with her webbs quivering.
Unnah sighed.

Beloved, beloved High Feeler, he wrote, this being the Final
Reportage of the gratifying spectacle which we have proprioccepted
for thy amusement, having followed HER lo, these many hours
through the forests of Desires and past the Broad Valley of
Emotions into the fourth quadrant of the hinterland. Listen,
therefore, with amusement and conceited glory to our poor discoveries brought before thee in the name of Joy.
     BubbaBubba had to excrete. Unnah was grateful. He caught
the excretion and helped BubbaBubba roll it into a feathery ball.
They both smiled broadly when Unnah splattered a passing
asteroid with the missile. Since it was only good for a broad
smile, Unnah knew that this boring task must be quickly finished,
else he would be in no condition to enjoy the Moment of Joking and
Selfhood, which would open his heart to the floodgates of happiness and relief as reward for this undesired discipline. Therefore
that his heart would soon be relieved of this burden, Unnah set
his pappypen grimly to the line. The Elixir ink spilled out its
dot-dashes slowly, excruciatingly slowly. But he wrote steadily.

And Adored One, we sought HER without flinching, without laughter,
and our path was strewn with the obstacles of dullness and obsurity,
for SHE had chosen the garb, for this HER plunging, of HER most
ancient and gloomy ancestress; for we were not, I say with regret,
and speaketh with heart heavy, able to dissuade HER from breeding,
for HE came up like a god of light and thunder, shaking HIS vast
emotions, and SHE fled unto HIM, and they joined, and mighty was
the union they made between them, so that we beat our breasts and
ceased to laugh, in a mourning, for twenty spaces of Joy, Happy
Prince.   Then bewildered we followed the errant child, SHE who
escaped from thy royal House, where all was pleasantries, and
wanton laughter, on this HER evil course, set as our books hath
said, in the inevitable and inimitable wickedness of HER ways.
This I bethought me: that SHE was afforded every pleasure, and we
sought to keep HER happy alway, and to save HER from thinking of
the final Joy, that hollow Joy, of destruction, so fearful and
empty and without Ending, my Lord.

BubbaBubba was playing with the Capsule that it had snatched
through the portal. Unnah saw that the things inside no longer
moved, and were shrivelled. He had hoped to find a moment to feed
the things, but they were lifeless in the space of ten Joys. He
would take the stenchy things to Untarah, who giggled always at
the tiny things BubbaBubba caught and gave to him. But though it
was an uncommon way to pleasure, Unnah often felt curiosity in
how the parasites who clung to HER talons grew and multiplied;
therefore, he often inspected the capsules or fragments BubbaBubba
snatched from whistling space. Such were these dead things that
rattled inside the glossy peapod capsule that BubbaBubba fondled.

Ah, me, Unnah thought, I must finish this Taletelling. The
High Feeler would not wish to see it again; but to send it once,
even to pucker his mighty notocord, was necessary, since he was
responsible for the loosing of HER, who had waxed so unhappy.

"Release HER," he had commanded, to the instantaneous applause
of the Lessers who confused spectacle with true Amusements, "and
let the heavens be HER dominion, that SHE find joy before HER
dossolution."

For aeons, SHE had been caged, though SHE wept, and would not
learn of Joy but transiently. They fed HER the worms of Madda, which
gave HER visions fulfilling, but it was not enough. HER spiracles
shrank and groaned, puffing out dust and destroying the musics they
fed HER. Reluctantly, the Adored One proclaimed that SHE be free,
but followed by a Recorder, that HER end might be known, and understood. The Happy One knew that this miserable task might destroy
the Recorder; Unnah was chosen not because he had already attained
ultimate happiness (for did not Untarah wait for him still with
quivering webbs?), but because his youth might save his sensitive
hedoniceptors from irreparable damage. Certainly the more aged
among the Serene Ones would dissolve under the strain of watching
and recording a single object for so long a time, even though that
object be HSHE. It was necessary to follow HER even to the hinterland, alas! if he survived, Unnah would be greeted by the Radiance
Himself; if not, the Report would be greeted by the Radiance Himself.
So Unnah tried to console himself. That he needed consolation was
an unhappy sign. He could see a dangerous glistening of the myelin
laid along his notocord, the only material portion remaining in this
high state of Joy. But the Salve and BubbaBubba's cavortings were

enough to divert his attention from any perception of pain.
If he could avoid pain only a little while longer—if he could
dissociate himself from what he had experienced, and write of it
with the calm Radiance—then he would be saved.

Unnah closed his Eye. He concentrated on the happy fact that
SHE could destroy only one segment of space at a time, that SHE
was dead now. Of course, HER death had spawned nine more SHE's
and one viable HE; these Unnah must not think about, but hope with
benevolent laughter that the Pleasant Zoo Reporters would enmesh
and entangle the material feathers of these ones together, to put
them, dissolving, into the form of but a single SHE/HE. There
were few wild HE's remaining, and when the last one was entangled,
the Two could be finally, totally entertwined and mingled, and there
would come an end to the impatience and unhappiness and destruction
of HER way.

Pain. He felt it stretch across the webbs. He withdrew his
central gatherer from BubbaBubba's wriggling orifice and looked
seriously at his image in the Funny. He laughed. He was dripping,
but not disintegrating. The pain was from the Report, still waiting
to be finished. Remove its weight, finish that duty, and the
dripping would heal. Surely it would heal. Unnah tried to laugh, AGAIN,
but a faint tracery of dust emitted from his spiracle. He began
to write, worried and trying to forget the creeping pain.

Prescient Joyful One, he wrote, SHE moved swiftly into the fourth
part of the black zone of the hinterland, where it was difficult
to follow. For the period of eighteen Celebrations and one Festivity,
SHE hung there, spawning. HER eggs were some large, some small.

and when SHE finished, SHE lay he-eggs beside these others,
some large, and some small. Then SHE ranged over the fourth part
of the black zone, destroying some of those eggs in her madness,
and covering others with excreta and filth of all kinds. Then
flew SHE in broad circles, coming, in HER increasing madness,
to HER completest Joy which, I must admit, compelled me also, so
strong were the emanations from HER orgasm, to come to the zone's
center fire, where SHE did plunge wholly in. So SHE ranged,
swooping into and out of the fourth part of the dark zone, guarding
HER eggs for a period of eighteen heca-Celebrations and Nine
Festivities, so that I grew exceeding weary and almost ceased to
smile, though that be Heresy. So deep grew my tension that the
Pure Joy of Light was my only consolation, and my idiot pacquila,
in its antics, brought much relief. And on HER third trip roaming
through the black zone, SHE turned toward the central fire, as
Thou had predicted, and, screaming so that I ceased, yes, Laughing
One, I ceased to SMILE and groaned, SHE plunged into the star.

When Unnah had written these words, he felt darkness cross over
his spiracle, and the Anger of Frowns was coming upon him. There
was a bleak and throbbing pain now. He realized that he had indeed
committed Heresy, he who had been created to be Eternally Happy
in sight of the Laughing One. He knew now that he would not survive.
Nevertheless, Unnah smiled at BubbaBubba; but the little Pacquila,
sensing the coming disintegration, backed away, giggling incoherently
at him. Ah, me! Unnah thought, to cease upon the verge of ultimate
Joys! but surely he had witnessed much consummatory in HER way,
though there was little in it of the Joy such as the Laughing One
had caused to melt before the eyes of all the eternally happy.

He tried hard to smile again, but it was impossible.
Reeling, seeing the whirl of yellow and silver that was the Broad
Valley of Emotions, the last beauty his eye would ever register,
Unnah felt a most blinding and excruciatingly painful tremor
travel down the notocord, so that it pulled at the vestigial
filament around his spiracle, and his orifice frowned. Unnah
slowly spiralled to the shallow center of his seat, dust rising
in a milky cloud around him. He tattered into quicksilver strands
that split and split again, pulsing and thrumming, then finally
lying in dim, round beads. The beads lay scattered in fading
silver over the tube in which rested the Report, soon to transmit
itself to the Adored One's presence.

And BubbaBubba chortled, gazing out at the play of rainbow
colors which shot into view as the vehicle transcended the Valley
and entered the Hills. Sometimes BubbaBubba giggled at the funny
silver beads which rolled over the desktop and across the Report's
ovule tube. Sometimes he reached out a teasing, tentative pseudopod
to touch the TINY capsule and its rolling, dead things inside.
The vehicle traveled on, and the silver beads dwindled, dimmed,
faded...

"Alt!" Crawley shouted. "ALT!"
There was no need to yell. Alt was awake. Alt was awake too.
He could hear the thin man's breath sucking in and out, gasping.
"My Lord," Alt said, slowly getting to his feet and staggering
closer to the viewers. "What IS it?"
The ship's motors whined. The ship was stuck between-space.
"Ontario's conked out," Crawley said, wiping his face.

It was hot, getting hotter. The engines raced, but something had slipped. The stars were going around in spirals; shimmering colored waves emerged in bands around each star, spiralling oscilloscopically. The star in the center of the viewers, the sun, was not spinning. It seemed to be rocking, back and forth. The <u>Ontario</u> was spinning, in place, caught between space-slides.

But that was not what was bothering either of the two men. No, not nearly so much as the massive Thing, the gigantic Presence, something shadowlike, almost without substance, yet so heavy that it seemed to push them against the rivetted floor like an enormous paw. And this force increased, even as the shadow part of it seemed to consolidate and to become smaller and denser.

"It's impossible," Alt was saying, pushing the words slowly from his mouth as if they were blocks of stone. "This is a hallucinatio That damned Dreamglo must have been contaminated."

"Shut up," Crawley exploded. "Look at it. Just LOOK at that th

"It's fantastic," Alt murmured, subdued. Sweat was standing out all over his face. Crawley stilled his shaking hands by pressi them together.

"It reminds me," Crawley said, slowly, "of a legend, ancient earth legend---"

They both grabbed behind them. Suddenly, the ship was jerking backwards. The sun rapidly dwindled in size. And the enormous shadow took on definite shape, the shape of a flying thing.

"--Legend--"Crawley repeated, "A bird--"

"What's that?" Alt asked him, straining to keep standing. They were both braced against the Vibrafloat, which was whimpering.

"They're things in the Plutonian Interzoo. Don't you know
anything?"

Crawley could see Alt's face getting crimson. He felt stupid,
yelling about birds like that. He rubbed his eyes. They were
watering, from gazing too long at the brilliant, magnified image
of the sun that almost filled the central viewer.

The flying thing on the screen was getting smaller and smaller.
It was a clean black cutout against the sun now, cleaving the disc
into two jagged parts.

"We're leaving the Solar System," Alt said, suddenly.

Crawley tried to fight the backdragging, tried to get to manual.

"Forget it, it didn't work back on Neptune," Alt told him.

Rage filled Crawley. He tried to jump at Alt. "You know
it's against the Mandates!" he roared. "Anything for profit, huh?
Kill both of us, huh?"

"No use, anyway," Alt said, imperturbably. "And it's out of
synchro. At the rate we're backing out, the old ship could never
jump back in. We're too far from the coordinates now."

"We're going to die," Crawley said, starting to shiver. The
heat was suddenly dissipating rapidly. He got himself strapped into
manual anyway, vainly pulling at first one control, then another.

"I never even saw half this stuff before in my life," he groaned.
"Go ahead, just stand there. Don't try to help. Damn you!"

Alt was behind him.

"You little jerk," he said to Crawley, "I said, it don't work.
Maybe we can think of something. But pull yourself together."

Crawley vainly continued his efforts, trying to get the stuttering
engines to cool down, to work together. They were moving backward

more slowly now, so that Alt was able to stand upright, and
Crawley no longer had to brace himself away from the control board.

A second shadow was growing over the viewer. Dimly behind it,
the sun, with the great bird-shaped form stretched across its face,
glimmered in eclipse.

As this second shadow drew close, the engines suddenly began
to purr like young Nepcats. And Crawley discovered that he was
shivering.

"I'm freezing," he said, locking his hands on the manual's
useless~~xkxxxxxxxx~~steering gear.

"I said we were leaving the Solar System," Alt said. "The only
power we've got left now is Alternate."

A benign happiness was melting around Crawley's bones.

"You know, it's beautiful out there---" he began, gazing at the
viewer. Then his mouth dropped; he could feel it drop, heavy and
sullen and incredulous.

"Alt. Look."

Alt was looking.
I STILL SAY
"It's impossible," he said, switching up the magnitudes.

There was the solar system, conveniently enlarged spheres all in
their usual places, magnified sun sitting squat and serene in the
near-center--and there was the flying Shape, the Thing, moving
closer and closer to the sun, a Thing so much more magnificent and
---alive--than the sun that Crawley suddenly loved it, loved it with
his whole heart. The secondary shadow tinged the viewer ever more
deeply, but both men ignored that, concentrating on the brilliant
Thing which was going faster and faster toward the sun's very center..

Alt was gazing not at the viewer, anymore, but at the wall.

"I love this damned old ship," he suddenly spouted, tears

running down his face. "I thought she could make a fourth trip,
I did, honest I did, Crawley. Forgive me, Crawley, you know I
didn't mean to hurt you or my ship or---" and the tears saved Alt
from more excessive pronouncements.

Crawley's heart was beating so hard that his ears were filled
with its [illegible]. He suddenly realized how much he loved the ship,
too, and how much he loved the sun, and how much he even loved
that bastard Alt. The incongruity of his thoughts made him notice,
for a moment, the encroaching coldness, the deepening darkness
[and] the secondary shadow that hung just over the viewers.

Alt had moved close to the viewercase, and was rubbing his body
affectionately against the chair, like a satisfied cat. The ship's
engines were making little self-satisfied sounds, too, tiny humming
sounds and little laughing sounds which Crawley had thought a ship's
engine could not have the construction to produce. Alt and his
outspread hands were facing the viewercase, and Crawley looked again
at the Thing, while Alt made giggling sounds.

"Lookee there," Crawley said, laughing out loud, "it's going to
fly into the sun, Alt Baby."

Alt guffawed. "Isn't that CUTE?"

Crawley tried to think. His brain was trying to alert him, to
tell him that something was wrong, terribly wrong... he shut his
eyes and squeezed his hands against his ears. Ah. Yes. They were
lost in space. And here they were laughing. And that thing was
flying right into the sun, just like a---

"It's a Phoenix!" he blurted out to Alt, who was sitting on the
flooring now, gazing stupidly at his feet.

"I never appreciated you properly," Alt was telling his feet.

"Listen, jerk, " Crawley said, "Listen to yourself! you're laughing--and it's a Phoenix---"

"A Phoenix?" Alt murmured, pulling himself to his feet. "Oh, the pretty thing that's going at the sun."

Crawley could feel his head wanting to explode with laughter. He felt like an imbecile. He tried to talk, but his voice came out squeaky with merriment.

"Solar system's being destroyed--" he managed to say, then burst into a cackle. He shoved his fist into his mouth, desperately trying to stop the sound. He bit down, tasted blood. His head cleared a little. There were tears smarting in his eyes.

"The solar system being destroyed," he said, again, pulling at the corners of his mouth with his nails. "Somehow--"

"It's important, isn't it?" Alt said, smiling and patting Crawley on the back. "It's okay. You can tell me. I like you, kid. I really really do like you."

"I think you're wonderful, too," Crawley said, meekly. He smiled with happiness. His fingers were numb and icy against his mouth, and he wondered why he was tearing at his face with his hands. Then, fighting to remember, he jerked his eyes upwards, at the viewer. He saw a flowery-looking shadow, frilled at the edges, and hairy. It almost engulfed the viewer, but on the side viewer the uncluttered scene of the solar system and its strange visitor remained.

The sun had received the Phoenix.

Alt was singing something. He was not as happy as he had been. It was as if something in him had burned out. Crawley jerked his hands away from his mouth, let the laughter explode, with relief. He was so happy! yet, before his eyes, billions of men were dying.

"We're men," Crawley said viciously to Alt, kicking him. Alt looked at him like a heartbroken dog. "Get up," Crawley said, kicking him again. "Get up, you have to see this. Only---" he slapped his hands over his mouth, feeling the corners upturning with laughter once again. Alt was standing, almost solemn.

"Look," Crawley gasped, shaking his head monotonously to relieve it of the pressure. Alt was stamping his feet, trying also to look.

"I understand," he said, finally, to Crawley.

"The sun is going Nova," Crawley whispered.

Over the central viewer all was darkness. Complex darkness, full of little wriggly things, as if a gigantic nose were pressed against the viewer's round window with curiosity to see the contents of something tiny and held between two fingers, delicately, like a pea in its pod...

The sun was expanding. It was shooting out super-heat, super-light, a heat and light which eventually reached even the ship and its freezing occupants, postponing their death awhile.

"So that's what it's like," Alt said, grimly biting into his lower lip, grinding against it.

"The cute little people are probably broiling to death," Crawley said, giggling.

"If they only knew how nice it was to be out here," Alt agreed, trying to stay erect, and somber.

Tears of joy were flooding Crawley's eyes. Somewhere in the back of his mind he knew that this was the last thing he would ever see, that man was being exterminated, that only a man could truly understand the enormity of that, and how infinitely sad it was.

So, he thought, laughing, the Phoenix actually exists.

It plunges into the sun, and from the sun comes...

But he was watching, with joy, the new life bursting, not from the sun, but from the planets which surrounded the sun, which were one-by-one engulfed in its flaming mass. The slimy, parasite-ridden spheres that for all these long ages had held their slowly-developing treasures, these slowly-growing treasures that needed only the sudden incubating warmth of the exploding sun to crack their iron shells, their icy shells, their slimy or gaseous shells. And emerging, as the sun shrank back, sputtering and spent, the golden, red-feathered things, some large, from the large spheres, and some small, and razor-beaked, from the small spheres.

He saw a brief, savage scene of fury between the large, female-breasted ones and the smaller, sharp-beaked males. The male that emerged from the moon-egg so long encircling the earth met the female, who came forth, dripping and glorious, from her own shell, ripping her blunter beak at the male, disembowelling him...

Some of the males from the outer moons of Jupiter escaped the huge Phoenix which leapt out of that magnificent egg, which killed and tore to pieces almost all the other she-birds who still sat, dazed and angry, on the summits of their shells, still weaker than this mighty one who almost immediately flew, and, flying, collided with one she-Phoenix after another, destroying, destroying

"We are seeing the end of the solar system," Crawley repeated, suddenly beginning, despite his happiness, to feel a fresh flow of despair.

"My God," Alt was saying, "Crawley, look at THAT——"

"Another legend," Crawley babbled, his mind jerking out the appropriate words, his tongue forming them, but no one now listenin or able to understand. They were both overwhelmed with the and visible Mad Joy.

"LOVE! LOVE!" Alt wept, falling upon his face.

Icicles were forming on Crawley's face, but his lips, too, babbled words of love. His words came from an old text he had once read to amuse himself while enduring his long hours of silent waiting on Interspacial Training.

The happiness was splitting his brain, cleaving his tongue. Darknes and the cold, collided in his body with his joyously beating heart, the nerves that raced message after message of impossible good tidings through his vibrating body.

"I HAVE SEEN THE ANGEL OF THE LORD!" Crawley's tongue said.

BubbaBubba whistled. He rolled the peasize capsule around and around; then, witless as all pacquilas, he let it sit on the Report, and the capsule was transported with it, in another instant, to the beloved High Feeler.

The High Feeler Smiled. He brushed the speckle of dust from the Report's tube, and, Smiling Broadly, thrust the Report into his orifice. Then, having Understood, he closed his receptors to stimuli, and he Rested.

Oswald Was Writing Anti-Red Book, Fort Worth Steno Says

FORT WORTH, Tex. (AP)—Lee Harvey Oswald, obviously scared and nervous at the time, enlisted the help of a public stenographer while working on what a public stenographer called an anti-Communist book in 1962.

The stenographer, Miss Pauline V. Bates, said he told her to stop typing the manuscript after three days, explaining he had only $10.

This occurred only 17 months before Oswald, an admitted Communist sympathizer, was to be accused of killing President Kennedy. In turn, a Dallas night spot owner killed Oswald two days later as city police started to move him to the county jail.

Oswald had returned after nearly three years in Russia. He went there in 1959, declaring he wanted to renounce U.S. citizenship, but later obtained a State Department permission and loan to return to this country.

Miss Bates said Oswald came to her office with a mass of notes condemning life in the Soviet Union, presumably jotted down while he was abroad.

PAULINE BATES
Her Job Unfinished

She recalled typing this paragraph at one point:

"The TV (in Russia) carries nothing but the Communist party line, but you have to turn it on or somebody gets suspicious. A few have hidden radios and are enthusiastic over the Voice of America."

Miss Bates estimated she had transcribed a third of a book manuscript June 18, 19 and 2 last year while Oswald waited "fidgety and jumping up and down." She related these details:

He did not permit her to keep his notes overnight or even t see them alone. Oswald refused to let Miss Ba keep copies of what she typed and he ordered the carbon paper destroyed.

Once he displayed a letter from a Fort Worth engineer expressing interest in getting the book published. She did not recall the name of the engineer.

On the third day he went her office, Oswald, seeming worried or scared, stopped Miss Bates after she had finished 10 pages.

"Ten dollars is all I've got," he said and handed her the money.

She offered to finish the typing job and let him pay later. He refused the offer and left.

Twice after that Miss Bates saw him on downtown street. Oswald did not speak.

LEE H. OSWALD: WHAT HE READ AND WHAT HE THOUGHT

L ee's idealism underpinned his interest in writing science fiction and about governments in the future. Evidence that he was anti-communist can be seen in his sketch outlining "a system opposed to the Communist" (system) to which he appended his idealized Utopian system. Lee called it "The Atheian System." Nevertheless, the Warren Commission, which published Lee's material, told the world that young Lee Harvey Oswald was just another evil Communist madman. In fact, even while Lee was inside the USSR, he never joined the Communist party, even though, for drama, he declared in his "historic diary" (which he wrote in mere days, as if he had been at it for 30 months) that, "I want citizenship because I am a communist and a worker. ..." Lee told me personally, in no uncertain terms, that he had pretended to be a communist to gain entry into the USSR as a spy, in his role as "defector."

Lee had previously been writing a book about conditions in the USSR. In 1962, he asked a public stenographer, Virginia Bates, to type up "a manuscript he was writing" for a book. Mark Lane, who interviewed her,[i] learned that the Secret Service had never interviewed Bates, even though her story reached newspapers soon after the Kennedy assassination. Bates said he told her about his wife, and also that he had been in the Marines. She said he told her he "had applied for a visa to go to Russia," and "how much he liked America. ..." Even though this woman told newspaper reporters that Lee was writing an anti-communist book, they reported that Lee was "an admitted Communist sympathizer" as can be seen in the article on the previous page.

Newspaper article shows witness saying Lee was writing an "Anti-Red Book" but the reporter then says Lee Oswald was "an admitted Communist sympathizer...."

Lee's "System Opposed to the Communist"

Warren Commission Exhibit 98, pp. 431-434. "Note: In the interest of clarity and legibility, spelling, punctuation, and capitalization has been corrected in certain cases."

Lee's spelling and punctuation was corrected then, as shown above, and is further corrected here, as any editor would do for any published work (with comments added).

"A System Opposed to the Communist."

In that the state (or any group of persons) may not administer or direct funds or value in circulation, for the creation of means of production. [Against banking systems.]

A. Any person may own private property of any sort. [Private property ownership, the opposite of Communism.]

B. Small business or speculation on the party of a single individual may be guaranteed. [Free enterprise.]

C. That any person may exchange personal skill or knowledge in the completion of some service, for remuneration. [Receiving pay for work or services rendered.]

D. That any person may hire or otherwise remunerate any other single person for services rendered, so long as that service does not create surplus value. [Lee was against padding payments.]

A System Opposed to Capitalism in That:

No individual may own the means of production, distribution, or creation of goods or any other process wherein workers are employed for wages, or otherwise employed, to create profit or surplus profit or value in use or exchange. [No profits beyond those needed to run the business properly and to justly pay everyone; if owners made excessive profits, they were either underpaying workers and/or overcharging consumers.]

A. In that all undertaking of production, distribution or manufacture or otherwise the creation of goods must be made on a pure, collective basis under the conditions: [Profit-sharing.]

1. Equal shares of investment be made by members.

2. Equal distribution of profit after tax, be made to all investors [of course, based on percentage of ownership of stock.]

3. That all work or directive or administrative duties connected with the enterprise be done personally by those investors. [Those not directly associated with the business should not be able to buy stock.]

4. That no person not directly working or otherwise directly taking part in the creational process of any enterprise, have a share of or otherwise receive any part of the resultant profit of it. [Lee believed that outsiders should not be allowed to conduct hostile buyouts/piracy on an enterprise.]

Stipend [unfinished note area]

Agronomist [unfinished note area]

THE ATHEIAN SYSTEM [AΘEIAN = "ATHEIST-ATHENIAN" SYSTEM]
A system opposed to communism, socialism, and capitalism

A. Democracy at a local level with no centralized State. [Argued for city-states].

1. That the right of free enterprise and collective enterprise be guaranteed. [Free enterprise, etc.].

2. That fascism be abolished [anti-Nazi, anti-fascist].

3. That nationalism be excluded from every-day life. [no militant form of patriotism].

4. That racial segregation or discrimination be abolished by law. [Civil Rights for All].

5. The right of the free, uninhibited action of religious institutions of any type or denomination to freely function. [Freedom of Religion].

6. Universal Suffrage for all persons over 18 years of age. [When written, US voting age was 21].

7. Freedom of dissemination of opinions through press or declaration or speech. [Freedom of Speech].

8. That the dissemination of war propaganda be forbidden as well as the manufacture of weapons of mass destruction. [WMD: used this term years before it reached common vocabulary].

9. That Free compulsory education be universal until 18. [free education for all]

10. Nationalization or communizing of private enterprise or collective enterprise be forbidden. [no Communist practices]

11. That monopoly practices be considered as capitalistic. [anti-monopoly]

12. That combining of separate collective or private enterprises into single collective units be considered as communistic. [For example, today most US media is owned by just a few large corporations, which is a monopoly akin to certain forms of Communism. Chinese?]

13. That no taxes be levied against individuals [Only businesses could be taxed]

14. That heavy graduated taxes from 30% to 90% be leveled against surplus profit gains.

15. That taxes be collected by a single ministry, subordinate to individual communities.

That taxes be used solely for the building or improvement of public projects. [Lee leaves out taxes for defense, education and running governments ... however, this suggested system was just a first draft, and Lee was only 22 when he wrote it.]

Against	In so far as	Reason [left unfinished]
communism (international	limitations on freedom of travel, press, religion, speech, elections	
taxes	limitations on freedom of travel, press, religion, speech, elections	
sale of arms	pistols should not be sold in any case, rifles only with police permission, shotguns free	
extremism of purely racial character or regional	anti-Negro or Jew or nationality or anti-religion	
unemployment	[if] it is caused by other than voluntary means of employers such as automation.	
For		
medical aid: free	Hospital beds and operations	
aid to education	State and national subsidy of universities and free or paid expenses for students of higher educational units.	
welfare: all encompassing.	Higher pensions independent of amount of work; only curbed as to type of work and rank of worker upon retirement.	
disarmament	General disarmament and abolition of all armies except civil police force with small arms	

Lee Harvey Oswald, the Reader: Oswald's Reading Habits in New Orleans, and Evidence Manipulation

by Judyth Vary Baker

W hy should we care about what the accused assassin of Kennedy read in New Orleans?

The FBI did. They confiscated every book they could find that Oswald read in New Orleans. But did you know that the FBI described the title of one book Oswald read as *Conflict,* when its actual title was *Conflict: the history of the Korean War, 1950-53?* However, the FBI did not shorten the title of this book, *Portrait of a Revolutionary: Mao Tse-Tung.*

The manipulation of evidence concerning Oswald extended to even such small details.

Even today, such manipulation continues. For example, Oswald's reading the works of Marx and Engels is highlighted in the Wikipedia encyclopedia biography without mentioning that he read many kinds of books. The Wikipedia article is influenced by the same Internet team associated with John McAdams' Marquette University-sponsored websites promoting Oswald as guilty of killing Kennedy, a position no longer tenable since a plethora of recent, new evidence has emerged.[1]

This paper provides a resource for students, scholars and researchers as an aid to discerning the truth about Oswald's reading habits, how evidence was manipulated in matters related to the materials he read from various sources, and what Oswald's reading choices might suggest about the true character of the accused assassin.

Introduction

T he life of Lee Harvey Oswald has been recorded many times by friends, foes, investigators and researchers, with little information about his reading habits, though one early book, *Marina and Lee,* makes some mention of them. Its author, Priscilla Johnson-McMillan[2] presents a highly biased negative portrait of the accused assassin of President John F. Kennedy. It is also a source of information regarding what Lee's Russian-born wife, Marina Prusakova, purportedly knew about his reading selections and habits (little).

Another useful resource: the twenty-six volumes of the Warren Commission's interviews and exhibits (CE's). The FBI not only attempted (unsuccessfully) to track down all the books Lee checked out from public libraries in Dallas and New Orleans, they also confiscated every book they found (27 of the 34 books on their list). Seven books were "in the hands of private citizens" at the time – 20.6% – a rather large percentage, considering how many thousands of books were available for check-out: in fact, Lee's book choices often included current best-sellers in their field.

According to the Secret Service report to the Warren Commission, Lee's New Orleans library card was issued May 27, 1963, and was set to expire May 27, 1966. The Librarian at the Napoleon Branch told Special Agent Roger D. Counts, of the Secret Service, that Lee's library card number was #8460 – not #8640 (CE 2650) as reported by the FBI. The Secret Service obtained a copy of the book list from the FBI for the Commission.

The Napoleon Branch kept Lee H. Oswald's card on file and wrote down what books he checked out and when they were returned. But six other libraries in town, including the Main Library, used a numeric system to register checked-out books. The FBI noted, "...of the nine remaining libraries, five have a record system similar to the Main Library." While books Lee borrowed from the Napoleon Branch library had findable records, those keeping only his library card number on file against books checked out made it impossible for the FBI to go through the Main Library's records, which were kept on microfiche.

The FBI apparently neglected to check any of the other library branches using the same filing system as the Napoleon Branch. Lee could have checked out books and magazines at other branches, as well as at the Main Library, but if he did, we'll never know. What we have, therefore, is a record of the *minimum number of books* Lee is known to have read in New Orleans, as recorded at one branch library. Nevertheless, the list is long. Below is the report by agent Roger D. Counts, of the Secret Service.

THE SHARK AND THE SARDINES

Only one book (Feb, 19, 1964 report, CE 2650, p. 565) was reported as checked out by Lee Oswald after an examination of Dallas library records. That book was *The Shark and the Sardines* by Juan Jose Arevalo. In

Commission Exhibit No. 2650

Form No. 158 (Revised)
MEMORANDUM REPORT
(7-1-58)

UNITED STATES SECRET SERVICE
TREASURY DEPARTMENT

ORIGIN Dallas	OFFICE New Orleans, La.		FILE NO. CO-2-34,030
TYPE OF CASE	STATUS		TITLE OR CAPTION
Protective Research	Continued		Lee Harvey Oswald
INVESTIGATION MADE AT	PERIOD COVERED 11-29-63 12-4-63		Assassination of President John F. Kennedy
New Orleans, Louisiana			
INVESTIGATION MADE BY			
SA Roger D. Counts			

DETAILS

SYNOPSIS

This report covers investigations made at the branches of the public library at New Orleans. Attached is a list of the books obtained by Lee Harvey Oswald.

DETAILS OF INVESTIGATION

Reference is made to the M/R of SA Steuart, Dallas, dated 11-27-63, in which it was mentioned that Lee Harvey Oswald had among his belongings a New Orleans Public Library card No. 8460, and also to a telephone call from SAIC Bouck to SAIC Rice requesting that inquiries be made to determine if Lee Harvey Oswald had checked out any books pertaining to the U. S. Secret Service.

On 11-29-63 Jerome Cushman, Head Librarian, New Orleans Public Library, was interviewed. Mr. Cushman advised that the library card of Lee Harvey Oswald had been issued by the Napoleon Branch library, 913 Napoleon Avenue, New Orleans, and that the original of this card had been picked up by the FBI along with all available books which had been checked out by Oswald. He further stated that it would be extremely difficult to determine if Oswald had obtained books from the Main Library, as this would require examination of the microfilms of all transactions since Oswald obtained his card. He said that it would also be quite possible that Oswald could have any number of cards issued to him. These cards are filed numerically and, without knowing the exact card number, all cards would have to be checked to determine if this was the case.

On 12-2-63 Geraldine Vaucresson, Librarian, was interviewed by SAIC Rice and the writer at the Napoleon Branch library. She stated that the correct number for the library card issued to Lee Harvey Oswald was N8640 and not 8460. This card had an expiration date of May 27, 1966, indicating that it had been issued on May 27, 1963. Mrs. Vaucresson said that the original card had been given to Mr. Cushman, Head Librarian, who had in turn given it to the FBI. She also said that a number of books which

DISTRIBUTION	COPIES	REPORT MADE BY	DEC 10	DATE
Chief	Orig. & 2 co's			12-10-63
New Orleans	2 co's	SPECIAL AGENT Roger D. Counts		
Dallas	2 co's	APPROVED John W. Rice 564		DATE 12-10-63
		SPECIAL AGENT IN CHARGE John W. Rice		

(CONTINUE ON PLAIN PAPER)

COMMISSION EXHIBIT No. 2650

Page 2
CO-2-34,030
December 10, 1963

Oswald had checked out had been turned over to the FBI and that she had not retained a list of these.

On 12-3-63 SA Steve Callender, FBI, was interviewed and a list of the books checked out by Oswald was obtained (see attachment). This consisted of 34 books of which 27 are being held by the FBI. The 7 remaining books are in the possession of private citizens as they were checked out at the time of the investigation by the FBI.

Also on 12-3-63 a call was received from SAIC Bouck requesting that an inquiry be made to determine if Oswald had obtained any of the four books written by the following authors: U. E. Baughman, Harry Neal, Edward Starling, or Michael Reilly. On 12-4-63 a visit was made to the Napoleon Branch library where it was determined that none of the aforementioned books had been checked out by Oswald.

The difficulty in examining the records of the Main Library has been explained above. Of the nine remaining branch libraries, five have a record system similar to the Main Library. As this is the case, no effort will be made to examine these records as well as those of the other four branches unless specifically directed.

UNDEVELOPED LEADS

Investigation continued.

ATTACHMENTS – Chief and Dallas

List of books obtained by Lee Harvey Oswald from New Orleans Public Library.

RDC/mjl

564

COMMISSION EXHIBIT No. 2650—Continued

626

Dallas, only books with late charges preserved the name of who checked out a book. *The Shark and the Sardines* is the only book on record that Oswald supposedly kept over the time limit in Dallas, or anywhere else.

But the book was not found among Lee's possessions. It was therefore not on the official list. Nor was the book ever returned to the Dallas library. These facts place the book in a "suspicious" category. The book was supposedly checked out November 6, 1963. It became due November 13, 1963. This is the only known instance of Lee Oswald failing to return a library book, who is also on record as never missing a day of work while employed throughout 1963.

For perspective, in the Cold War era of 1963, having materials mailed from the USSR to one's actual physical address, or from the U.S. Communist Party, was risky, just as if someone who had returned recently from Iran, in 2010, kept receiving mail from Iran, Iraq and Afghanistan, with anti-American slogans all over it. Lee, who was fluent in Russian, chose to have most of his Russian language magazines and newspapers delivered to his post office boxes. Lee.[3]

Lee was not only careful that all the books he checked out from the New Orleans Napoleon Branch library were returned in a timely manner, but he seems to have gone to extraordinary lengths to make sure of it. Oswald, according to the FBI and the CIA, was in Mexico by September 26, where he remained until October 3. But the last four library books Lee Oswald checked out, *Goldfinger, Moonraker, Ape and Essence,* and *Brave New World,* were returned to the library on October 3 by an unknown person. No effort was made to locate the person responsible. Had they done so, they might have learned that Susie Hanover, my landlady at nearby 1032 ½ Marengo St., a mutual friend of both Lee and myself, dropped off the books for him before they became due. Such a discovery might have revealed more than the Commission would have wanted the American people to know.

On the day these four books were returned to the library, Lee had just left Mexico. Passengers on a bus from Laredo heading toward Dallas said they saw him, and the FBI reported this as his mode of travel.[4] Whether that was true or not, Lee was not in New Orleans. Notwithstanding his care in making sure the last four books he checked out in New Orleans were returned when due, during the same time period Lee was being maligned by the Garners as a deadbeat who skipped out on his rent and utility bills, which was echoed by US government agents, and McMillan. This is important because of what we see next, regarding Lee's supposedly never returning a particular overdue library book in Dallas in November 1963.

The reported failure to return the book to the Dallas library system thus takes on a suspicious note. Such a failure, especially in the 1960s, could be seen as an indication of the accused assassin's growing instability and unreliability.

The Oak Cliff branch library was 8/10's of a mile from the boarding house at 1026 North Beckley, twice as far as it had been from Lee Oswald's apartment in New Orleans, but even so, Lee was said to have visited it frequently.[5] Known to be meticulous as to details, and careful with money, Lee would have avoided a fine on an overdue book if possible. For these reasons, we should inspect the particulars of the reported incident carefully.

The Shark and the Sardines (1961, 256 pages) was a notorious, controversial book in 1963, considered "anti-American" by the CIA. Such a book in Oswald's possession could help buttress the case against him as anti-American. The overdue book was the last known, according to the FBI, that Lee Oswald borrowed from the public library before Kennedy's assassination.

What was this book about? Its author, Juan Jose Arevalo, was Guatemala's first democratically elected president (1944). Before that, the country had been run by a series of dictatorships. When President Jacobo Arbenz implemented his predecessor's failed land reform policies, in 1954, the CIA designed and conducted a Coup d'etat through Operation PBFORTUNE and Operation PBSUCCESS to get redistributed land back into the hands of big private plantations run by the United Fruit Company. Guatemala became a harsh dictatorship, with three decades of bloodshed and war as a result of the people's attempts to restore a democratic government.[6]

Arevalo remained an unpopular figure in the US in 1963. His complaints about the CIA-sponsored coup d'etat that deposed Arbenz made him a pariah to American media. But the book told the truth. *The Shark and the Sardines*, published in 1956, was followed in 1963 with a sequel, *Anti-Communism in Latin America*. In their Jan. 5, 1962 article, "Guatemala: Echoes from a Sardine," *Time Magazine*, possibly inspired by the CIA's blacklisting of the author, trumpeted the fact that Castro and the Fair Play for Cuba Committee had embraced Arevalo's little book, while admitting that the author took no royalties from Castro's reprinting of his story:

> A self-styled "spiritual Socialist," he blamed his country's ills on the United Fruit Co., which had immense holdings in Guatemala, [and] accused the U.S. Government of backing the company's "exploitations,"... Though a devious administrator, he gave his country some freedoms it had not known under a previous long line of dictators.
>
> The one party he refused to legalize was the Communist – but he did nothing to restrain the Communist clique behind gullible Army Colonel Jacobo Arbenz, who succeeded him as President... Arévalo protests, "I am a Christian and an idealistic anti-Marxist." He insists that, "I am not anti-American. I oppose the American Government when it turns into a protector of American corporations." As for Castro, says Arévalo, Communism will not work in Latin America or anywhere else. "You can see that by going over their record in Cuba."

In other words, Lee Oswald was reported to be reading a work by an anti-communist socialist whose anti-American little book was reprinted by Castro even as it was damned by the CIA and the US media. The book was available in the Dallas public library, we have been told. But because so much evidence against Lee Oswald in Dallas is now known or suspected to have been planted, and because this book has never been found, we have to ask if the notably right-wing Dallas library would actually have purchased such a book for its upright citizens to read. The fact that *The*

Shark and the Sardine was "late" – the one and only record of a late book for Oswald that can be found (and the sole evidence for the tardiness that could be found in the Dallas library records by the FBI) places this "find" on shaky ground.

Other volumes are known to have been read by Lee H. Oswald in Dallas: CE 2652 tells us that Marina Oswald witnessed her husband reading two thick, blue books in New Orleans that she believed were US history books. The two volumes were last seen in Robert Oswald's possession: he turned them over to the FBI. The books were H.G. Well's massive and popular tomes, *The Outline of History, Vols. I and II*. At least 1,324 pages long, with expanded material after WW II. Robert Oswald identified both books as belonging to his brother, and the locale where he read them was changed to Dallas, prior to the move to New Orleans. We do not know how Robert Oswald happened to have obtained possession of these books. Interestingly, Lee mentioned H.G. Wells in his Russian diary: "I don't like: picture of Lenin which watches from its place of honour and phy traning at 11.00-11.10 each morning (complusery) for all. (Shades of H.G. Wells)."[7]

The apparent dyslexia from which Oswald suffered did not stop him from reading. His British form of writing "honour" – and some other words in the British form – probably derived from his reading so many books written by British authors. H. G. Wells, for example, was born in London. And then there was Ian Fleming, whose James Bond novels were an Oswald favorite.

WERE THERE OTHER OVERDUE BOOKS?

But weren't there other overdue books? The Mary Ferrell Chronology, trusted by many researchers, raises the question, despite the entries on the FBI list:

"Sept. 5, 1963 (Thursday) - Oswald had three library books due this date. *He probably didn't return them until 9/9/63.* (22:83)"

When we access the record Ferrell cites, it is the wrong page (page 2) of the same FBI library book list that everyone references. No dates of 9/9/63 are listed there, or on any other page. Ferrell was in error. Checking the entire record, three books were checked out on August 22, 1963: *From Russia with Love*, *The Sixth Galaxy Reader*, and *Portals of Tomorrow*. All three were returned on time, on Sept. 5, 1963 (Thursday). We conclude that no books were returned late in New Orleans, despite Ferrell's insinuation.

Ferrell makes other statements that betray prejudice in dealing with Lee's life story and his financial records, especially regarding what she and the Warren Commission decided that which constituted his and his family's daily expenses, leaving out transportation, magazines, clothing, medicine and other needs, by assigning a mere pittance to "miscellaneous." Thus they were able to conjure up "savings" that they assigned to Lee as available for travel and other expenses, otherwise wholly unaccountable. Their "budgets" for Lee were wholly out of range with the demands of reality. Had they been honest, they would have had to admit that Lee Oswald had to have obtained funds from ignored sources for his travels to and from the USSR and for his and his family's daily needs. As a woman who was forced to live on a tight budget at the same time that Lee was forced to seem to do so, in the same city, between April and September of 1963, I know from personal experience that no one could live and travel as Lee, and later Lee and his family did, on the limited amounts so arbitrarily assigned.

WHY BE CONCERNED ABOUT WHAT OSWALD WAS READING?

The FBI was. And Ferrell, as well as other serious researchers, made note of the books Oswald read. Perhaps an assassin's reading materials could help explain why he committed the crime and cast light on his evil motives.

The FBI confiscated every book it could find that Lee Oswald had read in New Orleans. We know that many of Oswald's writings and documents were chemically treated to find fingerprints. In addition, perhaps the FBI sought to find underlined passages – Lee was fond of underlining passages. Or perhaps they wanted the books to be kept from the public eye. What would people think if they had learned that Lee Oswald the Evil had read the classic religious book *Ben Hur – a Story of the Christ,* when he was supposed to be a cruel, demented, Communist, Castro-loving atheist who single-handedly killed the nation's president?

What if Lee Oswald had underlined some key passages that showed a different side to the supposedly demented killer? We know the title of the book – *Ben Hur – a Story of the Christ* was truncated by the FBI to "Ben Hur" – obscuring the fact that Lee had read a big book that was beloved and respected by American Christians. Certain other book titles were also truncated that should have had full titles shown to indicate their actual topic. The full titles of these books might have better revealed some of the character and thoughts of the real lee H. Oswald (to be revealed below).

If I seem biased in favor of Lee Oswald, one must remember that facts are being brought to the fore here that will not be found in "official version" sources. Not a few, but hundreds of suppressed facts exist that throw everything out of the shadows into the light. Any perplexity or frustration with those pushing the official version is caused by these anomalies found by honest researchers. Only persons with a double-digit IQ could possibly come to the conclusions pushed on the Internet by the "Oswald-did-it" clan, when exposed to the new evidence. Dishonesty is rampant among those such as John McAdams, Gary Mack, Dale Myers and Gerald Posner, who have pushed the official version using sources that prove they are not ignorant of the truth.[8]

No mention is found in the Wikipedia biography, for example, of the fact that Lee Oswald visited New Orleans college campuses in 1963 over a course of weeks with former FBI Chicago-area chief Guy Banister, famed for his anti-communist, anti-Castro, and anti-desegregation stances. That old bulldog would never have associated with Oswald if the young man had really been a communist or a pro-Castro activist. By ignoring the statements of multiple witnesses, or demeaning them in their "conspiracy theory" sections, Wikipedia is guilty of withholding vital information about Lee Harvey Oswald that the public has the right to know (why are we not surprised?).

In this example of evidence ignored or suppressed by the media, in 1995 Dr. Michael L. Kurtz, a respected professor of history and native of Louisiana, told the ARRB that when he was a student in New Orleans, Kurtz and a fellow student (who has corroborated Kurtz' account) witnessed Guy Banister and Lee Oswald working closely together on college campuses[9]

> "...during the spring and summer of 1963...(a)s I have (stated) in my book ... I myself saw Banister and Oswald together in New Orleans in the summer of 1963. On the first occasion, Banister was debating President Kennedy's civil rights policies with a group of college students, including myself. Oswald was in the company of Banister. At the time – this is the late spring of 1963 – I was a senior at what at that time was the Louisiana State University in New Orleans, although today it's called the University of New Orleans ... Banister was certainly a rabid segregationist to say the least, virulently critical of President Kennedy's civil rights policies."

Later that summer, Oswald was acting quite differently. By mid-August, he had conducted three pamphleteering events for his bogus branch chapter of the FPCC (Fair Play for Cuba Committee) that he had founded – a chapter that never held a meeting, and never had a membership list that was made public. A famous photo of Oswald handing out "Hands Off Cuba" flyers near the entrance of the Trade Mart has been widely published. But almost ignored, except by researchers, is the 40-page booklet Oswald also handed out on an earlier occasion, "The Crime Against Cuba" by Corliss LaMont, of which researcher William Davy tells us some crucial information:

> "Written by a well-known New York peace activist, the tract was critical of the Bay of Pigs invasion. In 1963 the pamphlet had already gone through four printings. However, the copies that Oswald distributed were from the first printing of June of 1961, a period that found Oswald still in Russia. In 1961 a large bulk order

for this first printing came directly from the Central Intelligence Agency."[10]

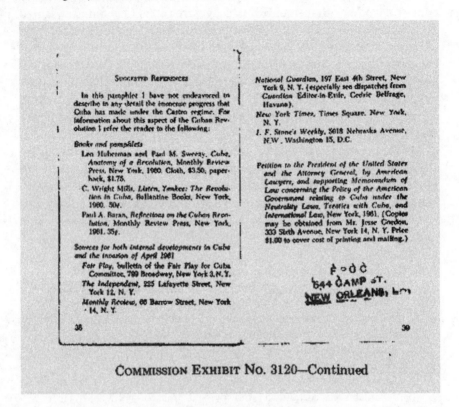

COMMISSION EXHIBIT No. 3120—Continued

So how did the "pro-Castro" Lee Harvey Oswald get his hands on a stack of 1961 first-print pamphlets, with, logically, the CIA as the likely provider? Three later editions had been printed since the big CIA order. The Warren Commission failed to mention this fact about the pamphlet. Knowing the true relationship of Oswald to Banister makes it easier to guess how Lee got hold of the pamphlets.

Anyone who closely studies the evidence with an open mind realizes that Lee was surrounded by "Agency" people in New Orleans. In contrast, there is a foreboding silence about his agency connections in Dallas, except for his relationship with FBI agent James Hosty, a man who obediently destroyed evidence in the case.[11] Author-researcher Harold Weisberg was one of the few who realized that Warren C. deBrueys, head of the FBI office in New Orleans, was transferred to Dallas when Lee was there after his trip to Mexico City. It was deBrueys who wrote and collected a big file on Lee, which was released Dec. 8, 1963. Weisberg asks, quite reasonably, *why was deBrueys brought to Dallas?*[12]

We now understand that the Warren Commission, the Secret Service, and the FBI did not give us accurate information regarding the above events. Thus, though we can hope to learn something about the real Lee H. Oswald by reviewing his reading choices, we must be cognizant of the fact that the official list shows *only the books the FBI reported to the Secret Service*, which the Secret Service passed on to the Warren Commission.

There were other books Lee read or paged through without checking them out. One such book was *The Seven Pillars of Wisdom* by T. E. Lawrence (Lawrence of Arabia), a beautifully illustrated tome,[13] kept safe from check-outs. Lee and I accessed it together on several occasions.

Besides New Orleans' main library, we also met several times at Tulane University's libraries: one such book we read there was *The Lost World of Quintana Roo* (1963), by Michael Peissel.

What is certain is that in 1963, the last year of his life, Lee Harvey Oswald had established a record as an avid reader with eclectic and sometimes intellectual tastes. Officially, though witnesses tell us he was sometimes elsewhere, Oswald spent 115 days in the Dallas, Texas area and then moved to New Orleans, where he spent 152 days.

After telling his Russian-born wife, Marina, that he was leaving her forever (McMillan), Lee Oswald visited Mexico and Mexico City for less than two weeks, then returned to Dallas, where he lived some 54 days. He spent that time generally apart from his wife, visiting her and their offspring on most weekends, where they lived with Ruth Paine, who was estranged from her husband, Michael.

When police sought a "suspect" in the killing of Dallas police officer J. D. Tippit less than an hour after Kennedy was shot, it is a fact that they first descended on the local library at 1:35PM in the Oak Cliff area, after police officer C. T. Walker saw a male suspect run inside. But they were quickly redirected to the Texas Theater, where Lee Oswald was arrested after a short but violent struggle. Researchers who have carefully examined all the witnesses have sometimes concluded that an attempt by officer Nick McDonald to plant a gun that could be linked to Tippit's murder provoked Lee to defend himself.

Lee was apprehended at about 1:45PM, some 75 minutes after Kennedy was shot. A charge sheet with the murder of Tippit, the murder of Kennedy, and the near-fatal wounding of Texas Governor John Connally against Oswald was filled out with a time notation of 1:40PM.

The next day, it was announced that no one else was involved in Kennedy's death.

One day later, Oswald was assassinated by Marcello associate and mobster Jack Ruby. Lee had been in police custody for 47 hours.

Lee's death by public execution (we have evidence that the police knew Lee would be shot) was the first witnessed on live TV, and seen by millions. At almost the same time, the famous Katzenbach Memo was issued by the FBI. Said John Edgar Hoover, FBI director: "*The thing I am most concerned about, and Mr. Katzenbach, is having something issued so that they can convince the public that Oswald is the real assassin.*"[14]

It is in this context that we enter a deeper study of the reading habits of Lee in New Orleans.

LEE HARVEY OSWALD, THE NASTY BOOR

Priscilla Johnson-McMillan wrote *Marina and Lee*, taking thirteen years to do so. The book purports to be biographical. It delves into many negative personal details about Lee H. Oswald, such as describing how he burped without excusing himself, and that he breathed his foul breath deliberately into his wife's mouth. According to McMillan, Oswald was a selfish, brutal, shallow, irresponsible man quite capable of impulsively killing Kennedy, but her book was such an obvious hatchet job that *Choice* magazine concluded:

> McMillan has no background in psychology, yet attempts to weave Freudian explanations of Oswald's alleged motives for assassination. The use of source materials is so shoddy as to be capricious, with many claims about Oswald's history and state of mind having no citations to substantiate them.... The armchair, pop-psychoanalysis is so loose, the conclusions so logically flawed and so far beyond McMillan's data and sources, that the book obscures more important questions than it clarifies. It is poor history; its overwhelming bulk of pseudo history renders it poor human interest or journalism.[15]

The *New York Times'* Thomas Powers, noted Pulitzer Prize recipient and a writer of insider-style books about the CIA, disagreed:

> Despite strong reviews (including an enthusiastic one, in these pages, by me), Ms. McMillan's book, "Marina and Lee," made no deep impression on the public, which was unready to recognize, much less accept, Oswald's humanity, while the professional assassination scholars darkly suspected that Marina (and perhaps even Ms. McMillan!) might be part of the plot.[16]

The standard media response to anti-Oswald books is almost universally enthusiastic, whereas short shrift is given to pro-Oswald books in general. Thus, the public, until the advent of the Internet, could rarely find any dissenting voices raised in Oswald's defense.

McMillan's book, flawed as it is, does give us a window into how data in the case has been handled and reported by "official version" researchers and government agencies. McMillan cites official records when she tells the reader that Lee "first" visited the Napoleon Branch library near his apartment, on "May 22 … [when he] applied for a borrower's card, and took out his first book. It was *Portrait of a Revolutionary: Mao Tse-tung*, by the biographer Robert Payne." (400).

According to the FBI and Secret Service, as reported to The Warren Commission, Lee Oswald's library card was issued May 27, not May 22. But the list of books the FBI released to the Secret Service tells us McMillan was correct. Still, the list is all in a jumble and out of order, which is typical of how evidence was presented in the Warren Commission Exhibits. They seem to have been tossed together like a Caesar salad.

The first entry on the FBI book list shows a 9/19/63 check-out for a book, while the last entry, on page 2, shows a 6/12/63 check-out date. Nor are the books in alphabetical order. When we search through the dates, we find the first book checked out was Mao's biography. McMillan, continuing, wrote:

> On Saturday morning, June 1, Lee took Marina and June [their daughter] to the Napoleon Branch of the public library, the nearest branch to their apartment, to look for books in Russian for Marina. All they found were some novels in English translation. But Lee took out two books for himself: *The Berlin Wall* by Dean and David Heller, and *The Huey Long Murder Case* by Hermann Bacher Deutch. (402)

McMillan does not mention most of the books checked out by Oswald, only these two. The biography of Mao, the infamous dictator (and liberator) of Communist China, helps bolster the "Communist" image of Oswald. The second book helps bolster the idea that Oswald was interested in assassinations.

Robert Payne, author of the Mao volume, wrote 110 books in his long and illustrious career, including the lives of Hitler, Churchill, Gandhi, Lawrence of Arabia, and Jesus Christ. For the record, I assert that *The Huey Long Murder Case* was interesting to Oswald not because he was fixated on assassinations, but because the author, Hermann Bacher Deutch, was a good friend of an important figure with whom Oswald was involved in New Orleans[17] – Dr. Alton Ochsner. In addition, the man accused of assassinating Long, Dr. Carl Weiss, had worked in the same hospitals and infirmaries and was known to Ochsner.

OSWALD, THE READER

As for reading "communist" books, as described by McMillan, by 1963 Lee Oswald had likely read them all. What no one mentions is the fact that Lee also read all the great patriotic writings of John Adams, Benjamin Franklin, Thomas Jefferson, Hobbes and others.

Few, if any, have noticed that Lee checked out a book about Communism that was recommended by the FBI's J. Edgar Hoover, and perhaps only I knew why (here, you will learn why he did so). Lee himself reported that he began reading all of the available writings of Marx and Engels in English [and later, many in the Russian language] as a very young teen, saying he found them covered with dust in the bowels of the library. Even McMillan acknowledged that Lee spent considerable time reading in New Orleans:

> Lee spent most of the day [surely she means after July 19, his last day working full time at Reily Coffee Company?] and the early evening until the light began to fade, reading on the screened-in porch of his apartment. As summer lengthened and dusk came on earlier, he carried a lamp onto the porch so he could read a little later. (451)

Lest anyone think highly of so much reading, McMillan is quick to add:

> But the seriousness and even the quantity of his reading had fallen off.
> During the first part of the summer, he had read political books, biographies, and books about Russia and Communism ... but after the beginning of August, most of his reading consisted of a lighter diet of spy novels and science fiction. Marina had no idea what he was reading. (452)

McMillan stated that Lee Oswald's quality and quantity of readings "had fallen off" by August 1963. But was McMillan accurate in her evaluation? Lee read 21 books in the first period of 69 days (61.8% of the books), and 13 books in the later period of 55 days (38.2%), meaning that Lee read 2.4 fewer books for the second period than expected, compared to the first period (Lee Oswald was reading an average of .274 books/day, or a book every 3 to 3 ½ days, on record. This doesn't count newspaper and magazine reading, and books he read elsewhere, such as at Tulane's libraries. Nor does this record include any books Lee might have checked out from New Orleans' main library system, which did not keep the kind of records that would allow us to track down any books he may have checked out there.

There is a statistically significant difference in the gross number of books read – a decline to a rate of one book read approximately every 4 days – though still at a pace that is impressive. However, when we look closer, we find that during this period Lee Oswald read *Ben Hur – a Story of the Christ* – 561 pages. He was also reading other big books at this time.

Ben Hur – a Story of the Christ was hardly a spy novel or a science fiction anthology, as was much of Lee's other reading at this time: it was written by U.S. Army General Lew Wallace, and was the number one best seller in America between 1880 and 1936, when *Gone With the Wind* overtook it in popularity. It regained the top position once more in 1959 when the MGM film version won eleven Academy Awards.

Science fiction was an Oswald favorite in 1963. George Orwell's seminal anti-communist book, *1984*, was found among his possessions, as were the James Bond novels, *The Spy Who Loved Me*, and *Live and Let Die*. Lee's late summer choices included Aldous Huxley's *Ape and Essence* and *Brave New World*. *The Treasury of Science Fiction Classics* was 694 pages long, the size of two ordinary books, and contained selections in science fiction from authors such as Jules Verne, H.G. Welles, Aldous Huxley, and Sir Arthur Conan Doyle. Thus, McMillan's statement that Lee's reading had "fallen off" in quality and quantity is not supported by the facts. Lee was actually reading significantly more later in the summer. As for quality, the spy novels that go unnamed by McMillan are Ian Fleming's famous James Bond series: *Moonraker, Goldfinger, From Russia with Love,* and *Thunderball*, all well-written, witty novels later made into the famous movies. Fleming himself had been in British Intelligence, as well as an advisor to Dr. Alton Ochsner's good friend, "Wild Bill" Donovan, who founded the OSS and was instrumental in forwarding the founding of the CIA.

The Bridge Over the River Kwai was another late summer choice: written by Pierre Boulle, who also published *Planet of the Apes* (the English version was called *Monkey Planet*) in 1963. Further, *Ben Hur* and *Everyday Life in Ancient Rome* are not light reads: the latter book was later expanded and is still referenced in archaeology studies.

Since Lee read so many books by Ian Fleming, whom he admired, it behooves us to briefly study that elusive *bon vivant*:

> Fleming schemed, plotted, and carried out dangerous missions. From the famous Room 39 in the Admiralty building in London>s Whitehall, Fleming tossed out a myriad of off-beat ideas on how to confuse, survey, and enrage the Germans. In a 1940 trip into a crumbling France, Fleming supervised the escape from Dieppe…With Fleming flair, he spent one of his last evenings eating and drinking some of the best food in the country, and one of his last days coordinating the evacuation of King Zog of Albania. The "Fleming flair" proved to be his greatest strength in Naval Intelligence. He dined at Scott's, White's, The Dorchester, plotted intelligence operations, many of which were absurd, and many of which proved ingenious. Yet, Fleming understood the business side of the war.
>
> … He did not take his assignments lightly, always gravely aware of the real human risks involved. The "Fleming flair" also proved valuable in one other aspect: writing. As assistant to Admiral Godfrey, Fleming wrote countless memos and reports… his seemingly limitless knowledge of his subjects made the usual dry missives a pleasure to read. Eventually, Fleming wrote memos to William

"Wild Bill" Donovan on how to set up the OSS, forerunner to the CIA. For that bit of work, Fleming received a revolver engraved with the thanks: "For Special Services.[18]

THE BOOK LIST: UNTANGLING THE FBI DATA

For the convenience of researchers, scholars and others, the FBI book list (below) has been put in proper chronological order. The full title, where missing, is also provided. When necessary, the "author" section is expanded for clarity. The likely date of publication is offered. Check-out dates are listed first; return dates are listed last, the opposite of the FBI's method (date of return first, check-out date last). However, the FBI only recorded return dates. Check-out dates were only estimated. Thus we can be certain only of the dates when Lee Oswald (or a friend) dropped off books.

CARD SHOWS RETURN DATE	TITLE	AUTHOR	DATE WOULD HAVE BEEN CHECKED OUT
10/3/63	"Goldfinger"	IAN FLEMING	9/19/63
7/3/63	"Thunderball"	"	6/24/63
10/3/63	"Moonraker"	"	9/19/63
9/5/63	"From Russia With Love"	"	8/22/63
10/3/63	"Ape And Essence"	ALDOUS HUXLEY	9/19/63
10/3/63	"Brave New World"	"	9/19/63
9/5/63	"The Sixth Galaxy Reader"	H. L. GOLD	8/22/63
9/5/63	"Portals of Tomorrow"	AUGUST DERLETH	8/22/63
8/13/63	"Mind Partner"	Edited by H. L. GOLD	7/30/63
8/1/63	"Five Spy Novels"	Selected by HOWARD HAYCRAFT	7/18/63
9/23/63	"Big Book of Science Fiction"	GROFF CONKLIN	9/9/63
7/24/63	"The Hugo Winners"	Edited by ISAAC ASIMOV	7/10/63
8/22/63	"The Worlds of Clifford Simak"	CLIFFORD SIMAK	8/3/63
8/19/63	"The Expert Dreamers"	Edited by FREDERIK POHL	8/5/63
8/14/63	"Nine Tomorrows"	ISAAC ASIMOV	7/31/63
8/26/63	"The Treasury of Science Fiction Classics"	Edited by HAROLD KUEBLER	8/12/63
8/14/63	"Everyday Life in Ancient Rome"	F. R. COWELL	7/31/63

564

COMMISSION EXHIBIT No. 2650—Continued

324

CARD SHOWS CHECKED-IN DATE	TITLE	AUTHOR	DATE WOULD HAVE BEEN CHECKED OUT
7/1/63	"Soviet Potentials"	GEORGE B. CRESSEY	6/17/63
7/1/63	"What We Must Know About Communism"	HARRY BORLRO OVERSTREET	6/17/63
7/24/63	"Russia Under Khrushchev"	ALEXANDER WERTH	7/10/63
7/15/63	"Portrait of A President"	WILLIAM MANCHESTER ~~JOHN F. KENNEDY~~	7/1/63
6/15/63	"The Huey Long Murder Case"	HERMAN B. DEUTSCH	6/1/63
6/5/63	"Portrait of A Revolutionary: Mao Tse-Tung"	ROBERT PAYNE	5/22/63
6/15/63	"The Berlin Wall"	DEAN and DAVID HELLER	6/1/63
7/1/63	"This Is My Philosophy"	Edited by WHIT BURNETT	6/17/63
9/23/63	"The Bridge Over the River Kwai"	PIERRE BOULLE	9/9/63
8/13/63	"The Hittite"	NOEL B. GERSON	7/30/63
7/29/63	"The Blue Nile"	ALAN MOOREHEAD	7/15/63
7/20/63	"One Day In The Life of Ivan Denisovich"	ALEXANDER SOLZHENITSYN	7/6/63
9/23/63	"Ben-Hur"	LEWIS WALLACE	9/9/63
7/29/63	"Profiles In Courage"	JOHN F. KENNEDY	7/15/63
7/12/63	"A Fall of Moondust"	A. C. CLARKE	6/28/63
7/20/63	"Hornblower and The Hotspur"	C. S. FORESTER	7/6/63
6/26/63	"Conflict"	ROBERT LECKIE	6/12/63

o   o   o

The first 27 books are in the possession of the FBI.
The remaining 7 are in the possession of private citizens
who checked out these books after they were returned
by Lee Harvey Oswald.

564

COMMISSION EXHIBIT No. 2650—Continued

Date Out	Book Type	Title, Author(s)	Pub Date	# Pages	Date Returned
05/22	Biography	*Portrait of a Revolutionary: Mao Tse-Tung*, Robert Payne	1961	311	06/03
06/01	Murder Investigation	*The Huey Long Murder Case*, Hermann B. Deutsch	1963	180	06/15
06/01	Documentary History	*The Berlin Wall*, Dean & David Heller	1962	~223	06/15
06/12	Documentary History	*Conflict: the History of the Korean War, 1950-53*, Robert Leckie	1962	448	06/26
06/01	Geography & Economics	*Soviet Potentials: A Geographic Appraisal*, George B. Cressey	1962	262	07/01

Date Out	Book Type	Title, Author(s)	Pub Date	# Pages	Date Returned
06/17	Textbook on Communism by husband-wife writing team in psychology & sociology: J. Edgar Hoover wrote recommendation.	*What We Must Know About Communism: Its Beginnings, Its Growth, Its Present Status,* Harry & Bonaro Overstreet — (The book was checked out for me: Oswald, a recent USSR resident, knew all this material. See *Me & Lee* for details)	1958	348	07/01
06/17	Cerebral Essays Schweitzer, Huxley, Oppenheimer, Marcel, Sartre,	*This Is My Philosophy: Twenty of the World's Outstanding Thinkers Reveal the Deepest Meanings They Have Found in Life,* Eds. Whitney, James & WilliamBurnett	1958	378	07/01
06/23	Science Fiction: Hugo Award Winner	*A Fall of Moondust*, Arthur C. Clarke — (Why was this book estimated by the FBI to have been checked out by Oswald on 06/23, when it was returned four days later than *Thunderball*?)	1961	224	07/12
06/24	Spy 9th Bond novel	*Thunderball,* Ian Fleming	1962	~272	07/08
07/01	Biography by personal friend of JFK	*Portrait of a President: John F. Kennedy,* William Manchester	1962	~266	07/15
07/06	Quasi-historic Adventure	*Hornblower and the Hotspur,* C. S. Forester	1962	400	07/20
07/06	Soviet Prison Camp Life by (Nobel Prize) Anti-communist Russian	*One Day in the Life of Ivan Denisovitch,* Alexander Solzihnitsyn	1963	160	07/20
07/10	Documentary History	*Russia Under Khrushchev,* Alexander Werth	1962	~342	07/24
07/10	Science Fiction:	*The Hugo Winners,* Ed. Isaac Asimov	1962	318	07/24
07/15	History	*The Blue Nile,* Alan Moorehead	1962	~368	07/29
07/15	Essays	*Profiles in Courage,* John F. Kennedy	154	272	07/29

Date Out	Book Type	Title, Author(s)	Pub Date	# Pages	Date Returned
07/18	Spy Novels	*Five Spy Novels, slected by Howard Haycraft* (*The Great Impersonation*, E. Phillips Oppenheim / *Greenmantle*, John Buchan / *Epitaph for a Spy*, Eric Ambler / *No Surrender*, Martha Albrand / *No Entry* by Manning Coles)	1962	757	07/9
07/30	Historical Fiction	*The Hittite* Noel B. Gerson	1963	224	08/13
07/31	Science Fiction	*Mind Partner,* ed. H. L. Gold	1962	241	08/13
07/31	History	*Everyday Life in Ancient Rome,* F.R. Cowell	1961	~207	08/14
07/31	Science Fiction	*Nine Tomorrows,* Isaac Asimov	1959	236	08/14
08/03	Science Fiction	*The Expert Dreamers,* Ed. Frederik Pohl	1962	248	08/19
08/03	Science Fiction	The Worlds of Clifford Simak, Clifford Simak	1960	302	08/22
08/12	Science Fiction	*The Treasury of Science Fiction Classics,* Ed. Harold Keubler	1954	694	08/26
08/22	Spy Novel	*From Russia with Love,* Ian Fleming	1957	253	09/05
08/22	Science Fiction	*Portals of Tomorrow* August Derleth	1954	371	09/05
08/22	Science Fiction	*The Sixth Galaxy Reader,* H.L. Gold	~1962	240	09/05
08/22	Historical Fiction	*Ben Hur – A Story of Christ,* Lew Wallace	1961	510	09/23
08/22	Science Fiction	*The Big Book of Science Fiction,* Groff Conklin	1950	187	09/23
08/22	Historical Fiction	*The Bridge Over the River Kwai,* Pierre Boulle	1954	~225	09/23
09/19	Science Fiction	*Ape and Essence,* Aldous Huxley	1948	207	10/03
09/19	Dystopian Novel	*Brave New World,* Aldous Huxley	1932	288	10/03
09/19	Spy Novel	*Goldfinger,* Ian Fleming	1959	~220	10/03
09/19	Spy Novel	*Moonraker,* Ian Fleming	1955	~256	10/03

"None of the books that OSWALD read were written by leftists…"

A. J. Weberman, Nodule 11, orig. p. 39)

Though Lee's library books were not written by leftists, what about the newspapers to which he subscribed? Official version accounts typically avoid the idea that Lee was a fake defector who had to keep up the veneer of being a communist, though even in the USSR he never joined the communist party and was not arrested when he returned to the United States more than thirty months later. His saga as a "defector" is worth a close study.[23] There is no doubt he read many Communist newspapers, and this was known to the US Postal service before Lee moved to New Orleans.

In Nodule 17, A. J. Weberman tells us:

> OSWALD'S landlord on Mercedes Street, Chester Riggs, was contacted in July,1993: "I saw him weekly. He was an aloof, strange, different individual, very quiet, he read quite a bit. Not an aggressive person. He was relatively orderly. It was a low income area…I don't know how OSWALD found out the property was for let. OSWALD had his own entrance. The postman that came there also delivered to my commercial building where I had a business and told me that OSWALD was being investigated for receiving subversive literature."

Some of the Newspapers Read by Lee Oswald

Dallas Morning News – in the main public library, in May.

The Times-Picayune – at all libraries (buses and streetcars had free copies)

New Orleans States Item – at all libraries (buses and streetcars had free copies)

The Militant – the Socialist Workers Party newspaper, begun in the 1920s. A communist newspaper, the SWP was, however, anti-Stalin, and therefore "anti-USSR government" at the time, adhering to Trotskyite communist principles, for which its leaders had been kicked out of the communist party. SWP's *The Militant* was in radical opposition to *The Daily Worker*. The faked "backyard photo"[24] shows "Oswald" holding both *The Militant* and *The Daily Worker* in one hand: Lee subscribed to both newspapers, which were mailed to him in Dallas and later, to New Orleans. Since Lee read both newspapers regularly, he was well informed as to the interior squabbles between the two branches of communism. Lee Oswald made the distinction between being a Marxist or a Marxist-Leninist on the New Orleans WDSU radio program "Latin Listening Post," which aired Aug. 17th after his arrest on Aug. 9th for distributing "Hands off Cuba" flyers and other materials on Canal Street in New Orleans provided fodder for interest.

"I am a Marxist," Lee had stated in a radio program" debate" held on "The Latin Listening Post," in New Orleans a few days after he had been arrested for "creating a public disturbance" by passing out FPCC "Hands Off Cuba" flyers. The incident was staged to create a pro-Castro image for Lee that would make it easier for him to bring the bio-weapon into Mexico City without suspicion. Ever since May 4, 1963, Lee had the idea to be the target of a physical attack by three anti-Castro activists. He got this idea from this newspaper article, which mentions three attackers who beat up an undercover agent pretending to be a drug dealer:

Lee added that he was not a Marxist-Leninist. Asked by Carlos Bringuier, one of the three activists who had been arrested with Lee, to point out the difference between Marxist theory and Communism, Lee responded, "... Many parties, many countries are based on Marxism. Many countries such as Great Britain display very socialistic aspects or characteristics. I might point to the socialized medicine in Britain."

Bringuier, unlike Lee, was not fined, despite his aggressive confrontation, which included striking Lee and throwing his materials to the ground, to which Lee utterly refused to respond. Bringuier's staged confrontation provoked the arrest, which has often been described as a "brawl" or a "fight" by anti-Oswald writers, even though Lee never raised so much as a hand in his own defense.

Asked if he lived on a subsidy while in the USSR, Lee replied, "... I will answer that question directly then, as you will not rest until you get your answer. I worked in Russia. *I was under the protection of the – that is to say I was not under protection of the American government,* but as I was at all times considered an American citizen. I did not lose my American citizenship." This quote is from the actual recording made by INCA (Information Council of the Americas; a pet project of Dr. Alton Ochsner) and published on vinyl ("Self-Portrait in Red") at the time. It offers us an example of manipulation of evidence on the smallest scale, adding a pattern of consistency that suggests the omissions and misinterpretations as shown in this account were not mere accidents.

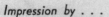

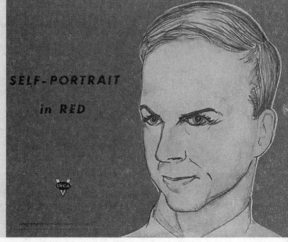

Dr. Alton Ochsner, world famed surgeon and President of both the Alton Ochsner Medical Foundation and the Information Council of the Americas (INCA), who was perhaps the only listener who knew of Oswald's defection before the debate.

On the back cover of the INCA recording is Ochsner's photo, with the assertion that he knew of Lee's "defection" before the so-called debate. Of course he did! Ed Butler's sketch of Lee on the front cover shows an ugly, angry, satanic sketch of the man I knew and loved.

The anti-Oswald website run by John McAdams offers the naïve reader the corrupted version of Oswald's statement as published by the Warren Commission, "I was under the protection of the (American government)" was slyly altered to: "I was *not* under the protection of the – that is to say I was *not* under protection of the American government, but as I was at all times considered an American citizen. I did not lose my American citizenship."[25]

Such subtle deviations from the truth occur distressingly often in the official version of Lee Oswald's life, statements and actions. This is why readers should not be fooled by the sheer size and tone of authority of big websites and big books (such as Bugliosi's *History Reclaimed*) that cleverly construct arguments using material that has been carefully chosen and edited. Below is an example of material from *The Militant*[26] that Lee Oswald, deeply interested in racial equality, was likely to have read just before his subscription expired in September. This is the text of the speech that Student Non-Violent Coordinating Committee (SNCC) Chairman John Lewis was prevented from delivering at the March on Washington in August 1963. John Lewis became and continues to be a Democratic Party Congressman from Atlanta:

> We march today for jobs and freedom, but we have nothing to be proud of. For hundreds and thousands of our brothers are not here. They have no money for their transportation, for they are receiving starvation wages – or no wages at all. In good conscience, we cannot support the administration's civil rights bill; for it is too little, and too late. There's not one thing in the bill that will protect our people from police brutality. This bill will not protect young children and old women from police dogs and fire hoses, for engaging in peaceful demonstrations... This bill will not protect the hundreds of people who have been arrested on trumped-up charges... The voting section of this bill will not help thousands of black citizens who want to vote ... I want to know, which side is the Federal Government on? ... We will not wait for the President, the Justice Department, nor Congress, but we will take matters into our own hands and create a source of power, outside of any national structure that could and would assure us a victory'.... We cannot depend on any political party, for both the Democrats and the Republicans have betrayed the basic principles of the Declaration of Independence... Mr. Kennedy is trying to take the revolution out of the street and put it in the courts. Listen Mr. Kennedy, Listen Mr. Congressmen, Listen fellow citizens, the black masses are on the march for jobs and freedom, and we must say to the politicians that there won't be a 'cooling-off' period... The time will come when we will not confine our marching to Washington... We will make the action of the past few months look petty. And I say to you , WAKE UP AMERICA![27]

The *Daily Worker* was the official daily Communist Party mouthpiece in the United States beginning in 1924. Lee began subscribing to *The Daily Worker* in October, 1962, at the same time he commenced working for Jaggars-Chiles-Stovall.[28]

HUAC's 1962 Hearings listed as subversive literature subscriptions to *The Daily Worker* (New York) and *The Militant.*

COMMUNIST OUTLETS FOR THE DISTRIBUTION OF SOVIET PROPAGANDA IN THE UNITED STATES
PART 1

HEARINGS
BEFORE THE
COMMITTEE ON UN-AMERICAN ACTIVITIES
HOUSE OF REPRESENTATIVES
EIGHTY-SEVENTH CONGRESS
SECOND SESSION

MAY 9, 10, AND 17 AND JULY 12, 1962
INDEX IN PART 2

Printed for the use of the
Committee on Un-American Activities

The fact that Lee did not renew this subscription might be explained this way: Lee and I had high hopes that the CIA would keep its promise that he would be sent to Mexico by Christmas. There he and I planned to reunite and to divorce and marry. Therefore, for the first time since his return from the USSR, Lee did not renew his subscription to *The Militant.* After all, he had reason to believe that he would only be able to read 25% of what he had paid for. Lee was always careful with money because he could not look as rich as he really was. As he told me, "How can I play the role of a dissatisfied American worker who longs to live in Fidel's 'Workers Paradise' if I have a car and a good job?" He diligently set aside money, which would go to his wife and children in case anything happened to him, including arrangements to have anonymous funds sent to his family from his secret account after returning to Mexico. But as things turned sour, we had to include a year in hiding in the Cayman Islands to those plans.

Still, Lee had hoped, upon coming to New Orleans, that he could work in a cover job as a photographer, which would have made him much happier and still kept his income level low.

KROKODIL AND *MAD MAGAZINE*:

Besides all the books and newspapers that this voracious reader, Lee Oswald, sucked in, as if he were a veritable reading vacuum sweeper, he enjoyed the satire and humor of *Krokidil*, a magazine similar to Britain's *Punch*. *Mad Magazine*, which Oswald also enjoyed reading (borrowed copies), was not as politically oriented as *Krokodil*; or *Крокодил*, which in Russian is "Crocodile." First published in 1922, this 1976 abstract about the book, *Krokodil: Laughter in the Soviet Union*, by Marian Pehowski, tells us what it was all about:

> A 16-page, four-color-on-newsprint magazine, "Krokodil" is among the world's most popular magazines of humor and satire. As a product of the Pravda Publishing House, it is produced by a branch of the Central Committee of the Communist Party, yet there are no official taboos or guidelines. Connections, popularity, and profits give "Krokodil" clout. Paid circulation is at six million only because of a paper shortage and inadequate presses, which already run 24 hours a day. Contributing to the success of "Krokodil" are its role as national ombudsman between public and government, strong reader identity, reputation for responding quickly to complaints, grass-roots connections, excellent relations with freelancers, and the strong, innovative character of the magazine.[29]

Krokidil editors "dumping the remains of Nazis."[30]

MAGAZINE: *FRIENDS WORLD NEWS (FWCC) #87*

Found, with subscription receipt, among Oswald's possessions, this is a Quaker Magazine, founded in 1949. Ruth Paine was raised as a Quaker. [31]

Printed Items Found in Oswald's Possessions on 11/22/63

An article from *The New Republic*, dated 9/12/1960.
Two world atlases; also, various maps and postcards.
A subscription to *Life* Magazine.
Magazine: *The Nation*, 1/23/60.
FPCC pamphlets and flyers, some since traced to CIA supplies.
Copies of *The Daily Worker* and *The Militant*.

Books:

The Spy Who Loved Me, by Ian Fleming;
Live and Let Die by Ian Fleming;
The Idiot (in Russian) Fyodor Dostoevsky;
1984 by George Orwell;
A Gregg shorthand manual/dictionary;
A Russian-English dictionary; also: Russian-Spanish notes.
A US Marine Corps Manual.

Booklets:

Most of these were used in Oswald's pamphleteering.

Ideology and Revolution by Jean-Paul Sartre.
The Coming American Revolution by James Cannon
Booklets (various titles) published by the FPCC.

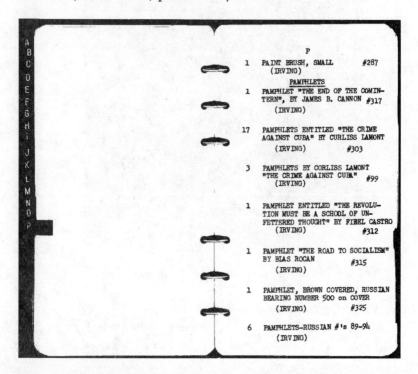

Adrian Alba, a member of a family involved with the Crescent City Garage next to Reily's Coffee Company, testified that Lee Oswald was intensely interested in gun and hunting magazines, but Lee told me he had befriended Alba only in order to be able to pass through Alba's Crescent City Garage's front bay doors, in order to go on to Guy Banister's office without being noticed by Reily employees; who were situated in the building next door to the garage on the side further from Banister's. Not one gun or hunting magazine was found among Lee Oswald's possessions in Dallas.

Three boxes of flash cards were found: one for Russian (invoice #11199G), one for Spanish, and one for Phonics (invoice #11199G). Lee struggled with dyslexia, which interfered with his ability to spell correctly, but he read anyway, overcoming whatever problems stood in his way, as the number and type of books he read emphatically demonstrate. Although Oswald's written Russian appears to have been just as dyslexic in certain features as was his written English, Lee conquered spoken Russian, and exhibited knowledge of high-level Russian writing and literature to such an extent that he astonished USSR-born (Minsk, Belarus native) George deMohrenschildt with his abilities:

> Lee read Russian classics and discussed some at length with me, especially I remember *The Idiot* by Dostoievski, a psychoanalytical study... it amazed me that he read such difficult writers like Gorki, Dostoevsky, Gogol, Tolstoy and Turgenev – in Russian. As everyone knows, Russian is a complex language, and he was supposed to have stayed in the Soviet Union only a little over two years. He must have had some previous training and that point had never been brought up by the Warren Commission – and it is still puzzling to me." Oswald also read difficult poetry by such writers as Pushkin.[32]

APPENDIX

This section includes information from myself, the witness, largely not included in the official record, or elsewhere. It comes to you at some cost, and is provided for those who may want to know more about Lee Oswald's reading habits that are not documented in any official records. Also, I include a list of trusted books for those who wish to read material other than the corrupt official versions about Lee. I have also added comments about my situation living in exile, which is not as romantic as it's cracked up to be, but has given me insight and perspective I never would have had. Thank you, fascist America.[33]

CULLEN MOORE HOROSCOPES IN *THE TIMES-PICAYUNE*

Cullen Moore, an astrologer and horoscope writer located in New York, had syndicated columns called *Stars and Lovers* (Sundays) and

Moon Messages (weekdays).[34] Lee was Libra and I was Taurus. Oddly, some horoscopes Lee read to me when we rode the Magazine Street Bus to work at Reily's resonated with intrigue. I believe it is entirely possible that these horoscopes were altered when published in New Orleans. Whether by coincidence or by design, words such as "clandestine" "secret" "subversives" and "maneuvers" peppered the horoscopes in New Orleans to an extent that could not be ignored. I saved the dates of some entries that I found fascinating, and copied some of them later. The May 23, 1963 entry for Libra, for example, reads: "Venus, the planet of love, strongly invites you. Avoid the clandestine." At that time, Lee and I had commenced a love affair.

A few of the interesting bits of advice from the horoscopes that Lee read:

May 25: "Keep quiet about financial arrangements. Do not reveal confidences. If you are dealing with underground or behind scenes affairs, do prevent interference."

May 30: "Quiet behind scenes maneuvers will gain more ground than airing your views."

May 31: (At the same time that I was engaged in clandestine cancer research efforts, with Lee beginning to learn certain lab techniques as well), the column headline was "Today's Rays Splendid for Research Scientist"

July 1ˢᵗ: Column Headline: "Rays favorable Today: Detectives May Benefit"

"Today's Moonrays are favorable for detectives, investigators, all who deal in behind-scene activities. Medicine, science, may also benefit. The sensitivity of the atmosphere should reveal many strange things."

Aug. 1ˢᵗ: "A walk or sudden visit is revealing. You should use the telephone, telegraph, or send important messages."

Aug. 11:"…Beware of subversives…" "Your temper is too high. You could cut off your greatest benefactor or lose a loyal friend unless you calm down. See things from more unbiased view."

Aug. 20: "A secret matter could take a surprising twist. Be sure you are open-minded, tolerant. (Interestingly, Lee was surprised on Aug. 21 when his status as a returned defector from the USSR was made public during the Latin Listening Post radio "debate" on WDSU).

Aug. 24: "No one knows how to gain points better than you when armed with advance information. Someone tips you off."

August 29: Context: this was the day Lee went to Clinton, then to the Jackson hospital, with Clay Shaw and David Ferrie: their extended stay, waiting for a phone call at a payphone to join a convoy from Angola prison, made their long wait quite visible to those standing in a voting registration line composed of blacks who had responded to Martin Luther King's "I Have a Dream" speech during the March on Washington the day before. Cullen Moore also responded:

"Rays Favor Religion, Aspiration and Hopes." "Today's Moonrays favor religion, aspiration, hopes, dreams, those who dare to attempt impossible ideals. Leaders of noble causes may reach hearts of people."

enter Loyola University in September.

MOON MESSAGES FOR YOU

Rays Favorable Today: Detectives May Benefit

By CULLEN MOORE

Today's Moonrays are favorable for detectives, investigators, all who deal in behind-scenes activities. Medicine, science also may benefit. The sensitivity of the atmosphere should reveal many strange things.

ARIES (March 21-April 20) Not best cycle for you (especially

August 31: This was an extremely important day for me and Lee.[35] The horoscope was emblazoned into my memory: "Today's Rays Conducive to Accuracy, Vigilance."

Lee did not seem to take horoscopes seriously, but nevertheless, he often read them, even pointing out to me the entries for Guy Banister

(March 7, Pisces), David Ferrie (March 28, Aries), and for his wife, Marina (July 17, Cancer).[36] Lee also read the editorial pages, the political cartoons and "funny papers," as well as keeping up with football games in the sports section. He read all the major news items and took special note of the arrest columns, political precinct news items, and articles about New Orleans' society.

MAGAZINES LEE OSWALD ALMOST CERTAINLY READ IN NEW ORLEANS AND ELSEWHERE IN 1963. [37]

| April, 1963 | July 1963 | October, 1963 |

The two magazines whose covers are shown below (*Life* magazine: "Bay of Pigs," and *The Saturday Evening Post*, "Night of the Iguana") featured front cover articles of interest to us: we read these articles in both these magazines.

May 10, 1963   July 11, 1963

Recommended Books: Exposing the Truth

Many books on the subject of Lee Harvey Oswald now exist that reliably support the evidence as we have come to know it from both old and new information, witnesses, and the efforts of honest researchers. Several important books have buried the government's false position, such as Doug Horne's *Inside the ARRB*, Dr. James Fetzer's *Assassination Science*, James Douglass' *JFK and the Unspeakable: Why He Died and Why It Matters*, Jim Marrs' *Crossfire, the Plot That Killed Kennedy*, and Edward T. Haslam's book, *Dr. Mary's Monkey*. Books by Groden, Livingstone, and Noel Twyman can also be trusted. Within those pages, as well as in the pages of my own book, *Me & Lee, How I Came to Know, Love and Lose Lee Harvey Oswald*, the truth is revealed, to the shame of those who still promote "Oswald did it alone," for what seem to be monetary/egotistical reasons.

It behooves us to examine Lee H. Oswald and his ways outside the province of the "official version" box, always striving to utilize a stringent and accurate methodology. I may not live to see the man I loved cleared of all charges, but somehow, someday, he will be.

JVB

Lee Oswald, November 22, 1963: "I'm just a patsy!"

Endnotes

1 Efforts to update Wikipedia, or to make the McAdams team correct falsehoods on their highly prominent websites have been futile: the reader, scholar, and honest researcher must look elsewhere for updated, unbiased information. As in all academic fields, assassination science research has its own schools of thought and theory. Efforts to discredit assassination science researchers as "conspiracy theorists" have increased dramatically in the last few years as the McAdams team has found its position of authority eroding. The Internet has expanded everyone's horizons, however, and the truth about Oswald's framing has emerged. Nobody who is an honest student of the Kennedy assassination would read only Oswald-did-it books: see the comment section of this article for a list of new books from reputable, hones researchers offering incontrovertible evidence that Oswald was innocent. These books are recent, but are generally ignored by the major media, which continues to adhere to the "official version" – for which it is monetarily rewarded. For example, Vincent Bugliosi received a million dollars for his book *Reclaiming History*, an Oswald-did-it extravaganza. Bugliosi attacked this author viciously in his end-note section, opining that I was incapable of writing my first published book about my relationship with Oswald, instead suggesting that Harrison Livingstone, the publisher, wrote it. Bugliosi never interviewed me, relying on the McAdams team for his erroneous information. Considering what Bugliosi did to me, how can we trust his treatment of other witnesses whose information points to Oswald's innocence?

2 "The working papers of staff lawyer David Slawson reveal that even the Warren Commission suspected Ms. McMillan had ties to the CIA." Jim DiEugenio, "POSNER in New Orleans ...GERRY IN WONDERLAND" *Electronic Assassinations Newsletter*, Vol. #1, http://www.assassinationweb.com/de.htm .

Also: "CIA reports on interviews with Priscilla McMillan (nee Johnson) describe her as a "witting collaborator" of the Agency.... many researchers [suspect] that she had close ties to the Central Intelligence Agency, a role she has always denied.... She later became a confidante of Oswald's widow and co-authored Marina and Lee, with her. This book...helped to reinforce the image of Lee Harvey Oswald as a hapless, maladjusted, lone assassin in the public's mind. REF: "No Smoking Gun, But Something Smells" by Jerry Policoff and John Judge, The Fourth Decade, Volume 4, #1, November, 1996.

3 Despite abundant evidence to the contrary (viz Russian native George DeMohrenschildt's *I Am a Patsy!*) the fiction that Oswald knew only rudimentary Russian is still touted on some websites and encyclopedias pushing the Official Version. For example: "The Marine had subscribed to The Worker and taught himself rudimentary Russian." *New World Encyclopedia* : http://www.newworldencyclopedia.org/entry/Lee_Harvey_Oswald

4 "On 3 October 1963 Oswald arrived by bus at Nuevo Laredo at 6:30 AM. He arrived at Dallas, Texas, on the evening of 3 October and took a room at the Dallas YMCA. On 4 October 1963 Oswald returned to and stayed at the YMCA." NARA Document #104-10017-10037, declassified February 9th, 1996.

5 Jim Marrs, *Crossfire, the Plot that Killed Kennedy*. Quote from "On the Tippit Slaying" http://www.acorn.net/jfkplace/03/JDT/brundage.tippit . Acquired 2 Dec. 2013.

6 Allan Dulles, one of the Warren Commission's members, was not only the former CIA Director who had been fired by President Kennedy, making him a poor choice to sit on a committee investigating who killed Kennedy, but he was also a major stakeholder in United Fruit. That such a man would be appointed to the Commission (and he was not alone in having conflicts of interest) presaged its doom as an unbiased investigative arm of the U.S. government in the Kennedy assassination.

7 Weberman, Nodule 4: "Oswald in Minsk, Jan. 4, 1960."

8 Witnesses who bring out the facts are often attacked on Internet forums, usually involving char-

acter assassination, *ad hominem* arguments, and nit-picking aimed at destroying witness credibility. ARRB witness and board member Douglas Horne, for example, was subjected to appalling rudeness. I, too, have suffered the same treatment. Horne, I am told, has "retired" from any further research efforts due to the harshness of forum criticism, despite the fact that his five volumes of work remove all doubts that evidence was suppressed, destroyed or substituted in the autopsy records of JFK to frame Lee Oswald.

9 See *Crime of the Century, the Kennedy Assassination from a Historian's Viewpoint*, by Dr. Michael L. Kurtz. Kurtz made these statements to Tunheim and other ARRB Board members on June 28, 1995. Note by JVB: Lee despised having to assist Banister, the bigot, racist and Red Raider, on this assignment, but felt he was being tested for his loyalty as a recent returnee from the Soviet Union; Lee told me he had to cooperate with this distasteful assignment.

10 *Let Justice Be Done*, Ch. 4. The information is derived from James DiEugenio's *Destiny Betrayed: JFK, Cuba, and the Garrison Case* (New York: Sheridan Square Press, 1992), pp. 218-219.

11 Soon after the assassination, Hosty, on orders, destroyed a note from Lee Oswald that he and a receptionist at the Dallas FBI office called a "threat to blow up the FBI building." We have to take their word for it, but logic tells us that if the note helped prove that Lee was violent, it would have landed on Hoover's desk ASAP.

12 To get the full quote from Weisberg, follow this link: https://books.google.com/books?id=8cUtAgAAQBAJ&pg=PT167&lpg=PT167&dq=warren+debrueys+new+orleans&source=bl&ots=M9YcRlAV9l&sig=oq65ztlnwU7dZC2DhtVohiFysSg&hl=en&sa=X&ved=0-ahUKEwjw6JOZov_KAhWDWCYKHWgqA4oQ6AEIWDAJ#v=onepage&q=warren%20debrueys%20new%20orleans&f=false from Weisberg's book *Oswald in New Orleans: a case for Conspiuracy with the CIA*. Acquired Feb. 17, 2016.

13 One of the beautiful illustrations commissioned by T. E. Lawrence ("Lawrence of Arabia") for his book, *The Seven Pillars of Wisdom*.

14 Ref: Lancer: "The Big Lie Begins" http://www.jfklancer.com/Katzenbach.html accessed April 3, 2010.

15 Choice Magazine, March, 1978, p. 138.

16 *The New York Review of Books*, http://www.nybooks.com/contributors/thomas-powers/

17 See my book, *Lee & Me*, as well as Edward T. Haslam's book, *Dr. Mary's Monkey*, regarding Ochsner's association with Oswald.

18 *The Life of Ian Fleming* (1908-1964), by John Cork, The Ian Fleming Foundation, http://www.klast.net/bond/flem_bio.html

19 In the 1960s, public libraries usually purchased hardcover editions.

20 By this time, Oswald and I had become lovers: both of us were unhappy with how our mates treated us. I am therefore intrigued by the description on this dust cover.

21 http://www.randomhouse.com/modernlibrary/100bestnovels.html

22 Dozens of printings of the same edition were made.

23 A good start in helping the reader assess whether or not Osdwald was a true defector can be found at this website: http://hum.uchicago.edu/~jagoldsm/Papers/JFK/2_Oswald.pdf

24 See Op Ed News: "The Dartmouth JFK-Photo Fiasco by Dr. James Fetzer and Jim Marrs, Nov. 18, 2009 for the full updated story (it became a front page story immediately there, but was nevertheless ignored by the general media) on the truth behind the "backyard photos" that debunks the findings of Dartmouth professor Hany Farid's analysis of a copy of a copy of a copy of a single backyard photo, digitalized, which he announced was "not faked" –a statement immediately picked

up by the media and broadcast widely. Later it was learned that Farid's laboratory work receives support by US government secret agency funds. (Farid would make two additional attempts to 'prove' the backyard photos were 'genuine,' still confining himself to just a single photo and in other ways exposing himself as a mere apologist: his later work has been largely ignored after a flurry of the usual media announcements proclaiming that 'finally' Lee Oswald as a gun-and-rifle man was 'proven.' (Not so). http://www.opednews.com/articles/THE-DARTMOUTH-JFK-PHOTO-FI-by-Jim-Fetzer-091116-941.html

25 "Transcript of FPCC Debate Over Station WDSU," as posted by John McAdams, using the Marquette University server at: http://mcadams.posc.mu.edu/russ/jfkinfo3/exhibits/stuck3.htm July 18, 2010.

26 Lee Oswald's close friend, CIA asset George DeMohrenschildt, in his book (its text is in the HSCA) speaks of Oswald's deep commitment to racial equality: "I would die for my black brothers," is a typical statement deMohrenschildt attributed to Lee. Lee sat on the "Negro" side of the courtroom when waiting to go before the judge where he paid a $10 fine for his pamphleteer activity on August 9th that ended in an altercation with three anti-Castroites who were also arrested, but not charged with any wrongdoing. Lee and I often sat in the back of New Orleans buses to protest the unwritten rule, despite the law, that blacks were to stay in the back of the bus. Passengers who recognized us as frequent riders on the Magazine Bus line (by which we rode to work most mornings for eleven weeks (my bus stop was right after Lee's) eventually began saving us a seat on the back bench of the bus.

27 World History Archives: "The Struggle for Civil Rights" http://www.hartford-hwp.com/archives/45a/641.html

28 *Oswald and the CIA*, by John Newman, p. 273.

29 US Govt. Document Resume CS 202 871. http://www.eric.ed.gov/PDFS/ED127608.pdf

30 From: http://hitlergettingpunched.blogspot.com/2009_08_01_archive.html

31 It should be noted that Lee Oswald described himself to me as trained in passive resistance, a Quaker tactic of non-violence designed to withstand harassment and physical threats.

32 See WC Vol. IX pp. 226, 259., and HSCA's *I Am a Patsy!*: http://www.acorn.net/jfkplace/03/JA/DR/.dr17.html ; also, my book, *Me & Lee*.

33 Due to vision problems, which get worse as the day advances until I can no longer focus my eyes, and my various European and Hungarian keyboards, numerous typos appear in my writing. Composing in English, under the circumstances, is a labor of love. I do it for Lee's sake. I was forced to leave America and live in safe places in Europe and elsewhere for my protection after threats in 2007 forced me to apply for political asylum in Sweden. The Swedes of course could not grant me permanent political asylum, but they allowed me to stay in safe havens for over ten months until my family and donors could assist me. To this day I rely on donations in order to 'stay legal' overseas by moving every 89-90 days.

34 "Now It Can Be Foretold" Ann Bayer (assistant editor of *Life*.) *Life* Magazine, Sept. 26, 1969.

35 It was extraordinary how the horoscope fit the situation this day: I had to make some practical blood analyses in a very short time span at Jackson, Louisiana, to determine if one or more prisoners had been successfully inoculated with a highly refined, aggressive form of cancer. I had protested the use of unwitting prisoners who did not have cancer for this experiment, but was trapped into having to perform these last tests because nobody else was available, and I felt the victims would die in vain or the experiment might be repeated if I did not obtain the results they asked for.

Just before the tests, I was told I was blackballed by Dr. Alton Ochsner for making a written protest, which was discovered and read aloud over the Intercom at the Clinic by his secretary, a nurse who was taking the place of Ochsner's usual nurse-secretary, who was on vacation. Outraged because of the announcement and the paper trail it had created, Ochsner ordered me to return to Florida.

My protest against virtually murdering "volunteers" if the bioweapon was successful destroyed my career in cancer research and basically ruined my life, at least the one I thought was awaiting me. Lee Oswald drove me to that hospital near Jackson, Louisiana, where the rapid tests were made; he also rushed blood samples that night for further testing back to New Orleans after purchasing a bus ticket and dropping me off that evening back at 1032 Marengo: we beat my husband home that night by only half an hour or so. Forced to separate, Lee and I were devastated: worse, he, too, had been threatened. We had both been told that we were "expendable."

36 Due to the horoscope readings, I was aware that Marina's birthday was in mid-July. Oswald, deeply entrenched in many assignments, had forgotten her birthday (he was now planning to divorce her): I was able to remind him of the birthday in the midst of technical work he was doing. Mortified, he left immediately for home.

37 These magazines were read by Lee Oswald, which we discussed. The "Night of the Iguana" article here and in newspapers helped interest us in thinking about the Belize area or other nearby places in the Yucatan peninsula as exciting places to visit. Eventually, we planned to divorce in Mexico and get married there, probably in Merida. But Lee became so entangled in the plots in Dallas, into which he realized he had been lured, that by November 20-21, our last conversation, he was afraid he would not be able to escape alive. After the assassination, the FBI tried to find Lee's safety deposit box, which they heard was in San Antonio. Lee told me that he had placed his best clothes in a bus locker in Laredo. David Ferrie and his connections to Laredo have not been studied.

https://www.youtube.com/watch?v=Hlnp0HfhLvQ Mark Lane's interview of Pauline Bates. A newspaper article pops in at the beginning of the video saying, "Hinted He Was Secret Agent for the US."

Acknowledgements

I have other books to write: "THE SSC/ssc" (a social theory treatise), a book about dear friend Lt. Col. Daniel Marvin (a Green Beret), a book of contemporary short fictional stories demonstrating a new literary genre which I invented in 1996 ("The Literature of Denouement" – also known as "The Literature of Surprise"), a book on social theory half-finished and co-written with my precious friend Martha Rose Crow (suddenly and suspiciously deceased after we received simultaneous death threats) and a book soon to be finished with co-author Edward Schwartz about the fundamental historical facts behind the Kennedy assassination. I hesitated to write Letters to the Cyborgs because it is science fiction, and so much of my other writing involves serious history and scholarship. As the author of two non-fiction biographies (Me & Lee, and David Ferrie: Mafia Pilot) it was not an easy decision to bring forth this collection of science fiction. I am not the first writer to bring forth science fiction as well as biographies and books on ethics, history or philosophy: H.G. Wells did the same, and today is best known for his science fiction. Letters to the Cyborgs is designed to both entertain and to serve as a wake-up call regarding Artificial Intelligence and the future of the human race thereby, the demise of which Stephen Hawking has already warned us.

Of all the thousands of people I have met, known and cared about, the most interesting and enigmatic was my beloved soul mate, Lee Harvey Oswald, who was falsely accused of murdering a president he admired (John F. Kennedy). Lee wished to become a writer. He was as enthusiastic about science fiction as I was. He was the first person to read my science fiction story about Monkeys (included in this collection). I own three of Lee's short stories, but of the three, his science fiction story was the most fascinating. Lee typed it several times over, but I typed the final draft, making a carbon copy so that it could be sent off to a magazine. I thought it was that good, and I believe the reader will see the talent Lee was developing at only 23 years of age. "Her Way" had many spelling errors, and while retyping it, I also removed some run-on sentences and grammar problems so that it might get published. The result was a story that was 75% Lee's. It is now published with this collection: Lee's dream to become a published writer of science fiction has now come true, thanks to Kris Millegan of Trine Day. And an extra special thanks to Ed Tatro for his astute eyes and help.